Dedication

This book is dedicated to the good people of Old St. Andrew's Episcopal Church in Charleston, South Carolina. Thank you all for your kind hospitality to me and my wife, for your help, and for your warmth of heart.

Stephen F. Clegg

THE FIRE OF MARS

AUSTIN MACAULEY
PUBLISHERS LTD.

A CIP catalogue record for this title is available from the British Library.

ISBN 978 1 78455 188 9

www.austinmacauley.com

First Published (2015)
Austin Macauley Publishers Ltd.
25 Canada Square
Canary Wharf
London
E14 5LB

Printed and bound in Great Britain

Acknowledgments

Thank you to my wife Jay, my daughter Nicola, and to my loyal friends and test readers Jayne Miles, Jean Dickens, Lorraine & Kevin Middleton, Michele Norton, and Ted Wylie. You all know how much you mean to me.

<u>Fact:</u>

On the 19th March 1863, in the second year of the American Civil War, the Confederate Cruiser, *SS Georgiana*, sank after being scuttled by her Captain. It had been fired upon and damaged by one of the Union's blockading vessels, the *USS Wissahickon* whilst it was attempting to enter Charleston Harbour.

On board was 350 pounds in weight, of gold, with a present day numismatic value of 15 million dollars.

On the 19th March 1965, marine archaeologist E. Lee Spence discovered the wreck near the Isle of Palms.

So far, sundry items totalling 12 million dollars have been recovered from the hold – but the gold has never been found…

Preface

Monday 20th November 2006. St Andrew's Church, Charleston, South Carolina, USA

Everybody stared at the exposed entrance door to the burial holding vault. Some were wide-eyed in disbelief, some were making the sign of the cross, and others, including Naomi and Carlton, were shocked. But nobody was more horrified than Reverend Hughes; he was stunned into silence, and for a while, didn't know what to say.

The vault door was metal, it was padlocked, and it had a large, black, inverted cross painted on it.

Taffy Brewer, who'd been working on the trench, walked over to the vault and saw the entrance door. He said, "Whoa!" He looked at the shocked faces and then walked across to the Deacon. He said, "I'm sorry to have to tell you, but Ryan and the guys don't want to go anywhere near that."

Carlton looked at Naomi and said, "Does that mean what I think it does?"

Naomi said, "I don't know."

"Surely it's not witchcraft or anything like that?"

"Unlikely. This type of vault was constructed around 1820, and most of the witch executions, including the famous Salem Witch Trials, were over by 1700."

"But what about individual, narrow-minded, communities dealing with what they saw as a local problem?"

Naomi looked up and nodded. She said, "Hmm, maybe… "

"This isn't part of what you heard is it?"

Naomi looked at the door and tried to focus her psychic radar, but nothing happened. She said, "I don't think it is, but it may be connected."

The Sheriff spoke up and said, "Reverend, sir, this is your church and your jurisdiction. Have you ever come across anything like this before?"

Reverend Hughes raised his eyebrows and said, "No, I have not."

"And can you give us any inclination about what might be in there?"

"No I can't."

"Then do you have any objection to us proceeding?"

"And opening the door?"

"Yes sir."

Reverend Hughes considered the situation and then looked at all the expectant faces. He said, "I think that I should say a short prayer first." He walked to the top of the stairs, made the sign of the cross, and then put his hands together and bowed his head.

Everybody followed suit.

"Lord, we ask your blessing to enter this place. Please protect us and guide us, and give us the wisdom to handle this situation with understanding and compassion. Amen."

Everybody repeated, "Amen."

Reverend Hughes looked up and said, "Okay, now you can proceed."

The Sheriff looked at Taffy and said, "Sir, will you?"

Taffy was unsure. He looked at the door, and then at the Sheriff. He said, "I don't know ma'am. It looks a bit...well, you know... "

"I'll do it."

Everybody turned and looked. "I've had experience of this type of thing before," said Naomi, "so I'll do it... "

Chapter 1

Thursday, 2ⁿᵈ November 2006. Deacon Del Morrison's house, Charleston, South Carolina.

Deacon Del Morrison looked at the email on his bedside table and noted the date. It had been nearly six months since he'd solved the final part of a nineteenth century puzzle leading to the whereabouts of a very rare and valuable ruby, and he hadn't done a thing about it.

Alan Farlington was a distant cousin of English professional historic researcher, Naomi Wilkes, through his side of the Chance family. In the early 1800s, one of his forebears named Valentine Chance, had sent two enigmatic clues to his father in England, leading to the hiding place of a very large and very rare ruby named 'El Fuego de Marte', or 'The Fire of Mars'. The first of the clues had been solved by Naomi and her colleagues in England, and had led the Farlingtons to Old St. Andrew's Episcopal Church in Charleston, where Del was a Deacon. But the second clue hadn't been solved because nobody had been able to find the place to which it led.

The search hinged on being able to find a grave that bore the name 'Matthew' or 'Chance' and when one had been found with the name of 'Chance Mathewes', everybody had thought that the ruby would be found; but when the Farlingtons, aided by their friends the Robiteauxs, had arrived from Dunnellon to investigate, they'd been informed by the local feisty Sheriff, Bonnie-Mae Clement of Charleston Police, that the grave had two nights' earlier, been desecrated.

It had turned out that the location of the grave had been disclosed by an ex-work colleague of Naomi's in return for a large sum of cash.

A few days later, and in order to be able to capture the people who'd carried out the desecration, a trap had been set by the Sheriff, and most of the perpetrators had been arrested, including the man behind the whole operation, Adrian Darke.

But all of it had been for nothing, because the Chance Mathewes grave had been the wrong one.

Being a Deacon of St. Andrew's and one of the major participants in the arrest of the erstwhile grave-robbers, Del had been given a copy of the second clue by Alan who'd asked him to make contact if any further information had come to light.

And it had.

Through a caprice of fate, he'd learned the whereabouts of a hitherto unknown and unmarked grave bearing the name 'Mathews P. F.' and it had fitted, to the letter, with all of the clues – but despite his promise to Alan, he hadn't informed another soul about it, and right then, he'd known that providing it was still there, he'd got the exact location of The Fire of Mars.

He'd also known that he was a Deacon – a man of the cloth. A man in who people sought comfort and in whom they could place their trust. But, within weeks of establishing the ruby's whereabouts he'd changed. On the outside, he was the same. On the inside, he was a different beast altogether. He'd also met the exciting and bi-sexual Julie, and had started to experience a stimulating and sexy side of life that he'd never known before. Just the thought of her sleek, naked body writhing with another naked woman, and then the two of them, under, and on top, and wrapped around his naked body, would have him walking around with a diamond-hard erection that wouldn't go away for hours.

In short, he was now in the grip of lust and rapaciousness, and The Fire of Mars was the catalyst that empowered him. The thought of it lying in his churchyard waiting to be retrieved, and that he was the only person who knew where it was, was a potent aphrodisiac, and it had become all-consuming.

He looked down at the email again and saw that it was from Alan Farlington, asking him if he'd had any further clues to the exact whereabouts to the 'Matthew's P. F.' grave site, and informing him that he would be visiting St. Andrew's with Naomi sometime before Thanksgiving.

"Honey, check out the time!"

Del snapped out of his fixation and looked at his watch – it was 2:40pm and he had an appointment with his regional manager at 3:30pm.

"Okay, I'm coming," he called back to his wife. He checked his appearance in the full-length bedroom mirror, picked up his jacket, stuffed the email in its inside pocket, and headed downstairs.

Janet Morrison was waiting by the front door with the car keys in her hand and said, "Come on honey, you know how I hate you to be late."

Del looked at his wife; she was perfect, everything that a respectable man in his position could want. She was older now, granted, but she still had her looks, she had good dress sense, kept a near perfect house, and since the death of her mother, she'd been loaded.

The trouble was, that wasn't what he wanted any more. He wanted to discard the robes of the church, he wanted to move to a different part of the country, and he wanted to be with Julie. Being a parish deacon however, wasn't well paid, and his supplementary job, running a Christian bookstore in Charleston's French quarter wouldn't finance such a venture either, which was why The Fire of Mars could be his meal ticket; his gateway to the new and exciting life.

Now – how to get to it without being detected, and how to sell it if he found it, were the big questions.

Within fifteen minutes of the appointed time with his manager, he hit solid traffic as he headed south on King Street in downtown Charleston.

"Shit – just what I need," he said out loud. He paused for a few minutes and remembered that if he hung a right at nearby Fulton and then picked up Archdale, he could cut through the back to New Street.

Inch by inch his car moved forwards until he drew level with Fulton Street; he indicated right, waited until it was clear, and then accelerated into it.

What happened next took place in one continuous blur.

As he drove past one of the properties in Fulton Street, a man dressed in black lurched into the road from his left, and stopped straight in front of him.

He had no chance; he swerved to his left in lightning-quick time, but it was too late.

The car slammed into the hapless man and sent him spinning onto the right sidewalk.

He looked through his rear-view mirror and saw the man fall into a crumpled heap.

"No, no, no!" he said. He stopped the car fifty yards further up the road and prepared to jump out. He looked at his watch and saw that it was now minutes before his appointment. He said, "Damn," and opened the door.

He looked up the street and saw that nobody had come out of any of the other properties. He looked both ways – there were no vehicles, no pedestrians, and nobody at any of the windows. He looked one last time at the prone man, and then, in an act of supreme folly, climbed back into his vehicle and accelerated away.

As Del's vehicle sped out of sight, and turned left into Archdale Street, a swarthy looking man stepped out of the adjacent house and looked down Fulton in amazement. He looked across at the prone figure lying on the sidewalk and said, "Holy shit Lennie – the bastard's gone!"

Lennie looked up from his position on the sidewalk, looked left and right, and said, "No? – Did you get his licence plate?"

The swarthy guy, nicknamed Muz, because throughout his life folk had told him that he was 'angrier than a muzzled dog,' still couldn't believe his eyes. He said, "Yeah, but I can't believe that he just drove away like that."

Muz and Lennie had perfected a small-time scam that they'd named 'rolling the hood.' Lennie would step in front of a slow moving vehicle, roll over the hood, and Muz would witness it. Once the distraught driver had run back to his victim, Lennie would groan and say that he needed hospital treatment. They would then 'suggest' that the accident could be dealt with privately if the distressed driver paid as close to five-hundred dollars as he could, for the required medical expenses.

It was a ruse that had been very successful on numerous occasions – until today.

Muz stood rooted to the spot unable to believe what had happened, and then an idea started to form. He said, "Quick, run up to Bekkie and ask her to make you up like you was dead."

"What? – *Dead?*"

"You heard – dead; and move your ass, 'cos I've got an idea that's gonna cost that dude five big ones instead of five hundred."

Lennie nodded and ran up to the upstairs room. He knocked on the door and entered.

Bekkie looked at Lennie and said, "That was quick, what happened?"

"Muz wants you to make me up like I was dead."

Bekkie frowned but knew better than to argue. She said, "Okay sit down here." She pointed to a chair in front of a dresser mirror.

"And be quick Beks, we gotta get this done and get outta here."

Lennie sat down in front of the mirror on the dresser as Bekkie got to work.

Rebecca Fisher or 'Bekkie' to her friends was an ex-top rate Hollywood make-up artist who had worked with a lot of her big screen idols. The trouble was, she wanted more than they were prepared to give, and when the police had visited her apartment following reports from suspicious studio officials, they'd found more than three hundred pieces of personal belongings, including watches, jewellery, cigarette lighters, and more than seventy items of underwear from both the male and female stars. And the latter items had been her downfall when she'd sold numerous of them on the internet accompanied by a photo from whom they'd been taken.

Following her release from custody, she'd followed her long-term boyfriend, Muz Appleton, a serial offender of personal scams, across the southern United States, wherever there were easy pickings to be had, and wherever they weren't wanted.

Within less than five minutes, even Lennie was impressed. He looked at his reflection and said, "Sweet Jesus, if I didn't know better, even I'd think I was dead!" His skin was pallid and stained, and blood appeared to be emitting from his mouth, nose, eyes, and ears.

"Okay," said Bekkie, "go."

Lennie hurried down and said, "All clear?"

Muz looked and said, "Holy crap, she's good. You look like a zombie." He turned and opened the door, waited until a pick-up had driven past and then gestured for Lennie to take his position. He checked left and right, removed a digital camera from his pocket and took three photos of him lying in the place that he'd landed after being hit by Del.

Upon completion he said, "Okay, get in the car."

"What? Where are we going now?"

"To Wal-Mart. And keep out of sight!"

Thirty minutes later, and armed with a newly purchased shovel, they swept through a maze of streets, until they picked up Route 17. They crossed the Ashley River and headed west. They followed the highway for several miles until they reached an old and deserted shack set back in the trees.

Muz checked that no other traffic was around and then drove the car to the rear and switched off the engine.

Lennie looked around and said, "I don't know about this Muz."

Muz said, "Quit whining, the sooner we get it done, the sooner we can get out of here."

"Are you sure this place is deserted?"

"According to an old soak in one of the downtown bars, it's been empty for years. I'd noticed it on the way in, and was considering using it in case we ran out of cash."

Lennie looked around and then said, "Okay, let's get it done."

Muz opened the trunk, grabbed the shovel, the camera, and headed for the nearest trees. They found a suitable spot and dug a shallow grave.

When it was deep enough to be convincing, Lennie laid in it in a way that made him look as though his body had been dumped in.

Muz took several photos, and said, "Okay, job done."

They refilled the 'grave', returned to their car and headed back to the house in Fulton Street.

On route, Muz handed Lennie some wipes and said, "Nice one buddy, now wipe that crap off your face – we don't want any passing cop thinking that I'm driving with a goddamned murder victim."

Lennie removed the make-up and said, "Do you think it'll work?"

Muz turned and smiled; "Oh yeah," he said, "It'll work. I'll contact Pete the Pen in vehicle licensing and get that dude's name and address. By the time that we've finished with him, he won't know his ass from a hole in the ground."

Chapter 2

"O what a tangled web we weave,
When first we practise to deceive."
- Sir Walter Scott

Thursday, 2ⁿᵈ November 2006. New Street, Charleston.

Del waved goodbye to his bookstore regional manager and walked down the few steps from the front of his house to the sidewalk. He turned left and walked towards his car. Without wanting to draw attention, he looked at the front fender but saw no obvious signs of impact.

The meeting had gone well, but he hadn't concentrated on any of it. All he could think about was the man that he'd left lying in the road.

He reached his car, feigned needing to tie his shoelace, and knelt down. Whilst fiddling about with his left shoe, he inspected the whole area around the front of the vehicle and saw nothing.

A voice behind him said, "Is everything all right sir?"

Del looked round and saw a police officer standing behind him. He steadied his nerve and said, "Yes – thank you officer – I was tying my shoelace."

The cop nodded and said, "I thought so at first, but when I saw you looking at the front of this vehicle, I wondered if it was something else."

Del cursed his stupidity for not checking to see if the street had been clear before looking, but he'd been so obsessed with finding any damage, he hadn't.

"No, it's not," he said, trying to appear calm and collected, "it was just my shoelace; it had a knot in it and that was why it was taking so long."

The cop nodded, and said, "Is this your car sir?"

In a stupid knee-jerk reaction, Del said, "No it isn't." – And then realised what a huge mistake he'd made.

"And do you live locally?"

Del stood up and turned around.

The cop saw the dog collar and said, "Oh – I see that you are a man of the cloth."

"Correct, I am Deacon Del Morrison of St. Andrew's Episcopal Church on the Ashley River Road."

"I know it well sir, my wife and I have visited your beautiful church on more than a few occasions. Truth be known though, I would have liked to visit more often, but my duties often occasion me to work on the Lord's Day."

"I understand – the pressures of modern-day living show no regard for what day of the week it is."

"True enough sir," said the cop. He paused for a second and then said, "Do you mind me asking what brings you to this side of town?"

"Not at all, I run a small Christian bookshop in Calhoun Street, and I was visiting my regional manager who lives a few doors from here." He nodded down New Street in the direction of his boss's house.

"Strange," said the cop with a frown, "Calhoun is on my beat, but I don't recall seeing your establishment."

Del smiled and said, "That's not surprising officer er…"

"Beauregard Jackson sir." The cop extended his right hand and said, "I am pleased to make your acquaintance."

"Two very distinguished southern names," said Del. He took the offered hand and said, "And likewise, I am pleased to make your acquaintance Officer Jackson."

"No need to be so formal between us," said Jackson, "we are both officers in our own way, me of the people, you of God, so I'd be pleased if you'd call me Beau."

"Why thank you Beau, I'd be delighted. I am Del." He shook the cop's hand and then let go.

"Now as I was saying, it's not surprising that you haven't seen my establishment in Calhoun, because it is attached to Hildebrand's Candy Store, and everybody notices that instead."

Jackson smiled and said, "I have to admit to the same sir – Del – but next time I'm passing, I'll be sure to drop by and pay my respects." A moment of silence ensued and then he said, "Okay, it was nice to meet you – now I'd better be on my way."

"Yes, and it was a pleasure to meet you too."

Jackson touched the peak of his cap and turned to walk away; he then stopped and turned back.

"Please forgive my appalling manners Del; my car is just up the street a short ways, are you in need of a lift back to Calhoun?"

Del's mind went into turmoil; before he could think of anything else, he said, "Thank you Beau – that would be nice."

Fifteen minutes later, Jackson stopped the police car and looked at Hildebrand's Candy Store; he saw the small sign indicating the presence of the bookshop and said, "Here we are Del. You mind how you go – and I hope to see you at St. Andrew's real soon."

Del got out and thanked Jackson, who smiled and bid him farewell. He watched until the police car disappeared out of sight, and then turned to see if he could see a cab.

"Hey Del – I thought you were supposed to be meeting Cole this afternoon?"

Del spun around and saw his shop assistant, Lesley-Ann, standing in the recessed doorway. He walked over to her and said, "I just did LA, but then…" he hesitated as he tried to think of a reason for being at the store, "…I remembered that I'd left my new Cross pen at the store."

"Goodness me," said Lesley-Ann, "Janet would be less than thrilled if you'd lost your birthday present so soon."

"I know, why do you think that I'm here?" He followed Lesley-Ann into the store and then disappeared into the small office. Seconds later he re-emerged and said, "Got it!" and headed for the door. He turned and said, "See you tomorrow."

"Wait," said Lesley-Ann, "before you go, what did Cole say?"

Del looked at his watch, saw that it was getting close to 5pm, and knew that Janet would be wondering where he was. He said, "Can we talk about it tomorrow? If I don't leave now I'm going to get caught up in the downtown traffic."

"No problem." Lesley-Ann looked at her watch and said, "I'll close up now and you can give me a lift to Wragg Mall."

Del knew that his car was parked in the opposite direction; he faltered and said, "Sorry LA, I can't. Janet dropped me off and she's driven to Fulton Five to book a table for our anniversary dinner."

"Oh how romantic," said Lesley-Ann, "when is it?"

Del's heart sank. It was September and he knew that their anniversary wasn't until February – but he was in a hole, and digging. He smiled and said, "Next week, on the nineteenth."

"In that case I must get you a card!"

"No, please don't," said Del, "we don't do cards, we think that it's... it's er, exploitation by the card manufacturers."

Lesley-Ann said, "Oh tosh Del! It's just my way of saying congratulations to two of my favourite people."

"Really," said a desperate Del, "you know what Janet's like when she gets an idea in her head."

Lesley-Ann faltered and then said, "Okay, whatever you think." She hesitated and then added, "Never mind about the lift, the walk'll do me good. Say 'Hi' to Janet for me, and tell her that I'll see her next week as arranged."

Del's heart sank even lower. He said, "You're seeing her next week?"

"Yes, she's introducing me to the folks at St Andrew's."

Del was distraught. He couldn't think straight anymore and said, "Okay, I'll tell her.

Lesley-Ann followed Del to the door and locked it behind them. She headed off down Calhoun and said, "Bye – see you tomorrow."

Del smiled and waved, and waited by the shop until he was sure that Lesley-Ann couldn't see him. He then walked down Calhoun at a brisk pace, turned into King Street, and hailed a passing cab. Within fifteen minutes he was back at the top of New Street.

He looked down its length to see if Officer Jackson was about and then walked back to his car, and climbed in. As he sat there, the folly of the day flooded into his mind. He closed his eyes and leaned his head back on the headrest. He couldn't believe how stupid he'd been. First for driving away from the scene of the accident, second for denying that he'd been the owner of the car to Beau Jackson, and third for telling Lesley-Ann a pack of lies that could be exposed within a week.

In an agitated state of mind, he looked at his watch and gasped at the lateness of hour. He switched the engine on and engaged drive. He failed to check his mirror, failed to indicate left, and then pulled out and knocked a passing woman off her bicycle.

Chapter 3

Friday 27^(th) February 1863. The Nashville & Chattanooga Rail Road, Union Depot, Broad and Ninth Street, Chattanooga.

Captain Adam Holdsworth of the 72^(nd) Ohio Regiment stepped aboard the train. He walked through the carriage until he reached Officer Lieutenant General William Joseph Hardee, Corps Commander of the Army of Tennessee. He stopped at attention in front of the imposing desk, saluted, and said, "Captain Holdsworth reporting for duty sir."

Hardee continued writing for a few seconds, removed his spectacles, and then placed his pen on the small holder on his desk. He reached for a blotting pad, carefully dried the ink on the letter, and put the blotter back. He looked up at Holdsworth and said, "Everything in my world, Captain Holdsworth, has a place."

Holdsworth looked at the desk and saw that everything was symmetrical, and neat to within an inch of its life.

"Yes sir," he said.

"And in my world, there is no compromise."

"No sir." Holdsworth looked up and saw an oil painting attached to the bulkhead above the General's desk. It was of a semi-naked woman reclining on a chaise longue, and he wondered for a second, whether she was somebody of the General's acquaintance.

Hardee noticed the distraction – paused, and then said, "And I trust that I have your full and undivided attention for the duration of this meeting…"

Holdsworth dropped his gaze and said, "You do sir."

Hardee kept his eyes fixed on Holdsworth for a few seconds longer, and then undid the top buttons of his tunic. He reached under his voluminous beard into the neckline of his shirt and extracted a gold chain, attached to which was a small brass key.

He slipped the chain over his head, unlocked the top left drawer of his desk, and removed two sealed envelopes. He put his spectacles back on, looked at each envelope, and then handed one to Holdsworth.

"These are your orders," he said, and they have been signed by President Jefferson Davis himself."

Holdsworth looked down and saw the Confederate States of America Presidential Seal on the rear of the envelope. He extended his right hand, took hold of it, and said, "Thank you sir."

Hardee looked at the name on the other sealed envelope and said, "You and Lieutenant Charles Joliet have been recommended for this task by Colonel Buckland because of your exemplary behaviour over the last few months.

In your case, it was your bravery and quick-wittedness that attracted the attention of your commanding officers, and though some, I might add, saw your antics at Stones River as foolhardy and ill-thought-out, there was no denying, that your er...," he paused as he sought the correct word, "...actions, were noteworthy, and got you mentioned in despatches."

Holdsworth remained at attention and kept his eyes fixed on the nipples of the semi-naked woman in the oil painting. For the briefest of seconds he wondered how long it would be before he could see real female nipples again.

"So in recognition of your outstanding loyalty to the Confederacy," continued Hardee, "you have been entrusted with one of the most important missions of our cause."

Holdsworth looked down and raised his eyebrows.

Hardee saw the look and said, "Stand easy Captain." He waited until Holdsworth relaxed and said, "What you have in your hands is the trust of your President, the trust of me, and the fate of the people fighting to maintain the democratic ideals of the secessionist States."

Holdsworth looked at the envelope and said, "I don't know what to say sir. Shall I open it now?"

"No, that won't be necessary." He looked up and saw his private secretary writing at a small desk in the opposite corner of the carriage. He called, "George, would you please step out of the carriage and give me and the Captain half an hour to discuss some important business?"

George looked up and said, "Certainly General."

"And tell the guard that I don't want to be disturbed until I say otherwise."

George stood up, said, "I will," and departed.

Hardee waited until the door of the carriage had been closed and pointed to a chair opposite his desk. He said, "Sit down Captain."

Holdsworth said, "Thank you sir," and sat down.

"Would you care for a drop of bourbon?"

Holdsworth raised his eyebrows and would have given an eye-tooth for a drop of quality bourbon, but said, "That is most gracious of you – but no, thank you sir."

Hardee said, "Good – I like a man who remains focussed on his objectives..." he recalled Holdsworth's fascination with the oil painting and added, "...even if some are more noteworthy than others."

Holdsworth looked down for a second, half-smiled, and then said, "Thank you sir."

Hardee put the other envelope back in the drawer, locked it, and replaced the key and chain around his neck. He looked at Holdsworth and said, "Now, to business. You are to meet Lieutenant Joliet at a location in Charleston. He will give you a consignment of gold, and you are to take it by rail to Major General Robert F. Hoke in Wilmington, North Carolina."

Holdsworth was stunned. "Gold?" he said, "How much gold?"

"Fourteen bars, three-hundred-and-fifty pounds in weight, with an approximate value of one-hundred-and-forty thousand dollars."

Holdsworth sucked in his breath and said, "That is a lot of money sir."

"It is Captain, and it is being placed in your care."

Holdsworth thought for a few seconds and then said, "Would I be permitted to know where the gold is coming from?"

"If the President himself has placed his faith in your veracity Captain, then it would be indecorous of me to do no less. The gold is coming from Liverpool, England, via Nassau, and then into Charleston."

Holdsworth frowned and said, "And you want me to escort it from Charleston, to Wilmington?"

"Correct."

"You'll forgive me General, but that makes no sense."

Hardee wasn't used to having *his* orders questioned, let alone those of the President. He said, "Perhaps you'd care to enlighten me on your questioning of the President's orders and rationale?"

Holdsworth realised that he was verging on insubordination and said, "I apologise if I caused offence General Hardee, my natural exuberance sometimes overtakes my sensibility."

Hardee looked at Holdsworth through furrowed eyebrows and said, "And your reason for stating that the President's orders makes no sense?"

"Federal blockades sir. Charleston has one of the most concentrated blockades of the Union's Atlantic fleet, whereas Wilmington is one of the Confederacy's most accessible ports. Why not ship the gold directly there instead of risking it being seized at Charleston?"

"Smoke and mirrors Captain – smoke and mirrors."

Holdsworth sat back in his seat and repeated, "Smoke and mirrors?"

"It is no secret that nearly half of the North Carolinians put on the Union blue, and likewise there are Union sympathisers in England who will have been sending word to General Grant about our planned activities. Therefore, within the next few days, two vessels will leave two separate ports in England. The *SS Georgiana* will leave Liverpool on Monday the second of March, ultimately bound for Charleston, and three days later on the fifth of March, the *SS Cornubia* will leave Hayle in Cornwall bound for Wilmington. Both vessels will arrive at their destinations in the early hours of Thursday the nineteenth of March.

We have gone to extraordinary lengths to 'let it slip' that the *Cornubia* will be delivering the gold to Wilmington, and that the *Georgiana* will be attempting to deliver munitions and general supplies to Charleston, and we are hoping that the Union fleet will despatch its most capable commanders to intercept the *Cornubia* – while all along the gold will be aboard the *Georgiana*."

Holdsworth had always had faith in his mental acuity, but the plan still didn't make sense. He said, "Even if you are successful in fooling the Yankees that the *Georgiana* is only carrying munitions and supplies, it will still have to run the blockade at Charleston, and it could still end up being sunk."

"We are aware of that Captain, and we are expecting that."

Holdsworth raised his eyebrows and said, "I have to say General that I am puzzled. Puzzled and intrigued by your comments."

Hardee said, "Your orders are plain – follow them to the letter and you will understand what is required of you." He paused and then added, "And you are to tell nobody about this conversation either – is that understood?"

Holdsworth stood up and said, "Yes sir, you have my word."

Hardee looked up and said, "One last thing Captain."

"Yes sir?"

"Do you intend taking that nigger sidekick with you?"

Holdsworth blanched at the terminology and said, "Yes sir, Corporal Jones has been an invaluable aide to me over the years, and I trust him with my life."

Hardee glared with ill-concealed contempt and said, "Very well. I am prepared to accommodate your highly unusual taste in companions, but if I find out that he's compromised the President's orders, I will have him shot."

Holdsworth wanted to respond with equal contempt, but knew better. He looked at Hardee and said, "Will that be all – sir?"

"It will Captain – dismissed."

Holdsworth snapped to attention, saluted, and said, "Thank you sir, I shall now retire to my quarters and acquaint myself with these remarkable orders."

Chapter 4

Del watched as the patrol car pulled up outside; his heart was in his mouth as he waited to see who would alight. The driver's door opened and Sheriff Bonnie-Mae Clement stepped out. Seconds later, the passenger door opened and Beau Jackson stepped out.

He closed his eyes and said, "Shit…"

The front doorbell rang and he heard Janet let them in.

"Honey," called Janet, "Bonnie-Mae is here…" She ushered her visitors towards their living room and opened the door.

"Please sit yourselves down while I fetch you some home-made lemonade."

"Thank you ma'am," said Bonnie-Mae, "that would be most appreciated."

Del looked at Beau's impassive face and tried to figure out what he was thinking.

"Just because you're here on official business," said Janet, "doesn't mean that we should occlude neighbourliness does it?"

"No ma'am it does not – and I have heard that your home-made lemonade is particularly noteworthy."

Janet smiled, excused herself, and departed.

Bonnie-Mae and Beau walked across to a chair each and sat down.

In an attempt to postpone what was about to come, Del said, "Are you both happy sitting here, or would you prefer to sit on the porch?"

"Here is just fine," said Bonnie-Mae. She removed her notebook from her shirt pocket, studied it, and then looked at Del.

"You know why we are here sir," she said, and then waited until she'd received an acknowledgement.

Del knew that it was serious, because on most occasions she called him by his Christian name.

Bonnie-Mae looked at her notes and said, "At 5:25pm yesterday, the second of November 2006, you were involved in an accident on New Street in downtown Charleston; is that correct?"

"Yes ma'am."

"And at that time you knocked a lady, named Helene Gibsonne de Lyon, off of her bicycle occasioning her to be sent to hospital. Is that correct?"

"Yes – if you say so."

Bonnie-Mae frowned and said, "If I say so? Are you denying these facts?"

"No ma'am – I wasn't aware of the lady's name."

Bonnie-Mae stared at Del and then said, "And do you take full responsibility for the accident Deacon Morrison?"

"I do. I was temporarily distracted and pulled away from my parking spot without looking."

"And without signalling…"

"And without signalling," said Del. He paused and then added, "The lady didn't appear to be too badly injured, but I shall of course, pay for any medical costs that she has incurred."

"Hmm," said Bonnie-Mae, "We'll get to that in due course."

Del saw her pause, as she appeared to be considering her next question; he shot a glance in the direction of Beau, but he remained impassive.

"Now sir," said Bonnie-Mae, "the vehicle."

Del knew that this would be the crunch point.

"When questioned by Officer Jackson yesterday afternoon, you informed him that the offending vehicle was not yours. Is that correct?"

"Yes ma'am."

Out of the corner of his eye, Del saw Beau drop his head and look down at his shoes.

"And yet within the hour, you are involved in an accident driving that same vehicle."

"Yes ma'am."

"Now why would you lie to Officer Jackson earlier in the day, if it was indeed your vehicle?"

"Because it isn't mine, it's my wife's."

Bonnie-Mae looked through slits of eyes, and expelled a long breath through her nose.

"I see…" she said, "then…"

The living room door opened and Janet walked in carrying a tray with three glasses of lemonade on it.

"Here we are," she said, depositing a glass in front of everybody. She looked at all the faces, gauged the gravity of the atmosphere, and said, "Now if you'll excuse me, I have other things that require my attention."

"Yes, of course – thank you Janet," said Bonnie-Mae.

"Much obliged ma'am," said Beau.

Bonnie-Mae waited until Janet had departed, turned back to Del and said, "Without wishing to put too fine a point on it Deacon, wouldn't you say that informing Officer Jackson that the car was not yours, was being downright devious?"

"No, not at all; he is an officer-of-the-law, I respect that, and I was brought up not to lie."

Bonnie-Mae dropped her head and then looked back up.

"Very admirable qualities," she said, "but that doesn't explain why you didn't inform Officer Jackson that it was your *wife's* car."

Del shrugged and said, "Because he didn't ask me that."

"Nor did you proffer that information sir!" Bonnie-Mae's legendary prickliness began to surface.

Del remained silent. He was convinced that at any second, she was going to bring up the hit-and-run incident.

"If I may be permitted a question Sheriff?" said Beau.

Bonnie-Mae turned and nodded.

Beau said, "Why did you accept a lift to your shop in Calhoun, if your wife's car was so close by?"

"I explained to you that I'd been visiting my regional manager's house in New Street, but I wasn't working at the shop that day. Before you offered me a lift, I was planning to go there to pick up a pen that I'd left lying on my desk; a pen that had been an expensive present from my wife, which, if it had ever gotten lost, would have upset her no end. But I was also considering the extreme difficulty we have with parking in there. That and the zealousness of the meter maids…" he faltered for a second and then said, "…er, police personnel; so when you offered me the lift, I thought that that would be the perfect solution. I knew then that I could leave my wife's car in New Street, retrieve my pen, and then catch a cab back to collect it."

"An expensive way of tackling the problem," said Bonnie-Mae.

"But," said Beau, "it kind of makes sense."

Bonnie-Mae looked back at Del and said, "All right, I'll give you the benefit of the doubt on this occasion, but, I have to inform you that I am uncomfortable with your explanation. I have been doing this job long enough to know when a bug just crept up my pants leg and bit my ass." She glared at Del, and then added, "And if I ever discover bugs trying to bite any part of me, especially my ass – I always crush 'em…"

Del dropped his gaze, and in an instant, regretted doing so.

"And I see," said Bonnie-Mae, "that I have touched a raw nerve…" There was a charged pause until she said, "Now, about the lady that you hit…"

Del said, "Forgive me for interrupting Bonnie-Mae, but how is she?"

Bonnie-Mae said, "I would prefer it – sir – if you were more formal when I am here in the course of my duty."

Del lowered his head and said, "Yes of course, I apologise."

Bonnie-Mae glared for a few seconds and then continued, "In answer to your question – I cannot tell you."

"Can't tell me?"

"No – because I don't know where she is. Fact is, neither does anybody else. She was admitted for observation after the accident and advised to stay overnight, but when the hospital staff went to see her this morning, she had gone."

"Gone? Where?"

"We don't know. When the lady was admitted, she told the staff that her name was Helene Gibsonne de Lyon, but no more. She promised to provide her insurance and personal details after a short rest. When the hospital staff returned later, she appeared to be asleep so they decided to leave her be 'til this morning. When they returned just after 7am, she'd gone. Nobody had seen her go, and there is no sign of her leaving on any security camera footage."

Del looked at Beau who raised his eyebrows and shrugged. He turned back to Bonnie-Mae and said, "Surely, somebody must have seen her leave?"

"No – nobody did; which of course leaves me with my fait accompli dilemma. Whether or not I believe your account of yesterday becomes a by-the-by, because I cannot proceed with any kind of investigation if I have no injured or aggrieved party."

Del felt the pressure lift and said, "So is that it?"

"No sir, I don't believe that it is…" Bonnie-Mae held Del's gaze and then added, "Do you *know* this lady by any chance?"

"No ma'am."

"Could she have become acquainted with you through St. Andrew's?"

Del thought for a few moments and then said, "It's possible; lots of folk go there, but if I'd been introduced to a lady with such a distinctive name I feel sure that I would have remembered it."

Bonnie-Mae closed her pocket book, and said, "Okay, then that concludes our business for now." She leaned forwards, picked up her glass of lemonade, and finished it.

Beau finished his, stood up, and extended his right hand.

"Del," he said.

Del shook the offered hand and said, "Beau."

"Thank you for your time," said Bonnie-Mae as she shook Del's hand too. "Give my regards to Janet and please convey my compliments to her on her fine lemonade."

"I will – thank you."

Ten minutes later, Del sat with Janet in their living room having mulled over the main points of the interview. To his surprise, he thought she had been very tolerant about the whole affair. He ventured putting his head into the lion's mouth and said, "Thanks for being so supportive about this, er…business."

Janet didn't respond at first. She sat pondering for a few seconds and then said, "I'm sorry dear, what did you say?"

Del frowned and said, "Okay, this isn't like you; what's on your mind?"

Janet said, "What was the name of the woman you knocked off the bike?"

"Helene Gibsonne de Lyon."

Janet sat back and toyed with her necklace – something that she did whenever she was deep in thought. She then drew in a deep breath and looked at Del. She said, "Okay – after the meeting of church elders last night, I overheard one of our ladies talking to some others in a hushed tone; I approached and asked what was so interesting but they all clammed up and made out that it was just trivia. Later on in the car park though, Carole told me that they hadn't wanted to offend me, because they'd been planning to attend a séance that was to be held one night next week somewhere out of town."

Del was shocked. He said, "A séance? If Reverend Hughes gets to hear about it there'll be trouble."

"I know," said Janet, "but that's not what's distracting me."

"So – what is?"

Janet looked at Del and said, "The name of the lady holding the séance is Helene Gibsonne de Lyon."

Chapter 5

Tues 7th November 2006. Deacon Morrison's house, Charleston.

"For sweetest things turn sourest by their deeds;
Lilies that fester smell far worse than weeds."
- Shakespeare.

The telephone rang on the hall table; Del picked it up and said, "Deacon Morrison."

"Is that Deacon Morrison?" said Muz.

"Yes it is."

"We need to meet."

"Okay – where did you have in mind, St Andrew's church?"

"Only if you want your flock to find out what you did last week."

Del was stunned; he said, "I'm sorry, I don't understand."

"Yes you do," said Muz.

"No – I'm sorry. I have no idea what you're talking about."

"Then how about I contact the Sheriff instead?"

"About what?"

"About how you butt-fucked my buddy with your Ford in New Street last Thursday."

Del was shocked to hear the use of such language, but recalled how his denial about ownership of the car had gone so badly the last time. He decided to give it one more shot.

"Well I'm sorry; you must have the wrong person because I don't own a Ford car."

"I know you don't shit-for-brains, it's your wife's car."

Del was mortified; he didn't know what to say.

"So perhaps I should be talking to her then?" said Muz.

"What? – No – what do you want?"

"I want you to get your fucking ass in gear and credit me with some sense."

Del was horrified that somebody should be talking to him in such a fashion, and in his own home. He hesitated, and then said, "All right, apart from that, what do you want from me?"

"I want you to meet me and discuss some options."

"What kind of options?"

"My kind of options," said Muz.

Del heard the front door open; he clapped his hand over the telephone receiver and waited until Janet walked in.

Janet placed her car keys in the drawer of a casual table just inside the front door, put her handbag down, and said, "Everything okay hon?"

Del whispered, "It's a troubled person. I'm trying to help."

"Oh right," said Janet in a hushed tone. She then mouthed, "Would you like a coffee?"

"Please."

Janet walked down the hall and into the kitchen.

Del waited until he could hear her filling the coffee maker and then spoke in a whisper down the receiver. "My wife just came in...," he said.

"I don't give a fuck if the ghost of Mother Theresa just came in," said Muz, "are you going to meet me or am I going to take these photos to the Sheriff?"

"Photos? What photos?"

The photos I took of my buddy lying in New Street just after you hit him, and the photos I took of him in a grave off Route 17."

Del was mortified, he said, *"He's dead?"*

"Yes he is. Now stop fucking me about and tell me where we're going with this."

"What do you mean, 'where we're going with this'? We're going to the Sheriff, that's where!"

"So now you're admitting it then?"

"Of course I am! Sweet Jesus; I can't believe how stupid I was – and I never would have driven away if I'd thought he was dead."

Muz frowned; the call wasn't going how he thought it would; he said, "Well you did, and now it's payback time."

"Yes – and I hope that in time both you and God can forgive my callousness and thoughtlessness. I shall go to the Sheriff's office forthwith and hand myself in."

Muz said, "What? – *Why?*"

"Because I killed an innocent man for crying out loud – why do you think?"

It was Muz's turn to be stunned; he felt that he was losing control. He said, "But nobody *has* to know about this."

"What?" said, Del, "of course they do!"

"No they don't – 'cos I got rid of the body."

Del didn't think that he could take any more; he felt as though he'd been caught up in some sort of surreal fantasy. He said, "I can't believe that I'm hearing this. Why would you do that? Didn't he deserve a proper Christian burial?"

Muz began to feel edgy; he said, "Listen to me you piece of shit, meet me in the Old Harbor Bar on South Battery at two o'clock this afternoon, or you won't need to call the Sheriff, I will!"

Del heard the phone go dead and stared at it in mild shock. His first instinct was to confess all to Janet and then call the Sheriff, but the prospect was horrendous. He thought about it and wondered how he, a respected man of the cloth, could ever justify knocking an innocent man over and then driving away and leaving him to die in the middle of the road?

He took stock of the situation, and then decided that it might be worth hearing what the caller had in mind before handing himself in.

He walked into the kitchen and said, "Honey, I have to go out this afternoon…"

Just after 2pm, he stepped into the dark interior of the Old Harbor Bar in the French Quarter of Charleston. Unlike the brightly painted pristine interiors of the more visitor-orientated Inns and hotels nearby, it had retained a lot of its historical authenticity.

He left off his familiar dog collar and wore a red open-necked polo shirt and blue jeans. He looked around and saw nobody that seemed to fit the voice he'd heard.

He pushed through the tables, up to the bar and ordered a beer.

"Make that two," said a voice over his left shoulder.

Del turned around and saw Muz for the first time. He was big and bulky, and looked like a retired boxer; he had big shoulders, thick wrists, and ham-sized hands. His face was clean-shaven except for the first traces of dark whiskers showing on his jaw, his head was shaved, and he sported a gold earring in his left ear. He wore a navy blue T-shirt and blue denim jeans.

"Sir?" said the barman.

Del turned and nodded.

Muz inched up alongside and said, "I'm in that corner over there," he indicated with a nod of his head. "Bring the beers over when you've got them."

A couple of minutes later, Del walked to the table with the beers and sat down. He looked around and then said, "All right, let's get to business. What do you want?"

"Five grand."

"Five grand? You've got to be out of your mind. I haven't got that kind of money! Besides, I should go to the Sheriff and tell her what I've done"

This was the first time that Muz had had a reaction like that. He said, "What – you'd go to the Sheriff and tell her what you did? Are you fucking crazy? You'd lose your job and your self-respect. Your parishioners would think that you were a piece of shit, and you'd probably lose your wife. And looking at you, you'd more'n likely get your candy-ass stretched in the male shower-block if you ever ended up in the joint."

Del recoiled at that thought and shuddered.

Muz leaned closer and said, "Yes jerk weed, I see that you're getting it now."

Del thought for a second and then said, "But I don't have five grand, so how could I pay you?"

"Ain't my problem."

Del thought for a few minutes and then said, "And if I could get it, how do I know that you wouldn't put the price up, or come to me for more money at a later date?"

"'Cos if I'd wanted more, I'd have already asked for it!"

"And if I get you the money, what then?"

"I'll delete the photos, use the money to buy me a ticket somewheres, and get the fuck out of South Carolina."

"And if I don't believe you?"

"I don't give a shit whether you do or not."

"When would you want the money?"

"I'm not unreasonable, so let's say – Friday."

"Next Friday?" gasped Del, "You've got to be joking!"

Muz leaned over the table and said, "Do I look like I'm joking?"

Del leaned back and closed his eyes. The only person he knew with that kind of money was his wife, and there was no way that he would be able to ask her. He mulled things over for a few seconds and then something clicked in his brain – El Fuego de Marte – The Fire of Mars.

He sat bolt upright and an idea started to form. His demeanour changed in an instant.

He looked at Muz and said, "Wait here, I have a call to make."

Muz frowned and said, "Oi! Where are you going?"

Del leaned across the table and said, "If you want your money, you'll stay here and do as I say."

Muz was stunned by the change in the Deacon; he grabbed him by the shirt and yanked him over the table. He said, "You talk to me like that again and I'll kick your ass around the car park. Got it?"

Del remained calm and said, "Are you purposely trying to attract attention?"

Muz peered around and saw one or two barflies looking; he pushed Del back into his seat and said, "Who are you going to call?"

"It ain't the Sheriff if that's what you're thinking." He paused, looked around, and then said, "I've got an idea that could help us both."

"How?"

"I need to make the call before I can tell you, but I'm not going to do anything stupid."

Muz pondered for a few seconds and then said, "Go on then, but make it quick, I'll be watching you."

Del got up from the table, walked outside, and dialled a number. A few seconds later he said, "Hey, it's me."

Julie said, "Why, hi, me. This is a nice surprise – I was just playing with my soft, wet pussy and thinking about you…"

Del felt a movement in his pants right away. He said, "Honey, I can't stop long, but I might have a solution to our problem. Are you still interested in getting out of here?"

Julie couldn't believe her ears, she said, "Sure babe, but what are you talking about?"

"Us – being able to get away from Charleston, together."

"Are you serious?"

"Yes, I couldn't be more serious."

Julie said, "Well that would be amazing honey, but how…?"

"Never mind about that now; I have a few things to do over the next couple of weeks, but if everything goes according to plan, we could be together by the middle of next month."

Julie said, "Okay babe – I have no idea what you're planning, but don't go doing anything stupid."

Del said, "I won't. Now, I've got to go, but I'll be in touch."

Julie whispered, "Okay, bye honey." She rolled over and faced the naked young girl lying by her side squeezing her nipples.

"Anybody I know?" said the girl.

"No sugar, just a guy…"

Del walked back into the bar and saw Muz waiting with a suspicious look on his face. He sat down and said, "Okay, I have a proposal for you."

"What kind of proposal?"

"You help me with what I have planned, and instead of giving you five grand, I'll double it."

Muz said, "What are you talking about? Ten minutes ago you told me that you couldn't raise five grand, now you're offering me ten?"

Del nodded and said, "Yes, but what I have in mind won't be easy."

"Is it legal?"

Del leaned over the table and said, "It is, and it isn't. It's not a bank job or anything like that, but if we do pull it off, you'll get your money."

Muz looked at Del and said, "You ain't like no fucking Deacon I ever met before…"

Del leaned forwards and said, "And if we succeed, I don't plan on staying one."

"All right, then talk to me. Maybe we can come to a new arrangement…"

Chapter 6

Corporal Irate Jones, 72nd Ohio Regiment and ex-slave, sat on a cane chair and looked up at Adam Holdsworth.

The Jones' siblings, consisting of Irate – known to all as Ira, his sister Mary and brother Joseph had been indentured to the Holdsworth family on their estate in Catonsville, Maryland, but they had never felt like slaves. They had all grown up and prospered under the watchful and caring eyes of James and Rosalie Holdsworth, Adam's mother and father.

Adam and his twin brother Bart were now 27, the same age as Ira. Ned Holdsworth, now 25, had been the same age as Mary, and Joseph had been two years younger.

On the night of Mary's seventeenth birthday, the two families had been enjoying a party thrown in her honour, when four unruly brothers from a neighbouring farm had become drunk, and had attempted to rape Mary behind one of the barns. Rosalie had heard the screams, had tried to intervene, and had been shot dead by one of the unruly brothers.

The sound of the shot had attracted everybody, and in the resulting chaos, three of the offending brothers had been killed. Joseph had been killed, and so had Mary.

Within a few months, the remaining unruly brother had been hanged for murder and attempted rape, and James Holdsworth had died in prison after being jailed for killing three of the offending brothers.

Nothing had been the same at Catonsville after that. Neighbouring families, though professing to be staunch abolitionists, had distanced themselves from the Holdsworth brothers and two years later, towards the end of 1857, they had sold the estate and had moved south, to Richmond, Virginia, with Ira.

Four years later, Civil War had broken out.

In 1862 they had all joined the ill-fated Union Army of Virginia which had been defeated at the Second Battle of Bull Run by Stonewall Jackson and his Confederates, and following a defensive retreat into Washington D.C., the Army of Virginia had merged into the Army of The Potomac, and Bart and Ned had stayed with it.

But because of the way in which Adam and Ira had distinguished themselves in the various battles and skirmishes, they had been summoned to a secret meeting by General Ulysses S Grant and three months later they'd become enlisted as undercover agents, in the Confederate Army of Northern Virginia, commanded by General Robert E. Lee. Later that year they'd been dispatched to serve in the Army of Tennessee under General Braxton Bragg, and it had been their apparent noteworthy actions that had been brought to the attention of General Hardee.

Now, here, they were holding Presidential Orders to escort one-hundred-and-forty thousand dollars in Confederate gold from Charleston to Wilmington.

"If you're thinking about doing something with this gold, it's much more than we'd ever planned," said Ira.

"My sentiments too, and it sure as hell wouldn't be a cake-walk."

For one of the first times that he could remember, Ira felt a rush of uncertainty. He looked around and said, "Be careful brother – don't go too far. The gold arrives on the nineteenth, and that would give us less than three weeks to figure out what to do with it, without being caught." He shook his head and handed the orders back.

Adam took the papers, and leaned back in his seat. He said, "Is Ned still in charge of that unit overlooking the iron mines in Pittsburgh?"

"I believe so – why?"

Adam put his right hand up to his mouth and started tapping his lips with his middle finger.

The penny dropped with Ira. He said, "Hey, hold up one minute – you're not considering substituting iron ore for the gold are you?"

Adam didn't answer. He stared into the distance and continued tapping his lips.

"Come on Adam, there's only two of us. How much does one-hundred-and-forty thousand dollars in gold weigh?"

Adam stopped tapping his lips and said, "It's three-hundred-and-fifty pounds in weight, made up of fourteen bars, each weighing twenty-five pounds, and it will be transported in seven boxes."

"In that case, I made my point. At fifty pounds a box, there's no quick and efficient way that the two of us can steal it."

Adam looked at Ira and said, "Did I say that it would be just us?"

Ira frowned and said, "What? What on earth are you planning?"

"I'm not planning anything right now. I'm considering options."

Ira continued to look at Adam with a frown on his face and said, "Well in my reckoning, we only have two options. We either follow General Hardee's orders, get ourselves a pat on the back and lay low until we can pull off something more manageable, or we can try to steal the gold from the rebs, and dispatch it up north."

"Dispatch it up north? No, no brother, we make them *think* that we are planning to dispatch it up north, but at the last minute it will be stolen from under our noses."

Ira shook his head and said, "Ooh, I don't know if I'm going to like this, but what do you have in mind?"

Adam resumed tapping his lips with his finger for a few seconds and then said, "Right, I'm beginning to get the seeds of an idea, but for it to work, we'll need several things to be in place. First we need to get a message to Bart with the 104th Ohio in Lexington to proceed to Charleston by Saturday the seventh of March. Then we need to contact Ned in Pittsburgh to send seven fifty pound boxes of iron ore to Charleston before the seventeenth."

Ira thought for a second and said, "Does gold weigh the same as iron?"

"No it's lighter."

"Then how would we fool folk into thinking that iron is gold if it comes in bigger boxes?

Adam pondered for a second and then said, "I doubt that many folk, including me would know how big boxes containing gold were meant to be."

"But some will," said Ira.

Adam thought some more and then said, "I can't see what other option we have, so we'll just have to pray that providence is on our side and that nobody seeing our boxes suspects they're carrying anything other than gold."

"And how do you propose that we arrange all of these details – by carrier pigeon?"

Adam ignored Ira's sarcastic comment and said, "The rebs still control the railroad track from here to La Vergne, but the Union's Colonel Wolford and his 1st Kentucky Cavalry are camped a two-hour ride away south of Nashville. You can take the train, and he'll be able to get the necessary messages to Ned and Bart."

"*I* can take the train?" said a stunned Ira, "then just ride through heavily guarded Union lines into Wolford's camp…" he pointed to his uniform jacket and said, "…dressed like this?"

"No, of course not, you'll have to go in plain clothes. I can't go for the obvious reasons, but as long as you have a pass from me for the railroad to La Vergne nobody will question you. Then you ride to Nashville under the cover of night and report to Wolford with my request. If he questions you, show him the orders given to us by General Grant and inform him that we are on a secret mission. After that he'll contact Ned and Bart by telegraph to carry out our requests."

Ira sat back and said, "You make it sound so simple…"

"It is, sort of," said Adam, "and when you get back – if you get back that is… "

"Hey, thanks brother! Is that supposed to fill me with confidence?"

Adam smiled and said, "Just joshing. *When* you get back you'll need to meet up with a nice friendly USCT unit."

Ira sat straight up and said, "Whoa – a United States Coloured Troop unit? I'm kind of all right with the prospect of going to Nashville, but if you're asking me to go to one of those outfits, especially with my colour of skin, that's a different matter."

"Why? All the Union's USCT units are all made up of coloureds."

"Don't be so naïve Adam. I couldn't go see those folks dressed in my Confederate grey. And you know what would arise if I was to walk into one of those units in plain clothes – a coloured – and without seeming to have a cause."

Adam said, "Right, I see. Not that I could shimmy up in my suit of grey either, but, with the kind of proposition I have in mind, I reckon that we can get somebody's attention."

Ira said, "And why does it have to be the Union's coloured troops? There are plenty of coloureds working in the rebel army, why not approach them with what you have in mind?"

"Because they ain't regular soldiers, and that's what we need. I agree that there's plenty of coloureds working for the rebs, but none of them are allowed to put on the uniform. Indeed, I haven't seen one other black guy wearing the grey apart from you, so I'm guessing that there'll be a lot of mixed feelings about *why* they're doing what they are – and who they're doing it for."

Ira nodded and said, "That makes sense." He paused and then added, "But what are you proposing to approach the USCT's with?"

Adam sat forwards in his chair, and said, "I know what I have in mind, but until we steal Lieutenant Joliet's orders from General Hardee regarding his part in this endeavour, I have no idea how we are going to conclude it."

"Steal Presidential Orders from the General?" Ira was aghast. He said, "Are you out of your mind? We could be shot, or in my case even worse… "

"We have no other option. We know when the gold arrives in Charleston, and we know that we're under orders to escort it by train to Wilmington. But we don't know how or where it's coming ashore, and we haven't yet been told where it's being kept until it's given to us."

"So you want us to steal the orders from General Hardee, read them, then put them back, with the Presidential Seal unbroken, and in such a fashion as to make the General unaware that they've been tampered with?"

"Almost right,"

"Almost right?" repeated Ira.

"Yes," said Adam, "only *we* aren't going to steal the orders – *you* are."

Chapter 7

Janet Morrison, Carole Thompson and two other friends from St. Andrew's approached an unassuming house in a quiet road, not far from Jedburg cemetery. They planned to attend the séance being held by the mysterious Helene Gibsonne de Lyon.

It was 7:30pm and Carole and the other two women from St. Andrew's had been amazed at Janet's request to join them. At first they'd thought that she was only going so that she could disrupt the meeting, but when she'd asked Carole to go with her out of what appeared to be genuine interest, they'd agreed. Everybody, including Janet, was aware that if Reverend Hughes had known about the séance, he would have been dead against it.

Under normal circumstances Janet wouldn't have been attracted to such a place either, but following the mysterious events with Del, and the strange disappearance of Ms' de Lyon after the accident, she'd felt compelled to come.

The friends entered, were ushered into a room where numerous others were in attendance, and were seated. Cold drinks were served by a young woman and then the door opened and two distinguished-looking ladies walked in.

"Good evening," said the first one, "my name is Helene – and this is my friend Samantha – Sam…" she pointed to a slim, fair-haired lady wearing a full-length white skirt, and white, embroidered blouse.

Helene who was fair-haired, slim, and shapely also, wore a calf-length, pale turquoise cotton skirt, and a white cotton blouse with colourful looking jewellery.

The assemblage nodded and said their various 'hello's' and watched as the two ladies seated themselves in one corner of the room.

"If I may be permitted?" said Helene quelling the small talk. "Sam is an accomplished psychic in her own right, but tonight she will be supporting me. It is difficult to explain, but certain psychics have the ability to draw power, or strength, from compatible colleagues, and we have found that when we are working together, our capabilities are increased.

But, as I am sure that you are already aware, it isn't just up to us. We also depend on our colleagues from the other side." She paused as she surveyed each of the watching faces until she knew that she had their understanding.

"We are not here to fool anybody; we abhor those cheap and nasty people who only tell folk what they want to hear, and we will not be informing you that there is an ancient nun, or an Indian Chief standing behind you..." she paused for a moment of pure theatre and then said, "...unless of course there is!"

A few nervous giggles came from the gathering.

"So, before we start, I have to warn you; I shall be conveying what I receive, warts and all, because I believe that if somebody from the other side has gone to the effort of getting a message to any one of you – then it is incumbent upon me to pass it on." Once again she paused and looked around. "Are we all in agreement?" she said.

"Ms' Gibson de Lyon..." said one of the gathering.

"Please call me Helene."

"Thank you ma'am – Helene – I was of the understanding that psychics weren't supposed to pass on bad news."

Helene looked at the enquirer and said, "It is an accepted rule that people in our position do not generally pass on bad news, but it is not a hard and fast one."

"So what would you do if you were told that somebody was planning to do something evil to one of us here tonight?"

Helene paused for a few seconds and then said, "Somebody *is* planning to do something evil to one of you here tonight."

A gasp erupted from the gathering.

Helene scanned the gathering and then stopped when she was facing Janet.

"You ma'am," she said. "It is you."

Janet was aghast; she hadn't wanted to attend the meeting in the first place, but to be picked out for special attention was too much.

Helene saw the look of indecision upon Janet's face and said, "He doesn't have to know that you are here."

Janet was doubly shocked; she knew that Helene was referring to Reverend Hughes, but she feigned ignorance. She gathered her composure and said, "I'm sorry, I don't know what you are talking about."

Sam, who'd been smiling and looking from face-to-face, turned and stared at Janet.

Janet felt it. It was weird and scary; Sam's eyes seemed to bore into her soul, and for a second she felt as though nothing was a secret any more. The combined look from both women felt like mental rape and she didn't know how to stop it.

Helene broke the energy flow. She made the sign of the Cross with her right hand and said, "You do know ma'am."

As soon as Helene had pronounced the words, Sam looked away and the ethereal grip was broken.

What had happened hadn't been lost on anybody. There was an incredible level of tension in the air, and everybody had been mesmerised.

Carole had been the most moved. She'd drawn an immediate parallel with people from Greek mythology that'd been caught in the fatal stare of Medusa. Completely out of character, she said, "My God."

Janet was shaken too; she sat in silence for a few seconds and then felt that she needed to take control. She said, "Why did you run away from the hospital after my husband knocked you off your bicycle?"

Carole was shocked again: she turned to Janet and said, "What? What are you talking about?"

Janet ignored the question and looked at Helene.

"Now that is a fascinating question," said Helene; she looked around the room and then turned back to Janet, " – because I haven't owned, or ridden a bicycle, since I was in college, and I'm sure that you can see I'm well past that age."

"So are you denying that you were in an accident in New Street last week?" said Janet.

"Yes ma'am, I am."

A silence descended on the meeting as the two women stared at each other for a few seconds.

Helene regained the initiative and said, "It is clear that we are at an impasse here, so let me make a suggestion."

Janet didn't respond.

"I think that you should go home, and ask your husband who 'Muz' is."

Janet looked down at her left hand and saw that it was out of sight, but then figured that her wedding ring could have been seen at any time before the meeting began. Almost in contempt, she said, "Did I say that I was married?"

"No ma'am, you did not. But then again, I guess that Del would be shocked if you denied it."

Janet was stunned. She hadn't mentioned her husband's name to anybody. She stared at Helene for a few electrifying seconds and then said, "If you haven't ever been in contact with my husband, how do you know his name?"

"I haven't been in contact with Muz either, but I know his name too."

Janet opened her mouth to speak, but was cut off.

Helene stood up and raised both hands in the air. She said, "Ma'am, I can feel your hostility, and I can understand that you may harbour doubts about my veracity, but I am telling you now…"

As Helene uttered the words, "telling you now…" Sam turned her head and stared once more at Janet.

Janet reeled again. It felt as though her inner core had been breached.

"…that," – Helene faltered and repeated, "…that…"

Images started flashing in her mind. Her breathing rate increased, and then she felt something or somebody rip her blouse open from the back and start tearing at her bra. Her eyes widened, she opened her mouth to speak and then saw Sam spin around and look at her in horror.

Sam leapt up and stared at a point behind Helene's right shoulder. She shouted, *"Holy Christ – get the fuck away!"*

Helene grabbed the collar of her blouse as she felt it being ripped away. And then whatever it was, suddenly let go, and disappeared. Sam yelled some more abuse and then lowered Helene to her seat.

You could have heard a pin drop.

Helene allowed Sam to comfort her for a few seconds and then she looked up at Janet.

"You need to ask Del who Muz is," she said again, "and when he tells you – you need to come and see me"

Janet was dumbstruck.

Carole leaned across and said, "Hot damn – that was spooky!" She paused and then said, "I haven't ever heard of Del mention anybody by the name of 'Muz,' have you?"

Janet ignored the question, stared at Helene, and then stood up. She hadn't heard the name 'Muz' either, but she had no intention of dignifying what she'd just seen with a question. She picked up her handbag and cardigan and threaded her way through the stunned assemblage.

Carole hesitated and then stood up and started to follow Janet.

"Ma'am!" called Helene.

Carole stopped and turned around.

"Use the green canvas bag with the long white handles, it will save your life."

Carole didn't know what to say; she couldn't recall a green canvas bag, and said, "I don't… "

"No," said Helene, "but you will."

Carole stared at Helene for a few seconds and said, "I'm sorry, I have to go… "

She walked outside and found Janet leaning against the fence by the front gate.

"Are you all right honey?" she said.

Janet turned to her friend and said, "How could she have known Del's name?"

Carole thought for a moment and then said, "It's not a massive stretch to think that she may have known Del, especially if she *was* knocked her off her bike by him -which by-the-by, I shall be questioning you about on the way home!"

Janet bucked up and said, "Yes – yes! I hadn't thought of that!"

"And it's possible that she disappeared from the hospital to avoid paying her bills."

"But Del offered to pay them," said Janet.

"Maybe, but did she know that at the time?"

Janet said "Of course! Thank you honey, I do believe that you've restored my utter disbelief of this kind of nonsense."

Carole smiled the faintest of smiles and linked arms with her best friend.

They headed towards their car,

lost in their own thoughts until Carole could hold back no more. She said, "Have you ever heard of anybody named 'Muz' before?"

Janet remained silent as doubt started to fill her mind again; she'd seen the gesture from Helene indicating the sign of the Cross, she'd heard the use of her husband's name, and she'd felt the palpable intensity as both psychics had stared at her – and all of those things might have had a reasonable or rational explanation, but she hadn't ever heard Del speak of anybody named 'Muz' before, and that was an enigma.

She decided to stick to her resolute disbelief. She turned to Carole and said, "No I haven't, and I'm not about to ask either; that would be an acceptance on my behalf that all of this ungodly stuff had some sort of credibility. I'm already shocked that I agreed to come here in the first instance, so I am not going to give further credence to these ridiculous goings-on by acting upon information received from what could at best be described as a cheap, circus side-show."

Carole raised her eyebrows and was surprised by her friend's vehemence. She said, "Well good for you," and continued to walk down the street in perplexed silence.

Unknown to Janet, Carole, too, had become ravaged by doubt; she was desperate to know why her life could be in danger, and even worse, how using a green canvas bag that she'd never seen before could be the only thing that would save it.

Chapter 8

Del threaded his way through the tables to where Muz was sitting with another man; he looked around and then sat down. He nodded to Muz and then looked at the stranger.

"This is Lennie," said Muz, "he's the guy that you killed in your wife's car."

Del's mouth fell open. He said, "What?"

"You heard me – I told you we could come up with a new arrangement."

Del looked at Lennie and shook his head. He said, "I can't believe it. So he wasn't dead at all?"

Muz said, "Fucking get over it and tell us what you've come up with."

Still in daze, Del said, "Have you told him any details?"

"Most of 'em, but if I've missed any out, he can ask as we go along."

Del saw Lennie nod; he cast a quick look around and then leaned over the table.

"Okay, I've been making some discreet enquiries since I last saw you, and the only person left at St. Andrew's who knows where the old graveyard boundary used to be is Casey Peters, the groundsman."

Lennie said, "Back up a minute cowboy, Muz told me that the jewel was buried in the graveyard, so what's all this about boundaries?"

Del said, "The graveyard used to be bigger than it is now, but a few years ago they enlarged the car park, and the three graves that were near the old boundary were covered over, including the one we're interested in."

"Can folk just do that to make room for car parks?" said Lennie.

"Not easily, but they can after a lot of due process."

"Due process?" said Muz.

"Yes, it's complicated and extensive including trying to locate the families of the folk buried there, but if there's none existing, or the family don't object to their ancestors being relocated, the ground can be de-consecrated, and everything can go ahead."

"So how do we know that this guy's remains weren't removed? 'Cos if they were, someone could have found that stone already."

"Because of Casey Peters."

Muz said, "How do you figure?"

"He was the groundsman at the church when all this took place; he removed the headstones, and he'd been told that he didn't need to relocate any remains, because no living relatives had been found for them."

Lennie looked at Muz and said, "I thought you said that this – what was it? – Matthews guy…?"

"Chance Mathewes," said Del.

Lennie nodded and said, "…yeah – that this Mathewes family came looking for him."

"They did; but they all live in Florida, so when the Church Elders posted notices about their plans for the car park, I guess that they never saw them 'cos they lived out of state."

Muz said, "So the bottom line is – there's a good chance that ruby might still be there."

Lennie nodded and said, "And how big did you say it was?"

"I'm not sure;" said Del, "I recall being told that it was in excess of eighty carats, but I doubt it. I did some research on the internet and the highest price per carat ever paid for a ruby was set last year for an 8.01 carat, faceted stone, that sold for 2.2 million dollars at Christie's in New York. Prior to that, the record price was for a 15.97 carat, faceted stone that sold at Sotheby's in 1988 for over 3 million dollars – or just under 230,000 dollars per carat. " He paused, looked at each mesmerised face, and then added, "So unless we are talking about something really exceptional, and with good clarity, I doubt that the ruby is anything like as big as I was told."

Lennie made a 'whewing' sound and said, "Holy shit." He paused and then added, "So how come it ended up being buried in the car park of St. Andrew's?"

"It's a long story…"

"And it don't need telling," interrupted Muz, "the point is, however it got there is horse shit, all we need to know is that there's a good chance it's still there – and how to get to it without being seen."

Del said, "That part I can figure. What I can't figure, however, is what to do with it if we ever do find it." He paused and looked at each man in turn, "'Cos it's not like we can just turn up at a jewellers or an auction house and ask them to buy it from us, or to sell it for us."

Muz looked at Lennie and said, "Are you thinking what I'm thinking?"

"Beks?" said Lennie.

"Yep," he turned back to Del and said, "We may be able to help there; one of our associates has some very wealthy contacts in the film industry who are always on the look-out for something extra-special, and they ain't none too fussy about where it came from neither."

Del nodded, paused, and then said, "I've got to say something that you might not like."

"Go on…" said Muz.

Del considered his words and then said, "If we're going to do this, I need to know that we can trust each other. I don't want to be leaving here today wondering whether we'll recover the stone and then you'll double-cross me, or even worse, maybe kill me, and take it for yourselves."

Once again Muz looked at Lennie who just shrugged. He turned back to Del, and said, "That's fair enough I suppose. I'll be honest with you and say that it may have crossed my mind, but Lennie here knows, if ever I swear an oath on the life of Connie my sweet mother, I would never break it." He turned to Lennie and said, "Ain't that right?"

"Sure is," said Lennie.

"Right then," said Del, "do you swear?"

Muz looked around and then raised his right hand in the air. He said, "I swear on the life of my dear mother Connie that I won't double-cross you... " he leaned forwards and said, "...or anything else – if we ever get a hold of that stone."

Del nodded and said, "All right – I've heard that there's honour amongst... " he hesitated as he saw frowns begin to appear, "...guys like you..."

Muz leaned forwards and said, "What, thieves?"

"No, no, that's not what I meant... I meant – oh you know what I meant! Anyway, I accept what you say." He reached over and extended his right hand to Muz. He said, "Shake... "

Muz stared at Del for a few seconds and then shook the offered hand.

"Good, now let's get down to business.

Either we've got to include Casey Peters in our plans, or, we've got to get rid of him for at least a week. Then, I've got to get back in touch with a guy named Taffy Brewer from the SCDHEC about their stormwater programme."

Lennie frowned and said, "SCDH what?"

Muz said, "Taffy Brewer? What kind of name is that?

"South Carolina Department of Health and Environmental Control," said Del to Lennie. He then turned to Muz and said, "Taffy Brewer, he's from Wales in England."

"Wales isn't in England," said Lennie, "it's next to it."

"So what's a Welsh guy doing with the SCD whatever, in South Carolina for Chrissakes?" Muz paused and then said, "He's not a rag head is he? 'Cos I ain't..."

Del couldn't believe his ears. He said, "It wouldn't matter a damn if he was a fully paid up, pig-screwing redneck from the Appalachians. If he's the guy I've got to contact, he's the guy!"

"I don't know," said Muz, "I've heard that the English don't trust the Welsh 'cos..."

"Muz!" said Del, "get off it."

"Leave it bro," said Lennie, "he could be worse than a Welshman – he could be a vegetarian."

"Jesus Christ!" said Del, "What is it with you guys?"

Muz looked at Lennie and said, "A vegetarian? Shit – that is weird...and unnatural." He shook his head, turned to Del and said, "Now – why do you have to contact that guy?"

"Because South Carolina Environmental Control have been pushing the Rector of St Andrew's about a problem we have with the car park."

Muz and Lennie leaned forwards.

"Okay," said Del, "when the car park was constructed it was done as a favour by one of the parishioners, but he didn't do it properly. When we get a storm or even prolonged rain we end up with a mini-lake. Maybe the run-off was badly calculated or the ground sank – whatever, nothing has been done about it. And the project was going to be so large and so expensive to cure, that it was decided to leave it until more funds had built up to do it.

Anyway, following a bad hurricane season it finally drew the attention of the SCDHEC stormwater guys and they asked the Rector for permission to sink something known as an MS4, or, a Municipal Separate Storm Sewer System."

"Why would they want to do that just 'cos some rainwater built up in a car park?" said Lennie.

"Because of where the car park is."

"What, next to a graveyard?" said Muz.

"No, next to the Ashley River tributaries."

Both men frowned at Del.

"Wait a minute – let me read this to you..." he extracted a piece of paper from his pocket and said, "This is a printout from the stormwater guys' website.

He read; *"What is Stormwater Runoff?*

During a Storm Event, rainfall is either absorbed into the ground or it flows across the surface of the ground towards a downstream point once the ground becomes saturated with water. The rainfall that does not percolate into the ground and flows across surfaces to a downstream point is commonly referred to as Stormwater Runoff.

As Stormwater Runoff flows across various surfaces it has the potential to accumulate and transport pollutants like sediment, debris, and chemicals. If left untreated, Stormwater Runoff can impact water quality, harming or killing fish and other wildlife, and may even flood downstream areas."

He paused and said, "So you see, they've been anxious for us to allow them to sink an MS4 so that the stormwater runoff won't go into the Ashley River. But, because the car park was built on part of the old graveyard, the Rector has been procrastinating and telling them that he wants to be sure about where they'll be allowed to dig, before letting them to do so."

"Right," said Muz, "so what's changed now?"

"This Brewer guy phoned last week and I took the call. They'd had a two-week job cancel out on them and they wondered if they could send their guys to St Andrew's to sink at least one MS4, and until you guys er, entered my life, I'd completely forgotten about it."

"And?" said Muz.

Del looked at Muz and said, "Reverend Hughes goes on vacation on the thirteenth, next Monday that is – for a fortnight. If we do this right, we can get the stormwater guys in, tell them where we want them to dig – and to what depth – and I'll guide them right over where the ruby should be lying. Then we can come in one night, dig further down and try to find it!"

Lennie looked at Muz and nodded.

Muz turned to Del and said, "For a church Deacon you're a devious bastard."

Del said, "Was that supposed to be a compliment?"

Lennie said, "It's as good as you're going to get."

"So," said Del, "we've either got to include the groundsman in our plan, or we have to get him away until the stormwater guys are done."

"And what about the Rector?" said Lennie, "Won't he absolutely shit when he comes back from vacation and sees what you've done?"

"First off I don't plan to be there when he comes back, but if I am, I'll tell him that I was put under pressure by the stormwater guys, and acted on my own initiative."

Muz shook his head and said, "Like I said, you sure are a devious bastard."

For the next half-hour minor details were discussed and mulled over until everybody was satisfied that nothing further could be done; they then parted company with a promise to get back in touch once the plan started to roll.

Del left with a satisfied smile on his face, looking forward to being able to get away with Julie, whilst Muz and Lennie headed back to their hotel rooms to tell Bekkie about their plans.

On route, Lennie thought of something. He turned to Muz who was driving and said, "When we were back in the bar, you swore on your mother's life that you wouldn't double-cross the Deacon."

"And?"

"You said your ma's name was Connie."

"And?"

"Your ma's name isn't Connie – it's Ellen."

Muz turned and said, "No shit, Sherlock?"

Chapter 9

Sunday 1ˢᵗ March 1863. Big Eve's Bar, Brown's Alley, Chattanooga.

Big Eve and Adam Holdsworth stared at the unconscious body of General Hardee, and then exchanged glances.

"He don't look all that now, does he?" said Eve.

Adam looked back at the General and said, "What did you give him?"

"One of O'Shaughnessy's Mickey Finns."

"How long will he be out?"

"An hour, maybe two."

"Will he know that you doctored his drink?"

"No. He'd drunk so much of Pete's special whisky that he won't suspect a thing when he comes to."

Adam retrieved his pa's old pocket watch and looked at the time. "Right," he said, "it's a quarter after two, I expect to be back by a quarter after three, but if I'm not, and the General wakens up, I need you to delay him until I return."

Eve nodded and said, "Okay, but I don't want to know what skulduggery you're up to this time Adam Holdsworth, so I'll just keep myself to myself." She nodded and then swept out of the room.

Adam waited until Eve had closed the door and then he removed the gold chain and key from around the unconscious General's neck. He put it into his shirt pocket, made sure that the General was lying on his side in case he vomited, and then departed, and locked the door behind him.

Less than five minutes later, he, and Ira tied up their horses and walked across the deserted railroad depot at Broad and Ninth. Looking and listening all the time, they sidled up to the door of the General's personal carriage.

"You wait here until I'm sure that we're alone," said Adam.

Ira nodded and looked down at the key. He felt a wave of apprehension spread over him. The thought of what could happen to him if he was caught with it was bad enough, but what he was about to do with it, could have consequences that would be horrific in the extreme. He patted his trouser pocket for the umpteenth time to make sure that the equipment he needed was safely in place.

Adam cast a last glance around the yard, and then opened the General's carriage door and stepped inside. As he entered the cool interior his heart nearly stopped.

Sitting at his desk with a puzzled expression upon his face, was George Albright, the General's personal clerk.

"Captain Holdsworth, whatever brings you here on the Lord's day?"

Adam steadied his rocked equilibrium and said, "I am so glad that I found you here George."

"Why?"

"Because we've received news from the Fort Payne telegraph office that General Hardee's daughter is aboard the afternoon stage."

George frowned and said, "And why would that be any business of mine?"

Adam walked across to George's desk and placed both palms upon it. He leaned forwards and said, "Because we know that of all the people on the General's staff, you can be relied upon the most."

George frowned again and said, "I'm sorry Captain, I don't follow."

Adam looked around and said, "Are we perfectly alone George?"

"We are."

"Then I should tell you – the General did a mite more imbibing than he may have intended at Big Eve's this lunchtime, and he is er – currently indisposed…"

George stared at Adam and said, "What? 'Old Reliable' drinking? Are you sure?"

"These are difficult days George, and 'Old Reliable' has a lot of responsibility since General Kirby Smith got posted to

Mississippi. Who are we to disapprove of him having the odd drink now and then?"

George stared with incredulity at Adam and said, "And exactly what form does 'currently indisposed' take Captain?"

Adam looked from left to right once again, leaned forwards, and said, "Right now he is sleeping his current indisposition off."

George made a gasping sound and said, "And you say that his daughter is arriving on the afternoon stage?"

"Correct."

George shook his head and said, "This is intolerable. We cannot allow her to see the General like that, she is propriety itself. What time is the stage expected?"

Adam removed his pocket watch and looked at it. It was 2:28pm. He said, "In less than half-an-hour, outside of the Grand Hotel on Seventh."

Indecision spread across George's face. He said, "What are we to do?"

Adam stared at George as though deep in thought and then said, "I think that you should go to the Grand Hotel and wait there for Miss Hardee. You can tell her that the General is temporarily indisposed and that he has asked you to attend to her immediate needs whist I try to, er..." He glanced at George and saw him raise his eyebrows. "...enlighten the General about the pending approach of his daughter."

George nodded in approval, and then doubt spread across his face again. He said, "But I can't leave this carriage, the General placed it in my trust and it would be more than my life is worth to leave it unattended."

Adam moved around George's desk, took hold of his arm, and indicated that he should stand up. He waited until George was on his feet, moved closer to his left ear, and said, "I may be able to help you there."

"How so?"

"You are no doubt aware, that I have the full confidence of the General *and* the President?"

"I am."

"Very well – my aide Corporal Jones is outside waiting for me. I shall instruct him to stand guard in front of the carriage and let nobody in until you return."

"Corporal Jones the nigger?"

Adam hesitated before answering. He then said, "Irate Jones is my personal aide George. He is a decorated, Field Promoted Corporal in this man's army and I trust him with my life. Therefore, by association, so does the General and the President."

George looked embarrassed and said, "I'm sorry Captain Holdsworth – I meant no offence."

"Good – then none's taken. Now shall I ask Corporal Jones to guard the carriage, or shall we shilly-shally some more and hope that Miss Hardee doesn't find the General at Big Eve's?"

George hesitated one second longer and said, "All right, but Corporal Jones must not leave his post until I return, is that clear?"

"Perfectly." Adam opened the door of the carriage, gestured to Ira, and waited until he stood close by. With a minute movement of his eyebrows he conveyed a need for Ira to play along. He waited until George stepped out of the carriage and said, "Corporal, you are to remain here until Mr Albright returns, and you are to allow nobody to enter the carriage. Is that clear?"

"Yes sir, it is."

"Good, then we shall be back within the hour."

"Very good sir."

Adam turned to George and said, "I'll try to get the General to the Grand Hotel within the next half-hour."

George nodded and scurried across the depot in the direction of Seventh Street.

Adam waited until he was out of earshot, turned to Ira, and said, "Okay, you know what you have to do?"

Ira nodded and said, "And you'll wait by the depot gates?"

"I will." Adam looked around the depot, and then said, "Right – jump to it."

Ira waited until Adam took up his position by the gates and then entered the carriage.

He looked down at his hands and saw that they were shaking. He took in a deep breath, removed the key and chain from his pocket, and unlocked the drawer. The Presidential Orders were there. He picked them up, saw that they were addressed to Lieutenant Charles S Joliet, and then turned them over. His heart sank. The Presidential Seal was huge.

From his trouser pocket he removed a sheet of paper, a cutthroat razor, a piece of solid wax, and a box of percussion safety matches.

He examined the Seal and saw a small gap where the wax hadn't taken properly. He unfolded the sheet of paper, placed it like a mat on the General's desk, and then teased the edge of the cutthroat razor into the gap, and began sawing backwards and forwards with the slightest of pressure. The minutes ticked by as the gap got wider until he reached a point when the seal detached.

He opened the orders and read the words. He made sure that he had missed nothing out, and then folded the orders back, leaving the underside of the Presidential Seal exposed.

Now was the tricky bit. Using his razor, he cut a small hole into his piece of paper. He then put it in place, over the exposed underside of the Presidential Seal. He then lit a percussion match, and held his piece of red, solid wax over the hole. One-by-one the drops fell through and onto the underside of the Presidential Seal. When he was satisfied that he had just the right amount, he removed the paper with the hole, and carefully folded the document back together. He pushed, and prayed that the new wax would cover the whole of the exposed Seal without oozing out.

It did.

He blew onto it, made sure that it had secured the orders once more, and then replaced them, the right way up, in the same place that he'd found them.

He looked at the clock on the wall and nearly had a fit. It was 3pm, and he knew that Adam would be desperate.

At 3:08pm, the afternoon stage pulled up outside of the Grand Hotel.

George Albright stood up, straightened his necktie, wet the palms of his hands, and ran them over his hair in an attempt to hold it in place. He stepped outside onto the wooden boardwalk and watched as the passengers alighted.

A frown spread across his face as the last of the passengers stepped down, and Miss Hardee was not amongst them.

"George!"

George turned around at the call of his name and saw Adam Holdsworth running towards him.

"George," repeated Adam as he drew up alongside, "it's good news! I've just received a second telegraph informing us that Miss

Hardee never boarded. She had to stay at Fort Payne for personal reasons."

"Personal reasons? What personal reasons?"

"I don't know – the second telegraph didn't go into detail."

"And did you manage to er, revive the General?"

"He is currently making himself presentable with Big Eve."

"Then I should get over there and inform him that his daughter isn't coming."

Adam looked at George and said, "Do you think that's wise? Won't the General wonder why you left his carriage unattended?"

George looked shocked. He said, "Oh my! Thank you Captain. I momentarily forgot about that!"

"It's of no consequence. You get back to the carriage, tell Corporal Jones to meet me at Big Eve's, and I suggest that we speak no more of this whole incident, to spare the General any embarrassment."

"What about Miss Hardee?"

"She too will be none the wiser."

"And you'll make sure that the General is okay?"

"I will, and he will emerge from this affair knowing nothing of his daughter's current situation. When she finally acquaints him with the facts, it will come only as a surprise, and he will act in pure innocence."

George looked at Adam's face with a renewed respect and said, "You are a bright and resourceful man Captain Holdsworth. I can see why the General holds you in such high esteem."

Adam said, "Thank you George – and I can see why the General places so much faith and trust in your loyalty."

They shook hands and parted company – each breathing a huge sigh of relief.

Adam approached Big Eve's bar and saw Ira standing outside. "Is the General okay?" he said.

"A bit groggy but none the wiser."

"And are you sure that you can remember all the fine detail of Joliet's orders?"

Ira looked askance at Adam and said, "Of the two of us I may have been the fighter and you the thinker, but I was born with a reasonable brain too… "

"Good," said Adam, "then we'd better get back to our office and prepare for your journey tomorrow."

Four-thousand-three-hundred miles away, on a cold, wet, windy, night, the *SS Georgiana* departed Liverpool docks for its four-and-a-half thousand mile, two week, journey to Nassau in The Bahamas.

Aboard were Captain A. B. Davidson and his crew, numbering one-hundred-and-forty souls.

Chapter 10

As Janet Morrison sipped her mid-morning coffee, she was racked with indecision; she looked across at Del for the umpteenth time and couldn't work out what had happened. In sixteen years of marriage she thought that she knew everything about him, but within one weekend, all of that had changed. All through the Sunday church celebrations at St. Andrew's, instead of being his usual caring, concerned, and interested-in-others self, of all things, he appeared to be happy.

Miserable, unwell, sceptical, angry, and frustrated, she could deal with – but happy? She knew that he was content, and well fed, and to within certain acceptable levels, which thank Heaven, no longer included anything oral, was satisfied in the bedroom department. But it was curious – and disconcerting, that he appeared to be happy.

She took another sip of coffee and sat back in her seat. The brief thought of oral sex reminded her of the excruciating episode that she'd had to endure when Del had come home with 'a suggestion' one night.

She was very well aware that being a wife, even a Deacon's wife, meant that she was expected to deliver singular duties, maybe even up to once a month – and with a modicum of enthusiasm. But when he'd suggested trying something 'oral,' she hadn't fully understood. Oral sex to her had been as mysterious, and alien, as quantum physics.

She shuddered when she recalled that Del had asked her to completely disrobe, to leave the bedroom light on, and to lie on her back on top of the bedclothes with her legs wide open!

She knew that her modesty would be obscured by her generous 'naturalness'. But then Del had descended upon her like something possessed. She hadn't been sure what had gone on down there, but when she'd felt herself being penetrated, and then she'd seen both of his hands on her hips, she'd decided that it was the devil's work and that it wasn't going to happen to her.

Then it had all gone downhill.

As she'd struggled to free herself from the demented creature making hell-sent slurping and grunting sounds she'd wiggled her hips back and forth as she'd edged back up the bed. In doing so, some of her pubic hair had gone up his nose and had made him sneeze. He'd then bitten her – right on the lady button.

She could still recall how horrified she'd been at Del's suggestion that she present her savaged pudendum to the local, young male doctor who was no less than a very well regarded member of St. Andrew's church community! She'd made it clear there and then, that from that day on, nothing with teeth in it was getting any closer than two feet from her private parts – and that was how it was going to stay.

She looked at her husband and shook her head. Something else niggled too. She couldn't stop thinking about Helene Gibsonne de Lyon's suggestion that she ask Del who 'Muz' was. It might start to put her on the track of finding out why her husband was so happy, but – and it was a big 'but', – it would be an acknowledgement that she had paid some credence to the 'circus side-show' of six days' earlier.

Unaware of his wife's inner turmoil, Del looked across at her and said, "It's a beautiful day honey, why don't you and Carole go into town, have some lunch and buy yourselves some new clothes?"

"All right," said Janet, "that's it. What's going on?"

Del looked at his wife with a puzzled expression and said, "What hon? What do you mean?"

"Why are you so happy?"

Del faltered and said, "What do you mean why am I so happy?"

"For the last few days you've been…" Janet faltered as she realised how ridiculous she sounded, but then said, "…just – happy."

Del walked across to the kitchen table and sat down. He made a sweeping gesture with his left arm and said, "Look around you; what's not to be happy about!"

Janet looked through the conservatory and out onto the patio; she saw the corner of their medium-sized swimming pool, the reflections of sunlight dancing on the surface of the water as the pump cleansed it. She saw flowers, pot plants, chairs, and occasional tables, plus a myriad other signs of a comfortable life-style, but right then, she appreciated none of it.

She turned back to Del and said, "Who's Muz?"

Del was stunned; he wanted to ask her how she knew who he was, but he couldn't. Instead, he said, "Who?"

"Muz – who is Muz?"

Del gathered his wits and said, "I don't know babe, is he somebody from the church?"

"I don't know! That's why I asked you?"

"Well I'm sorry hon, it beats me." He hesitated for a second, and then added, "Should I know him?"

Janet spun around and said, "Did I say that Muz was a he? – You do know something don't you?"

"Of course I don't!" Del could have spat at his own stupidity. He said, "I just presumed that 'Muz' was a he, because 'Muz' is hardly a feminine name, is it?"

Janet realised that she was in an untenable situation and faltered once again; she looked at her husband, and wasn't sure how to proceed. If for one second she took the word of the psychic over her Deacon husband of sixteen years, it was not only disloyal, but ungodly too. She pursed her lips and looked down at her feet. She seethed and ruminated, but underneath it all, she knew that something wasn't right.

Del was filled with questions too, and the two most prevalent ones were 'how the hell did Janet know about Muz?' And 'does anybody else know about him?' He tried to assess everything at once. What were the ramifications of failure? Was anybody else aware of his plans to dig for El Fuego de Marte? Had Muz or Lennie had one too many one night and blabbed to a barfly? Whatever – it was clear that somebody else knew about Muz, and it was now of paramount importance to find out who – without alerting Janet.

He stared at his wife's troubled face for a few seconds longer and then said, "Talk to me hon, who is this Muz?"

Janet looked up and said, "I don't know!"

"Well if you don't know, how do you expect me to?"

"Because I was told to ask you – there, are you satisfied now?"

Del frowned and said, "Who told you?"

"Helene Gibsonne de Lyon."

"Helene Gibsonne de Lyon?" Del was stunned. He said, "You went to see her?"

Janet explained that she and Carole had attended the séance but had left before it had properly started. She explained that she'd asked Helene why she'd disappeared from the hospital after the accident, and that Helene had denied being knocked off a bicycle. She then told him that Helene had asked her to question Del about the mysterious Muz.

Del was flabbergasted. He said, "She said *'ask Del who Muz was'*? – She called me Del?"

"Yes."

Del was rendered speechless. He couldn't believe that Janet and Carole had gone to the séance. He was staggered by Helene's denial of the accident, and he was brimming with questions about how she knew who Muz was. Was she in cahoots with him? Was this some sort of elaborate con being perpetrated by Helene, Muz, and Lennie, or had Helene really been psychic?

He dismissed the psychic link as balderdash and became convinced that Helene must have been a part of the original plot to con him out of money… But – that didn't add up either.

His wild ponderings were interrupted by Janet. "Well?" she said, "say something…"

Del shook his head and said, "Huh! The only thing that I can say, is that I'm staggered that you even went to see a psychic because you know how the church views that."

"I went because of who she was; and I wanted to know why she'd disappeared out of the hospital."

"And a lot of good that did, by all accounts."

Janet said, "You stop being so high-and-mighty here Delbert Morrison. You were the one who started all this nonsense by knocking somebody off their bicycle in New Street. Now – who the hell is Muz?"

"I have no idea! I already told you that!"

Janet glared at Del and then stormed away. She was convinced that he was lying. She picked up the coffee pot and her cup, turned and said, "I'm going out by the pool, please leave me be."

Del realised that this was an opportunity; he said, "I have to go back to St. Andrew's to sort out some stuff with Casey, I'll be back before lunch."

Janet nodded but didn't speak. Within minutes she'd decided that she'd contact Carole and go to see the circus freak once more. But this time it would be for a personal audience.

Two-hundred yards down the street, Del spoke to an agitated Muz on his mobile.

"No," said Muz, "I don't know any broad by the name of Helene Gibsonne de fucking whatever!"

"So how did she know your name? Have you and Lennie had a few beers and blabbed?"

"It's a good job that you're on the end of a phone," said Muz, "'cos I'd shut your blab if I could reach you."

"Yeah whatever," said Del, "if we're going to do this, I need to know that I can trust you, and that includes you being discreet!"

"You fucking asshole!" bellowed Muz, *"you're gonna pay for this!"*

Del ignored the threat and said, "If you really haven't said anything, we've got a problem, 'cos she sure as hell knows about you."

Muz's anger subsided as he racked his brain to see if there had been a time when he and Lennie had had a few beers and may have said something, but nothing came to mind. He said, "All right – you find out where your wife saw that bitch, and we'll pay her a visit."

Del panicked and said, "You're not going to do anything stupid are you?"

"Of course not asswipe – and if you're inferring that I'm stupid, I swear I'll…"

"And how am I supposed to find out where she lives without alerting anybody?"

"Not my problem."

Del closed his eyes and began to question the wisdom of getting in any deeper when his thoughts were broken by Muz.

"And did you contact the water people yet?"

"No, the Rector only started his vacation today, so that's next on my list. After that we've got to decide what to do about the groundsman."

Chapter 11

Monday 13th November 2006. Orlando, Florida.

At 5.30pm Naomi and Carlton walked across the lower concourse of Orlando airport to the Dollar Car Hire desk and checked in. They'd endured the flight, the interminable wait to pass through US Immigration Control, complete with its dozen or more stations with only five manned, and now they wanted to get to their hotel.

They filled in all the required paperwork, chatted with the friendly staff, and then made their way to where the cars were parked.

"Hi folks," said another friendly attendant, "Got your slip?"

Carlton smiled, said, "Hi," and handed the car hire slip over.

The attendant scrutinized it, said, "That's fine guys," and pointed to the line of cars. He said, "Pick any vehicle from those over there."

Naomi saw a smile of delight and anticipation spread across Carlton's face. As he turned to look at her, she knew what he was about to ask, but pre-empted it by saying, "You choose, you'll be doing all the driving so any is okay by me."

Carlton walked down the line looking at the tempting array of new cars until he found the one he wanted. He walked back to Naomi with a big grin upon his face and said, "Oh yes – it's not big, but it feels really nice. I love it!"

Naomi grabbed hold of her suitcase and wheeled it down to the car. As she saw it, the feeling of a thumb pressed down on her left shoulder. She knew that this indicated that psychically she was no longer alone or that something significant was about to, or had, just taken place.

To her, a car was a car, and the male pre-occupation with them was as alien to her as mascara and foundation to the average man, but as she looked at it, the pressure from 'the thumb' increased. She listened, but heard nothing. She walked to the rear, left Carlton to load the suitcases into the trunk, and instinctively walked around to the left-hand side to get in. Once there she saw the steering wheel, remembered where she was, and walked to the other side. She climbed in.

As she looked out of the windscreen, the thumb pressed harder and she recalled an episode that she'd had in the previous July where she'd heard the words of a song named *'The Kennesaw Line,'* by a songwriter named Don Oja-Dunaway, and she'd seen a tree-lined, single-carriageway road, where the trees appeared to be festooned in Spanish moss. She also recalled the colour of the car she'd seen.

She sat forwards in the seat, looked out of the windscreen and a shiver ran down her spine. The car was exactly the same colour. She shook her head and realised that she hadn't even registered the colour before climbing in. She drew in a deep breath and felt a shift in her perception of reality. Straight away she knew that she was at the start of some sort of pre-ordained episode, and that by association; it also meant that her unborn son had not been destined for the world either. In a weird kind of way, that was a small comfort.

A few seconds later, a beaming Carlton climbed into the driving seat and they set off for their hotel.

Just after 7pm, they stepped out of the Quality Inn on International Drive. The turning back of their watches five hours to accommodate for the time difference hadn't altered how their bodies had felt, but it had been dinnertime in Florida, and instead of heading for bed, they headed out for a likely restaurant.

"It would be midnight in the UK right now," said a reticent Carlton, "so wouldn't you rather…"

"Get an early night, you old stick-in-the-mud?" said Naomi pulling her husband's linked arm closer.

"Well, yes. If we go and eat a full meal now, it could be too rich for us and our bodies won't know what's going on."

Naomi turned and said, "Our bodies won't know what's going on?"

"You know what I mean."

"I know that if you didn't have me with you, you'd turn into a regular old gimmer. You'd probably make yourself a cup of cocoa, pull on a woolly hat and long nightgown, and traipse up the stairs each night with a lit candle on a saucer."

"Gee," said Carlton, "since when did I transport back to Dickensian times?"

Naomi looked up and said, "Transport back? You were born then weren't you?"

Carlton smiled, said, "Hey! Watch it you!" and playfully smacked Naomi's bottom.

They arrived at a junction in the road and looked left and right. To the right, the venues appeared to be roadside shops, to the left, there seemed to be several likely candidates for eating.

They turned left and sauntered down the road until they came upon a Chinese restaurant.

"Fancy this?" said Carlton.

Naomi peered in and saw that the place was empty. She nodded towards the interior and said, "Are we just early or do the locals know something that we don't?"

Before Carlton could answer, a jolly looking Chinese-American appeared at the door and said, "Hi Folks, I'm the owner! Come on in and make yourself comfortable, we have the best Chinese food in Orlando!"

"Did we beat the rush?" said Naomi.

Carlton gave Naomi a sideways look.

The owner hesitated, and then smiled. He said, "Ah, yes – it's a bit early now, but by the time you've finished your meal, the place will be full."

Following a tasty, but distinctly average meal, Naomi leaned forwards and said, "This place is a dump..."

"The food was okay...," said Carlton trying to be upbeat.

Naomi looked up and said, "Yeah, okay, but look around you, we're still the only ones in here apart from the staff."

Carlton said, "It's not that bad." He paused and then added, "What about the scintillating company?"

"Yes," said Naomi, "that might have been good if there'd been any..."

Carlton raised his eyebrows and said, "I'll pretend I didn't hear that!" He saw Naomi smile and said, "It's nice to be back, and for nearly three weeks this time. Are you as excited as I am?"

Naomi hesitated and said, "Yes, I suppose so." She looked at Carlton and said, "I wished that I wasn't for other reasons, but you know…"

Carlton saw the look on Naomi's face and cast his mind back to the events of July and the emergence of the Malaterre Estate. It was at that time that Naomi had lost their baby son, and although he was pleased to be in America to re-unite with his old friends and Naomi's distant relatives, he too would have swapped the status quo in a heartbeat. Life, and love life, had been good between them, but he was aware that something was missing – a feeling as though part of Naomi had died along with their unborn son.

He leaned forwards and said, "Not meant to be honey."

"I know, but I can't help thinking how different our lives might have been."

"And still could be. You didn't suffer any permanent injury when you lost him, so if we're lucky, all of that could be just around the corner."

Naomi smiled and said, "You always cast light into the dark Cal Wilkes, and I think that maybe, until I find my perfect, ripped, stud-muffin, I'll hang on to you."

Carlton smiled and said, "And aren't I a stud-muffin?"

Naomi scrutinised her husband for a few seconds and then said, "No. You're more of a blueberry muffin."

Carlton burst out laughing and said, "Talking of dark, you know whose trial we'll be missing by being here?"

"How could I forget? It's one week today on the twentieth."

Both lapsed into silence as they recalled the forthcoming trial of Naomi's biggest adversary, the rich, and powerful multi-millionaire businessman, Adrian Darke. A man who blamed the exposure of his secret drug manufacturing facility, and his subsequent imprisonment awaiting trial, fair-square on Naomi's shoulders.

"Do you think that he was responsible for those weird notes we found?" said Naomi.

"What the single word things?"

"Yes, 'Brahma,' 'hive,' '2 Delta 2,' and 'male.'"

"God knows," said Carlton, "but they did stop after he was locked up…"

"True."

"And neither you nor Helen worked out the meanings did you?"

"No, because once they'd stopped, we dismissed them and put them down to the deluded Darke or one of his cronies."

"Well, it all starts next week for him, so let's hope he gets banged up for a very long time."

Naomi nodded and said, "Come on, drink up; I've had enough of this place, let's get back to the hotel."

At 5am Carlton watched as Naomi climbed out of bed and headed for the bathroom. He'd been awake for half-an-hour, and didn't feel in the least tired. He knew that if he'd been back in the UK it would have been 10am, and he realised that his body hadn't fully adjusted.

He heard the toilet flush and saw Naomi walk back in, perch on the side of the bed and attempt to look at the time on her watch in the darkness of the room.

"It's just after 5am," he said.

Naomi turned and said, "I'm sorry if I woke you."

"You didn't. I've been awake for at least half-an-hour."

"Me too, but it's only five o' clock and nowhere will be open for breakfast yet."

Carlton thought for a second and said, "Do you want to go back to sleep?"

"No, how about you?"

"No, I don't want to either."

"So why don't we get dressed, check out, hit the road early and head up to Dunnellon? We can stop for some breakfast on the way."

"Ooh yes," said Carlton, "and it has to be an American breakfast with pancakes and maple syrup!"

Three-quarters of an hour later they were on the Florida Turnpike heading towards Dunnellon and the Farlington house.

They sat in silence, deep in their own thoughts as the car streaked northwest through the darkness – on a venture that would not only shock and horrify people in two States, but one that would impact the lives of their American cousins forever…

Chapter 12

Wednesday 4th March 1863. 72nd Ohio Temporary Regimental Field Quarters, Chattanooga.

Ira knocked on the door of the small office that had been allocated to Adam in the newly constructed warehouses adjacent to Union Depot, and looked around before walking in. Satisfied that nobody was nearby, he stepped inside.

Adam looked up and said, "What took you so long? I was expecting you back last night." He saw the look on Ira's face and said, "And why are you looking so furtive?"

Ira sat at the chair in front of Adam's desk and said, "I think that I was followed."

A shiver ran down Adam's spine. He leaned forwards and spoke in a low tone. "Why do you think that?"

"We've been doing this unusual work for a long time now, and I've come to trust my senses. And I know that you understand because I've seen you react the same way whenever we find ourselves in a tricky situation…"

"Okay," said Adam, "but…"

"As the train was about to leave for La Vergne last Monday, a guy I hadn't ever seen before entered my carriage and sat a few seats behind me. He was dressed like any other guy except for his boots."

"Go on…"

"Each boot had three leather tassels, hung below red discs with Indian markings on."

Adam frowned and sat back in his seat. "Maybe an Indian tracker?" he said.

"No… maybe – but he didn't look Indian."

"So what makes you think that he was following you?"

"After the train journey I checked into one of the hotels in La Vergne, and when I came down for a drink, he was in the bar."

"How many hotels were there in La Vergne?"

"I don't know."

"Was yours the closest to the railroad station?"

"Maybe…"

"Well that's it then, it's…"

"No, it's not that," said Ira, "when I came down to the bar, even though I was wearing my uniform, some guy said something about 'niggers in bars where white folk was drinking' but before anybody could respond, the guy with the tassels jumped up, said something to the other guy, and he immediately sat down and ignored me after that."

"And did you attempt to make contact with tassel man after that?"

"No. He sat down and ignored me too; but all the time I was there, so was he."

"And then what?"

"Sometime after 10pm I went upstairs, waited half-an-hour, then lit out for Nashville."

"And was he in the bar when you left?"

"I don't know, I went out by the back stairs."

"Then what?"

"All the way to Nashville I felt like I was being followed. I stopped several times, hid behind trees and rocks, but I didn't see or hear anybody else. Just after 1:30am I reported to Colonel Wolford and passed on your messages. At 2.45am I made my way back to La Vergne."

"Did you see or hear anybody on the way back?"

"No."

"And did you get the impression that you were being followed?"

"No."

"So what's got you so spooked?"

"I arrived back in La Vergne around 6am. I stabled my horse, went back to the hotel, and aimed to get some sleep, but just as I was drifting off, I heard another horse ride into town. I jumped up, looked out of the window, and saw tassel guy disappearing into the stable on his horse."

"Are you positive that it was him?"

"Yes."

Adam put his right hand up to his mouth and started tapping his lips with his fingers. He remained silent for a few minutes and then said, "And did you see him again after that?"

"Yes – when I caught the train back to Chattanooga yesterday morning. I didn't see him in my carriage, but when I went to stretch my legs he was in the one behind."

"Did you acknowledge each other?"

"No, he appeared to be asleep."

"So what did you do?"

"The train stopped in Winchester to take on fuel and water. I looked into the next carriage and saw tassel man in his seat; I waited until the train started moving again then jumped off on the opposite side of the track.

I reported to the local C. O. and told him that I was on special orders from you and General Hardee. I don't think that he believed me at first, but after a couple of hours he let me go. After that I set off, but it isn't easy getting from Winchester to here, and that's why it took me so long."

"Who was the C.O. in Winchester?"

"A Colonel I haven't heard of before by the name of Lafayette Baker."

"Lafayette Baker?" said an astounded Adam. "Lafayette Curry Baker?"

Ira looked surprised and said, "That's what he said…"

"And did he ask you what you were doing in La Vergne?"

"No."

Adam sat back and began to tap his fingers on his lips again.

"Is there a problem with that?"

Adam looked at Ira and said, "Tell me again what happened when you reported to Baker?"

"I already told you. I told him that I was under orders from you to go to La Vergne, he told me to wait in another office. Then two hours later he let me go and supplied me with a horse and provisions for the journey."

Adam expelled a long breath and said, "Okay, maybe it's that the good Lord is watching over you, but Lafayette Curry Baker is a Union spy working for General-in-Chief Winfield Scott, and the last time I heard he wasn't a Colonel; he was working undercover in Virginia. How, or why, he was in Winchester Tennessee posing as a reb Colonel is a complete mystery to me, but I can say that you could not have happened upon a man who could have been more helpful to you."

Ira said, "Do you think that he knew me?"

"I'm sure that he did. But my concern now is that another top spy in the Union army is aware that we are in Tennessee and probably planning something; and he might start poking his nose in."

"And could that be such a problem?"

"I hope not, but the fewer the people who know about our presence the better I'll like it. Both sides of this conflict are awash with spies – military and civilian – so we'll need to keep our mouths shut and our wits about us. Which brings me to my next question – since getting back have you seen anything of tassel man?"

"No, nothing."

"Right," said Adam, "from now on we'll be extra careful, and if you see him again, don't let on, come and see me."

"I will, I promise." Ira looked at Adam and said, "Now, considering that I've risked my life for this hare-brained mission of yours several times in the last few days, are you going to tell me what you have planned for the gold?"

"I'm not sure about the last part yet," said Adam, "but here's what I have in mind. We know from Joliet's orders that the gold will be taken from the *SS Georgiana* in the early hours of the nineteenth. Joliet will take it to Charleston railroad depot, load it onto a secure coach, and keep it under guard until it's handed over to us at 0500 hours on Saturday the twenty-first.

Ira said, "I know all of that! I read Joliet's orders and gave you the information."

"I know," said Adam, "but you asked me, and I'm trying to convey my thoughts in a chronological order."

"Okay, but then?"

"We will escort the coach to Wilmington and hand it over."

Ira remained silent, expecting more, but when Adam said nothing else, he said, "And that's your plan? We accompany the railroad coach to Wilmington and hand the gold over?"

"That's not what I said brother."

Ira frowned and said, "Then what did you say?"

"I said that we would escort the coach to Wilmington and hand it over – I said nothing about the gold…"

Chapter 13

Tuesday 14th November 2006. Helene Gibsonne de Lyon's House, Goose Creek, Charleston.

At 9:05pm Muz and Lennie watched in silence as several women departed the unassuming home of Helene Gibsonne de Lyon; the main body appeared to leave first, and then ten minutes later two others departed.

"That's twelve in, twelve out," said Lennie.

Muz glanced at his watch and said, "Right, let's see what's going on." He leaned forwards, switched on the engine of their car, and then paused as he saw a police car pull up outside of the house.

"Shit!" he said, "that's all we need. We've been here too long already. If anybody starts looking out of their windows and gets suspicious, we could be asking for a visit from the cops as well."

"So what should we do?"

"I think that we should…" Muz suddenly leaned forwards and said, "…hey, wait one goddamned second, what the fuck is that all about?"

Lennie looked across to the house, saw two police officers – a woman, and Del Morrison. "Ain't that…?" he said.

"The Deacon – yes it is." Muz frowned and stared across the street. "If that bastard is screwing us over, or trying to lay some sort of trap he'll…"

"So what do you think we should do bro?"

Muz looked around and said, "Right now we get out of here – we could be attracting all sorts of attention."

"And then what?"

"We'll come back after we've spoken to Deacon fucking Devious." Muz paused for a second and then turned to face

85

Lennie. He said, "In fact, thinking about it, when was the last time you went to church?"

Across the street, Sheriff Bonnie-Mae Clement, Officer Beau Jackson, Janet, and Del Morrison walked up to Helene's front door and rang the bell.

The door opened and Helene said, "Good evening, I've been expecting you."

Jackson looked at Helene, waited until everybody was walking into the house, and then leaned across to Bonnie-Mae. "This isn't the lady I saw in New Street on the day of the accident," he said.

Everybody walked into the parlour; Helene excused herself, and then returned a few minutes later with some iced water, freshly squeezed orange juice and five glasses on a tray. After helping everybody to a drink, she sat down and said, "Now Sheriff, I take it that you're here because of the accident in New Street?"

Janet stared across at Helene and said, "Let's cut to the chase," she turned to Del and said, "Was this the lady you knocked off the bicycle?"

Del looked at Helene and said, "No."

Janet said, "Officer Jackson – was…"

"Ma'am – Janet," said Bonnie-Mae, "I would be most obliged if you would leave the police work to the police."

Janet looked across to the Sheriff and said, "I'm sorry Bonnie-Mae, I let the moment overtake me."

Bonnie-Mae nodded and said, "Very well – now, I do believe that you were about to ask Officer Jackson if this was the lady he saw involved in the incident in New Street too?"

"Yes ma'am," said Janet.

Bonnie-Mae turned to Jackson and said, "Beau?"

"No ma'am, it was not."

"Then we have ourselves a situation," said Bonnie-Mae, "and one that does not lend itself to easy explanation."

Janet turned to Del and said, "So who did you knock off the bike, and why did she say that her name was Helene Gibson de Lyon?"

Bonnie-Mae looked at Janet with disapproval and said, "Ma'am, please – if *I* may be permitted?"

Janet looked down at her feet and said, "Sorry Sheriff."

Bonnie-Mae continued to stare at Janet for a few seconds and then turned to Helene.

"Ms. De Lyon," she said, "would you have any notion why somebody would pretend to be you?"

Helene looked at Bonnie-Mae and said, "Do you mean psychically?"

"I mean it any way you'd care to look at it."

Janet frowned and said, "Oh please Sheriff; don't tell me that you believe all of this fanciful psychic hoo-ha?"

Bonnie-Mae turned to Janet and said, "Ma'am, unless you permit me to continue this investigation without further interruption, I will ask you to sit in the patrol car until we are finished."

Janet pursed her lips and looked back down at her feet.

Following a few more seconds of intense staring, Bonnie-Mae turned back to Helene and said, "Ma'am?"

"What?" said Helene.

"Do you have any idea why anybody would be riding round downtown Charleston on a bicycle, and pretending to be you?"

"I'd have thought that was obvious," said Helene.

Bonnie-Mae waited, but when Helene said nothing more, she took a deep breath and said, "And?"

"They were pretending to be me to conceal their own identity."

Bonnie-Mae closed her eyes for a second and then said, "I think that we could all have deduced that Ms de Lyon…"

"Please do call me Helene, Sheriff; Ms de Lyon is so formal."

"Very well, Helene – what I perhaps should have asked is, why of all people, do you think that they used your name, and not any other?"

"I don't know Sheriff, maybe it was somebody who knew me and just used it because it was the first name they could think of."

Bonnie-Mae stared a Helene for a few seconds and then nodded. "Okay," she said, "I can see that this line of enquiry is getting us nowhere, so we'll trouble you no further." She placed her hands on the arms of her chair and started to push herself up.

Beau started to follow suit, but halted when he heard Helene say, "There may be another way that I can help."

Bonnie-Mae looked and sat back down.

"Would you like me to see if I can get any help from my contact on the other side?"

Janet opened her mouth to object, but remembered the Sheriff's threat.

Bonnie-Mae paused and then said, "I have to tell you that I am a God-fearing Christian, and that by nature I do not hold with this type of activity, but I am aware that there have been recorded cases where the police have been helped by psychics, so I will endeavour to listen to what you have to say with an open mind."

Helene smiled and said, "How refreshing – an open mind indeed." She looked at the others, lingered on Janet for a nano-second longer, and then said, "Now, all I need is silence."

Del watched with a racing heart as Helene first stared across the room, and then closed her eyes.

For several minutes everybody sat still until Helene opened her eyes and looked up. She nodded a couple of times, and then turned to face Del.

"Connie is not his mother's name," she said, "it's Ellen, and she passed over in 2004."

Del felt as though his head would explode, and that his reaction would give the game away. He saw Helene turn towards Beau and heard her say, "He knew Officer Jackson – when you first approached him, he knew…"

Beau opened his mouth to speak but he too was cut off when he saw Helene turn to the Sheriff.

"The lady on the bike was a man, and he used my name by pure chance." She turned to face Janet and said, "But this is no pure chance – sometime within the next few days you will see a green canvas bag with long white handles. You must buy that bag because it will…" A sudden terrifying vision crossed her mind, she faltered and then said, "… save yours, and your friends' lives. If you disbelieve me and do not buy the bag, you will survive, but you will blame yourself for their deaths for the rest of your life."

Everybody was stunned. Even the sceptical Janet was speechless. For a few seconds they swapped glances, and then it sounded as though everybody tried to speak at once.

Beau said, "How did you know my name ma'am?"

Janet said, "I don't believe it…how could…"

Bonnie-Mae held her right hand up and said, "Hey, hey, wait one moment…" and waited until the room fell silent. She turned back to Helene and said, "That was er, very revealing ma'am…"

The only one who hadn't responded had been Del, and Beau clicked on to it. He looked at Del and saw him frowning. He then turned to look at the others. Janet was glaring at Helene and muttering disparaging remarks, and Bonnie-Mae was sitting with a puzzled expression upon her face.

Helene sat forwards in her seat and said, "Would anybody like another cold drink?"

Beau said, "Ma'am, Helene, you say that the lady on the bike was a man?"

"Not strictly me Officer Jackson, I was informed."

"And did your informant say *why* the man on the bike was dressed as a woman?"

"No, but I think that you'll find that he's an illegal immigrant, and that is how he conceals his identity."

"Goddamn! No wonder he lit out of the hospital like he did," said Beau.

Bonnie-Mae spun around and glared. She said, "Watch your language! There's church folk here."

Beau said, "Sorry Sheriff," and then lapsed into silence as he imagined describing to his colleagues how they'd learned about the cross-dressing, hospital-skipping, illegal immigrant. He looked at Bonnie-Mae and said, "This'll be fun to explain to the boys at the office…"

Bonnie-Mae raised her eyebrows and said, "You don't say?"

Janet finally found her tongue and turned to Del. She said, "Who's Connie?"

Del felt his cheeks flush but said, "I don't know." He cast a nervous glance across to Helene and saw her raise an eyebrow.

"You just mark my words Deacon," said Helene, "his mother's name *isn't* Connie."

Janet stared at Helene for a few seconds, turned to say something, but was cut off.

"I thought that you didn't believe in all this psychic mumbo-jumbo?" said Del.

Janet was in utter turmoil; she wanted to persevere about Connie, Ellen, and Muz, but her religious conviction held her back. She stared at Del through slits of eyes for a few seconds and then said, "I don't."

Helene looked at Janet and said, "Maybe you do, maybe you don't..."

"I don't!" repeated Janet.

Helene shook her head and said, "...okay, but don't you go walking past that green bag when you see it, or you will surely regret it until the day you die."

Janet said, "I've heard enough of this nonsense." She turned to Bonnie-Mae and said, "Sheriff – please take me home."

Bonnie-Mae put down her drink and said, "Sure thing. I think that we've all heard enough for now, so..." she turned to Helene and said, "...thank you for your hospitality ma'am, it was a, a – fascinating experience." She stood up and extended her hand.

Helene stood up, shook the offered hand, and said, "I hope that I've helped."

As everybody filed out of the front door Helene tapped Bonnie-Mae on the shoulder.

Bonnie-Mae stopped and turned.

Helene leaned close to her ear and said, "That gold cross of your mother's – it's in the filter of your sister Darlene's swimming pool."

Chapter 14

Del smiled at the ladies who'd prepared a tasty lasagne and side-salad meal for the volunteers who'd be manning the stands at the 'bring and buy' sale that evening.

"Thank you ladies," he said, after wiping his mouth on a paper serviette, "that lasagne and salad is as good as I've tasted in any of Charleston's finest Italian restaurants. My compliments to you all for this fine repast."

The ladies smiled back with genuine affection.

Del turned and walked back into the main body of the hall to greet the volunteers as they filed in. He nodded left and right, acknowledging various comments, and then his heart leapt into his mouth. Looking like fish out of water, he watched as Muz and Lennie shuffled in.

His heart rate went through the roof. The sight of them made him recall Helene's remark that Muz's mother was named Ellen, not Connie.

As Muz approached he said, "Evening Deacon, I hope that you don't mind two lost souls visiting your homely-looking establishment for a small bargain or two?"

Del smiled and offered his hand. He said, "Not at all; all are welcome in God's house."

Muz said, "Thank you Deacon. Before the sale, might we have a private word?" He gestured with his head to the outside.

With a racing pulse Del scanned the room and saw no sign of Janet or Carole, he smiled, leaned towards them, and said, "Round the back of the Parish House is Casey Peter's shed. I'll meet you there in ten minutes."

Muz leaned forwards and said, "Five, shit-for-brains, or I'll come looking for you."

Del looked around, saw that they hadn't attracted any attention, and then nodded in agreement.

Carole, who'd been chatting to an older couple out of Del's vision, caught sight of him and the two seedy, out-of-place-looking men, and watched as they parted company. She terminated her conversation with the elderly couple, moved across the hall in an attempt to follow them, but was waylaid by the officiating guest preacher Reverend Iain MacLean.

"Excuse me Carole," said Reverend MacLean, "I take it that you are aware that the new temporary lay preacher arrives tomorrow aren't you?"

Carole said, "Yes I am thank you Iain, and I know that she'll be staying here until Marshall returns from his vacation."

"Excellent. I know that you'll make her welcome."

With one eye on the disappearing men Carole said, "Of course I will." She then looked at the Rector and added, "As a matter of fact I'm looking forward to meeting her."

Reverend MacLean nodded and said, "Good." He paused for a few seconds and then said, "I have heard that she can be a bit controversial."

"Me too."

"We, er – don't want her upsetting any of the older folks mind."

"I don't think that we have anything to worry about on that score. I've heard that she can be different, but I feel sure that the folks at St. Andrew's will take her to their hearts." She smiled, and then turned to pursue the two men, but was stopped again.

"What exactly do you mean that she can be different?" said the Rector.

Filled with growing exasperation Carole said, "I understand that she has a reputation for being very liberal within her Christian beliefs, which has in the past caused a few eyebrows to be raised."

The Rector frowned and said, "Go on..."

Carole gave up on the idea of trying to follow the men, turned to face Reverend MacLean and said, "According to Bob Hoath, the Rector of St. Patrick's in Williston, she once officiated at the wedding of a couple who insisted on getting married in the er, altogether."

The Rector stood looking at Carole without responding for a couple of seconds and then the gravity of what he'd heard sank in. He said, "Saints preserve us! She didn't…Reverend Burch wasn't…? – You aren't trying to tell me that *she too* had no..."

"No, no, nothing like that! – Ali was fully clothed throughout the service. It's just that nobody else was."

Reverend MacLean was shocked; he said, "What? – Nobody at the service was clothed but her? – Nobody? – Not even the bride and groom's parents?"

"Correct, nor any of the staff who served at the reception afterwards."

Reverend Maclean put his hand up to his mouth and said, "My my – I see what you mean when you say that she's controversial."

Carole leaned closer to the Rector and said, "I do believe that she was invited to remove everything but her dog collar, but she did politely decline."

"My oh my!" said the shocked Rector, "We do live in strange times." He paused and then leaned down to Carole's ear and said, "I take it that you haven't got a copy of the wedding album then?"

Carole smiled and said, "Why Reverend MacLean! What would your parishioners think if they'd heard that question?"

"Heard what question? I never said anything! You must be hearing things Mrs Thompson!"

Carole smiled and nodded as she saw Reverend MacLean wink. She said, "Well you can rest assured that nothing like that will be happening at St. Andrew's while Marshall is away!"

"I surely hope not," said Reverend MacLean, "I surely hope not…"

Del stepped out of the Parish House, cast a nervous glance around, and then headed straight for the shed. He opened the door, stepped inside, and was slammed against Casey's bench with such violence that several objects fell off and scattered across the floor.

"What the fuck were you doing at that weirdo's house with the Sheriff?" said Muz.

Del stared into the wild-looking eyes and said, "I was ordered to accompany my wife there while the Sheriff asked her some questions."

"What kind of questions?"

Del realised that he hadn't mentioned the bicycle episode to Muz and Lennie, and knew that it would be complicated to explain, but he decided to come clean.

"A couple of hours after your, your charade with me in Archdale Street, I knocked a woman off her bicycle in New Street. The police were called and the woman gave her name as Helene Gibsonne de Lyon..."

"What?" said Muz, "You never..."

"Wait," said Del, "it gets more complicated, "It turns out that the woman I knocked off the bike wasn't a woman, it was a man..."

"What?" repeated Muz.

"...and he'd used the name Helene Gibsonne de Lyon. But then he disappeared from the hospital and..."

"Whoa, whoa, back up cowboy! What hospital?" said Muz, "And why did a man give a woman's name?"

"Because he was dressed as a woman, and according to Helene Gibson de Lyon's contact from the other side, he was an illegal immigrant who always dressed that way to avoid capture."

Muz turned and looked at Lennie, and then turned back to face Del. He said, "And I thought I was messed up. You're so far off the path I doubt you could find your ass with both hands and a road map."

Del hesitated and then said, "Right – okay – however you want to view it, or me, those are the facts."

"So I repeat – why did you go to the psychic's house with the Sheriff?"

"Because my wife went to one of her séance's thinking that she was the person I'd knocked off the bike, and she wanted to know why she'd disappeared from the hospital. She was then told by the de Lyon woman that she hadn't been anywhere near New Street that day, and to ask me who Muz was. Then yesterday we we're all instructed to accompany the Sheriff to de Lyon's house to confirm or deny whether she was the person I'd knocked off the bike."

Muz looked at Lennie again and said, "Do you believe all this crap?"

Lennie shrugged.

Muz looked back at Del and said, "So what then?"

"The Sheriff believed her when the other officer confirmed that it wasn't her he'd seen at the scene of the accident, and because the person I'd hit had disappeared, they hadn't got a case against me. So it's all over."

"So how did the psychic bitch know my name?"

"Don't ask me!"

Muz stared at Del for a few seconds and then turned to Lennie. He said, "We gotta pay her a visit."

Lennie nodded and said, "Whatever."

Muz turned back to Del and said, "From now on keep away from that bitch, we'll deal with her."

Del opened his mouth to speak but was cut off.

Muz pointed a stubby finger close to Del's face and said, "I mean it…" He waited until he'd seen an acknowledgement and then said, "You should be concentrating on those stormwater guys – did you contact them?"

"Yes, they're sending their surveyors to mark out the boundaries tomorrow, and if all goes according to plan they're hoping to start digging the drain on Friday."

Muz said, "Right, good. Now get back to your 'bring and buy' sale before anybody misses you."

Del nodded, and was about to head out of the open door when he remembered something. He said, "When you swore on your mother Connie's life that I could trust you, you did mean it didn't you?"

"I fucking said so didn't I?"

Out of the corner of his eye Del saw Lennie open his mouth to speak, and then saw him freeze. He frowned, turned to where Lennie was looking, and saw Casey Peters standing in the doorway.

"And who's trusting who, for what? And what are you guys doing in my shed?" said Casey.

All three men were startled but Muz was the first to respond. He fumbled about behind his back, until his hand alighted upon a heavy plant pot. He held it up towards Casey and said, "I've just been questioning the Deacon about these pots," he said.

Casey frowned, looked at the pot, and said, "What about them?"

Muz pointed to the base and said, "See this inscription? It shows that they've been stolen."

Casey looked at the pot and said, "What are you talking about?"

"Here," said Muz, lifting the pot up higher, "look for yourself." He waited until Casey leaned forwards, and then in a blur of movement, smashed the pot into his left temple.

Casey dropped like a stone.

Del gasped as he watched Muz and Lennie grab his arms and yank him into the shed. He said, "What the hell are you doing? Are you crazy?"

Muz looked at Lennie and said, "Get the pickup."

Del repeated, "What the hell are you doing? You can't..."

Muz grabbed Del by the jacket and said, "Shut the fuck up. Do you hear me?"

Del said, "But what..."

"I said, *shut the fuck up!*" He slapped Del hard on his left cheek and stared into his eyes. He said, "Got it?"

Del nodded and Lennie disappeared.

Del watched spellbound as Muz bound Casey's wrists and then gagged him with a dirty-looking neckerchief.

A few minutes later a dark grey Ford pickup reversed to the shed and Lennie hopped out.

"Is the coast clear?" said Muz.

Lennie scrutinised the area and said, "It's okay right now."

Muz looked at Del and said, "Get his ankles."

Del was astonished, he said, "What, me?"

"Yes you – get hold of his fucking ankles!"

"I'll do no such thing! I won't be a party to this."

Muz grabbed hold of Del's jacket with his left hand, yanked him closer to his face, and slapped him again.

"You're already a party to this you piece of shit, now get hold of his ankles or I'll kick you all around the fucking car park."

Del was petrified and almost stumbled as he was propelled violently forwards. He bent down, grabbed Casey's ankles, and heaved him up as Muz lifted him by the armpits.

"All clear?" queried Muz.

"All clear."

Del thought that his heart would stop. He was terrified of being seen, and he couldn't believe what he was doing with his friend.

"Del! Del – are you there honey?"

Del heard his wife call; he said, "Shit, that's all we need," he looked at Muz and said, "Quick, get him into the pickup and get out of sight."

Muz nodded. They bundled Casey's limp body onto the bench seat of the cab, Lennie covered him with a large grey blanket, and the two men disappeared into the shed.

"Del, honey…?"

Janet caught sight of Del and said, "Oh, there you are. What are you doing back here? You should be in the Parish House, the sale's about to start."

Del walked towards her and said, "Sorry honey, I caught two boys fooling around back here so I packed 'em off to their families."

Janet looked over her husband's shoulder and saw the front of the pickup; she said, "Casey got a new truck?"

"Beats me honey, you know him, he never holds on to any vehicle for more than a few months."

He walked with Janet to the front of the Parish House, held the door open for her, and followed her in. He turned right and looked over his shoulder as he heard the pickup growl past and head for the Ashley River Road.

He saw that Janet hadn't taken any notice and gently ushered her in to the main hall.

Whilst wrestling with his thoughts about the fate of Casey he walked slap-bang into the back of Janet. He recovered his composure and said, "Sorry honey I wasn't looking…"

Janet was standing with her right hand clasped to her mouth and staring at one of the stalls.

Del said, "What is it hon, what's wrong? You look as though you've seen a ghost."

Janet didn't speak at first. She looked up at Del and then pointed to an item on the nearby stall. It was a green canvas bag with long white handles.

Chapter 15

"*Dilemma* is a Greek word signifying a double proposition from
di or *dis,* meaning twofold – and *lemma*, a thing taken or received.
A *dilemma* therefore, is a position before which there are two
alternatives – equally good or equally bad."

Thursday 5th March 1863. Union Depot, Chattanooga.

Henry Thomas Harrison, known to all as 'Harrison,' aged thirty-
one years old, hesitated for a few seconds, looked around, and
then stepped through the door of General Hardee's personal
railroad coach.

Unused to folk entering without knocking, Hardee looked up
and saw who had stepped inside.

"George," he said to his industrious private secretary, "it's a
lovely morning – why don't you go get yourself a cup of coffee
from the hotel for the next hour?"

George knew when he was being dismissed and said, "I will –
thank you General." He put on his jacket, removed his hat from
the nearby hat-stand, said, "Sirs," and left.

Hardee looked at the slight figure before him.

Harrison's boyish face sported a thick and bushy moustache
over a goatee beard. He was dressed in a long, dark brown, riding
coat, wore a flax-coloured cotton shirt, a dusty-looking red
neckerchief, light brown trousers, and he was carrying a battered
Stetson cowboy hat. Altogether unremarkable dress except for his
light tan boots complete with distinctive red-topped tassels.

Hardee pointed to the chair in front of his desk and said, "Sit
down Harrison."

Harrison sat down and crossed his legs. Like Holdsworth
before him, he too noticed the half-naked woman on the chaise

longue behind the General, but unlike Holdsworth, he didn't linger on it long enough for the General to notice.

"Do you have anything to report?" said Hardee.

In his distinctive southern drawl, Harrison said, "In my opinion the nigger's a spy."

Hardee couldn't take it in at first. That meant that by association, it was possible that Holdsworth could be a Union spy too. He frowned as he recalled Holdsworth's exploits and bravery on the battlefield, and the thought that the man in whom President Jefferson Davis himself had placed his trust could be a traitor, was almost too much for him to bear. As he wrestled with his thoughts, he suddenly realised that it could be possible that Jones was acting under his own volition, and that Holdsworth too, was unaware.

He looked at Harrison and said, "And just how do you arrive at that contentious opinion?"

Harrison placed his hat on the General's desk and said, "There ain't no other way to explain Jones's nocturnal activity."

"Go on," said Hardee.

"As per your orders, I followed the suspect…"

"Suspect now is it?"

Harrison stopped speaking, looked down, and then looked back at Hardee. He said, "I am not trying to be offensive General, but I concluded that you 'suspected' Corporal Jones of something – considering how you put me on his tail, that is."

Hardee opened his mouth to respond, but decided against it.

Harrison saw the gesture and then continued, "I followed *Corporal Jones* on the railroad to La Vergne where he alighted and checked into Brown's Hotel on Front Street. Just after 10pm he left the hotel dressed in civilian clothing and rode to Nashville. There he reported in to the field headquarters of Colonel Frank Lane Wolford of the 1st Kentucky Cavalry and stayed until a quarter before 3am. He then rode back to La Vergne and went back to his hotel just before 6am. Yesterday he took the train back to Chattanooga."

"Did you find out *why* he had reported to Wolford?"

"No sir. I was born and raised in Nashville, and more than a few of my kinsfolk ride with the Yankees. Despite not being a member of either army, I didn't want to ride into Wolford's camp and risk the possibility of being recognised."

"Hmm," said Hardee. "So where did Jones go after he returned to Chattanooga?"

"I don't know sir."

"Why, didn't you keep a tail on him?"

"I couldn't because he wasn't on the train when it arrived back."

"Not on the train?" said Hardee. "Then where was he?"

"I don't know sir." For the first time since entering the coach, a shadow of doubt crossed his mind. He hesitated and then said, "The train stopped in Winchester to take on water and supplies, and it is there that I presume he slipped away."

"You presume?"

"Yes sir."

"And on what grounds do you base that presumption?"

"That Jones was no longer aboard the train once we arrived in Chattanooga."

"That sir – is stating the obvious," said an exasperated Hardee. He looked at the impervious face of Harrison and said, "Perhaps I should have said – why do you suppose that he departed the train at Winchester, and not somewhere else?"

"Because Winchester was the only stop after La Vergne – and considering that the locomotive travels at approximately twenty-five miles per hour when it's in motion, if he'd jumped off anywhere else at that speed, I expect I'd be reporting his untimely demise right now." He paused and then added, "Or maybe *timely* demise if we were to look at it from another, more agreeable angle."

Hardee started to grow impatient with Harrison's off-hand manner and said, "You appear to have an attitude to authority that would not be tolerated in the army Harrison, so I'd thank you to keep your sarcasm on a short leash."

Harrison said, "I apologise General, I did not mean to offend."

Hardee looked at Harrison and said, "I am forty-eight years old and a General. Unlike you, I have never met your mentor Secretary of War, James Seddon, so you are in a unique position to distinguish yourself. Don't let that smart mouth spoil your chances before you learn that a big part of being successful is winning over influential people by flattery, regardless of what you perceive the truth to be, instead of treating them with contempt."

Harrison looked at Hardee with a glimmer of respect and said, "No sir. Thank you, I will try to follow that laudable advice."

Hardee continued to stare at Harrison for a few seconds and then said, "Do you have any idea why Jones got off the train at Winchester?"

Harrison shook his head and said, "There are no Yankee units anywhere near there, so I doubt that it was to meet up with anybody like that. He may have been going to meet some other folks – who too could be up to something – or maybe he has some 'nigra' family near there. Simple answer is, I don't know, and all of this is pure conjecture."

Hardee sat back in his seat and said, "Do you think that he could have seen you?"

"He did see me – several times. But that don't automatically mean that I'm following him. La Vergne isn't awash with hotels, and because the damn Yankees keep on scuppering our railroad tracks there's only one train running a day, so everybody travelling would have seen all the other folks travelling that day."

Hardee frowned and said, "Hmm," again.

"If, however," said Harrison, "he got off the train because of me – that is an entirely different matter. That would mean that he was on to me, and that he was being evasive."

"So now we have the watcher being watched."

Harrison nodded and said, "Maybe…"

"So what now?"

Harrison leaned forwards and said, "Am I missing something General?"

"Like what?"

"You never explained to me why you wanted Corporal Jones followed."

"And should I? If I instruct you to follow somebody, you do as you're instructed. It's up to me to decide who I take into my confidence."

Harrison's eyes narrowed. He said, "Sir, I have the trust of the Minister for War. I do believe that you too can trust me with confidences."

Hardee paused and looked at Harrison for a few seconds. He then said, "Very well – Corporal Jones is the personal friend and aide of an officer who has been entrusted with a very important mission for the CSA."

Harrison listened but didn't respond.

"The mission," continued Hardee, "is vital to the Confederacy, and has been authorised by the President himself. When the officer informed me that he would be taking along Corporal Jones, I wanted to make sure that he was completely trustworthy and up to the task, so I contacted Major Sorrell who recommended that I employ your services. Now you have informed me that in your opinion, Jones could be a Union spy."

"No sir," said Harrison, "I did not inform you that he *could be* a spy. I informed you that in my opinion *he is* a spy."

Hardee took in a deep breath and said, "Damn it to hell. What am I supposed to do now? Arrest the nigger and have him shot for treason?"

"No sir – we do nothing to arouse anybody's suspicion. If the officer's involved too, we'll want to establish that and have them both shot. And if the mission involves something vitally important to the CSA we'll need to ensure that if anything untoward occurs, we'll have that covered as well."

Hardee looked with a new respect at the man before him. He said, "For a man of diminutive stature Mr. Harrison, you surely do command a presence."

"Thank you sir."

"Very well, we will do as you say. Now, would you like me to take an active part in this process?"

"No, thank you General, I know what I have to do, and no traitorous nigger nor anybody in cahoots with him will escape my notice from now on; not until we bring this distasteful and highly repugnant episode to a satisfactory conclusion."

Chapter 16

Thursday 16th November 2006. St. Andrew's Church, Charleston.

At 9:30am the workmen from the South Carolina Department of Health and Environmental Control arrived at St. Andrew's church.

Del saw the vans pull up outside the Parish House and several men alight. He walked outside and watched for a few seconds as a rugged-looking man in his early forties directed the others. He knew that the man had to be Taffy Brewer because of the lack of American accent.

"Mr Brewer?" he called.

Taffy turned around, smiled, and walked across to Del with his hand outstretched. "You must be Deacon Morrison," he said.

"I am." Del took the offered hand and shook it. He got straight down to business. He said, "I want to stress how important it is that whatever work you start must be completed by the end of next week."

"No worries there squire," said Taffy, "it's Thanksgiving Day next Thursday so most of the guys will want to be done by next Tuesday so that some of them can head off home to different parts of the country."

Del was surprised. He said, "Oh, I didn't think that you'd be finished so quickly."

"We won't. This car park needs more than one drain, which we'll have to do at another time, but we should be able to complete the one across the car park providing that you can ensure that we'll have clear access to it at all times."

"And what if you hit any snags?"

"Then we could always work through the weekend."

"Not on the Sunday you couldn't," said Del. "We have a full programme of events every week, and it gets very busy here."

Taffy rubbed his chin and said, "Hmm…but the car park will remain cordoned off if we do hit a problem?"

"Yes, I can ensure that."

"Okay – if it does hit the fan then, we could always finish off after Thanksgiving Day."

"But you will be finished by Saturday the 25th?"

"Yes, we're booked in somewhere else the following Monday, so we have to be out of your hair by then."

"Excellent, and…" Del stopped speaking as he caught sight of the Sheriff's car pull off the Ashley River Road, and turn into the drive.

Taffy turned too and said, "Trouble?"

"Not that I'm aware of." Del recalled the episode with Casey, and swallowed hard as he saw Bonnie-Mae behind the wheel. He walked up to the patrol car and waited until she stepped out. He saw her look at Taffy and then turn to look at him.

"You got something planned Del?" said Bonnie-Mae.

Del was relieved to hear her use his Christian name and said, "The stormwater guys are here to put in the first of a series of drains."

"I wasn't aware you had a problem."

"Ma'am," said Taffy stepping forwards and offering his hand.

Bonnie-Mae shook Taffy's hand and said, "And who might you be sir?"

Taffy pointed to the SCDHEC vans and said, "Taffy Brewer, I'm in charge of this bunch of merry men."

Bonnie-Mae looked at Taffy and said, "That accent isn't from around here."

"No it isn't ma'am, I'm Welsh. I do, however, have the good fortune to be a resident of South Carolina, and I relish in helping to preserve the county's natural resources through my chosen profession."

"And you have a slick tongue to go with it Mister Brewer. Does Reverend Hughes know that you're here?"

"I don't know Sheriff; I just turn up where I'm instructed and get on with the work."

Del started to feel uncomfortable. He said, "Marshall's been considering allowing the SCDHEC to put a drain across the car park for some time, but he never got around to it. Mr. Brewer here informed me that the boys had a window of opportunity to make a start on the project this week, so I agreed to let them."

Taffy frowned about the sequence of events, and was about to set the record straight, but was cut off by Bonnie-Mae.

"And are you positive that Father Marshall will be happy with you taking things into your own hands an' all?"

"Certainly," said Del with a lot more confidence than he felt, "anything that benefits both the church and the environment is good for us all."

Bonnie-Mae looked at Del and then said, "Very well, if you say so." She stepped closer and said, "Might I have a word inside?"

Del pointed towards the door of the Parish House and said, "Sure, we can use Marshall's office."

Once seated in the office Bonnie-Mae said, "I am sorry to say that I have some bad news."

Del felt as though an invisible belt tightened around his temples. He said, "What kind of bad news?"

"Earlier this morning Casey Peter's body was found in the Cooper River near Bushy Park Boat Landing."

Del gasped. He couldn't believe that Muz and Lennie had made the leap from small-time hustlers to murderers. He said, "No! – How? Why?"

"The 'how' we aren't sure of yet, but the Coroner's due to carry out an autopsy this afternoon. The 'why,' is why I'm here."

In an act of supreme stupidity, Del blurted out, "You don't think that I had anything to do with it do you?"

Bonnie-Mae frowned and said, "Now, that is an interesting response." She sat back and stared at Del for a few seconds, and then continued, "Why on earth would you think, that I would think you had anything to do with Casey's death?"

"I, er, I…"

"You er, what Deacon Morrison?"

Del noted the change of address and said, "It was just a natural reaction…"

"*Natural reaction?* To think that because I want to ask you a few questions about your groundsman, you would assume that I think you are guilty of killing him?"

Del could tell from the heat of his face that his cheeks were flushed, and he knew that the Sheriff could see it. He said, "Please

Bonnie-Mae – you know how close we are at St. Andrew's. I would never harm anybody. I'm the Deacon here. When you told me what you did, I just..." He hesitated as he realised that he was in a hole and digging deeper with every sentence.

"You just what? Thought that I'd think you were responsible for Casey's death?"

"I don't know...I'm getting befuddled now and not thinking straight."

Bonnie-Mae stared in silence at Del for a few seconds and then said, "Okay – let's start again. Have you any idea what Casey could have been doing twenty miles north of here at Bushy Park?"

"No ma'am..." he thought of something, "...unless he was fishing." He'd done it again! He knew that Casey hated fishing, but the mouth had engaged before the brain...

"Fishing?" said Bonnie-Mae, "I didn't know Casey liked fishing."

Del felt the hole sink down another twenty feet. He said, "Yeah, he did – not often, but he did go. Maybe he went to that jetty on the left where the fishermen go."

"You know that jetty do you?"

"Yes, I've fished off there myself."

"And when was the last time you went there?"

"When I was a boy, with my pa – and sometimes with my school buddies."

Bonnie-Mae removed her notebook from her shirt pocket and made a few notes. She then looked up and said, "Okay, let's make this official. Have you seen Casey in the company of anybody who might have held a grudge against him?"

"No."

"Do you know whether anybody had any kind of grudge or ill-feeling towards him?"

"No."

"Have you seen him with any strangers recently?"

"No."

"Have *you* seen anybody that you don't know at St. Andrew's recently?"

Del felt the walls of the office close in and said, "No." He looked at the Sheriff and heard her say, "Hmm..."

He sat in silence as the Sheriff pondered, and then said, "What's on your mind?"

Bonnie-Mae looked up and said, "Apart from my all-too-infrequent personal visits to St Andrew's, I can't hardly recall a time when I had to come here on business, but within one six month period we had a grave desecration, an attempted desecration, and now I'm investigating the mysterious death of your groundsman."

Del remained silent.

"And I'm beginning to see the glimmer of a common denominator here…"

"What common denominator?"

"Church ground."

"What do you mean church ground?"

"Or maybe what's buried in it."

Del frowned and said, "Like what?"

Bonnie-Mae flicked back through the pages of her notebook and then looked up. She said, "El Fuego de Marte – The Fire of Mars."

Del was horrified. He said, "What? How on earth do you make that kind of connection?"

Bonnie-Mae looked at Del and said, "Are you taking me for a complete fool Deacon? – Do I have the word 'dumbass' or 'hick' printed on my forehead?"

"No, of course not! How could you…"

"How could I think that any of this might be to do with a very rare and valuable ruby that might be buried in your church yard? – And you ask this when I turn up here in Father Marshall's absence and find another group of men about to start digging up more church ground?

Del became indignant and said, "Just what are you suggesting Sheriff?"

"You know damn well what I'm suggesting, and if I had a scrap of proof I'd have your ass in the back of the car right now!"

Del was mortified. He said, "This is ridiculous! The guys outside are here to put in a stormwater drain not go digging for non-existent jewels!"

"Non-existent? – Now why would you say 'non-existent' – have you looked?"

"No I haven't!" He suddenly thought of a way out of his dilemma. He said, "But not because I couldn't."

Bonnie-Mae frowned and said, "Whoa, whoa – what do you mean, 'not because I couldn't'?"

"I mean I know that I could have checked because Casey showed me where that old Mathewes grave was months' ago."

"He, actually told you, where it was?"

"Yes ma'am."

"And you did nothing?"

"That's right – I did nothing."

"Not even tell the family from Florida?"

Del opened his mouth but realised that he might have made a mistake. He stammered, "Well no, because, I, er…"

"Because you, er, what?"

"I was going to tell them, but…"

Bonnie-Mae frowned and said, "But you thought you'd keep it to yourself? – And now Casey's wound up dead…"

Del leapt to his feet and said, "That's outrageous! How dare you insinuate that I'm involved in any of this?"

Bonnie-Mae remained calm and said, "I'm not insinuating anything Deacon, I'm trying to fathom the fact from the fiction – and your whole manner has my mind positively floundering with questions."

"Well let me put you straight! I didn't inform the family from Florida because in my heart, I don't believe it's there. As you pointed out, we've already had one desecration and I didn't think it right that we should have another, so rightly or wrongly I held my council."

Bonnie-Mae sat in silence for a few seconds and then said, "Hmm, maybe…" She looked into Del's eyes and said, "…I guess I can live with that for now, but…"

"Thank you," interrupted Del.

Bonnie-Mae nodded and then continued, "…but you had no right to withhold that information from the family."

Del looked down and said, "Well I'm truly sorry about that."

"And unless I'm very much mistaken, they will want to hightail it up here and check it out."

A subdued Del said, "Yes, I guess so."

Bonnie-Mae stood up and said, "Okay, let's move on from here. Before I go, you can show me where that grave is. Then at least I can see that the contractors with the slick-tongued Brit won't be going anywhere near it."

Del's alarm bells started to ring. He knew that the workmen would be marking the site of the trench so he had to show Bonnie-Mae a grave somewhere well away from them. He also knew that being an early burial, the plot would have to be close to the church.

He tried to recall which of the graves was unmarked, but then remembered that the graveyard directory listed all the family names close to the church.

"Shall we?" Bonnie-Mae pointed towards the door.

"Sure."

They stepped out of the Parish House and into the drive.

Del looked across to the white painted, pristine old church with its distinctive pale green roof. All around, the long fronds of Spanish moss wafted slowly from the trees in the warm, gentle zephyr. The sight never failed to captivate him as the building gleamed with a rare purity in the South Carolina sunshine.

As they walked towards it, he had a sudden brainwave – something that the now dead Casey could not dispute.

"There," he said pointing to a spot near the southwest corner, "that's where it is…"

Bonnie-Mae frowned and said, "Where?"

Del continued walking and then pointed down. He said, "There, that's where Casey said the old grave was."

Bonnie-Mae said, "What? – *Here?*" She pointed to an old, brick-built, burial holding vault. It was a construction so familiar to everybody that it had been noted as one of the places of historic interest in the church's visitor guide.

"No ma'am – there." Del pointed to a spot above the head end of the vault.

Bonnie-Mae said, "I'm confused, are you saying that the Mathewes grave is attached to this vault, or maybe an extension of it?"

"No I'm not. According to Casey, God rest his soul, the Mathewes grave was aligned to this vault, several feet from the head."

Bonnie-Mae looked at the expanse of the church grounds and graveyard and said, "And given the amount of space available, do you think it feasible that it could have been sited so close to another?"

"I don't know – maybe at one time the two sites were linked, or perhaps they were constructed at the same time…"

"But," said Bonnie-Mae, "if the church records show all the early burial sites, including this holding vault, surely they would have recorded the Mathewes site too?"

"Ah," said Del, now letting his mind have a free reign, "according to Casey, that may be part of the mystery. *'Why he said, weren't there any records? – Were they concealed because of the presence of 'El Fuego de Marte?'"*

He recalled the old gravestone in the shed behind the Parish House, but dismissed it because he didn't think that any links could be made to where it came from.

Bonnie-Mae turned and stared at the ground and then turned back. She shrugged her shoulders and said, "Then I guess there's only one way to find out."

"Wait," said Del, "you aren't suggesting…?"

"That I request permission to disinter? Yes."

Del was shocked. In an effort to postpone the rushed decision whilst he thought about the consequences, he said, "But isn't that rushing things a mite?"

"Not if we're going to get this done."

"But what's the panic?"

"No panic; I just think that we should do it before Father Marshall gets back."

Del frowned and said, "Why?"

"Because we both know that he is a procrastinator. If we can get the digging done and the investigation completed before he returns he will be presented with a fait accompli situation that has already been resolved."

"And you'd be happy to apply to the South Carolina Department of Health and Environmental Control for permission to disinter?" said Del.

"Yes, and being from the Police Department I can usually get it within twenty-four hours."

"Don't you also need permission from the Rector?"

Bonnie-Mae looked sideways at Del and said, "Looks like you've already adopted that role in his absence." She nodded in the direction of the contractors. "And considering that they're from the same SC Department, we should be able to get things moving quickly."

Del began to panic. He wasn't a person to do anything in a rush. He knew that mistakes were made when that happened. He said, only just managing to keep the hesitation out of his voice, "Well, okay – if you say so…"

"I do. I'll go back to my office, contact the SCDHEC, and the family from Florida, and you can ask the guys here to mark out the exact location of the Mathewes grave."

"And then what?" said Del.

"It's Friday tomorrow, I'll leave you and the guys to get on with the stormwater drain for the next two days. That'll give me time to arrange things at my end. I'll get the family up from Florida – if they want to be in attendance – and arrange the state registered contractors and forensic archaeologists for Monday.

Del's panic level increased. He could feel his world spiralling out of control. He didn't want any part of what was happening and he didn't know how he'd managed to get himself so deeply in. All he wanted to do was to be with Julie, and out of Charleston.

Filled with self-doubt, he looked across to the Sheriff and said, "Okay."

Bonnie-Mae saw a subtle change in Del and her eyes narrowed. She stared at his troubled face for a second and said, "I gotta tell you Del, right now I have the darnedest notion that the next seven days are going to unfold in a way that I never would have imagined…"

Chapter 17

At 11:03am the phone rang in the kitchen. Debbie picked it up and said, "Hi, Farlington household." She listened for a few seconds, looked at Naomi and said, "Sure, she's here now, I'll pass you across."

Naomi frowned and mouthed, *"Who is it?"*

Debbie mouthed back, *"Sorry hon, I didn't catch it..."* She handed the phone to Naomi and sat back down at the breakfast bar.

Naomi took the phone and said, "Hello?"

"Ah, Naomi it's Bob Crowthorne – sorry to disturb you on your holidays but I have some news for you."

Bob Crowthorne was a Police Superintendent in the Lancashire Constabulary who had assisted and worked alongside Naomi on several projects since her investigations into the Whitewall Farm mystery. They had become friends, and he was aware of her psychic side. His earlier avid rejection of the phenomena had given way to him seeing it as 'an interesting aspect' of any investigation.

"Bob!" said Naomi, "It's always a pleasure to hear from you, but I didn't expect a call whilst I was in Florida."

"No, and normally I wouldn't have bothered, but I think that you'll want to hear what I have to say."

"Sounds intriguing. Nothing bad I hope."

"I suppose it's how you look at it," said Crowthorne.

Naomi frowned and then saw Carlton enter the open-plan kitchen and perch down at the breakfast bar opposite her. She covered the mouthpiece of the phone and said, "It's Bob Crowthorne."

Carlton frowned and cocked his head to one side. He said, "What does he want?"

Naomi shrugged, removed her hand from the mouthpiece, and said, "So what's so important?"

"Adrian Darke has been found dead in his prison cell."

The shock of the statement hit Naomi like a hammer blow. Her eyes widened in disbelief, her mouth fell open, and she clasped her right hand up to it. She didn't know how to respond. She sat for a few seconds making gasping sounds.

"My God Mimi," said Carlton, "what's happened?"

Naomi stared at Carlton, swallowed deeply, and spoke to Crowthorne. She said, "How? Why?"

Carlton said, *"Mimi?"*

Naomi covered the mouthpiece again and said, "Adrian Darke's been found dead in his cell."

Carlton was shocked too. He said, "No?"

Naomi nodded, and removed her hand from the mouthpiece. She'd been aware that Crowthorne had been speaking, but she hadn't heard any of it. She said, "Bob, Bob – I'm sorry, I missed that last part. Can you start again?"

Crowthorne realised that Naomi would be in shock and said, "Would it help if I gave you half an hour?"

"No, no, please tell me what happened."

"We don't know what happened. We haven't carried out the post-mortem examination on his body yet."

"Did he appear to have been attacked or anything?"

"Nothing obvious – a cursory examination was carried out by the attending doctor and coroner, but neither found anything that could have accounted for his death."

"Could he have been poisoned by an inmate or a warder?"

"As I said, we won't know the cause of his death until after the post-mortem, but as to who may have been responsible? That's something that's being looked into as we speak."

"My God Bob, what a turn-up, I'm finding it difficult to believe. I thought that he'd be a constant thorn in my side, and I never expected to receive news like this."

"Nevertheless," said Crowthorne, "it's happened. Finding out how he died or who had a part in his demise won't be an easy investigation given the number of people who may have wanted rid of him, but without sounding disrespectful, there is a positive aspect to his death."

"Yes, I suppose so – this may sound awful, but I for one, won't ever have to look over my shoulder any more."

"Exactly – hence my call. It would be crass and distasteful to say that this was good news, so let's just say that his passing may have brought us all some closure."

Naomi nodded and said, "Yes."

On Route 17, the Savannah Highway, fifteen miles west of Charleston, Muz, Lennie, and Bekkie were parked behind the deserted shack, and they were in turmoil.

"It was plumb stupid!" yelled Bekkie, "Goddamn it Muz, I've had to put up with some shit from you in the past but this beats all!"

Muz seethed. "So what was I meant to do – put him in a fucking hotel?"

"You weren't meant to kill him you jackass!"

Lennie sat as quiet as a mouse in the back seat. He knew better than to get involved when Bekkie and Muz were at each others' throats.

"For the thousandth time – I didn't mean to kill him. I…"

"I know," yelled Bekkie, *"for the thousandth bitching, fucking time, you only meant to mess him up a bit! – Only you didn't mess him up a bit, you fucking killed him, you moron!"*

Muz looked down and bit his lip.

"And then – you absolute king-sized pile of dumbass dog shit, you didn't bring him here and bury him like any sensible, straight-thinking, normal person – you threw him in a river! *A fucking river for Chrissakes!* And at a place where any mother-fucking, dozy-ass, son-of-a-bitch could find him!"

"Shit, Beks," said Lennie plucking up the tiniest morsel of courage, "you sure gotta mouth on you…"

Bekkie spun around and said, "And you can shut the fuck up unless you want your nut-sack for a wallet! You should never have let him do this!"

"I didn't let…"

"I said – *shut the fuck up!"* Bekkie stared at Lennie with fire in her eyes until she saw him close his mouth and settle back into his seat. She then turned and glared at Muz.

Muz saw what was happening and said, "What?"

"You know what! – We get the fuck out of here now!"

Muz whipped round and said, "And leave that stone? After what we've been through? Are you out of your mind?"

"Me out of my mind? – *Me?* – Holy shit, if you aren't the dumbest fucking puppy of the litter.

You just killed a guy – a guy you snatched from a church full of people – in front of a Deacon. And instead of trying to disappear before anybody can find you, you want to hang about, in case, and I mean *'in case,'* there's a ruby dating from the 1820's lying in a grave in the middle of the car park of the same godamned church you snatched the guy from!! – And you have the nerve to ask *me* if I'm out of *my* mind? Jesus*, fucking,* Christ!"

Muz looked down again. Inside he was raging and full of indecision. He mulled everything over that Bekkie had said, and then with a face contorted in anger, growled, "Fuck! – *Fuck!"*

He switched the car engine on, reversed onto Route 17, and seconds later roared away from Charleston towards the I-95 interstate highway.

At the Morrison household Janet stared in silence at the green, white-handled bag. It represented a world of staggering and bewildering perplexity to her. Everything about her Christian beliefs led her to disapprove of psychics and what she perceived to be their ungodly behaviour, but – and it was a monstrous but – there was the green bag. She should have walked past it, but she hadn't. She could have ignored it, but she didn't. She should have stuck to her guns and not believed one iota of what she'd heard – but she hadn't. And therein lay the dilemma. In a way, the buying of the bag had been an acceptance of the psychic woman and what she had said.

But how could she have walked past it, if it was going to save anybody's life? And damnably enough – that meant that she believed that too!

She made a 'Gah!' sound and ground her teeth in anger and frustration. Because, if she was going to accept *those* things –

with its default acceptance that the psychic was telling the truth, who the hell was 'Muz'?

And what about Del? His personality seemed to be changing. He had knocked somebody off a bicycle, he'd been out on more than one mysterious assignation about which he'd been – well – vague – and worst of all, he'd had bouts of inexplicable happiness – *happiness* for goodness' sake! She could cope with the former oddities, but the latter? What had he got to be happy about?

And the more than maddening thing that bugged her to distraction? – She was actually beginning to consider going to the damnable psychic woman to see if she could shed some light into her darkness!

She sat back in her seat and shook her head again. She picked up the green canvas bag and held it in both hands. She then put it down, expelled a long breath, and reached for her phone. She dialled Carole's mobile number.

"Hi honey!" said Carole, "You okay?"

"Not really."

"Why, what's the problem?"

Janet paused, and then with conviction said, "I want to go and see that psychic again. Will you come with me?"

Just after 12 noon, back at the Farlington house in Dunnellon, the phone in the kitchen rang again.

Debbie got up from the recliner by the pool and said, "Phone's ringing – back in a tick."

Seconds later she walked out with the phone in her hand and said, "It's for you Alan."

Alan looked up from his sunbed and said in a quiet voice, "Who is it?"

"It's the police."

Naomi raised her eyebrows, looked at Carlton, and said, "More police!"

Alan took the phone, and said, "Alan Farlington, how can I help?"

Debbie, Naomi, and Carlton watched as Alan listened, and then they were all surprised when they heard him gasp, *"No, never!* – Yes, yes, we can. We'll come up tomorrow. Yes, I understand, no, that's okay, we'll still come tomorrow." Pause. "Yes we will – thanks again. Yes – bye, see you then."

Debbie said, "What was all that about hon?"

"It was the Sheriff from Charleston, South Carolina." Alan had difficulty controlling his emotion. He stuttered, "You'll never believe this, they've – no, not *they* have, the police that is – I mean that the people from the church have…"

"The people from what church, have what?" said Carlton.

Alan turned to face Naomi and said, "The people from St Andrew's church in Charleston have located the Matthews P. F. grave, and they're going to start the disinterment proceedings on Monday morning!"

A stunned silence fell onto everybody, and then they all began talking at once.

As Alan looked from face-to-face, he held up his hand and said, "Wait guys, wait. I've told the Sheriff that we'll go up to Charleston tomorrow morning, so we'll get all the answers we want then."

Chapter 18

Adam knocked on the door of General Hardee's coach and entered. He saw George sitting at his desk and nodded in his direction. As usual 'Old Reliable' was at his desk writing, and didn't look up as he entered. He walked across to the General with his eyes fixed firmly on the pretty pink nipples of the semi-naked woman in the painting, and said, "Sir, if I might have a word?"

Hardee's eyes remained on the document in front of him. He said, "You might – if I can have your full attention this time Captain Holdsworth…"

Adam dropped his gaze straight away and was surprised that Hardee even knew who he was, let alone what he was looking at.

"You do indeed sir," he said.

Hardee continued writing for a few seconds longer and then replaced his pen in the holder. He looked up and said, "Now Captain Holdsworth?"

"I want your permission to go to Charleston sir."

Hardee recalled Harrison's suspicion and said, "Why?"

"To familiarise myself with the territory."

"Why?"

"Because I've never been there before sir."

Hardee sat back in his chair and said, "Oh, so where are you from?"

"Catonsville, Maryland sir."

"Maryland? A Union State – and you joined the Confederate Army?"

"Yes sir, but nearly half of the men from Virginia and North Carolina put on the Union blue. That was their choice, mine was mine."

"And what influenced that decision?"

"I'm a rebel sir. I rebelled at school, I rebelled at work, and I'm a rebel in my heart. I was even considered a rebel by my neighbours and kinfolk for having Corporal Jones as my best friend."

"And for that you sided against the Union?"

"No sir – I took exception to the Federal government interfering in the lives of people. I sympathise with its stance on emancipation, but I thought that they went too far when they tried to force good, law-abiding citizens to abandon years of order and structure.

Then when I heard that some States were seceding, my empathy was with their ideals." Adam paused and then added, "And if you don't mind me speaking frankly sir, I am not impressed by that dour Kentucky farmer Lincoln, and believe that the country would be better served by our President Jackson."

Hardee nodded in approval and then said, "All right, if I let you go to Charleston what would be your plans?"

"To acquaint myself with the surroundings."

"A reconnoitre?"

"Yes sir, this mission is so important that I need to be satisfied that I have all the bases covered."

Hardee raised his eyebrows and said, "Why, are you expecting trouble?"

"No sir, but *should* it happen, I want to be prepared."

Hardee thought about Harrison's resolve to catch anybody implicated with 'the nigger spy'. He said, "And do you want to take Corporal Jones with you?"

"No sir."

Hardee was surprised. He said, "No?"

"No sir. He has a sick sister living near Franklin and has asked if he could go visit her."

Hardee's eyes narrowed. He said, "Did he say what was wrong with her?"

"Diphtheria sir."

"And this is Franklin Tennessee?"

"I know of no other sir."

Hardee said, "You are of course aware that that's close to Union lines…"

"Yes sir, I am. I believe that Jones has planned to go in civilian clothes, to avoid raising suspicion, if you give your permission."

Hardee's mind went into overdrive. He mulled things over for a few seconds and then said, "Very well Captain – you can take the train to Charleston tomorrow morning but make sure that you're back here by Tuesday night. Jones can go to Franklin too, but tell him he's to be back here by the same time."

Adam snapped to attention and said, "Thank you sir, that's very understanding. I'm sure that Corporal Jones will appreciate your compassion."

Hardee called across to George and said, "Did you catch that George?"

George nodded.

"Please issue Captain Holdsworth and Corporal Jones with the appropriate authorities and railroad passes."

George said, "Very good General." He turned to Adam and said, "Your papers will be ready in half an hour."

Adam said, "Thank you George. What time does the train to Charleston leave?"

"O500 hours sharp, and Corporal Jones can take the 10am train to La Vergne. It stops at Smyrna Camp Ground which is about twenty miles from Franklin."

"Thank you. I'll be here at 0430, Corporal Jones at 0930." He turned to acknowledge the General but saw that he'd already resumed writing. He turned back to George, nodded, and left the carriage.

Hardee waited until Adam had departed and then said, "George, I need you to go to the Bay Tree Hotel on Sixth and get Mr. Harrison. Tell him that there's been a change of plan."

Half an hour later Adam and Ira sat in Adam's office.

"We have to assume that tassel man saw you ride into General Wolford's camp," said Adam, "and that he'd been despatched to tail you by Hardee."

"Why? Why would he do that? I haven't said or done anything to make anybody suspicious."

"You know how much I love you as a brother, but that is naïve."

Ira frowned and said, "Why?"

"Because you're black and this gold run is a top-secret mission."

Ira took exception and said, "You would automatically say that to me?"

"Don't you get uppity Ira, 'cos I won't even defend what I just said."

Ira looked down, and then back up. He said, "Sorry, I get mad when I'm singled out because of my skin colour."

"I can understand that, but we're sitting in slave country here, and most white folks don't trust blacks."

"So if you're right, and tassel man saw me go into Wolford's camp, why haven't I been arrested?"

Adam mulled it over and then said, "Maybe to see if I was implicated too."

"So in your opinion, if I was seen, I'm already a condemned man, and the only reason I've not been arrested is to see if you're implicated?"

"That is my belief, yes."

"Which means, that it matters not whether you're finally implicated – I could at some time in the future be shot?"

"Yes – unless Hardee gets unequivocal proof that you are innocent."

"And how could we provide that?"

"I don't know."

Ira's heart sank. He said, "I'm glad that you're taking this so calmly brother."

Adam looked at his friend and said, "I'm not. Trust me – I'm not."

Ira shook his head and said, "Okay…what next?"

"When I approached General Hardee I had to assume that I'd be followed to Charleston, so I said that you wanted leave to visit a sick sister in Franklin…"

"Sick sister – *in Franklin*? That's within twenty miles of Wolford's camp again!"

Adam said, "Correct. Now I hope that tassel man will follow you instead of me."

"So now all I have to do, is to go to a place I've never been to before, to visit a sick sister I haven't got?"

Adam raised his eyebrows and said, "But – because you haven't got a sick sister there, I've had to plan it in a way that ensures your safety. So – this is what you have to do…"

Back at Hardee's railroad coach, Harrison knocked and entered. "You wanted to see me General?"

"Ah yes," said Hardee. He put down his pen. "I've just given Corporal Jones leave to visit a sick sister near Franklin…"

"Franklin Tennessee? Near Wolford's camp again? That's an interesting development."

"My opinion too – that's why I want you to follow him."

Harrison sat down on the seat in front of Hardee's desk and stared at the ceiling. Seconds later he said, "And did Corporal Jones request this leave in person sir?"

"No, Captain Holdsworth did."

"The same man who you suspect of being in cahoots with Jones?"

Hardee took exception and said, "I don't suspect Captain Holdsworth of anything Mr Harrison – otherwise he would have been arrested by now!"

"My apologies General – that was indiscreet."

"And an indication of what you're thinking."

"I cannot deny that sir."

"Well let me put you straight one more time; if President Jefferson has faith in Captain Holdsworth, I have faith in him too. So until you can supply me with incontrovertible evidence of his treachery, I'll thank you to keep your distasteful and unbefitting comments to yourself."

Harrison took the rebuke and said, "My apologies again General."

Hardee let his feathers unruffle and then said, "So now – please make your preparations to follow Corporal Jones as per my orders."

Harrison turned to Hardee and said, "You haven't heard then?"

"Heard what?"

"I've been recalled to Richmond by Mr Seddon. I leave tomorrow."

"What about Jones?"

Harrison thought for a second and then said, "Please leave that to me General, by the time I leave – I will have *all* of eventualities covered."

Just after 9pm, two weather-beaten, swarthy characters crossed the pontoon bridge over the Tennessee River north of Moccasin Point and rode to the old Saw Mill on the eastern bank. They dismounted, made sure that nobody was around, and then walked into the main cutting shed.

"Howdy boys..."

The two men turned and looked into the darkest corner and saw a figure step out of the shadows.

"...anybody see you?"

The taller of the two, a vicious ex-army deserter named Thaddeus Polk who'd left the Union Army of the Potomac before being dishonourably discharged for raping and murdering innocent women said, "No."

Harrison walked over and looked at the smaller, slightly built man and said, "Gil?"

"Nope, I didn't see nobody neither." Gilbert Weims was a southern-born, ex-detective from the famous Pinkerton Detective Agency who'd left the company after Allan Pinkerton had allied himself to Major General George McClellan and the Union States.

Harrison said, "Good." He reached into his jacket pocket and gave each man a bulky envelope. "These are your papers, some spending cash, and a letter from me if you're questioned by anybody carrying out my orders."

Each man looked at the envelope and felt how heavy it was.

"Feels heavy Mr Harrison," said Weims.

Harrison looked down at Weims and said, "Sign of the times boys. The Confederacy seems to be printing more and more money as the days go by, but you cain't buy more with it."

"So what's the plan?" said Polk.

"You still riding with Carson?"

"Yep, matter of fact he's holed up in the woods near Stringers Point waiting for me to return."

"Good. I want you to follow a nigra Corporal named Irate Jones, to Franklin where he's supposed to be visiting a sick sister. In reality, he may be using the trip as an excuse to report classified information to General Wolford in Nashville."

"So you think he's a spy?"

"I know he is. I followed him to Wolford's camp last Monday, and now he's going to 'visit sick relatives' in Franklin? I reckon something big's going on that I don't know about yet, and it could be real soon."

"Okay," said Polk, "so you want me to tail him and report back his movements?"

"No. I want you to kill him at the first opportunity you get."

Even the stoic Polk was surprised. He said, "Kill him dead?"

Harrison looked sideways and said, "Is there any other way?"

Polk ignored the sarcasm and said, "Why kill him if you want to find out what he's up to?"

"Because he's a goddamned nigger spy and I want him eliminated."

"And how will we ever prove that to the Generals if we kill him before we find out what he's up to?"

"Because of what you've got in your package."

Polk looked down at his parcel and then back at Harrison.

"In there you'll find some papers containing actual Confederate troop strengths, planned movements, locations, the siting of ammo dumps and the like. When you report to General Hardee that the nigger's dead, give him the papers and tell him that you caught Jones riding into Wolford's camp with them."

Polk was surprised and shook his head. He said, "But don't you want to find out what he's *actually* up to?

Weims said, "And what if he *is* going to visit a sick sister, and he's innocent?"

Harrison snapped around and said, "He isn't!" He glared at both men and then said, "If you must know, I think that the nigger's being used as a feint and that the real problem is with somebody else."

"Oh, right," said Weims.

Harrison stared at the two men for a few seconds longer and then turned to Polk. He said, "So – you and Carson get on the same train as Jones tomorrow morning, and make sure that he's dead by this time tomorrow. Clear?"

"Clear," said Polk.

Harrison turned to Weims and said, "And I want you to follow a Captain Adam Holdsworth to Charleston tomorrow and watch him for the next few days..."

"The real problem I take it," said Weims.

Harrison nodded and said, "…keep out of sight, and make a note of everywhere he goes."

"And do you want him dead too?"

"No – I want to find out what that bastard's up to, and then we'll watch him swing."

Both men nodded and said, "Okay."

Harrison turned to Polk and said, "Jones will be on the 10am La Vergne train and he'll be wearing civilian clothing."

Polk nodded again.

Harrison turned to Weims. He said, "Holdsworth will be on the early train to Charleston and as far as I know, he'll be in uniform."

Weims said, "Right, noted."

"Okay," said Harrison, "I'm leaving for Richmond tomorrow." He turned to Polk and said, "When you've finished there's money in the envelope to pay off Carson. Report your findings to General Hardee and then meet me up in Richmond."

He turned to Weims and said, "Once Holdsworth returns to Chattanooga come straight back to Richmond and report only to me. Got it?" He saw Weims acknowledge him and then said, "Okay, good luck both of you, and don't be seen. Now, after I've gone, wait here for ten minutes, then make yourselves scarce."

He looked at each man in turn, nodded one last time, and then disappeared into the night.

In the small North Cornwall port of Hayle, the fast, iron, paddle steamer *SS Cornubia* set sail for The Azores on its four thousand mile journey to Wilmington in North Carolina.

Chapter 19

As Naomi and Carlton's hire car cruised up Route 61 on the Ashley River Road something triggered in Naomi's brain. A feeling of déjà vu crept over her and she began to look at everything around her. She sat up higher in the front seat and stared at the single carriageway road as it snaked ahead between the trees. They passed the odd sign advertising residences and small businesses, and then another advertising the Church Creek Shopping Mall ahead.

Her eyes opened wider, she sat bolt upright and looked at the hood of the car. It was the grey that she remembered. Without saying a word she reached across to the centre of the steering wheel and pushed the button that switched on the radio.

Carlton looked at Naomi and said, "Hey, have you got to? You know that I don't like..." He stopped speaking as the radio cut in.

The distinctive sound of a female country and western singer filled the air, and almost right away Naomi heard the words, *"...the day that hell broke loose just north of Marietta, all along the Kennesaw line."* She ignored Carlton's protestations and looked up. She saw Spanish moss festooned over the trees and remembered the psychic episode that she'd had back in June. She also recalled going upstairs to inform Carlton that they'd been invited to Florida by Alan, but that they wouldn't be able to attend because she'd been pregnant.

As the car swept past Church Creek Shopping Mall Alan leaned forwards and said, "St Andrew's is just up ahead on the right."

Carlton looked at Naomi and realised that something was happening. He remained silent until the song had finished.

Naomi reached across and turned off the radio. She said, "That song was written by a guy named Don Oja-Dunaway."

"Yes," said Alan, "and he's a really nice guy."

Naomi turned round and said, *"You know him?"*

"Yes, he's a long-time buddy of my friend Steve Robiteaux from Gainesville, and he introduced us when we went to see him play in St. Augustine last year."

The thumb pressed down on Naomi's left shoulder letting her know that something was about to happen or that she was not alone. She remained silent for a few seconds but heard nothing. She turned back to Alan and said, "We haven't ever been there, is it as pretty as everybody says?"

"Pretty?" said Alan, "it's exquisite."

Debbie and Alan were about to describe the delights of America's oldest city when a white roadside marker indicated that they'd arrived at St. Andrew's.

"You need to hang a right just before we get to that white stone," said Alan.

Carlton switched on the right indicator, slowed down, and turned into the drive.

The thumb pressed harder on Naomi's shoulder and then almost from the depths of time she heard a single far-off sounding groan. A groan as though somebody had been disturbed from a deep sleep. At first she couldn't distinguish whether it was the sound of somebody in pain, but then she heard another groan – and then another. She frowned as more groans joined the first.

She looked at both sides of the drive as the car crunched over the small grey stones, and for a second or two, she got the impression that the entire deceased population was wakening, and that they might at any second start emerging from the ground.

The look on Naomi's face told Carlton that something was wrong. He said, "Are you all right darling?"

"No – please stop."

Naomi waited until the car stopped, and then got out. She looked all around, and homing in like a human compass, she realised that the sounds were coming from a place near the far corner of the church.

She leaned down, looked through the open door, and pointed. She said, "I'll meet you over there."

Carlton nodded and said, "Okay."

As Naomi closed the passenger door she heard Debbie asking Carlton what was wrong, and gathered that he'd explain things to them.

The pressure from the thumb increased as the sound of the groans got louder. It was as though a multitude of people had awakened, and had found somebody who could hear their pleas.

The hair on her body stood on end as the sounds increased and she wondered how loud it could get before at least one other person would hear it. She drew in a deep breath, gathered her resolve, and set off up the drive.

As she turned towards the southwest corner of the church, she saw a group of workmen digging a trench. One or two men nodded and smiled, and she acknowledged them all by saying, "Hi."

She continued walking to where Carlton was standing next to the parked car, when out of the blue; it felt as though something pushed her backwards. The feeling was so intense, that she wondered at first whether a gust of wind had blown her. She stopped and looked up into the trees. She saw that the Spanish moss wasn't moving. With a frown on her face she set off towards Carlton. It happened again. The experience was so real, that even though she knew it wasn't so, she looked down to see if a small child had pushed her. She stopped again and turned in the direction of the workmen.

The pressure on her shoulder magnified, and then it felt as though a breeze was blowing her towards the workmen. She went with the pressure and set off towards them.

Carlton saw Naomi falter a couple of times and then turn, and head in the opposite direction.

"Where's Naomi going?" said Debbie.

Carlton kept his eyes on his wife and said, "I'm not sure…"

"Should we go and see where she's going?"

Carlton thought about it for a second and then said, "No – let's leave her be."

As Naomi approached the shallow trench, one man looked up, smiled, and hopped out."

"Morning Miss," said Taffy Brewer, "can I help you?"

Naomi looked over Taffy's shoulder and then at him. "What are you doing?" she said.

"Are you English?"

"Yes, and unless I'm mistaken you're Welsh?"

"Correct, but when I go back home, all my old buddies think I have an American accent."

Naomi smiled and said, "Well I can tell that you're Welsh." She looked over Taffy's shoulder and said, "Is there a problem?"

"Not anything life threatening; we're putting in a stormwater drain to stop contaminated surface water entering Church Creek and the Ashley River."

Naomi looked at the odd alignment of the trench and said, "Why here? Does it flood or something?"

"Does it rain in South Carolina? Oh yes, Miss…er,"

"Naomi." She offered her hand.

Taffy shook it and said, "…and in case you hadn't guessed, I'm Taffy!"

"But not named that by your parents I'd guess."

"No, but all the guys here know me as Taffy and I've got used to it. And in answer to your question – yes – it can really pour down here. What with Hurricanes, Tropical Storms and all sorts of weird and wonderful weather patterns off the Atlantic, South Carolina can get very wet indeed."

"Hence the drain…"

"Hence the drain," repeated Taffy. He paused and then asked, "You on holiday?"

"Yes, I'm here with…" The pressure on Naomi's shoulder shot sky high. She made an involuntary gasping sound, and grasped her left shoulder.

Taffy saw it, and so did Carlton.

Carlton turned to Debbie and said, "Can you wait here with Alan? I'll just see if Naomi's okay."

"Yes sure." Debbie looked over towards Naomi and said, "Do you think that something's not right?"

Carlton thought about his answer and said, "I think she's okay, but I'll check anyway."

Debbie turned to Alan and raised her eyebrows.

Taffy said, "That looked painful, are you okay?"

Naomi rubbed her shoulder and said, "Yes thanks – sometimes I get twinges."

"Me too, I think that it goes with getting old."

Naomi smiled and said, "Nice to chat with you, but I'd better get back to my husband." She turned to go, and then experienced the same feeling of being pushed back. It was so intense that it made her waver.

Taffy saw it and reached out towards her left arm. He said, "Hey, steady on – perhaps you need to take more water with it!"

Naomi ignored the remark, said, "Sorry," and walked towards the trench.

Taffy and Carlton saw her look into it, and then start to walk along its length.

The various workmen acknowledged her as she went past.

As Naomi walked away from the church, the pushy feeling was against her. She turned and headed back. The feeling changed – as though she was being ushered forwards. She continued walking to a point just over three quarters of the length of the trench, and then the feeling changed direction again. She stopped, turned, and walked back to a point approximately three fifths of the way along, and then stopped again. She looked into the trench and said, "What's down there?"

Taffy looked down and said, "Nothing – it's just part of the car park."

As Carlton arrived at her side, Naomi said, "And has this always been a car park?"

"No, at one time it formed a part of the old graveyard, and we had to be shown by the Deacon where we were allowed to dig, to avoid disturbing possible graves. Why?"

"Is everything okay Mimi?"

Naomi turned to Carlton and said, "Yes – it's just me – you know."

Taffy extended his hand and said, "I'm Taffy, I'm in charge of this lot."

Carlton shook the hand and said, "How do you do. I'm Naomi's husband, Carlton." He then looked back at Naomi and said, "Are you all right?"

Naomi stared at the pivotal point in the trench and then said, "Just bear with me a minute."

She started to walk away, expecting to experience the pushy feeling again, but nothing happened. She turned and walked in the opposite direction, but as before, nothing happened. With a frown on her face she walked back to Taffy and Carlton as the semi-bemused workmen watched on.

Taffy scratched the back of his head, looked at Carlton, and shrugged.

Carlton looked back and didn't respond. He didn't know how to.

Naomi looked one last time at the spot in the trench, oriented it with a couple of recognisable transit points, and then said, "We'd better get back to Alan and Debbie." She turned to a still bemused Taffy and said, "Nice to meet you Taffy, we're going to be here for the next few days, so we may meet again."

"And I hope that it'll be as interesting as this," said Taffy. He turned to Carlton and said, "What was that all about?"

Carlton shook his head and said, "No idea."

As they walked back to the car, Carlton said, "Care to explain?"

"I can't," said Naomi, "I really can't."

Chapter 20

"Come here honey..." Julie's honey soft, seductive voice said, "...I have a surprise for you."

Del looked around the inside of the trailer. All of the windows had been covered in blackout curtains, and dozens of scented candles flickered atop numerous surfaces. The overall appearance was how he imagined the inner sanctum of a harem to be. Three diaphanous net curtains were hung at intervals along the interior from ceiling to floor, stretching two-thirds of the way across the room alternatively left and then right, so that he could see through one curtain to the next, but not any further.

"But," said Julie, "as you pass each veil, you have to take something off."

Del felt a wave of excitement flush over him. He looked at Julie and said, "What about you?"

Julie stepped closer and said, "Of course me too."

The alluring smell of Julie's perfume swept over Del and he gulped. He said, "Before we start, can I have a drink of iced water?"

Julie smiled and said, "I can do better than that." She opened the door of her refrigerator and took out a large jug of homemade lemonade. She poured them both a glass and handed one to Del.

Del took a sip, then another, and then looked at the glass. "Mmm," he said, "this tastes good – what's in it?"

"Just a special ingredient of my own, otherwise nothing; it's the same recipe my ma used to give to my pa, before they retired upstairs."

Del took a deeper draft of the 'special' lemonade and said, "Did it help him sleep?"

"No honey, it didn't help any of us sleep." She paused for a second when she saw Del frown. She stepped closer and half-whispered, "None of us could sleep for at least an hour after pa drank ma's home-made lemonade 'cos their bed head had a tendency to bang on the wall when they got into full swing…"

Del's eyes widened in surprise; he glanced at the innocuous looking liquid and drank it all. He put down the glass, wiped his mouth, and said, "If it worked for your Pa, who am I to question?"

Julie smiled, took hold of Del's arm, and led him behind the first veil. She looked up at him, and then slowly undid the buttons on her white silk blouse.

Del watched as she slipped it off her shoulders and dropped it onto the floor.

Set into the roof of the trailer were several ultra-violet lights which highlighted the whiteness of Julie's pretty white bra against her silky olive skin.

Julie stepped closer and lifted her face up to his.

Del expected a kiss, but instead, he felt Julie touch his penis with her fingertips, and then step back to look at him.

Just the touch of her hand on his stiffening manhood made him gasp. He said, "You're asking for trouble touching the womb raider like that."

Julie stepped forwards again and gave his penis a squeeze. She said, "I'm not *asking* for trouble babe, I'm banking on it…"

Del looked into Julie's lascivious eyes and then removed his shirt and dropped it onto the floor.

Julie led Del to the second veil and said, "Part two – your turn first, remove two items."

Del looked down, shrugged, and slipped his sandals off his bare feet.

Julie looked and said, "I should have made you take those off before we started." She put her hands behind her back, undid the top buttons of her pencil-line, red, medium length skirt, wiggled, and let it drop to the floor. She kept her eyes on Del's face and then undid the back of her white suspender belt, unclipped it from her white stocking tops, and let it fall to the floor.

Del's penis was now pushing against the inside of his boxers, and was desperate to be free.

Julie looked down and said, "Seems I have an admirer…"

Del looked at the shape of Julie's bulge through her white silk panties. The material was stretched and indented as it swept down over her vagina. He felt his heart rate increase as he reached down and stroked his own growing bulge.

"Man," he said, "you look so goddamn hot…"

Julie looked at Del and said, "There's no *man* in me tiger…" she paused and then added, "…yet." Her eyes sparkled. She reached out, took hold of his hand, and led him behind the third and final veil. In front was the door to her bedroom. She said, "Part three, and I go first. This time we take off three things."

Del was beside himself with lust as he watched Julie slip first one stocking, and then the other, off her silky-smooth, exquisitely shaped legs. He saw her look up at him and smile, as she put her hands behind her back and undid her strapless bra.

As the two loose ends fell, Julie gripped her arms to her sides so that the bra didn't fall. She looked into Del's eyes, and then squeezed her breasts together so that they pushed out towards him. She held it for a second and let the bra drop.

Del stared at Julie's beautiful small breasts, with pert, pinky-brown, perfectly proportioned nipples, and he wanted to stop playing games – he wanted her, there and then. He said, "So help me, I want to fuck you so bad, you won't walk straight for a week…"

"First things first honey – take off your three things."

There was no finesse. Del undid his trouser belt, snatched it out of the belt loops, and dropped it. "One…" he said. He undid his trouser belt button, unzipped the fly, and pulled off his trousers. "…two…" He then yanked down his boxers and said, "…three!"

Julie looked down and said, "My, my, Del Morrison. I do believe it's rude to point."

Del grabbed her and pressed his rock-hard penis between her legs. He arched upwards and rubbed it through the material of her panties along the length of her vagina. He leaned down and started to kiss the left-hand side of her neck…

Julie gently pushed him away and said, "Wait babe, you haven't seen my surprise yet."

Del stepped back and watched as Julie opened the bedroom door. He saw her step inside, and then signal for him to follow.

At first he couldn't see because the windows were fitted with blackout curtains and the room was lit by a single ultra-violet light in the centre of the ceiling. His eyes adjusted and then he looked over to where Julie was pointing.

"Del – this is my very special girlfriend Lorraine."

Del's first reaction was to cover his massive erection, but then he saw that Lorraine was completely naked and lying on her back. The ultra-violet light highlighted the white cotton sheet on which she was gently writhing and gyrating.

Lorraine said, "My – you were right about him Jules, he is a big boy." She turned to Del and said, "That thing looks all red and swollen honey – why don't you come here and let me see if I can find something to ease it for you?"

Pure, one-hundred-percent lust gripped Del. He turned to Julie to speak, and then heard her say, "Haven't you forgotten something?"

Del looked down and saw Julie pointing at her panties.

"Aren't you going to help me get these off?"

Del dropped straight to his knees and attempted to grab hold of the close-fitting side panels, but saw Julie step back.

"Not here silly – over there..." Julie waited until Del stood up, and then walked towards the bed knowing that his eyes would be glued to her beautifully toned rear.

Del was spellbound. He watched Julie climb onto the foot of the bed, arch her beautiful backside up, and then push Lorraine's legs apart. He'd never felt his penis so hard. He looked down at it and saw how swollen it was. Every vein in it seemed to be standing out and rippling with frantic desire.

He stepped closer to the bed, took hold of each side of Julie's panties, and eased them down.

Julie wiggled her little bottom as they were removed, and then parted her legs. She knew that Del would be staring at her smooth, swollen clitoris and labia. She dropped down onto her stomach and then ran her hands up the inside of Lorraine's soft, suntanned thighs.

Lorraine moaned with pleasure as Julie reached her vagina, and then parted it so that Del could see.

Del gasped. His heart was hammering in his chest. He saw Julie lick her right forefinger, run it over the tip of Lorraine's clitoris, and then slide it between her soaking inner lips.

Julie arched her backside up again, parted her legs, and turned to Del. She said, "What's up honey, can't you find anything to do?"

Without saying a word, Del fell onto the two writhing women in blind, lust-crazed, frenzy.

At the Christian bookshop in Calhoun Street, Lesley-Ann looked up as Janet walked in. "Hey Janet!" she said, "I wasn't expecting you, what are you doing here?"

"I've come to see Del."

Lesley-Ann frowned and said, "I don't understand – what do you mean, you've come to see Del?"

"What's not to understand?"

Lesley-Ann faltered and said, "Wait, let's start again. Did you say that you've come to see Del?"

It was Janet's turn to frown. She said, "Yes, I was supposed to be meeting a girlfriend in Market Street but she phoned and cancelled at the last minute, so I dropped by to let Del know that I'd be free for lunch."

"Now that's just plain weird!" said Lesley-Ann.

"Why?"

"Today was supposed to be my day off, but Del called and said that he wanted to go out with you 'cos it was the anniversary of the day you first met."

Janet perched down on the chair at the side of the shop and thought for a few seconds. She looked up and said, "I have absolutely no idea what he's talking about. Today isn't the anniversary of our first meeting, and he told me that he would be working here all day."

"And you aren't going to Toast for lunch?"

"Toast Restaurant in Meeting Street? – No."

Lesley-Ann sat back in her seat and said, "I don't know what to say. Why would Del say those things if they weren't true?"

Janet didn't answer at first. She thought about all of the unusual occurrences in the last few weeks – somebody named Muz, the green bag, Del's 'happiness' and now this. She looked up at Lesley-Ann and said, "I don't know honey, but I sure as hell am going to find out…"

She removed her mobile phone from her handbag and dialled Carole's number.

Carole answered and said, "Hi Janet, y'all okay?"

"Yes, thanks. Have you made an appointment to go see that psychic yet?"

"Yes, odd thing is, I just got off the phone with her few minutes ago."

"What's odd about it?"

"She phoned me."

"She phoned you?"

"Yes, she told me that we both need to go see her."

"And you made the appointment?"

"Yes, I told her that we'd go next Friday night, 7:30pm."

"What, Black Friday, the biggest shopping day of the year?"

"Yes, I thought that we could check out the bargains, have an early dinner, then go and see her. Our partners never want to go shopping with us, so they won't know where we've gone."

Janet thought about it for a few seconds, and though she'd have preferred to go earlier, she said, "Okay, that's a date then."

Chapter 21

The Charleston train lurched away from the depot at the start of its gruelling three-hundred-and-eighty mile, nineteen-hour journey. It consisted of the locomotive, the tender, and three passenger cars.

There were numerous stops along the way, but the two most important were in Covington and Augusta, Georgia. There they had to pick up full loads of fuel and water.

Adam sat in the front coach. He hadn't seen anybody follow him, nor had he seen anybody wearing red, tassel-topped boots. He carried with him his overcoat, hat, and his brown leather valise which contained a change of clothes, and his few toiletries.

Weims sat in the middle coach, close to the door that led to the front coach. He had seen Adam, sitting in the middle of the front coach, wearing his best uniform.

The train crept up to its 25 – 30 miles per hour speed limit as it cleared the outskirts of Chattanooga, and Adam settled down into his seat, to see if he could grab another couple of hours sleep whilst it was still dark.

At 10am the train departed Union Depot for its one-hundred-and-thirty mile journey to La Vergne. A journey made longer than it should have been by first having to go southwest to Stevenson, Alabama, to pick up the northbound track to Nashville. The train make-up was the same as Adam's; a locomotive, tender, and three passenger coaches.

Ira had followed Adam's instructions to the letter. He sat in the middle coach, right-hand side, in the two-seater seat facing the forward bulkhead, near the door. He wore black dusty boots, which were mostly covered by a pair of brown, thick cotton trousers. He wore a long, tan-coloured poncho, a battered straw hat, and he carried a bulky hessian sack, tied around the top with twine.

In an effort to deter anybody sitting next to him, although not many people chose to sit next to a black, he placed the sack on the seat by his side.

He had not seen tassel man. Nor had he spotted Polk sitting in the rear coach on the left-hand side by the forward door, or Carson in the front coach, sitting on the right-hand side by the rear door.

He settled back into his seat, pulled his straw hat down over his face, and pretended to be asleep.

One-and-a-half hours later, he lifted the rim of his hat and looked around. To his intense good fortune he saw that nobody had sat in the left-hand front seat alongside his. Everybody else appeared to be engrossed in card-playing, reading, sleeping, or looking at the scenery. He looked at his pocket watch. He knew that the train would be arriving at Stevenson within the next ten minutes, and he wanted to be ready.

He opened the sack and removed the uniform slouch hat that Adam had given him and a small valise which he slid under the seat. Next he slipped off the brown trousers to reveal his uniform trousers and calf-length boots. He screwed up the trousers, rubbed the dust off his boots exposing the shiny blackness of them, and stuffed them into the sack. He slid down the seat, removed the long poncho, revealing Adam's Captain's uniform jacket, took off the straw hat, and stuffed both into the sack. Making sure that he hadn't drawn any attention to himself, he removed the valise from under the seat, and pushed the sack back in its place.

The train slowed as it approached Stevenson station.

Ira knew that any potential tails wouldn't be expecting him to disembark if they thought that he was going to Wolford's camp in Nashville, but he also knew that if he made one wrong move, he could blow it.

The train ground to a halt.

Ira saw several people get up and make for the doors. He pulled his slouch hat down on his head and slipped amongst the passengers disembarking.

As per their arrangement, Carson watched the right-hand side of the train for anybody trying to escape over the tracks, but he saw nothing unusual.

Polk watched the passengers disembarking at the station, and didn't see anybody wearing brown trousers, a poncho, and straw hat.

Satisfied that Ira had remained aboard, Carson and Polk settled back into their seats ready for the next scheduled stop in Winchester, Tennessee.

Ira shuffled along the platform heading for the exit gate when to his dismay, he saw a Confederate Lieutenant surveying the passengers as they passed by. He knew that he wasn't allowed to wear an officer's uniform and that he would be arrested as an imposter, or even worse, a deserter, if he were seen.

He looked to his left and saw an office door. As quick as a flash, he stepped inside, and shut the door behind him.

Inside was a single black telegraph clerk.

Ira put his right forefinger up to his lips and made a shushing sound. He snatched off the hat and jacket, opened the valise, removed his own uniform jacket and kepi hat – put them on, and then stuffed Adam's jacket and hat back in the valise. He smiled at the bewildered clerk, whispered, "Thanks," and departed.

Ten minutes later he stood outside the station looking at the unfamiliar sights of Stevenson Alabama knowing that he had to find a horse, and then ride thirty-six miles back to Chattanooga before nightfall.

At 11:30am Bart Holdsworth rode along River Road, north of Bear Swamp, towards Fort Bull. Despite the war having started in Charleston and the obvious build-up of defences and fortifications, he could still recognise the familiar landmarks that he, Adam, Ned, and Ira had become used to on their odd but memorable visits to see his old gran'ma Prevost in her small plantation home, north of Wappoo Creek, close to the junction of River Road and Bridge Road. He recalled her obvious discomfort of the brothers' choice of friend in Ira, not least of all because she still owned several slaves herself.

In appearance he was identical to Adam except for his voluminous facial hair. He sported the in-vogue thick, droopy moustache and full beard, whilst Adam and Ned remained clean-shaven. Although he was still a Captain in the Union's Army of The Potomac, he was dressed in civilian clothing and looked to the world, like any other young man thereabouts.

He passed the magnificent plantations of Magnolia Garden and Drayton Hall; both owned by Doctor John Drayton and he was surprised to see that two yellow flags had been posted at the end of the drive to Drayton Hall indicating that it was being used as a smallpox hospital. He recalled Drayton's ingenuity and found himself wondering whether the wily doctor was using the Hall as a genuine hospital, or indeed stating that it was such to deter folk from getting too close.

He turned left near Fort Bull, crossed Bee's Ferry to the north side of the Ashley River, and then headed west into Charleston. Within the hour he'd checked into The Bell Hotel in King Street, the one that he'd been instructed to go to by Adam – close to the Washington Racecourse.

He knew that Adam had planned to check into another hotel in King Street, but his choice was one about a mile further south near the terminal of the South Carolina Rail Road. The thought of that place made him wonder how Ned was going on in Pennsylvania trying to arrange the delivery of iron ore there.

He took out his pocket watch, made a note of the time, and then headed out for something to eat.

Just after 9pm, Ira rode into Chattanooga, and headed straight to Big Eve's Bar in Brown's Alley. He crossed his fingers that the General would be there, and he wasn't disappointed. He stood poised at the swing doors for a few seconds until he knew that the General would see him entering, and then strode purposefully across to the bar.

Hardee had just finished drinking a slug of whisky, when to his utter amazement he saw Ira walk across the room.

"Corporal Jones!"

Ira heard the General call and walked across to his table with his head bowed down.

"I thought that you were going to see your sister in Franklin."

"I was sir, but not how you thought."

"What do you mean, not how I thought?"

Ira pursed his lips and looked down. He said, "'Cos she was already dead sir."

Hardee frowned and said, "I don't understand. What are you talking about?"

"I wanted to go and pay my respects sir."

"Go on."

"When I found out that Mary, my sister, was already dead, I was distraught sir, so I went to Captain Holdsworth and told him that she was sick, and that I wanted to go and visit her."

Hardee stared up at Ira in astonishment. He said, "So you lied to Captain Holdsworth?"

Ira sunk his head lower and said, "Yes sir, I did."

Hardee was dumbstruck. The Corporal's frank confession meant that Holdsworth was innocent. He felt a mixture of shame for doubting an officer that the President had faith in, and anger at Jones for putting him in this reprehensible position. He also recalled Harrison's revelation that Jones had visited Wolford's camp in Nashville, and his anger level grew.

He said, "So what are you doing back here now? I gave you permission to have the leave. You could have stayed away until next Tuesday, said nothing, and I'd have been none the wiser."

"Because it was dishonest, and I'm not a dishonest man sir. All the time I was on the train I was wrestling with my conscience and I knew that my beloved Mary would be ashamed of me lying, even if it was to go pay her my last respects, so I got off the train at Stevenson, and rode back here as fast as I could."

Hardee wanted to say, 'And did you see anybody following you?' but knew that he couldn't. He opened his mouth to speak, but was cut off.

Ira said, "I came in here for a drop of Dutch courage sir, then I was going to report to you and take the consequences of my disgraceful behaviour."

Hardee didn't know what to say. He tried to think what Harrison would advise, but he couldn't. He fell back on his old faithful edict, 'if in doubt, do nothing.' He said, "I need time to think about this. Get back to your quarters, and report to me at 0700 sharp. I'll deal with this then."

Ira snapped to attention, saluted, and said, "Yes sir."

Ten minutes later he sat on his bunk and shook his head. He was amazed at Adam's reasoning. Everything had gone exactly as he said it would. He lay down, put his hands behind his head, and knew that Adam's train would be nearing Charleston and he wished him the best of luck. If Adam was right about tomorrow too, Hardee would still be filled with indecision, and he would be allowed to go about his duties until Adam returned.

Back in the bar, Hardee wasn't filled with indecision. He'd had enough of all the underhand, subterfuge stuff and he'd decided that when Jones reported for duty in the morning he'd be arrested for treason.

Chapter 22

Saturday 18th November 2006. St. Andrew's Church, Charleston.

As Naomi approached the southwest corner of the church with Carlton, the pressure on her shoulder became unbearable. She could hear the groans, and the closer she got to the corner, the louder they became.

"You all right honey?" said Debbie.

"She's fine," said Carlton.

Debbie cast a look at Alan as Naomi appeared to take no notice of her and walk straight past.

Naomi's eyes were fixed on the brick-built vault. She pointed to it and said, "What's this place?"

Alan said, "Hang on a minute; I've got one of the church leaflets in the car from our last visit." He reached into the car, retrieved the leaflet from the glove compartment, and opened it up. "Here we are," he said, "it's a holding vault constructed sometime around 1800 that was used to hold bodies prior to burial."

Naomi looked at the vault, but for some odd reason, the psychic homing device in her brain kept on causing her to look at the empty ground above the head end closer to the church.

She turned to Alan and said, "May I see that please?"

Alan handed the leaflet over.

Naomi studied it for a few seconds and then said, "I don't get it. According to this, the burial holding vault is described as item number seven in their walking tour. Item number six is the grave of John Ernest Gilchrist whose grave is behind the chancel, but the area I'm being drawn to isn't noted at all."

"Perhaps your radar is a bit out of kilter," said Carlton.

Naomi stared at the vault and felt something – she didn't know what – but her eyes were drawn away again and she became fixated on an area several feet above it. "No," she said, "it's there." She pointed to the same spot that Del had shown the Sheriff two days earlier.

The weirdest thing was the moaning. The volume seemed to increase when she looked at a certain spot, and then decrease when she looked away from it. She took in a deep breath and turned to explain what she could hear to Debbie, Alan, and Carlton, and then without warning, it ceased. She wheeled around, said, "What?" and stared at the ground above the vault.

Debbie, Alan, and Carlton were mesmerised. They looked at where Naomi was staring until Debbie turned to Alan. She said, "I don't like this honey, it's freaking me out."

Alan had a frown on his face too, and said, "Okay…we can leave if you want, but let's give Naomi a few more minutes – okay?"

Debbie nodded.

Carlton was frowning too. He said, "Mimi…"

Naomi appeared to be wandering aimlessly over the ground above the vault.

Carlton repeated, "Mimi?"

Naomi looked up and said, "I don't get it. From the minute that we arrived I was drawn to this place, now, it's as though the signal has switched off! I can't pick up anything at all."

Debbie cast a sideways glance at Alan and said, "Honey?"

Alan looked down at her and said, "I know…"

"I don't like this. It goes against my beliefs."

"I know," said Alan, "I know."

"Then do something about it!"

Alan glared at Debbie and said, "And what am I supposed to do? You know that we came here for a disinterment, so I'm sorry, but you're going to have to put up with it."

Debbie glared and said, "Nobody said anything about Naomi being… well, you know! – And, I don't *have* to put up with it. Maybe I'll do some shopping instead."

Alan said, "Whatever – your choice…"

Debbie stared at Alan for a few seconds and then turned to walk towards their car. Ahead, she saw a small woman staring at them.

"Hi folks," said the woman, "can I help you?"

Naomi, Carlton, and Alan turned.

A smallish, older lady stood before them. She was dressed in an ankle length dark blue skirt, white blouse, and black waistcoat, covered in part by a long white apron. In a soft, southern lilt, she said, "My name's Jackie; I'm one of the wardens here."

Carlton was the first to respond. He walked across with an outstretched hand and said, "Hi, my name's Carlton." He turned and indicated to the others. "That is my wife Naomi, and these are our friends Debbie and Alan."

Jackie smiled, said, "Hi," to everybody and then asked, "Did you want to see the Rector, or are y'all just visiting the churchyard?"

"We're here for the disinterment next Monday," said Naomi.

Jackie nodded and said, "I see." She paused for a few seconds and then repeated, "Did you want to see the Rector?"

"It's not really necessary if he's busy," said Naomi, "because we'll be back here on Monday for the er…"

"Disinterment," said Jackie.

"Yes, indeed."

"It's not our usual Rector who's with us at this time," said Jackie, "he's on vacation until after Thanksgiving. At the moment we have the Reverend Ali Burch officiating."

"Ah," said Carlton, "well in that case, we wouldn't want to disturb Reverend Burch right now, because no doubt we'll be taking up more of her valuable time next Monday."

"And will y'all be attending service tomorrow?"

"We'd love to," said Debbie.

Naomi and Carlton's hearts sank. Neither of them was religious, but they were aware how much more their American cousins were, compared to the English.

"Well in that case let me go get Ali, I'm sure that she'd be delighted to meet with y'all."

Debbie smiled at Alan as Jackie wandered off.

Carlton raised his eyebrows at Naomi.

"It won't do any harm to get friendly with a few of the locals," said Naomi, "considering that this is their church – and one of the oldest in America – that we'll be messing up."

She watched as Jackie headed off in the direction of the parish house and said, "I hope that she isn't too…"

The minute that Jackie disappeared into the parish house, the moaning started again. Naomi whirled around and said, "Whoa!"

Carlton frowned and said, "What?"

"It's started again."

"What has?"

Naomi cast a quick glance in the direction of Debbie and Alan who appeared to be deep in conversation, and said, "The moaning."

"Moaning?"

"Yes, it was coming from under the ground where I was pointing."

"God, that sounds spooky – what on earth's moaning?"

"I don't know, but it sounds like a lot of voices."

"Good grief, and that's where we'll be opening up."

Naomi shrugged.

Carlton thought for a few seconds and then said, "You don't suppose that we could be letting something out that we shouldn't do you?"

Naomi shook her head and said, "I don't know, I've never had an experience like this before."

"And was it linked to that business over there?" Carlton nodded in the direction of the trench.

Naomi looked across and said, "No, I don't think so."

"And can you hear the moaning right now?"

Naomi turned towards the burial vault and said, "Yes."

"Can you point to where?"

"I can try." Naomi walked towards the vault. The sound magnified the closer she got. She looked down to where she thought the sound was coming from and said, "It's…"

The sound stopped again.

Naomi frowned and said, "…it's stopped again." With a frown upon her face she turned to look at Carlton, and then out of the corner of her eye saw Jackie walking down the steps of the parish house with another woman. "My God," she said, "it can't be…"

Her sentence was cut off as Debbie turned towards them and called, "Jackie's here with the Rector."

Carlton didn't know which way to look first, at the approaching church officials or his wife. His mind was in riot.

Everybody remained silent until Jackie and the Rector arrived.

"Y'all," said Jackie, "this is Reverend Ali."

Everybody was introduced.

Ali smiled and said, "So you're the guys who've come to oversee the disinterment on Monday?"

"We are," said Carlton, "do you know the history of why we're here."

"Yes, Deacon Morrison explained it to me, and it sounds fascinating, but there's a bit of a problem."

Naomi frowned and said, "What kind of problem?"

"In order for the disinterment to take place, the Rector of the church has to give his permission for it to proceed."

"And?" said Naomi.

Ali turned to Naomi and said, "Reverend Hughes has refused it."

Naomi was stunned. She said, "Why? Why has he done that?"

"He was worried about the speed at which the proceedings have taken place in his absence. It would seem that our Deacon, Deacon Morrison, has organised all of these events in what can only be described as record time, and when he heard that the procedures were all due to take place over the period leading up to Thanksgiving, he was concerned that the increased number of churchgoers, and their children, might be concerned if they were going to arrive and find contractors digging up the resting places of their ancestors."

Carlton said, "I can understand that."

"But we came here because the Sheriff's Department informed us that they would be disinterring on Monday, and they asked us if we'd like to be present," said Alan.

"And I'm sorry about that Mr…"

"Farlington," said Alan.

"…Mr. Farlington. But when the Sheriff contacted you, permission hadn't been given by the Rector."

"But surely," said Naomi, "the procedure would be over within a day wouldn't it?"

Ali turned to Naomi and said, "Wouldn't that depend upon what you found ma'am?" She paused and then added, "Especially if it was something as important as a large, rare, historic ruby."

"Reverend Burch has a point," said Carlton, "What if the press get a hold of it?"

Ali turned to Carlton and said, "My sentiments sir – and calling me Ali's just fine."

Carlton smiled and turned to Naomi. He said, "Come on you can see what she…"

Naomi turned to Ali and said, "You said *'digging up the resting places of their ancestors'* – what did you mean? We're only proposing one."

Ali said, "I was talking figuratively ma'am."

The thumb pressed down on Naomi's shoulder with such violence that she grabbed hold of it and groaned. She looked straight behind Ali and saw that she was staring at the trench again.

Aware that everybody was looking at her, in particular Carlton and Debbie, she said, "Sorry, I slept wrong last night and I keep on getting twinges." She looked up at Ali and said, "I'm sorry to hear that Reverend Hughes hasn't given his permission, because we're only here for another week and we'll be gone by the time that he returns."

"That's not so now."

Naomi raised her eyebrows and said, "No?"

"No, when I told him the extent of what was going on here, he informed me that he would be cutting his vacation short, and that he'd be back this Monday. He also asked me to ask you guys if you could stick around until then, to see if he could accommodate at least some of your wishes too."

"So it's not all lost then?" said Carlton.

"No sir, but you will have to wait until Monday." Ali waited until she'd seen nods of assent all around and then said, "Now, please feel free to wander around the church and grounds; I'm sure that Jackie would be happy to escort you and fill you in on the history of this beautiful old church."

"I'd be delighted," said Jackie, "in fact I…"

Everybody stopped talking as a car turned off the main road and into the drive. It swept past the contractors at such a speed that it threw up a shower of small stones and caused one or two of them to yell at the driver.

The car drove towards them at speed, and then stopped. A determined-looking woman got out.

Jackie recognised her, and said, "My my, that was an entrance Mrs Morrison. Is everything all right?"

"It will be if you tell me that my husband is here," said an angry Janet.

Chapter 23

Del stood looking at the Christian Bookshop and felt guilty.

He'd approached it with a spring in his step fresh from his encounter with Julie and Lorraine, and prior to his feeling of guilt; he'd been on cloud nine. In the trouser department he was wrecked. He couldn't ever recall a time when he'd ejaculated so much, and for so long. The thrill of the two girls mauling every square inch of his naked body, and his ability to be able to maul theirs without any inhibition had been mind-blowing, and although he knew that he wouldn't have been able to do another thing by the time that he'd left, he'd wanted more before he'd driven more than a couple of miles from Julie's trailer.

As he'd turned into Calhoun Street, he'd been reminiscing over the encounter, and he'd been thrilled at the thought of being the secret lover of two such gorgeous women at his age. But then the bookshop had come into view, and he'd stopped dead. He couldn't rationalise it, he just felt guilty. The sight of it represented the good side of his life; the Deacon, the respected member of the community, the honest, loyal, and faithful husband, and not the lying, secretive, cheating, sex-crazed animal that he'd become.

He drew himself up, crossed the street, and went inside.

He saw Lesley-Ann sitting behind the counter and said, "Hi LA, everything okay?"

Lesley-Ann looked up and said, "Did Janet enjoy your surprise?"

"She loved it. She had no idea what I'd had planned, so thank you very much for helping me out today."

Lesley-Ann looked at Del and marvelled at his audacity. She said, "Toast is one of mine and Mark's favourite restaurants but we've not been there for a while. What's this week's special?"

Del hadn't considered that he'd be questioned about the menu and cursed his stupidity for not being prepared. He remembered something from a previous visit and said, "Charleston Cheese Steak."

Lesley-Ann frowned and said, "I haven't had one of those before, what is it?"

"It's grilled, shaved steak served with sautéed peppers and onions, topped with pepper jack cheese, served on a hoagie roll."

Lesley-Ann was impressed with Del's front. She said, "And did you have one?"

"Not today, I had a fried green tomato BLT, and Janet had a crab cake sammie."

Lesley-Ann sat down on the seat behind the counter and frowned. She said, "That's strange."

"What is?"

"You saying that Janet had a crab cake sammie."

"Why?"

"'Cos she told me that she'd had the chargrilled chicken…"

Del was stunned. He stared at Lesley-Ann and tried to steady his emotion. He said, "Janet told you that?"

"Yes."

"When?"

"About half an hour ago – why do you ask?"

"Janet was in here half an hour ago?"

"Yes, and when I asked her what she'd had with you at Toast, she said the chargrilled chicken."

"And then what?"

"She went silent for a bit, like she was thinking about something, and then she said that she needed to get home to arrange a special thank you for such a wonderful surprise."

"She said that?"

Lesley-Ann winked and said, "She sure did. And hey, don't tell me that you've been married so long that you don't know what that means?"

Del shuddered at the thought but smiled a weak smile and said, "Of course not…"

"So you'd better be ready honey, 'cos she looked like she was going to go for it."

Del looked at his watch and said, "And that was about half an hour ago?"

Lesley-Ann was revelling in Del's discomfort; she decided to up the ante. She said, "Maybe you'd better head on down to the pharmacy and get some of that Viagra!"

Del recalled his last few hours and said, "That I don't need…"

Lesley-Ann said, "If you say so." She reached down, picked up her bag, stood up, and said, Right – I'm off."

"You're off? I thought that you were standing in for me today?"

"Good Lord Del Morrison, one hint of sex and your mind goes to mush! Don't you even recall what you told Janet at Toast this lunchtime?"

Del was lost; he said, "Er, no, it must have slipped my mind…"

"Janet said, that you'd said, that if you came in this afternoon, you'd take over the rest of my shift."

"*I did?* – Er, yes – that's right, I remember now…"

Lesley-Ann winked at Del as she walked past and said, "I hope that I'm not letting the cat out of the bag, but Janet said that she wanted to be good and ready for you when you got in." She turned as she got to the door and said, "Bye hun, I hope that you get what you deserve after today's surprise…"

Del smiled and waited until Lesley-Ann had gone. His mind was in turmoil. He started repeating, "Shit – shit – shit…" as he paced up and down.

Back at the Morrison household Janet was beside herself with anger and frustration. Every bit of instinct that she had was warning her that something wasn't right, but something that Lesley-Ann had said, had her racked with indecision. She had mooted the idea that Del might be being furtive because he was planning a surprise for their impending fifteenth wedding anniversary.

She was now forty-two, and three years older than Del, and she'd known that he was attractive to the ladies; indeed she'd had to see more of them off from the church than she'd have liked, yet she'd always believed him to be honest and faithful. But since the accursed visit to the psychic, everything had changed. She was plagued by suspicion – the name 'Muz' – the damnable green bag – and Del's out-of-character behaviour, and she hated it.

She looked at the clock on the wall and saw that it was 5:25pm. She writhed at the thought that Del might be stringing out the time until 6pm before coming home, so that it gave the appearance that he'd been at work. She pursed her lips and almost snorted out an exasperated breath, as she got up to make a fresh pot of coffee.

No sooner had she picked up the water jug to fill the coffee maker, than she heard the front door close. She shot another glance at the clock, saw that it was 5:29pm, and heard Del call, "Hi honey – I'm home."

She steadied her volatile emotion, called back, "In the kitchen," and waited to see what he'd have to say.

Del walked in, went straight across to Janet, and took hold of her hands. He said, "I have a confession to make."

Janet said, "Go on…"

Del looked down, and then back up into Janet's eyes. He said, "I've lied to you **Note this!=>** and LA, because I didn't go to work today."

"Oh – and where did you go?"

"I've been doing something else."

Janet frowned and said, "What?"

"Something I needed to do on my own."

"I say again – what?"

"It was something for a very special lady and a forthcoming date…"

Janet remained silent.

"…the first of December?"

"Our wedding anniversary – yes, what about it?"

"It's not just *any* wedding anniversary, it's our fifteenth!"

"So?" Janet couldn't muster up any enthusiasm, in truth, she felt even more aggravated by his dithering.

"You're not making this any easier," said Del, "you have a face like a rat catcher's bait box."

Janet wasn't amused, she said, "And what's that supposed to mean?"

"I mean that it's… it's, not your usual attractive and appealing face."

"Well it's the only one that I have, so get to the point, I have a busy evening ahead, and I want to know why my husband has been lying to me."

"All right," said Del, "if you're not going to indulge me by showing even a little enthusiasm for…"

"*Enthusiasm?*" said Janet, "For what – lying to me?"

Del stopped speaking for a second and then said, "Okay, let's cut to the chase. I've booked us a two week Caribbean cruise commencing December second."

Janet didn't know how to respond. She wanted to say, 'And that took you all day?' But she didn't. She could see the look of anticipation on Del's face, and she didn't believe him, but, she couldn't dismiss the idea that he could in fact, be telling the truth.

She said, "Oh…"

"*Oh?* – I spend all day trying to get the detail exactly how I think you'll like it, and I get 'Oh.'?"

Janet was lost for words. She looked at Del's disappointed expression and stepped forwards. She put her arms around his neck, pulled him closer, kissed him on the lips, and said, "Sorry honey – that was very thoughtful of you." She then hugged into the side of his face and held him there.

Del held on and thought, *Damn – that was close…*

Janet had made her mind up. She didn't swear at any time, ever, but on this occasion she thought, *"And you are a lying, conniving, asshole, Del Morrison, and I am going to prove it…"*

Chapter 24

Without drawing any attention to himself, Bart Holdsworth walked to the back of The Drum Hotel and waited. Seconds later the rear door opened and he slipped in, unseen.

Adam looked through the door that led to the kitchen and saw that it was still empty. He turned to Bart and said, "Okay, let's go."

They crossed the kitchen to the door on the opposite side, and darted up the back stairs to the first floor.

Once they were in Adam's room they embraced each other.

"It's so good to see you brother," said Adam, "and just look at that facial hair! You could have a Pinkerton detective hiding in that beard!"

Bart laughed and said, "And so good to see you too!"

The brothers caught up, filling each other in on their latest adventures and developments until Bart said, "Will you go see granny while you're here?"

Adam sat back and thought about granny Prevost on her small plantation near Wappoo Creek.

She was now seventy-four years old, and bodily, as tough as old boots, but even on the brothers' last visit prior to the war; they'd noticed that her mind had been going. She'd seemed to be more insular, and less able to recognise them. She'd often sat alone talking to herself, and she'd become more and more irascible as the time had passed.

To her great good fortune though, she'd had an excellent friend and protector in Lucius and his wife, known to all as Mammy, who had been brought up as slaves on the Prevost

Estate, but both of whom had declined, along with six others, to leave once they'd been given their freedom.

"I don't know," said Adam, "it's been three years since we last saw her and she hardly recognised us then."

"What about Lucius?"

"Oh, I'll go and see him for sure, and Mammy. Indeed, part of my plan involves most of the guys from the estate if they're willing to help. I want to ensure that their lives will be properly catered for if we succeed."

For the next hour the brothers discussed the minutia of the plan, until Bart said, "Do you think that you were followed from Chattanooga?"

"I didn't notice anybody, but I wouldn't bet a brass cent against it."

"So you weren't joshing when you asked me to bring a jar of horse glue and some scissors?"

Adam said, "No – did you get some?"

Bart removed a small glass jar from his leather shoulder bag and held it up. "I did, and it smells disgusting!"

"Wonderful…" said Adam, "…I can't wait."

"Your plan," said Bart.

At 7:30am Gilbert Weims walked down the front stairs of The Drum Hotel and into the restaurant. He hadn't made any particular effort to conceal himself, and he positioned himself at a table that would allow a view of anybody walking in to eat, or exiting the hotel via the front entrance.

At 7:50am he saw Adam Holdsworth enter the restaurant in his full uniform and sit at a table on the other side of the room. He noted the way that Adam walked, the food that he chose, whether he was right or left-handed, the number of coffees he had with his breakfast, and how long he took to eat it. Upon completion of the meal he saw how Adam wiped his mouth and deposited his serviette on the table, and he watched which leg if any, was the dominant one when he stood up from the table. Finally, he watched how Adam departed, and whether or not he made any attempt to thank any of the waiting staff before leaving.

He saw Adam cross the saloon, and then ascend the stairs towards the guest rooms.

He waited for a few seconds and then departed the restaurant too. He walked across to the reception desk, picked up a news-sheet, looked at it, and turned back. He walked back into the saloon, sat at an empty card table in the corner, and waited.

He saw three civilians, two men, and one woman, depart the hotel, and then his quarry reappeared. He watched Adam exit the front entrance, turn left, and head down King Street towards the railroad depot.

He folded up the news-sheet, placed it on the card table, and then set off in pursuit.

Ten minutes after Weims had left following Bart, the real Adam walked down the front stairs dressed in Bart's clothing, and hoped that the thick moustache and goatee beard that they'd fashioned out of Bart's facial hair, wouldn't fall off. Furthermore, he hoped that nobody would get too close to him, because Bart hadn't been wrong about the foul stench of the horse glue, holding it to his face.

He went to the stables, picked up Bart's horse and set off for the Prevost plantation.

One hour later he stopped in Bridge Road before turning into the estate and cast his eyes across to the Prioleau plantation.

As children he, Bart, Ned, Ira, Mary, and Joseph, had all played with the kids from the Prioleau family. They too had had the same friendly and caring attitude to their slave families, and had freed them all years before the war. They had another plantation opposite Church Creek on the old Fort Dorchester Road, and all the children, black and white, had had free reign over anywhere they wanted to play as long as their individual chores or homework had been done.

The war had exacted its toll however. Kit Prioleau, two years older than he, and Abel Prioleau, one of his playmate ex-slaves who'd adopted the family name, had been killed in the Battle of Fort Pulaski in Georgia, in April 1862. Thereafter, the head of the family, Alexander Prioleau, had paid to have his other two sons, and the remaining son of an ex-slave, de-conscripted from the Confederate Army, and returned to the family estates.

Adam spurred his horse forwards and road down the long straight drive towards the house. Nothing seemed to have changed since the land had been halved after the Charleston & Savannah Rail Road had purchased the rights to run its tracks through the land towards the railroad bridge. He could see that the house looked in good repair and he knew that that would have been down to Lucius and the rest of the guys.

He dismounted, tied his horse up to the front rail, and saw the door open.

Lucius stepped out with a shotgun tucked under his right arm, and then he recognised one of the twins. At first the facial hair fooled him, but as Adam approached he knew who it was. A huge grin appeared on his face, and he leaned the gun against the porch rails.

"Well if it ain't the prodigal son, come to see his old pappy!" he said.

Adam smiled with genuine affection for the man who had been another father figure for most of his life. He ascended the three steps of the porch and embraced Lucius. He said, "Go on then pappy, which one am I?"

Lucius stepped back and said, "Adam – but you smell like Bart's horse."

Adam laughed and said, "That's 'cos I'm hoping to fool some folks by wearing Bart's moustache and beard, and we could only find horse glue to stick it on!"

"You boys don't change do you – always up to mischief? But before you explain, come and see granny. I do have to warn you mind, that she hardly recognises anybody nowadays, so don't be surprised if she doesn't know who you are."

Adam nodded and said, "So she's worse?"

"I'm afraid so, but she's happy in her own world, and despite the war, she's safe enough with us for now."

"Okay, let's do that now, because I have a serious proposition for you and Jacob."

Lucius nodded and led the way to the front door. He said, "I can't wait to see Mammy's face, and the rest of the boys come to think of it, when they see that hilarious disguise of yours."

Adam smiled and followed Lucius into the house.

Two hours later, and following an emotional but sad visit with granny Prevost, Adam explained to Lucius, Mammy, and Jacob, who was second only to Lucius in seniority on the plantation, what was planned for the gold.

"The gold which will be in seven, fifty-pound boxes will be landed by a Captain Davidson and eight men from the *SS Georgiana* on Long Island. They will be met by a Lieutenant Joliet who will take it to the South Carolina Rail Road Terminal and deposit it in a special railroad car that will be stopped in siding number four close to Hutson Street. Nobody but Joliet will know what the car contains, but it will be guarded overnight by a detail of six men. I am supposed to arrive at 5am the following morning with six men and escort it to Wilmington."

"And why are you telling us this Adam?" said Mammy.

"Because I want us to steal it."

Mammy, Lucius, and Jacob looked thunderstruck.

"Steal it?" said Jacob, *"Us?"*

"And from six Confederate guards?" said Lucius.

"Yes," said Adam, "don't ask me how, but Ned has somehow worked his genius and has arranged that a goods truck supposedly loaded with medical supplies, but containing seven boxes of iron ore will be arriving in Charleston two days before the gold, and it will be parked in one of the sidings nearby. He is going to mark the truck with a large red cross so that we know which it is.

During the night we have to swap the gold for the iron ore, and get the gold away along the old Fort Dorchester Road and leave it somewhere safe, so that Bart can collect it a couple of days later and take it away."

"Lord save us," said Lucius, "and you want us to do that? We could all be shot, and then who'd look after granny?"

Adam turned to Lucius and said, "Have you ever heard of William Tecumseh Sherman?"

Lucius and Jacob said, "No."

"He is a general who operates something known as a 'scorched earth' policy; a policy whereby everything that is captured is totally destroyed – houses, shops, factories, mills, railroads, everything."

"But why would anybody do such a wicked thing to people who have surrendered or who have been defeated?" said Mammy.

"To teach them a lesson that war is never to be considered by them again, 'cos that is the consequence – total destruction and total devastation."

"And why are you telling us this?" said Jacob.

"Because whilst the south seems to be retaining the upper hand through the efforts of Jackson and Lee at the present, the Union's armies are being filled to overflowing with ex-slaves fighting for the north since Lincoln's Emancipation Proclamation."

"Emancipation Proclamation?" repeated Lucius, "What's that?"

"In short, Abraham Lincoln has declared that if the north wins the war, all of the folk enslaved in the ten remaining rebellious states, will be freed."

Mammy, Lucius and Jacob were dumbstruck until Mammy said, "President Abraham Lincoln said that?"

"Yes he did. His proclamation has given justification for the north's war on the south, and it has stopped foreign countries like Great Britain recognising the Confederacy as a separate country because of their stance on abolition."

Lucius said, "This is all very interesting Adam, and I can see why black folks would be anxious to help free their families and all, but what has this to do with us and the gold?"

Adam turned to Lucius and said, "I believe that the south will be defeated. And if the general leading the attack on Charleston is Sherman, he will operate his scorched earth policy and destroy everything in his path, including the Prevost Plantation. That is why I want you all out, with granny, to somewheres safe, and with some of that gold, until Bart, Ned, and I can join you."

Silence descended until Lucius said, "Whew – that's a hard one to swallow, but considering that you're here, a northern officer, risking your life to tell us this, we'll all do what we can."

Mammy and Jacob nodded their assent too.

"Good," said Adam, "I believe that I know what we have to do, but I do have a weak point." He looked at the inquisitive faces and then said, "If we succeed in getting the gold away from the railroad depot, I don't know where to hide it for a couple of nights before Bart takes it past Fort Bull on the River Road."

Jacob looked at Lucius and raised his eyebrows.

Lucius turned to Adam and said, "We might know somewhere."

"You do?"

"Yes – we've been working on a top-secret project at St. Andrew's church."

Adam frowned and said, "What?"

"It's an escape tunnel that leads from the church to Church Creek."

"An escape tunnel?" repeated Adam, "why would anybody want that?"

"It was for the officers at Fort Bull, so that they could retreat a ways down River Road, take sanctuary in the church, and then escape through the tunnel to a boat at Church Creek."

An idea started to form in Adam's brain. He said, "And is the boat already in the creek?"

"I guess so," said Lucius.

"It is," confirmed Jacob, "I saw it the other day…"

"One of my problems was how to get across the Ashley River and past Fort Bull without using Bees Ferry. If the boat is moored in Church Creek, and it's big enough, that would be perfect."

"It's big enough all right," said Jacob, "it could take eight men and two of us could row it across to Jim Prioleau's estate on the north bank."

"*Our* Jim Prioleau?" said Adam.

"Yes," said Lucius, "his father gave him charge of the riverside plantation after he came out of the army, and he's lived there ever since."

"Excellent," said Adam, "then it looks as though we might have a plan…"

Chapter 25

Naomi reached into her handbag and removed her mobile phone. She looked up at Carlton and said, "Let's see if there are any texts from home before we go across to the IHOP for breakfast." She switched it on and waited for it to connect. Straight away the signal sounded indicating that she'd received a text. She clicked onto it and read; *"Hi Naomi, sorry to disturb your holiday again, but please call me when you can. Thanks, Bob C."*

"Anything interesting?" said Carlton.

"Bob Crowthorne wants me to ring him."

Carlton raised his eyebrows and said, "I wonder what now?"

Naomi looked at her watch and said, "It'll be early afternoon in the UK so I might as well call him before we go to breakfast."

Carlton said, "That suits me, I'll finish off in the bathroom."

Ten minutes later, with the bathroom tidied up and all of his shaving gear put away, he returned to the bedroom and saw Naomi sitting on the edge of the bed with a shocked expression on her face. He frowned and said, "Everything okay?"

Naomi looked up and said, "Darke's body has disappeared from the mortuary."

"What? Bodies don't just disappear from morgues – how the hell has that happened?"

"Nobody knows. His body was last seen on Friday, the mortuary had been locked up for the weekend and the post-mortem was scheduled for today, but when the Coroner's Assistant went to retrieve it, it had gone."

"That's truly shocking," said Carlton, "I've not heard of anything like that since the days of Burke and Hare."

Naomi looked at Carlton and said, "Oh – that's a thought…"

"What is?"

"Your comment about Burke and Hare."

"What about them?"

"You obviously think that his body has been stolen…"

Carlton looked at Naomi and said, "What other explanation could there be? Dead people don't just get up and walk away."

"Hmm…"

"What?"

"The mortuary attendant's missing too."

"What?"

"The mortuary attendant's gone too."

Carlton frowned and said, "Him too? Has Bob any theories?"

"Not yet; it was a man, and he started work at the mortuary two weeks' ago, but apart from that they have nothing."

"No CCTV coverage?"

"Nothing."

"And do they have any info on the missing attendant?"

"They're looking into that now."

Carlton walked across the bedroom and plonked himself down on the bed next to Naomi. He said, "Weird…"

Naomi turned and looked at Carlton and said, "And a bit scary."

"A bit scary – why?"

"It is Adrian Darke that we're talking about here."

"No," said Carlton, "it was Adrian Darke's body."

Naomi looked down for a second and said, "I wish I could be as certain as you are."

Carlton turned towards Naomi and took hold of her right hand. He said, "It may look suspicious with the attendant going missing too, but don't forget that the doctor who examined Darke's body pronounced him dead long before he was taken to the mortuary."

Naomi remained silent for a few minutes and then stood up. She walked across to the window and looked out; seconds later she turned to face Carlton and said, "What if it was all a scam? What if the doctor, the attendant, and maybe even the prison warder who found his body were all in the pay of Darke?"

"Whoa – that's a stretch isn't it?"

"Is it? What other chance did he have of escaping? How would such a high-profile figure, known to the press and public alike, get away? He would have been taken in convoy to and from court, he would have been in a secure dock in the courtroom, and he would have been secure in prison."

Carlton lapsed into silence for a few seconds and then said, "Well – you've got me thinking, that's for sure… Did you put all of this to Bob?"

"No, but I'll bet a pound to a penny that he's already considered the same things."

Carlton looked at his watch and said, "Look at the time; let's go to the IHOP and we can discuss this on the way over."

Naomi nodded and picked up her jacket. She said, "Yes, okay. You still having pancakes?"

"You bet," said Carlton, "brekky here wouldn't be the same without them!"

"I can always do them for you at home you know. Pancakes and Maple syrup *have* made it across the pond."

"I know," said Carlton holding the bedroom door open for Naomi, "but if I did have them at home, it wouldn't be so special when we came here."

The couple held hands as they walked across the busy junction towards the IHOP and just before entering Carlton said, "I suppose that if Darke has somehow faked his death and escaped, at least he won't be bothering anybody like you. He'll want to perpetuate the myth and keep well away from anyone who could identify him."

Naomi stepped inside the restaurant in front of Carlton and smiled at the friendly-looking assistant.

"Ma'am, sir, welcome to the IHOP north Charleston," said the young waitress, "is it just the two of you?"

"It is," said Naomi.

"Okay, this way please…"

Naomi and Carlton sat where indicated and smiled at the waitress.

"Can I get you folks a coffee while you're deciding?"

"You can," said Carlton, "thank you."

The waitress smiled and nodded and then headed towards the bottomless coffee pot.

Naomi leaned forwards and looked into Carlton's eyes. She said, "You might be right about Darke keeping away from people who could identify him, but you could be wrong too."

"How so?"

"What if he's planned his escape to get revenge on those who put him behind bars?"

"Including you."

"Right."

Carlton frowned and said, "That's an awful thought… "

"Yes maybe – but we have no idea what state of mind he was in after being locked up for so long…"

Carlton sat back in his seat and stared at his pretty wife in silence.

At St. Andrew's church Del had a quick look around the parish house and made sure that everything was, as Reverend Hughes would like to find it. Satisfied that all was well, he stepped outside to talk to the contractors who had now brought in three extra men to accommodate the opening of the burial vault.

"Morning Deacon," called Taffy, "what time's kick-off?"

Del frowned and walked across to the trench. He was surprised to see how deep the men had gone. He looked at Taffy and said, "I'm sorry, what did you say?"

"I said, what time's kick-off?" he saw the lack of understanding spread across Del's face and then added, "What time does all the action start? The disinterment and so on?"

"Oh, of course – sorry," Del looked at his watch and saw that it was 9:45am. He said, "The Sheriff and Reverend Hughes are meeting us here at 10am, and we're expecting the family of the deceased between 10:30 and 11am."

Taffy looked at Del's white smock and said, "You're taking a risk wearing that smock Deacon, these excavations can get very dirty, and with this breeze blowing, it could come out second best."

Del looked down and said, "Yes, you're right, I'll remove it before the work begins." He looked down into the trench and said, "How much deeper have you got to go?"

"About a foot and that should be it."

Del cast his eyes towards the spot that Casey had identified as the 'Matthews P. F.' grave and wondered whether any of the ruby had been exposed. He walked towards it and kept his eyes down. He got to the spot and looked around.

"It's going to get worse," said Taffy.

Del turned and said, "What is?"

"The ground's getting boggier and boggier the further we go down."

Del looked into the trench again and saw the difference in ground texture at the bottom."

"It's the water table," said Taffy, "the deeper we get, the slimier it's going to get."

Del hadn't considered that before and stared more intently at the place he thought should be the grave.

"That's odd," said Taffy.

Del turned and said, "What is?"

"Well – we have a sixty-five foot long, by four feet deep, soak-away trench, and when you stare into it, you do so in exactly the same spot as the English woman last Saturday."

Del looked up and said, "I don't understand – what do you mean?"

Taffy walked across to Del and pointed down into the trench. "There," he said, "where you're looking. That's the same place that the woman was looking."

"Which woman?"

"The English woman who's come to see the disinterment."

Del said, "So what was she doing looking in here?"

"I don't know – maybe she was just interested in what we were doing."

"And you say that she was looking at the same spot as me?"

"Yes."

Del began to regret his action and said, "But I wasn't looking at anywhere in particular, I was checking out the water table like you said."

"Maybe so," said Taffy, "but she wasn't. She walked up and down the full length of the trench a couple of times, and each time, she ended up looking where you were." He paused and then said, "Is something down there that I should know about?"

Del was shocked; the last thing that he wanted was to draw any attention to the Matthews grave. He said, "No, I was very careful to lead you between the burials."

"So we're not likely to unearth anything we shouldn't then?"

Del looked at Taffy with a frown on his face and said, "No you're not. Besides, all of the burials near here dated to the early part of the nineteenth century, so it's unlikely that anything would ever have been found, even if we'd gone that deep."

He could have kicked himself! He couldn't believe that he'd uttered the words, 'even if we'd gone that deep' – but he had.

Taffy looked into the trench and then back at Del. He nodded and said, "I get it now – you're hedging your bets by having us only go down five feet."

Del could have spit.

"Is that because you aren't sure about the location of the burials?"

Del said, "No, we're sure of the locations, and you're nowhere near any of them. But, I can see your logic in thinking that by not going down the full six feet, we'll guarantee not to disturb anything."

"Right," said Taffy, "so where were the burials?"

Del couldn't believe it again. He hadn't thought that he'd be asked that question. He looked around and pointed in the direction of the parish house. He said, "One's over there…"

Taffy turned to look where Del was indicating, and then turned back when he heard a car approach.

"Looks like they've finally caught up with you Deacon," he said.

Del said, "Sorry? What?"

Taffy pointed towards the approaching car and said, "There – isn't that the Sheriff?"

Chapter 26

The police car pulled up in one of the parking bays and Sheriff Bonnie-Mae Clement stepped out. She surveyed the area, caught sight of Del and Taffy, and walked across to them.

"Gentlemen," she said.

"Ma'am," said Taffy, "how are you today?"

"I'm well, thank you." She turned and said, "Del?"

"I'm well too, thank you Bonnie-Mae."

"Are we the first to arrive?"

"We are," said Del.

"And what time are you expecting the family?"

Del looked at his watch and saw that it was 10:05am. He said, "Within the next half hour or so."

Bonnie-Mae turned to Taffy and said, "Will you please excuse us sir?"

"Sure," said Taffy. He smiled and headed back to the trench.

Bonnie-Mae waited until Taffy was out of earshot and said, "I need to ask you a couple of questions about Casey."

Del felt an imaginary belt tighten around his temple. He said, "What kind of questions?"

"We've had the autopsy report from the Coroner's office and Casey didn't just fall into the creek and drown. There were injuries to his head consistent with repeated and sustained blows."

Del winced at the thought and said, "No – poor Casey."

"Indeed," said Bonnie-Mae, "and there was a particularly nasty bruise on his left temple where he'd been struck by something big."

Del recalled Muz hitting Casey with the large plant pot, but remained quiet.

"The report also confirmed the time of death being somewhere between 8pm Wednesday 15th November and 2am Thursday 16th November." Bonnie-Mae stopped speaking, turned to Del, and said, "Can you account for your movements between those times?"

Del was horrified; he said, *"Me?* Can *I* account for *my* movements?"

"Yes sir, it's nothing personal – just a matter of elimination."

Del didn't hesitate, he said, "I was at home with Janet."

"And can Janet confirm that?"

"Yes, she can."

"Okay…" Bonnie-Mae made a couple of notes in her pocket book and then said, "…and you had no knowledge of anybody who might want to harm Casey?"

"No."

"And are you right, or left-handed?"

"What? – What has that to do with anything?"

"Please just answer the question. Are you right or left-handed?"

Del frowned and said, "Right-handed."

Bonnie-Mae said, "Thank you," and then looked into her notebook. She looked back up and said, "Now, who is Muz?"

Del felt a rush of blood go to his head, but tried to remain as calm as possible. He said, "Who?"

"Muz."

"I've no idea."

Bonnie-Mae stared into Del's face, saw his pupils dilate, and his eyes flash up to the right. A signal that, as a right-handed person, he was not trying to recall something; he was lying or trying to make something up. She paused and then said, "Okay." She didn't believe Del, but decided to change tack. She said, "Is Father Marshall here?"

"No, but he should be real soon."

Bonnie-Mae closed her pocket book and put it back in her shirt pocket. She looked around and said, "Do you mind if I have a wander round until the others get here?"

"Of course not," said Del, "or would you like a coffee? There's a pot freshly brewed in the parish house."

Bonnie-Mae said, "No, but thanks – I'll be fine." She nodded at Del and then turned and walked towards the church deep in thought.

Del stared at Bonnie-Mae's back as she walked away and wondered how much she knew. The urge to get away from Charleston jumped up a notch.

The Farlingtons and Reverend Hughes arrived in their vehicles at the same time. Everybody alighted, and introduced themselves. Minutes later, a low-loader delivery truck carrying a mechanical digger turned into the drive and parked near the end of the trench.

Marshall looked around and shook his head. He caught Del's eye and waved him to one side. Out of earshot of everybody else he said, "What on earth were you playing at arranging all of this unnecessary activity before Thanksgiving?"

Del stepped closer and said, "We did it for you."

"For me? How in the Saint's names do you work that out?"

"We weren't expecting you back until this time next week, and we thought that we'd get all of this done while you were away."

"Who's 'we'?"

"Sheriff Clement and me."

Marshall looked around and all he could see was disruption. He looked back at Del and said, "But you had no right, no authority."

"None of this is costing the church any money."

"That's not the point! The point is…"

"The point is," said Del interrupting, "that the water people have been trying to get in here to sink a stormwater drain for months. The Sheriff had ordered a disinterment, and the family from Florida have brought other family members here from England, and they will be gone by this time next week. So, by our reckoning, we thought that it would be good to get all of this done while you were away, so that you wouldn't be under any stress to do it when you got back."

Marshall faltered, but before he could respond Del upended the apple cart.

"But as usual, your signature procrastination has lost us at least a day now, and we may not be finished in time for Thanksgiving after all."

Marshall didn't often feel cross, but when he heard Del's insulting remark about his 'signature procrastination' he felt it rising to the surface. He said, "What do you mean – my signature procrastination?"

Del stepped back and looked at the Reverend. He said, "Oh come on Marshall, let's at least be honest with each other. Nobody could ever accuse you of making a 'spur of the minute' decision could they?"

Marshall frowned and said, "Well, how about this for size? From now on, you are to ask my permission before you do anything, ever again, at this church. Do you understand?"

Del was shocked. He said, "All right – If that's what you wish."

"It is."

"And what about everything that's been arranged?"

Marshall looked around; he saw how deep and how long the trench was, at the delivery truck off-loading the digger, at the family chatting in the corner of the car park, and at the approaching Sheriff. He exhaled a long breath through his nose and said, "I suppose that there's no sense in sending this lot away now that you've arranged it, and if I'm honest, I can see that you may have been trying to help in my absence, so it can stay." He turned and looked into Del's eyes and said, "But from now on, I mean it – don't do anything without consulting me first."

Del nodded and said, "Thanks Marshall. Does that mean that we can open the ground above the burial vault now?"

Marshall thought of something. He said, "No, but while all these contractors are here, you can open up the vault if you like. We've long considered doing that; we've no record of what it looks like inside and we don't know what condition it's in, but I want it closed again by Wednesday afternoon."

Del could have kissed Marshall. The opening of the burial vault would be another distraction from the trench.

Marshall saw the look of anticipation on Del's face. He said, "And I don't want anybody on Thanksgiving Day seeing anything untoward. The rest of the work will have to wait until after then."

"And what if the drain isn't finished?"

"That I can cope with; to all intents and purposes folk can only see work going on in the car park – though I am expecting you to apply all the pressure that you can to get the men to complete the job by then."

Del nodded and said, "Okay. Leave that with me. Right now, with your permission, we'll get on and open up the vault."

Marshall looked at the innocuous-looking vault and drew in a deep breath. He turned to Del and said, "Okay, go ahead – if you need me I'll be in my office. Now I have to phone the church council and explain what's happening."

Del said, "Good luck with that…"

"Yeah? Tell me about it."

Del called to everybody and said, "Folks – if I could have your attention?" He waited until everybody was looking and then said, "Reverend Hughes has given his permission to open the burial holding vault now, but he has not agreed to open the ground above the head of it, until after Thanksgiving."

Naomi's heart sank; she raised her hand and said, "Excuse me."

Del looked and said, "Yes ma'am?"

"What's the point of that?"

Del floundered and then thought of something. He said, "When the groundsman told me where the old grave was, he said that it pre-dated the vault, and that a part of it may have been under it."

"That won't help us today though, will it?"

"No ma'am, but if we open it up, it may give us an idea how far down it goes, so that we'll be prepared for the next stage after Thanksgiving."

Naomi nodded, turned to Carlton, and said, "True enough." She then faced Del and said, "Sheriff Clement's office was adamant that the actual disinterment would be carried out today, and we've travelled all the way from Gainesville to be here. So why can't that go ahead?"

"I'm truly sorry for your inconvenience ma'am," said Del, "but we've experienced what you might call crossed wires. Reverend Hughes has agreed that the disinterment can go ahead, but not until after Thanksgiving."

"But my husband and I won't be here after Thanksgiving, that's why we're here now."

"And I hope that you will accept my sincere apologies for our blunder ma'am, but there really is nothing that I can do about it now. The Reverend's mind is made up."

Bonnie-Mae sidled up to Naomi's side and said, "Trust me ma'am, when Father Marshall makes up his mind, Heaven and earth won't move him."

Full of disappointment, Naomi looked up to Carlton and said, "I can't tell you how frustrated I am. All the work everybody put into solving those contrivances, the time and cost of getting here, and now we'll be going home before we get to see if El Fuego de Marte is here!"

Carlton looked down at Naomi and said, "That doesn't have to be the case."

"What do you mean?"

"I do have to go back, but you don't. Helen can run things in your department if you're held up here for a few days' longer."

"But what about the plane tickets, car hire, and accommodation?"

"Easily sorted," said Carlton, "so if you want to stay, then do so. I'm sure that Alan will put you up if you want, otherwise we can book you into the Quality Inn for a few days after Thanksgiving."

Naomi smiled and said, "That's fantastic – I will stay. I'm not coming this far and then going home before we've resolved the mystery one way or the other."

Carlton opened his mouth to say something, but was cut off.

"Okay folks," called Taffy, "please make way for the guys, and let's get this thing done…"

Chapter 27

Gilbert Weims sat in the restaurant at breakfast time and knew that something wasn't right. He'd followed 'Adam' around numerous venues in Charleston and nothing appeared to be suspicious. He'd watched as 'Adam' had visited all of the planned operation locations; he'd seen him take notes and look at things from various angles, and he'd seen him doing everything that he'd have expected him to do. Every day he'd noted the same idiosyncrasies and habits, and they all checked out. But – whatever it was, something was not right, and so far, he had nothing whatsoever to report to Harrison in Virginia.

He took a drink of coffee and tried to figure out if he'd missed something, or if he'd been spotted, but if he had, and 'Adam' had known that he was being followed, he'd made an exceptional job of not letting it show.

He shook his head and ground his teeth together. He was missing something – he knew it, and they were supposed to be going their separate ways the next day.

He saw 'Adam' walk into the restaurant and sit at the same table as he had each of the previous days. He watched 'Adam' order the same food, eat it, drink the coffee, thank the young waitress, and leave. Nothing suspicious. He saw him go up the stairs, come down the stairs, and go out of the front door. Same same...

He got up to follow, and then stopped dead. He realised that he was about to repeat the same procedure that had been fruitless for the past two days. He stared at the front door to the hotel and then turned and looked back into the saloon. He couldn't see a back door. He looked at the stairs leading to the guest bedrooms – and then it hit him like a hammer blow. He knew that a chambermaid had been into his room each day, but he'd never seen one use the front stairs.

He threaded his way through the tables and then saw a door behind the piano in the corner of the room. He made sure that nobody was looking and then turned the handle, and pushed. It was locked.

He scanned the saloon and saw another door on the left-hand wall just inside the entrance. He walked across to it, checked that he was still alone, and then turned the handle. It was unlocked.

He stepped inside and saw that he was in a corridor that led to the back of the hotel. Keeping as quiet as he could he followed the corridor around the back of the saloon and saw another set of stairs. He was about to ascend them when he heard a door open at the top. He backed up the corridor, moved around the corner and waited. He heard the footsteps come down the stairs and then walk away from him. He leaned forwards, peered round the corner, and saw a man disappearing in the opposite direction. He waited a couple of seconds and then followed.

Beyond the stairs was a left-hand turn that led to the kitchen. He opened the door and walked through.

Inside were two white guys, one black woman, one Chinese man, and another woman who appeared to be Mexican. They were all busy at their kitchen duties and because he was wearing a suit, they shot him a cursory look and then continued with their work.

The kitchen was 'L' shaped, and around the bend, he heard a door close. He threaded his way through staff, turned the corner, and walked across to the door. He opened it, and saw a man a few yards in front. Without hesitation, he snatched his pocket book out of his jacket pocket, and called, *"Wait – sir! You dropped this!"* He saw the man stop and turn around. He held the pocket book up in the air and waited.

Adam frowned but saw a man holding something in his hand. He walked back and straight away saw that he was one of the men who'd been on the train from Chattanooga.

Even with the false beard and moustache, Weims knew who it was.

"Good morning Captain Holdsworth," he said, "this is a mighty interesting development…"

Adam knew that excuses would be pointless. The simple act of walking around in a disguise would have been enough to have his activities questioned, and Bart arrested for impersonating a Captain in the Confederate Army.

"The name is Gilbert Weims." Weims extended his right hand. "I am an ex-Pinkerton Detective, and a very good one, but for the last two days you have given me a good run for my money."

Adam shook the offered hand, peeled off the facial hair, and threw into a nearby rubbish bin. "Adam Holdsworth," he said. He paused and then added, "And if nothing else, I am at least glad to be rid of that disguise – the smell of the glue was repulsive."

Weims nodded and said, "I don't suppose that you'd care to enlighten me about your fascinating activities over the last two days?"

Adam looked at Weims' face and saw something in his eyes. He said, "Why don't we go back inside and talk over a cup of coffee?"

"And you won't force me to use this?"

Adam looked down and saw that Weims was pointing what appeared to be a small pistol at him through his right-hand jacket pocket.

"No sir, I won't."

Weims nodded and said, "Okay, then since you're familiar with the rear of this establishment, you'd better lead the way."

Two-hundred yards south on King Street, Bart hadn't seen his customary shadow. Up ahead he saw a gents outfitters'. He stopped, looked in the window, and then looked back up the street. Nobody was there. He slipped into the recessed doorway and waited. Several minutes later he turned and headed back towards the Drum Hotel. He didn't notice anybody cross the road as he approached and he didn't see anybody suspicious on the opposite sidewalk.

He got to the hotel, walked through the front door, and was about to pass the restaurant when he heard somebody call his name.

"Mr. Holdsworth – sir!"

Bart pretended that he hadn't heard the call and continued to walk towards the stairs.

"Bart, it's okay..."

The second call stopped Bart. He turned and saw Adam, minus the facial hair, sitting with the same man who'd followed him for the last two days. He drew his right hand into the cuff of Adam's jacket and let his middle finger hover over the spring mechanism that would snap a Derringer pistol into his right hand.

Adam watched as Bart approached and saw what he was about to do. He looked into his brothers' face and with the faintest of movements, shook his head.

Bart removed his finger from the trigger mechanism.

"My name is Weims, Gilbert Weims, and your brother and I are engaged in conversation. Would you care to join us?"

Bart sat down, stared at Weims, and said nothing.

Weims looked at the brothers and said, "Ah, twins – of course..."

Bart looked at Adam and said, "What's going on?"

Weims said, "Isn't this nice? It's just a shame that General Hardee couldn't see us sitting here together like this, he'd be captivated."

Bart shot a glance at Adam and then turned to Weims. He said, "Right now I have a gun aimed at your balls..."

"Then we have ourselves a Mexican stand-off Mister Holdsworth because my pistol is aimed directly at your brother's private parts too."

"Gentlemen, stop," said Adam. "Let's sit here like civilised people and see what can be made of this interesting situation."

Weims raised an eyebrow and said, "Well I'm all ears, but I don't know about...?"

"My twin brother Bart," said Adam. "And we are going to steal fourteen bars of Confederate gold and then disappear."

Bart was staggered; he couldn't believe that Adam had told Weims.

Weims sat in silence for a few seconds and then leaned back in his seat. He looked at Adam and said, "And I guess that I am to conclude from your use of the future tense, that you intend to either silence me, or cut me in."

Bart's mouth fell open, but before he could respond, he heard Adam say, "That is correct." He didn't think that he could be more shocked. He turned to Adam said, "What? Are you crazy?

He's a reb. Whatever deal he makes here, he'll turn us in at the first opportunity!"

Adam turned to Weims and said, "Is that right Mister Weims?"

Weims looked into Adam's eyes before answering. He said, "I guess that that depends on what you're offering…"

"One bar of gold."

"One fourteenth?"

"Yes sir – that's as much as any of us will have."

Weims was shocked. He said, "Your plan involves fourteen people?"

"No, it does not, but if we are successful, those who help will receive one bar each, and the rest will be divided amongst dispossessed southern families, white and black."

Weims said, "You're planning to give some of the gold to niggers?" He then recalled Harrison mentioning that Holdsworth's closest friend was black. He moderated his language and said, "You cain't go giving no nigra families bars of gold, if they're found with it, they'll be hanged."

Adam said, "I had no intention of giving them bars of gold. I will sell it first and then distribute whatever I get."

"And how much is each bar worth?"

"Gold is selling for twenty-five dollars per ounce in New York. Each bar weighs twenty-five pounds and is therefore worth ten thousand dollars."

Weims gasped. He leaned forwards and said, "Holy Mother! That's a total of one-hundred-and-forty thousand dollars in all!"

Adam nodded.

"And my cut would be ten thousand?"

"It would."

Weims sat back in his chair and stared at Adam. His mind was racing.

Bart frowned in question at Adam, but saw him dismiss it.

Adam leaned towards Weims and said, "By my reckoning, there are going to be a lot of losers by the end of this war, with a lot of unhappy northerners if the south wins, and a lot of unhappy southerners if the north wins."

"And there's going to be a lot of dead folk on either side," cut in Weims.

"I agree, but whichever side wins – there's going to be a lot of people needed to put back the infrastructure, and the pay for all of that back-breaking work isn't going to be worth writing home about." He paused and then added, "And would there be a job for a private detective at the end of it all?"

Weims was about to say, there's always work for a good detective, but then had a flash of inspiration. He thought that it would be one thing to be employed as a private detective – but it would be something different if he was to be the proprietor of his own agency.

He looked at Adam, then Bart, and then back to Adam. He said, "If I was to consider your offer, how do I know that you would keep your word, and not try to kill me at the first opportunity?"

"Because we could do this better with your help, than without it, and if I give you my word, I'll stick by it."

Bart said, "You wouldn't give this reb your word?"

Adam looked at Bart and said, "I would if he gave his."

Weims looked from face-to-face and said, "I see that you boys pay a lot of heed to giving your word."

Adam said, "It is one of the few graces left to us in this blood-thirsty world Mister Weims, and yes, we do."

Weims sat back in his seat and stroked his chin for several seconds; he didn't feel honour-bound like the brothers but the more he thought about the gold, the more he liked it. He leaned forwards and placed both of his hands on the table. He looked at the brothers and saw an innate honesty in their eyes. He turned to Adam and said, "And do I have your word that you won't betray me if I help you?"

Adam said, "I give you my word."

Weims extended his right hand and shook Adam's. He said, "Then I give you my word too." He turned to Bart and said, "And do we have the same accord?"

Bart extended his right hand and said, "The name's Bart Holdsworth and you have my word."

Weims shook the offered hand and said, "And I give you my word too Bart."

He looked at both brothers again and then said, "Now – how on earth do you intend pulling this off?"

Chapter 28

Monday 20th November 2006. St. Andrew's Church, Charleston

Taffy Brewer looked at Marshall and said, "There's no obvious entrance to the vault, does anybody have any idea which side the original door was on?

Marshall shook his head and said, "No, not really. I suppose that it would have been the side closest to the church, but that's only a guess."

"Can I help?"

Everybody turned round and saw a man approaching.

Marshall said, "This is Peter Purewell folks; I invited him along today because he's been involved with a lot of the restoration works on the church, and he probably knows more history about this place than anybody else."

Peter smiled and said, "Maybe Marshall's overstating things a bit, but I do have some knowledge if I can be of help."

"Perfect," said Taffy, "which side was the entrance door on?"

Peter winced and said, "Sorry – no idea."

Taffy scratched the back of his head and said, "Okay..." He walked around the vault and saw that the earth appeared to be stacked a couple of courses of brickwork higher up on the side furthest away from the church. He looked up and said, "From a practical point of view, I suppose that the less digging, or disturbance we create, the better. Therefore, might I suggest that we start at the side closest to the church as Marshall suggested?"

"No, please don't."

Everybody turned and looked at Naomi.

Taffy frowned and said, "Why?"

Naomi felt awkward. She knew that she couldn't explain away the groans that she'd heard when she'd arrived, especially as she was unsure about how her kind of experiences would have been viewed by her much-more religious American friends.

She said, "For those who don't know it, I am a professional historic researcher from England, and whilst I've never been involved with the opening of an American burial vault before, I have had experience in various other funerary excavations." She turned to Peter and said, "When was the last time that the vault was opened?"

"Nobody knows. We have an anecdotal reference to a young woman who walked the grounds sometime around 1912, who said that she saw bats flying out from one of them, and that she could see bones inside – but it may have been apocryphal, and we don't know which of the two vaults she was referring to either."

"What about the church records?" said Naomi.

"Can't help there either," said Peter, "All of the early church records, with the exception of the colonial register, are missing and the extant vestry minutes only begin in 1950."

"What – with all the history of this church?"

"Yes, in 1865, at the end of the Civil War, it was mostly abandoned, and when the incumbent Reverend Drayton died in 1894, regular worship here ceased altogether. It wasn't until the middle of last century, when the local population had increased, that the church began to be restored."

"So none of the known and recorded history of this place can help us with the vaults?"

Peter shook his head and said, "Sorry, no. I have read and studied references to other brick-built burial vaults, and know that they proliferated around the 1820's, and looking at ours, they do look similar, but below our feet we have pluff mud."

"Pluff mud?" said Alan, "I've never heard of that before."

Peter turned to Alan and said, "It's our grey South Carolina mud, a gooey, sticky substance that can suck the shoes right off your feet."

Naomi looked down at the ground.

Peter saw Naomi look and said, "It's because of our proximity to Church Creek. The water table here is very high. In

2004 to 2005 we did a lot of digging around the church whilst carrying out major restoration works, and in places we didn't have to go far down to get to it."

Naomi looked back at the vault and said, "So how far down do you expect the vault to go?"

Peter said, "I don't know for sure."

Carlton looked at the top of the vault and said, "From here it doesn't look as though the apex is much above two to three feet above the ground and that's not including how thick the construction is. And look at the shallow angle of the vaulting, it doesn't look self-supporting, so it may even be supported by wooden framework too. Wouldn't that suggest that excluding the roof, the vault is at least four or five feet down?"

Everybody looked at the vault and could see Carlton's point.

Marshall stepped in to Peter's rescue. He said, "Come on everybody, Peter's told you that there aren't any historical records of the church prior to the 1950's, and even those make no reference to structural works, so it's kind of unfair to put him on the spot."

Carlton said, "I'm sorry Peter, that wasn't my intention, it was just an observation."

Peter smiled at Carlton and said, "It's fine, really, and I don't feel put on the spot."

Naomi said, "I can see Carlton's point though. If this was a burial holding vault, and it's only shallow, how would the persons using it in the 1800's have accessed it? It's not as though they could have just opened the roof. They must have had to go through one end. Therefore, if the depth is only shallow because of the water table, the users must have been, either very short, or they must have slid the coffins in and out."

Taffy spoke up. He said, "So, the sooner we open her up, the sooner we'll learn the truth." He turned to Peter and said, "Before we start, are there any other things that I should know?"

"The only other thing I know is that in 1989 the churchyard was devastated by Hurricane Hugo, and that work was done to stabilize everything on the grounds. I presume that included the vaults."

Taffy nodded and then said, "Okay," he turned to Peter and said, "so which end do you want me to go in?"

Peter looked at Naomi and said, "Why did you suggest that we go in at the end opposite to the church, when the earth is deeper there?"

"Because the earth is deeper there."

"And that makes sense because…?" said Taffy.

"Because we all agreed that access to the vault had to be at one end or the other."

"And?" said Taffy with a frown upon his face.

"Why can't we see any obvious entrances?"

One-by-one, everybody looked at each end of the vault, and nobody could see any sign of an entrance.

Peter looked at Naomi and said, "Ah – interesting…"

Taffy said, "Okay, you've lost me! What's interesting?"

Peter looked at Naomi and said, "Will you tell him?"

Naomi nodded and turned to Taffy. She said, "Because someone, at sometime in the past, didn't want anybody to access this vault again. Whoever ordered it, went to great trouble to extinguish any signs of an opening, and I am guessing that they would have piled more earth at the end where the door may once have been, to discourage even further, anybody curious enough to look."

Bonnie-Mae turned to Naomi, shook her head, and said, "I don't often say this ma'am, but I am impressed. That is sound and logical thinking, something that I could do with a lot more of in my department."

Naomi blushed and looked around. Everybody appeared to be looking at her and nodding with the same kind of look upon his or her face.

Taffy broke the silence and said, "Okay, Reverend? Peter? – The final decision is yours."

Marshall looked at Peter and said, "Your call."

Peter looked at Naomi, and then back to Taffy. He said, "Right, go in where Naomi said."

Two of the SCDHEC contractors walked to the end of the vault furthest away from the church and removed small hammers and masonry chisels from their bags. They noted that the first four courses of brickwork rose up from ground level and then recessed one brick-width in, before going up another three courses. At the top of that level, the brickwork recessed another brick-width in before meeting the brickwork that rose up in a diminishing width, to the apex of the vault.

The first contractor, a guy named Ryan, lifted up his chisel and placed it in a joint between two of the bricks at the top recess and raised his hammer.

"Stop," said Naomi.

Ryan stopped and then looked at Taffy.

Taffy shrugged.

"I'm sorry," said Naomi, "but that may be putting the cart before the horse."

Nobody said a word; they all stared in baffled silence at Naomi.

Naomi looked at all of the expectant faces and then said, "Just please give me a moment."

They all watched as Naomi went back to the car, removed a notebook from her handbag, and appeared to be writing something. Still in complete silence they watched until she returned.

"Right," said Naomi, "put those hammers and chisels away for now, and get a couple of shovels."

Looks were passed all round until Naomi spoke again.

"If the actual floor level of the vault is say, five feet down, which to me is more than likely, and, if the door is on this side, there would have to have been steps leading down to it."

"Of course…" said Peter.

"And those steps would not have been steeper than a forty-five degree angle if folks were having to manhandle heavy coffins down there. Therefore, estimating that the vault sinks five feet below ground level, and using the angle of forty-five degrees, the first step would have to be five feet back from the vault." She pointed to a spot on the ground and said, "There."

Everybody turned and looked at where Naomi was pointing.

"And if nothing is there," continued Naomi, "we can assume that the entrance is on the other side, and we won't have damaged any of the historic brickwork on this side."

Taffy nodded and said, "Hmm, good thinking..."

Carlton looked at his wife in amazement. He'd known about the type of work that she'd done for years, but he hadn't ever seen her in action like this before.

"Ma'am," said Bonnie-Mae, "if ever you consider giving up your line of work and coming to live in Charleston, you let me know. I'll have a job proposition for you."

"Right lads," said Taffy, "you heard the lady, break out the shovels."

Chapter 29

Naomi had been right. In less than thirty minutes the contractors had exposed stone steps. What shocked everybody was how many there were. They went down at a forty-degree angle and there were eight of them.

As the men continued to expose more of the entranceway Peter watched with a puzzled expression on his face.

"Something bothering you?" said Naomi.

"Yes – I can't understand why the men haven't hit the water table yet. They're approximately six feet down now, and the ground still looks dry."

Naomi looked at the external width of the vault and said, "Maybe the steps are in a brick-lined well…?"

"I'd expect that," said Peter, "but submerged bricks aren't waterproof, so how come everything else in the churchyard was sticky and gooey at this depth, but not here?"

"The only way we'll properly know is when the guys reach the walls. Perhaps then we'll be able to see what's stopping the water permeating through."

Fifteen minutes later Ryan said, "Hey guys – look at this."

Everybody gathered round.

Marshall looked into the exposed entranceway and said, "What is that?"

Peter walked down the steps and looked at the interior of the brickwork. A few seconds later he looked at Naomi and said, "It's asphalt." He looked below his feet, took a spade off Ryan, and exposed what he was standing on. He bent down, cleared away more soil with his hands and then said, "This is asphalt too."

"Very clever," said Naomi, "whoever constructed this made it watertight by lining it."

"I still can't see any sign of a door," said Taffy.

Peter ascended the steps and said, "It must be there, so we'll leave you to it for a while." He looked around and said, "Anybody for a coffee in the parish house, I believe that Jackie has been badgering away in preparation."

As everybody began to file away, Naomi felt a pressure on her shoulder and looked at the area of ground above the head end of the vault.

Carlton noticed and said, "You okay?"

Naomi heard the first few groans start, and said, "This is weird. I've become accustomed to my unusual feelings, but I've never felt spooked before. This lot creeps me out a bit."

Carlton frowned and said, "You're not hinting, or being hinted at, that we should leave well alone are you?"

Naomi cast a look over her shoulder as she headed towards the parish house and said, "I don't know – I can't call it one way or the other. It..." She suddenly felt something push her from behind and she banged into Carlton's side. She blurted out, *"Jesus Christ!"* and then saw a few others turn and look.

Carlton staggered to his left and said, "Whoa! What happened there?"

Naomi recovered her footing, looked at the people in front, and said, "Sorry! I went over on my ankle."

Alan said, "Are you hurt?"

"No, I'm fine thanks – I feel embarrassed more than anything else."

The onlookers turned and continued to walk towards the parish house.

Carlton looked down at Naomi and said, "Okay, what's going on?"

Naomi could still feel the pressure pushing her away from the vault and towards the trench in the car park. She looked up at Carlton and said, "I haven't got the foggiest idea."

"So what just happened?"

"It felt as though somebody pushed me again."

Carlton felt concerned but remained calm. He said, "I can't ever recall you feeling anything physical before."

"No, neither can I," said Naomi.

"So should we be worrying about what's going on here?"

Naomi called out to the people in front. "Guys – we'll be with you in a minute, I want to have a private word with Cal."

They saw a few nods and waves, and then Naomi led Carlton to a low boundary wall adjacent to the car park. They perched down and she said, "I really don't know what's going on. It's as though I'm experiencing two events at once. When I'm near the vault, I can hear something from an area above it, yet when I come over here, I feel as though I'm being pushed towards that trench."

"And do you think that the two events are related?"

"I've no idea."

"Do you hear anybody saying anything?"

"No."

"Just groans by the head end of the vault?"

"Yes."

"And you can't make out anything distinguishing – a single voice, or odd word?"

"No, nothing."

"And do you get anything from within the vault?"

"No – maybe – I don't know."

"That doesn't sound too clear."

"It isn't – that's the problem."

"So what's the point of going to all the trouble of opening the vault if nothing's there?"

"I didn't say nothing was in there, I said I'm not sure. And don't forget – the head end is close to where I can hear the groans."

Carlton nodded.

"I can also see the Deacon's point about opening it up. It's already revealed a couple of surprises, the depth and the asphalt, so it hasn't been an entirely useless exercise – it just doesn't answer what we came here for."

"So where do we go from here?"

Naomi looked down and said, "I've no idea, and I don't get it. When I've been drawn to things in the past, I've at least had some notion of what's going on, but here, I'm getting nothing."

"Perhaps you're not meant to know just yet?"

"Maybe."

"And what about El Fuego de Marte – do you think that we're any closer to discovering it?"

"Huh! – Now you're asking. I hear people, not inanimate objects."

Carlton thought for a few seconds and then said, "What about the pushing feeling, and you banging into me like that?"

Naomi shook her head and said, "I'm sorry Cal, I'm really in the dark."

Carlton looked up as he saw one of the contractors approaching from the trench.

"Excuse me sir," said the man, "I'm sorry to bother you, but did you see where Taffy went?"

"He went with the others into the parish house – to get a free coffee no doubt."

The workman smiled and said, "That would be right! Thank you sir, sorry to disturb you."

Naomi felt the pressure on her left shoulder increase and said, "Is there a problem?"

The retreating workman stopped, turned around, and said, "Nothing for you to worry about ma'am," and turned to continue walking.

"In the trench, I mean…" said Naomi.

The workman stopped, turned, and walked back. He said, "Are you with the church ma'am?"

Naomi lied as the pressure increased. She said, "In relation to these proceedings, yes."

Carlton turned and looked at Naomi with raised eyebrows.

"Right, I see," said the workman, "I just needed to know if anybody else had been in the trench in our absence."

"Go on," said Naomi.

"I can ask Taffy myself if you'd like ma'am."

"No it's okay, I'll speak to him when we go in, what makes you think that somebody else has been working on it?"

"Not working on it – walking in it." The workman paused and then said, "Because of the high water table round here we've been opening up the trench in an equidistant way as we go down, and the lower we've got, the stickier it's got. That's why we ordered that baby over there." He pointed to the small mechanical digger that had arrived earlier. "Before we leave each night, we make sure that the base is real smooth. That way we can know if any animal, or snake, or even person has been in the trench in our absence – and last night, somebody was in there, you can see his footprints clear as day."

"You're sure that it was a man and not a woman?" said Carlton.

"Yes sir, you can see from the size and shape of the shoes."

"Can we see?" said Naomi.

"Sure." The workmen led the way, and then pointed into the trench. He said, "Down there, see?"

Naomi felt the hair on her neck stand on end. The workman was pointing to the same spot that she'd been drawn to two days earlier. For several seconds she said nothing, and then she turned to the workman. "Okay," she said, "I'll take it up with Taffy, but to the best of my knowledge, nobody else should have been down there."

The workman said, "Thank you ma'am – sir." He turned to walk away.

"What time do you leave in the evenings?" said Naomi.

The workman turned back and said, "Usually about 5pm, but because Thanksgiving is on Thursday, we've been working until dusk each day to try and get this done."

"So whoever went into the trench must have done so after dark?"

"Yes ma'am, that's what makes it so curious."

Naomi looked at Carlton, and then back at the workman. She said, "Yes   curious indeed."

Twenty minutes later, in the parish house, everybody had finished their coffee and homemade flapjack – courtesy of Jackie, and they'd fallen into small groups, chatting with some of the locals who'd attended the morning bible class.

Naomi had told a concerned Taffy about the mysterious footprints, and he'd disappeared outside, leaving her alone with Carlton.

Carlton wiped his mouth on a paper serviette and said, "Pressure still there?"

Naomi looked around and said, "A bit – not much…"

"What do you make of the footprints?"

"Odd."

"Me too."

"They're right over the place I was drawn to."

"Meaning what?"

"No idea…maybe…"

They were interrupted when they heard a voice say, "More coffee folks?"

They turned round and saw the Deacon standing next to them with a coffee pot.

"Yes please," said Carlton, "it's delicious. What brand is it?"

"Green Mountain," said Del, "it's a favourite round here."

"With me too," said Carlton.

"You folks enjoying your vacation?"

"Yes we are," said Naomi, "we love America…"

"Guys!"

Everybody looked across to the door and saw Ryan leaning in.

"You need to come and see this."

Nobody spoke. They put down their cups and plates and shuffled towards the door.

Carlton said, "Moment of truth time…" and then walked straight into the back of Naomi who'd stopped dead in front of him. "Whoa, sorry babe!" he said.

Naomi turned and looked at Carlton.

Carlton said, "What?"

"Look…"

Carlton looked at where Naomi was pointing. It was down at the back of the Deacon's shoes. They were caked in grey, dried, mud.

Chapter 30

At 6am Adam lay wide-awake in his bed and went over the plans that he, Bart, Weims and Lucius had discussed. One-by-one he poured over the fine details until he was satisfied that he had all of the angles covered. Next he thought about Gilbert Weims.

Weims was the loose cannon. With his help, the plan would work like clockwork. His ability to be able to distract, supply information on timetables, last minute changes of plan, and a host of other variables, would be invaluable, but if he'd been lying, and his sole intention had been to discover their plans and have them all arrested, then that would be horrific.

The thought of the trust that he'd placed in a man he hadn't met until a few days previously sent a cold shiver down his spine, and he knew that he was gambling with everybody's lives.

But the lure of gold was a powerful thing. By the time that half a day had passed, Weims had been speculating about owning his own detective agency in Charleston's French Quarter after the war. He'd spoken about the type of office he'd wanted, the number of staff, and even the type of house he'd have built off the south end of King Street if they were successful. And his enthusiasm, and suggestions to improve the original plan, had convinced everybody that he was being genuine.

He got up and dressed ready for 6:30am reveille.

At 6:20am, he walked across to Ira's billet. He saw that his bed was made, but saw no sign of him. He turned to a nearby young private and said, "Where's Corporal Jones, soldier?"

The young soldier snapped to attention, saluted, and said, "He was arrested for treason last Sunday sir."

Adam's mouth fell open. He said, "What? – On what grounds?"

"No idea sir."

"No, of course not. Carry on."

The young soldier saluted, said, "Yes sir," and headed off to the parade ground.

General Hardee was very strict about reveille. His nickname of 'Old Reliable' said it all. He liked his routine and he believed that all life should be built around it. Military and personal.

Adam waited until everybody had been dismissed from the temporary parade ground, and then knocked and entered General Hardee's private railroad coach. He looked at George and said, "I'm sorry to interrupt your routine George, but would you please leave the General and me alone for half an hour?"

George looked across at the General and saw him nod. He looked at Adam, said, "Very well, half an hour then..." He put his jacket on, reached for his hat and departed.

Adam walked across to Hardee's desk and didn't even look at the nipples on the girl. He said, "Might I have a word General, sir?"

"If it's about that nigger sidekick of yours, no."

"It is sir, and I don't accept that."

Hardee frowned and said, "Be careful soldier..."

"I demand to know why Corporal Jones was arrested."

"Demand eh?" said Hardee, "Who the hell do you think you're talking to boy? And stand to attention when I'm talking to you!"

Adam stood to attention and said, "I'm talking to you sir – with respect – but I'm not moving until I've had an answer."

Hardee bristled and said, "This had better be good Holdsworth..."

Adam nodded and said, "Sir, why did you arrest Corporal Jones?"

"Because he was caught going into a Federal camp in Nashville, in civilian clothing, in the middle of the night, and that's treason!"

"With respect, sir – Corporal Jones hasn't ever informed me that he has been caught by anybody, doing anything."

"Not literally caught, I mean, seen."

"Seen going into a Federal camp in Nashville?"

"Correct."

"In Nashville?"

"Yes."

"By whom sir?"

"Never you mind by whom. It is enough that he was seen!"

"With respect, it is not enough. I need to know who saw him."

Hardee was holding onto his legendary temper, but only just. He felt his blood start to boil and said, "You insolent cur – how dare you talk to me like that? Get out of my carriage before I have you arrested for insubordination!"

"No sir."

"What? – What did you just say?"

"I said, no sir."

"Right," said Hardee, "we'll see about 'no sir'!" He got up and started to walk across the carriage to call for the guard.

"Have you forgotten whose jurisdiction I'm working under?"

Hardee stopped and turned. He said, "What?"

Adam turned around and said, "Have you forgotten who I am directly answerable to?"

Hardee frowned but remained silent.

"President Davis signed my orders, and he gave me carte blanche to achieve the safe delivery of the Confederate gold by all means at my disposal – foul or fair."

"What are you saying?" said Hardee.

"I am saying, that for the duration of my current mission, ordered by President Davis himself, I am acting in accordance with his command."

"And what has any of this got to do with Corporal Jones?"

"He was acting under my orders."

Hardee was stunned. He said, "Acting under your orders? What in blazes' name were you doing ordering Jones into Wolford's camp in the middle of the night?"

"I will answer you General, but before I do, I have two questions of my own."

"And they are?"

"Number one – who saw Jones going into General Wolford's camp, and two, did whoever see him, see him by chance?"

Hardee suddenly realised that he was on unsteady ground. He said, "I, er…"

"Sir?" said Adam.

"He was followed, all right?"

"Followed? Who followed him?"

Hardee felt fit to burst. He said, "This is intolerable! Who's the commanding officer here?"

"Sir," said Adam, "who followed Corporal Jones when he went to General Wolford's camp?"

"Harrison – Henry Thomas Harrison. He's a, an undercover agent."

Adam frowned and said, "Working for whom?"

"He was working for me Goddamn it!"

"Working for you?" Adam was horrified. He said, "Harrison was working for you?"

"Yes, I wanted to know if the nigger could be trusted so I had him followed."

"So I receive orders direct from the President, instructing me to use any means necessary to ensure the safe delivery of his gold, and you compromise the clandestine nature of those orders by having my man followed?"

"I, I, didn't…"

Adam stared at Hardee with as much venom as he could muster and then added, "I hope to God, that you didn't tell Mister Harrison *why* he was following Corporal Jones, General…"

Hardee had never felt more vulnerable. He spluttered, "I, I…"

"…because, if you did, that would be treason."

Hardee felt the blood drain from his face. He opened his mouth to defend his actions but was cut off before he could speak.

"And the only thing that could have been worse – would have been to have had me followed too."

Hardee was distraught. The bottom was falling out of his orderly world. He walked back to his desk, opened a desk drawer, and removed a bottle of bourbon. He pulled the top off, and took a deep drink straight from the bottle. He flopped down into his seat and said, "I wasn't thinking right Holdsworth…I've been under pressure with this damned war, and I'm not getting any younger. I had offered my resignation to President Davis before it all started, but he refused to accept it."

Adam dropped down into the seat in front of Hardee's desk and said, "You're not telling me that…"

"You were followed too? Yes! But that wasn't my idea – that was Harrison's."

Adam shook his head and said, "This is not going to sit well with the President when I report to him…"

Hardee's head snapped round. He said, *"Report to him? To the President? –* When do you have to report to him?"

"In a few days' time. That was one of my reasons for coming here today, to inform you that I had been summoned to his office to apprise him of how things were going, and to give him an assurance that I was receiving as much help and support from you as I required."

Hardee snatched up the bottle and took another drink.

"But when I tell him that you have more than likely compromised the operation by divulging his plans to outsiders, I expect that he's going to be more than a little upset by your actions…sir."

'Old Reliable' was in bits. He dropped his head and couldn't speak for several minutes. He drew in a deep breath and said, "I know that this is a lot to ask under the circumstances Captain Holdsworth, but could you find it in your heart to forgive an old fool? If I am dishonourably discharged from my post, my wife, and my family would be devastated and I doubt they could live with the shame."

Adam took his time before answering and then said, "Could I be absolutely sure of your full cooperation from this day forward?"

Life sprang back into Hardee's eyes. He said, "Yes, of course!"

"And you would free Corporal Jones at once?"

"Yes."

"And not question whatever we request for the remainder of this Presidential assignment?"

"You have my word!"

Adam looked at Hardee, sat back in his chair, and stroked his chin. He pondered for a few seconds and then said, "All right, providing that you call off this Harrison character, and keep your word, I do believe that we could surmount this regrettable interlude."

Hardee jumped up and extended his hand. He said, "Thank you Captain Holdsworth, thank you. You are an officer and a gentleman and I will do as you bid immediately." He opened a drawer in his desk, removed two small crystal glasses, and poured two large bourbons. He handed one to Adam and said, "Your good health sir."

Adam took the glass, nodded and said, "And yours general."

One hour later, Adam and Ira were reunited.

Adam had told a shocked Ira about including Weims in their plans, and he'd just finished telling him about the exchange with Hardee.

"And didn't Hardee ask *why* I rode into Wolford's camp that night?" asked Ira.

"No – I don't think that he had the heart."

"Well that was too close for comfort brother, and we need to take extra care from now on."

"Yes," said Adam, "we still have a lot to do, and it's just seven days before the *Georgiana* arrives in Charleston."

Chapter 31

Everybody stared at the exposed entrance door to the burial holding vault. Some were wide-eyed in disbelief, some were making the sign of the cross, and others, including Naomi and Carlton, were shocked. But nobody was more horrified than Reverend Hughes was. He was stunned into silence, and for a while, didn't know what to say.

The vault door was metal, it was padlocked – and it had a large, black, inverted cross painted on it.

Taffy Brewer, who'd been working on the trench, walked over to the vault after he'd heard one or two gasps. He saw the entrance door and said, "Shit!"

He looked at the shocked faces and walked across to Del. He said, "I'm sorry to have to tell you Deacon, but Ryan and the guys don't want to go anywhere near that."

Carlton looked at Naomi and said, "Does that mean what I think it does?"

Naomi said, "I don't know."

"Surely it's not witchcraft or anything like that?"

"Unlikely. This type of vault was constructed around 1820, and most of the witch executions, including the famous Salem Witch Trials, were over by 1700."

"But what about individual, narrow-minded, communities dealing with what they saw as a local problem?"

Naomi looked up at Carlton and nodded. She said, "Hmm, maybe…"

"This isn't part of what you heard is it?"

Naomi looked at the door and tried to focus her psychic radar, but nothing happened. She looked at Carlton and said, "I don't think it is but it may be connected."

Bonnie-Mae spoke up and said, "Reverend, sir, this is your church and your jurisdiction. Have you ever come across anything like this before?"

Marshall raised his eyebrows and said, "No, I have not."

"And can you give us any inclination about what we may find in there?"

"No I can't."

"Then do you have any objection to us proceeding?"

"And opening the door?"

"Yes sir."

Marshall considered the situation and then looked at all of the expectant faces. He said, "I think that I should say a short prayer first." He walked to the top of the stairs, made the sign of the cross, and then put his hands together and bowed his head.

Everybody followed suit.

"Lord," said Marshall, "we ask your blessing to enter this place. Please protect us and guide us, and give us the wisdom to handle this situation with understanding and compassion. Amen."

Everybody repeated, "Amen."

Marshall turned to Bonnie-Mae and said, "Okay Sheriff, you can proceed."

Bonnie-Mae looked at Taffy and said, "Sir, will you?"

Taffy was unsure. He looked at the door, and then at the Sheriff. He said, "I don't know ma'am. It looks a bit…well, you know…"

"I'll do it."

All heads turned to towards Naomi.

"I've had experience of this type of thing, so I'll do it."

Naomi cast her mind back a few months and recalled going into the mausoleum at Elland with Helen. That though, didn't have a black inverted cross painted on the door.

Before anybody could respond, she walked down the steps to the metal door and examined it. It was approximately five feet high and two feet six inches wide. It was well constructed and had two hinges on its right-hand side. The door was secured by a steel padlock attached to a metal hasp. She inspected the edges and top of the door, and then felt along the bottom with her fingers. It felt about a quarter of an inch thick. She inspected the hinges and saw that they appeared to be free, and then the black-painted cross, and the facia of the door. There were no other discernible man-made marks.

She looked down at her feet, frowned, and called up to Taffy, "Do you have a soft bristled brush and small trowel?"

"In the pick-up, yes…"

Seconds later Taffy handed the brush and trowel to Naomi, and retreated back up the steps.

Naomi got down on her haunches and brushed away the loose detritus in front of the door. As she did so, she saw something scratched into the surface. Using the tip of her trowel, she traced it over the indentation. Backwards and forwards, and round and round she went until she was certain of what was coming. Once finished, she brushed the surface once more and stepped back.

Everybody crowded around and looked down to where Naomi was pointing.

It was a pentagram.

Deathly silence reigned until Bonnie-Mae said, "Please don't touch anything more ma'am, not until I've taken a couple of photos."

Naomi ascended the steps and looked at Carlton with raised eyebrows.

Alan walked up to her and said, "This is exciting isn't it? I never expected anything like this!"

"I don't like it," said Debbie, "it looks like witchcraft, and I think that we should leave well alone."

Carlton recalled his previous question to Naomi when he asked her if she was being warned to keep away.

"It's nothing to be afraid of Debs," said Naomi. "We don't buy into all of this superstitious nonsense nowadays and I have to agree with Alan. I think that it's a fascinating glimpse into the past."

"What's in the past should stay in the past," said Debbie.

"And then as a historic researcher, I'd be out of a job!"

Nobody noticed the glib expression on the face of the nearby Del. He was beside himself with joy; his red herring had turned into a veritable field day and he couldn't believe his luck.

Indeed luck seemed to have been on his side in more ways than one. Since learning of the death of Casey, he hadn't heard a thing from Muz and Lennie, and despite being almost caught out by Janet, she'd appeared to be pleased at the thought of the forthcoming cruise in The Bahamas. It wasn't true of course – there was no cruise booked, but that was beside the point.

The only fly in the ointment had been his Sunday night foray into the trench. But that had been his fault. He hadn't realised how deep four-feet-six inches was in a two-foot wide trench. He hadn't brought an adequate shovel, just a large hand trowel which would have proved useless in the gooey underfoot mud and he hadn't brought a torch. He'd extracted himself from the trench without so much as a scrape of the surface near the old grave site, but he was more than enthusiastic about the possibility of locating The Fire of Mars, and looking forward to his return visit on Tuesday night.

"Okay folks."

Everyone turned when Bonnie-Mae called.

"Ma'am – you can proceed now."

Naomi nodded and then walked across to Marshall who was standing with Peter. She smiled and said, "Are you guys okay with me opening up the vault?"

Marshall said, "Yes we are. I'm not sure that some of the other church officials would agree, but I find it fascinating in a macabre sort of way."

"So, no reservations?"

"Oh, I do have reservations. Thanksgiving is just around the corner and I want the vault covered long before that. I don't want any youngsters being upset by anything that resembles pagan or satanic symbolism, and I'm nervous about the press aspect."

"Press aspect?" said Naomi, "nobody's contacted them have they?"

Marshall leaned closer to Naomi and said, "Not yet, but I will."

Naomi was surprised. She said, *"You will?* I'd have thought that you'd want to keep something like this quiet."

Marshall looked around and then said, "Are you kidding? This could do wonders for our church. More visitors, more publicity, more converts, and between you, me and the Bishop, more income!"

Naomi warmed to Marshall and smiled. She said, "Well I'm very happy to have your blessing Reverend."

"Calling me Marshall is just fine."

"Thank you Marshall. Right, we'll carry on."

She walked back to Taffy and saw that he was holding a pair of bolt-cutters and a torch.

Minutes later everybody heard the loud bang as the cutters snipped through the shackle of the padlock.

Taffy pulled it off the staple, and threw it to one side. He indicated for Naomi to join him, and said, "Ready?"

Naomi looked back up the steps at Bonnie-Mae and saw her nod. She turned back to Taffy and said, "Right, let's go."

Together they leaned on the metal door and pushed. Nothing happened.

"Here, let me have a go." Taffy hunched up his right shoulder and then slammed into it. It moved a few inches. He repeated the exercise several times until finally, the door creaked open. He looked at Naomi and stepped to one side.

Naomi switched on the torch and stepped into the doorway.

The vault was cool, dry, and earthy smelling. The beam of light played across the side and back walls and Naomi could see that they had been coated in asphalt too. She couldn't see much in the way of spider webs, or insect damage, and considering the age of the vault, and the reports of decades of weather phenomena and seismic activity, she was amazed that everywhere looked so pristine. It was as though somebody had been expecting her visit and had tidied up before she'd arrived.

She took two more steps inside, swept the light behind the back of the open door, and then jumped back in surprise. She couldn't help herself, and said, *"Whoa!"*

Up above, everybody heard it.

Bonnie-Mae was the first to respond. She said, "Are you okay ma'am?"

Naomi stepped back out of the vault, and said, "Yes, but you'd better come and look at this."

Bonnie-Mae walked down the steps, entered the vault, and looked at where Naomi was aiming the torch light.

Huddled in the corner behind the door was a small skeleton draped in badly deteriorated female clothing.

Naomi looked at Bonnie-Mae and said, "That isn't a burial. She's been sealed in here and left to die."

Bonnie-Mae looked at Naomi with hawkish eyes, and then looked back at the remains in the corner. She said, "We need to get forensics down here."

"And they need to do a carbon 14 test to establish when she died."

Bonnie-Mae nodded and said, "Yes, and in the meantime I suggest we get out of here to prevent any further contamination."

Naomi said, "Okay…" She swept the light around the interior of the vault – walls, floor, and ceiling, and was about to depart, when something caught her eye. She said, "What's that?"

Bonnie-Mae looked and saw that the light was directed onto the back wall. She frowned and said, "What?"

"There."

Bonnie-Mae looked again and said, "Oh, I see…"

Naomi said, "Shall we?" She saw the Sheriff look at the floor in front of them, and then nod. She walked to the back wall and knelt down.

Something was scratched into it.

"Hold the light under it, so that it creates shadows," said Bonnie-Mae.

Naomi put the torch under the scratches and shone it upwards.

Gouged into the asphalt in spidery writing, were the words, '*through here*'.

It felt as though a belt tightened around Naomi's head. She realised that she was looking at the 'head end' of the vault, and that whoever had been buried alive had left an indication that something was on the other side of it.

Bonnie-Mae said, "Holy Mother…"

Naomi said, "You know what this means, don't you?"

"That we have to open up the ground the other side of this wall."

"Yes, and I don't mind admitting to you, that I haven't a clue about what could be there."

Bonnie-Mae drew in a deep breath and said, "Me neither ma'am, but right now I suggest that we go and tell Father Marshall what we've found, and then get the County Coroners down here."

Chapter 32

Del was on tenterhooks. On any given night of the week Janet went to bed at 10:30pm, but a favourite film had been aired on the television and it hadn't finished until 11:10pm. He looked at the clock, he looked at his mobile phone on the bookshelf next to him, and he looked at the landline phone on the arm of Janet's empty chair.

"I'm taking a glass of hot water up to bed," said Janet, "do you want a tea or coffee?"

"No thanks babe, I'm going to play a couple of games on my tablet, and then I'll join you."

"Okay."

Del opened his tablet and loaded a page with a 'connect three' game on it and dallied with it until he'd heard Janet go upstairs. He waited until she went into the bedroom and then grabbed his mobile phone. As quick as a flash he dialled their landline number. He decided to let it ring three times before answering it, and was about to do so when he heard Janet's voice on the upstairs extension say, "Hello." He cursed his stupidity, let her say "hello" twice more, and then clicked it off.

He gathered his wits and then walked to the bottom of the stairs. He called up, "Who was that at this time of night?"

"No idea, whoever it was hung up."

"Hung up? – If it rings again leave it to me, I'll deal with it."

"Okay."

He went back into the lounge and rang the number again. As soon as it rang he snatched up the landline phone, switched off the mobile, and said, "Hello – Yes it is – What? – Really, and nobody can... – no of course not, sorry – yes, okay, I'll be there as soon as I can – okay, bye."

Janet sat on the side of her bed with a puzzled expression on her face. When the call had ended she went to the top of the stairs and called down, "What was that all about?"

Del walked to the foot of the stairs and said, "It was St. Andrew's security service. One of the alarms has gone off and they want me to attend."

"Why you? You don't normally go."

"I know – Casey used to do it, but not any more."

"Oh, yes, of course. I'll come with you in case there's any trouble."

That was the last thing that Del wanted. He said, "No, it's okay. The alarm that's gone off is the church itself and according to Casey it was always going on and off. I'll sort it out tonight and then I'll get the company to check it out tomorrow."

"Are you sure you don't want me to come?"

"No thanks honey, I'll be fine."

Fifteen minutes later, complete with shovel, torch, wellington boots, an old towel, a black plastic bag, and a packet of moist wipes, he turned his car into the drive of St. Andrew's and parked close to the trench.

He got out and listened. It was a windless night and the only things that could be heard were the ubiquitous night creatures from their secretive locations. For several minutes he watched and waited, as not even a car passed by on the Ashley River Road.

He took a deep breath, opened the trunk of the car, and then put on the wellington boots. Next he extracted the shovel, torch, and plastic bag. He was ready.

With a hammering heart, he lowered himself into the trench and felt his feet sink into the gooey, pluff mud. He made a mental note to smooth the surface of the trench before leaving, something, he realised, that he hadn't done on his previous visit.

He squelched across to where he believed the ruby to be located, bent down, and started to scrape away at the surface.

Ten minutes later, things were getting out of hand. The deeper he went, the stickier the mud got. He knew that he had to go down at least twelve inches to get to the six foot depth of the burial, but by the time that he'd gone down six inches, the viscosity of the mud had dropped and it was almost akin to thick dough. Even worse, the lower he went, and the bigger the hole, the more he tended to slip into it. Within minutes of starting he'd nearly lost his right wellington boot, and he'd struggled to extract it from the goo.

He stood up for a few seconds' break, and felt the sweat run down his forehead. He looked around, made sure that he was still alone, and switched on the torch. He looked down and said, *"Fuck..."* He had mud all over his trousers, boots, and hands, and the hole looked tiny – as though a child had been digging in the sand at the beach. He looked at the width of the trench, and then tried to imagine how much goo he'd have to extract if he was going to remove an area two feet six inches wide, by at least eighteen inches long, and eighteen inches deep. It was much more than he'd originally imagined, and much harder to dig too. And even then, he considered, if he'd located the stone, how difficult, and how much further down could that be?

He looked at his watch and saw that the face was covered in mud. He knew that he had a limited time before Janet would start to worry, and then realised that he had to fill in the hole, smooth it over, and clean himself up before returning. He set about it, cursing and swearing to himself, and realising that what was needed was something more industrial to get the job done.

It was then that he remembered the mechanical digger.

He finished cleaning himself up, looked around, and saw it parked no more than thirty feet away from the trench. He sauntered over to it, clambered up onto one of the tracks, and tried the driver's door. It was unlocked. He entered the cab, sat down, and located the ignition. And then in a stroke of pure luck, he found the starting key above the windshield visor.

He gathered that the engine would be a diesel, and noisy, but the only person who'd lived within listening distance of the church had been Casey, so that wasn't a problem. He looked down at the puzzling array of levers, joysticks, and foot pedals. He pulled a couple, pushed a couple, and pressed down on the foot pedals and said, "Come on Del – how hard can it be?"

He put the key in the ignition and turned. The diesel engine roared into life and sent a jet of black smoke out of the exhaust stack. It sounded deafening, and he knew that he had to act quickly. He looked down between his legs and saw two long handles. He figured that one would be the gearstick, and the other a transmission control. Perhaps forwards for high, and backwards for low.

What he hadn't known, was that the driver of the excavator had swivelled the cab around to face the rear of the vehicle, so that the boom would be out of the way of the men exiting the trench. He also didn't know that the two long handles propelled the vehicle forwards, and that the foot pedal was an accelerator.

He felt about on the floor until his left foot was comfy on what he thought was the clutch control pedal, and then he pressed down, and pushed both long handles forwards.

The result was disastrous. The excavator shot off backwards, throwing Del forwards, out of his seat, and causing him to fall onto the two long drive handles. Within seconds the right-hand track dropped into the trench, and the whole machine fell on its side, roaring and bucking about like a mechanical monster trying to extricate itself from the bowels of hell.

Del fell out of the driver's seat, and dropped face first into a large dollop of pluff mud that he'd shovelled out earlier. His legs slipped over the side and got perilously close to the spinning track, but in the nick of time, he managed to yank himself out.

He jumped to his feet and stood looking at the scene. It couldn't have been worse. The excavator was lying on its side making a fearful racket, a whole side of the trench had collapsed, and he looked as though he'd been in a full-scale mud-wrestling contest. And he still hadn't got any closer to the ruby.

In blind panic he ran to his car, jumped in, and sped away.

Halfway home he saw a lone car heading towards him, and as they passed, he saw that it was Janet, no doubt heading to the church to find out what was taking him so long.

He yelled, *"Shit!"* hit the brakes and turned the car around.

Ten minutes later he turned back into the drive leading to St. Andrew's and saw Janet standing beside her car, talking on her mobile. He pulled up close to her, got out, and said, "You're never going to believe this…"

Chapter 33

Just after 7pm, Gilbert Weims and Reverend John Drayton stood with a lantern each, looking into the burial vault near the southwest corner of the church.

Drayton shook his head and said, "We're so grateful to you Captain Weims, this could have been a monumental disaster, but I don't mind admitting that I'll find it difficult to tell the volunteers who helped dig out this tunnel, that it has failed." He looked at Weims and said, "Have you had to do anything like this before?"

"What – seal a dangerous escape tunnel?"

"No, not that, – I mean tell folk that something they've just completed is dangerous and can't be used?"

"It's one of the burdens of being a structural engineer Father," said Weims.

Following the departure of Adam and Bart, Weims had been busy with plans of his own. He wasn't planning to double-cross the brothers, but he wasn't planning to be completely honest with them either…

He looked down at the Captain's uniform that Adam had given him, and still marvelled at how well it fitted. He said, "You can tell from the smell, that the asphalt we used to waterproof the walls and floor hasn't cured yet, so I would advise not using this vault for at least fourteen days."

Drayton looked at Weims and said, "That's no bother, we have another smaller one that we can use." He turned to leave and then said, "By the way, what did you do with the metal door that led into the tunnel from the back of the vault?"

I used it to support the roof of the tunnel on the other side of the vault wall. I figured that a few people over the years would be gathered around this structure, and I didn't want anybody falling through."

"Ah – very thoughtful." Drayton thought about that for a second and then added, "That's not likely to happen anywhere else along the tunnel is it?"

"Not likely Father – the tunnel descended further down as it drew away from the vault, which of course, was why the water table was worse down there and forced the seepage in."

"So the roof is safe further along?"

"Yes it is, and with the metal door over the original roof lining next to the vault, there won't be a problem there now either."

"Wonderful – are you finished now Captain?"

Weims looked at the three fake soldiers from the 'Engineering Corps' that he'd recruited for the task, and said, "Yes sir, but we will be back intermittently over the next two weeks to check the ground and asphalt linings."

"Excellent," said Drayton, "excellent; now if you'll excuse me I have matters to attend before visiting a couple of sick parishioners."

Weims saluted, said, "Yes of course – good day Father," and waited until Drayton was out of earshot. He then turned to his three sidekicks and said, "Right boys, we've done everything that we can for now. Are you clear about what you have to do on Thursday?" He waited for an acknowledgement from them all, and then said, "Right, so far, so good. Let's get out of here."

At 10:30pm that night, Captain A B Davidson, skipper of the *SS Georgiana*, sat in the lounge bar of the new Grand Victoria Hotel in Nassau, and looked around.

Following two weeks crossing the Atlantic, the noise level was almost unbearable. All about him revellers were celebrating and he knew from experience that the principal reason for celebration was making it unscathed through the Federal blockades of Charleston harbour. And any successful mission had winners on both sides. Other countries, in particular Britain, were desperate for the American cotton exports, and the Confederate States to replenish their dwindling equipment and resources.

He removed his gold pocket watch from his tunic and noted that it was less than three hours to embarkation.

Out of the blue, a well-dressed, attractive-looking lady sat down at the table opposite, and leaned forwards.

Davidson said, "Madam, I don't wish to offend, but I won't be requiring…"

"Sir, I am M C Dunaway, your agent for this trip."

Davidson's mouth fell open. He said, "You're M C Dunaway? I was expecting…"

"A man?"

"Yes madam, I was."

"Well clearly I am not. My name is Melinda Christine Dunaway, and I am a woman."

Davidson looked at the low-cut neckline of Melinda's dress and said, "Clearly indeed madam." He stood up, extended his hand, and said, "Captain Davidson, at your command."

Melinda shook the offered hand and said, "Thank you. Now, we need to get down to business because I have something important to tell you."

Davidson looked around and saw that nobody appeared to be paying them any heed, and that the nearest table was out of earshot because of the ambient noise. He said, "Are you happy to speak here, or would you prefer to go somewhere quieter?"

Melinda looked around, and said, "Here's fine."

"And before we proceed, would you like something to eat or drink?"

"No thank you." Melinda paused, looked a second time, and then leaned forwards. She said, "The day after you departed Liverpool, we found out that one of the Stevedores on Albert Dock was a Union spy, and that he'd been paying the men who'd been loading the *Georgiana*, for information."

"So what? We'd been feeding information to known spies about the *Georgiana's* manifest – and that of the *Cornubia*."

"True – but we'd been feeding them what we wanted them to know. What he found out was different."

"How so?"

"The spy in Liverpool knew…" Melinda stopped speaking for a second and looked around again, "…that the 'special cargo' was aboard the *Georgiana*."

Davidson leaned back in his chair and stared in horrified silence. "So," he said, "the mission is compromised?"

"As far as that particular cargo is concerned, yes. That is why some of it is being taken off her as we speak."

Davidson sat bolt upright and said, "*What? –* now?"

"Yes sir."

"But that's preposterous! We're supposed to be sailing in two hours' time!"

"And you will. But we are replacing six boxes of your original cargo with thirteen boxes of er, brass buttons… "

"Brass buttons?"

Melinda leaned forwards and said, "…boxes of buttons with an estimated value of ten thousand dollars each."

"Ah," said Davidson, "I see." He paused for a second and then said, "So why didn't you replace them all?"

"The power of illusion Captain, we wanted the replacement cargo to appear different to what was taken off in case of watching eyes. So now you have one original cargo, and thirteen replacements – fourteen in all."

Davidson did a quick calculation and said, "But that's one new box too many…"

"Yes – it's there in case you need to take drastic action."

"What kind of drastic action?"

"Your instructions are to enter Maffitt's Channel, steam towards Charleston Harbour as though you intend entering, but once you see the signal light, you are to stop, deliver your cargo ashore, and then turn round and get out if possible."

"And then deliver the rest of the manifest to Wilmington – yes, I know."

"But because the mission has been compromised, and because the Union agents will know by now, they will not be expecting you to attempt to land that special cargo. They'll be expecting you to try to enter Charleston Harbour minus that. And because Nassau is also awash with Union spies, I'm sure that somebody somewhere will be recording that at least six boxes of freight have been removed from the hold of the *Georgiana*, and replaced with thirteen boxes of buttons."

Davidson thought for a few seconds and then said, "And did the man captured in Liverpool have any idea what we had planned for the special cargo?"

"No, he only knew that it had been placed aboard."

"So anybody watching now will think that most, if not all of that special cargo has been removed?"

"Yes."

"So what's the extra box for?"

"If your mission goes wrong, and all looks lost, we don't want the *Georgiana* falling into Yankee hands. You are to scuttle her, and use that box to pay you all off."

Davidson was shocked. He said, "Scuttle the *Georgiana*? She's brand new for God's sake. Even if you think that there is a possibility of that happening, why don't we use an older craft?"

"Because getting that cargo ashore is the prime objective. It is of vital importance to the Confederacy, and the *Georgiana* will give you the best chance of achieving that goal."

"And if she's lost – won't that be a blow to the Confederacy too?"

"Of course it would, but the delivery of the cargo comes first, and the *Georgiana's* insured."

Davidson raised his eyebrows and said, "I doubt that any insurance company would pay for losses through acts of war… "

"And that would be for our legal department to worry about Captain. You should be concentrating on this."

Davidson leaned back in his chair and raised his eyebrows at the mild rebuke. A few seconds later he said, "And what about the *Cornubia*? Did the Union spy inform the blockading squadron in Wilmington that she wouldn't be carrying her stated manifest?"

"We don't know. When the gaoler went to his cell the day after we'd questioned him, he'd gone."

"Gone! Good Lord! How?"

"We still haven't established that, but until he is re-captured, we are taking these extra precautions."

"So in the end it's still up to us to do our best to get the cargo ashore at the rendezvous, and if possible get out?"

"Yes."

Davidson looked at Melinda and said, "In that case there's nothing more to be said."

"No sir, there isn't." Melinda stood up and extended her hand. She said, "Captain Davidson, it has been a pleasure meeting you."

Davidson stood up and shook the offered hand. He said, "Madam, the pleasure's been all mine."

Melinda smiled and said, "Then good luck with your mission – and God go with you."

Chapter 34

Thanksgiving Day, Thursday 23rd November 2006. The Robiteaux Land, Gainesville, Florida

Naomi and Carlton walked into a wooded clearing near Julie and Steve Robiteaux's house and their mouths fell open. Stretched out before them was a huge made-up table laid out in a single, continuous line. White damask tablecloths covered its full length and all of the place settings were laid with silver cutlery. Little pots of fresh flowers decorated the table from end to end.

"This is amazing," said Naomi to Steve, "and nothing like I imagined."

Steve smiled and said, "Eleven families own, and live on this three-hundred acre section of Paine's Prairie and we started this tradition a few years ago. Year-by-year, we've had to add extra places as it's grown in popularity."

Naomi said, "And I can see why." She tried to do a quick place count, but gave up three-quarters of the way down. She said, "How many people are coming?"

"Forty-one."

"Forty-one?"

"Yes."

Naomi turned and looked at the spread of ancillary tables beneath a huge live Oak and saw more and more foodstuffs, drinks, hors d'oeuvres, desserts, and nibbles being delivered as the guests arrived and placed their contributions on the tables. She turned, smiled at Steve, and said, "Well we can't thank you enough for your generous offer to join you. Just the sight of everything here will be enough to keep this implanted in my memory, and we haven't eaten yet!"

Steve smiled back, and said, "After the Thanksgiving dinner we all take off for a half-mile walk across the prairie, then the younger guys play games and so on, while others do their own thing 'til the bonfire this evening."

Naomi looked around at the woodland, the tinder-dry grass, and Spanish moss wafting from the trees in the gentle breeze. She said, "Isn't that dangerous here?"

"No – it's something that we've learned to cater for, and we do have a fire-truck on standby just in case." Steve saw more folk arriving and said, "Sorry to interrupt the conversation but I have to go lay out our contribution…"

"Of course," said Naomi. She walked across to Debbie, Alan, and Carlton who were chatting to a few of the other guests whilst sipping pre-dinner drinks.

Carlton turned and smiled as Naomi approached. He said, "All right pet?"

"This is incredible, and nothing like I imagined. I harboured the idea that it might be really informal and that we'd be sitting around at wooden bench tables, but to see everything laid out so formally, with forty-one matching dining chairs, the damask cloth and so on, is stunning."

Carlton turned and indicated to the food and drink tables. He said, "And I can't wait to sample the fare…" He leaned down to Naomi and whispered, "…and check out that delicious looking pumpkin pie – if there's only one piece left when I get up for a dessert, there's going to be a fight!"

Naomi smacked the back of Carlton's hand and said, "Behave."

Seconds later, a sound came from her mobile phone indicating that she'd received a text. She read it and said, "Bob Crowthorne wants me to call him."

Carlton raised his eyebrows and said, "That isn't going to be cheap…"

"But it must be important."

"When will you call him – now, or after the meal?"

Naomi looked around and saw that folk were still arriving and depositing their contributions where indicated by Julie Robiteaux. She said, "I'll do it now."

Alan saw the look of concern on Naomi's face and said, "Everything okay cuz?"

Naomi said, "A friend of ours, who is a police Superintendent, has asked me to ring him."

Alan looked at Carlton and then back to Naomi. He said, "Let's hope it's good news then."

Naomi nodded, said, "Excuse me guys..." and walked across to a piece of open ground with nobody nearby. She dialled the number and heard Crowthorne say, "Ah, Naomi, thank you for calling." She said, "Is there a problem?"

"Yes there is. You recall me telling you that Adrian Darke's body, and the mortuary attendant had gone missing?"

"Yes."

"We've found the mortuary attendant."

"Good – where was he?"

"At the bottom of Dunsteth Reservoir in a car."

Naomi clapped her hand up to her mouth, and said, "My God!"

"You recall the approach road to the reservoir that we used when we were dealing with the Malaterre investigation?"

"How could I forget it?"

"Right – a couple of dog walkers saw tyre tracks leading along it into the reservoir, and they phoned us. We got Hugh Kearns and Kev Middleton to investigate, and we made our discovery."

"Was Darke's body in the car?"

"No."

"Have you established how the attendant died?"

"He had trauma marks on the left temple, cheek bone, and ear, consistent with being struck by something large, abrasive, and heavy."

"Like what?"

"Current thought is a house brick, but forensics will confirm that or not. I should also say that it would have taken somebody very powerfully built to inflict such a devastating blow with something that heavy."

"Was the attendant dead before he went into the reservoir?"

"No, the amount of water in his lungs confirmed his death by drowning."

"So not an accident then?"

"No – that's why I asked you to call."

Naomi frowned and said, "You're not going to tell me that you think we're in danger here now, are you?"

Crowthorne paused before answering. He said, "We don't know – maybe. We can't get away from the Darke link. If he's managed to stage his own death, and he is now on the loose, he could be anywhere. After you exposed his drugs facility at Cragg Vale we found him in America mobilising a huge op to recover that Fire of Mars ruby from St Andrew's in Charleston, so it's not beyond the wildest stretch to consider that if he is alive and up to his old tricks – he may have you and that ruby on his 'to do' list."

"Nice terminology… "

"Sorry, that was the wrong thing to say."

Naomi looked around to see if anybody was watching and then said, "Still an awful thought though."

"It is – sorry, and I didn't mean to spoil your holiday, but it would pay to keep a weather eye out for anything suspicious, and I would advise you to stick to public areas alone, and not to go out at night, unless you need to."

"Bugger Bob – that puts the dampeners on the hols a bit."

"I'm really sorry Naomi; this is the last thing that I wanted to do."

"It's not your fault, and I appreciate the call. Have you told Helen about this too?"

"I have, and she's asked me to send you her best. She also asked me to let you know that everything's okay at the office, and that she's looking forward to a quality American gift. She said to tell you, more Gucci than Wal-Mart!"

Naomi smiled and said, "Cheeky so-and-so, she'll pay for that."

"That's the spirit, try not to let this spoil the rest of your holiday, keep a watchful eye out, and we'll see you next week."

"No you won't – things haven't gone as we planned, and I'm staying for a few days' longer."

"With Carlton?"

"No, he's going home."

There was an extended pause on the phone until Crowthorne said, "I can't say that I'm happy about that. Could you get Carlton's gay army buddies to join you?"

"What Auntie Rosie and the sewing circle?"

"Yes."

"I hadn't thought about that, but I could mention it to Cal."

"Yes, please do, I don't want you coming to harm when it can be avoided by a few sensible precautions."

"Mimi – are you going to be long?"

Naomi looked up and saw Carlton gesturing for her to join him. She said, "I have to go Bob, I'm about to eat."

"Okay – look after yourself; keep your wits about you and no more daft forays like that Lone Ranger act into Cragg Vale!"

"I won't, I promise – bye for now."

"Bye."

Naomi walked back to Carlton filled with uncertainty. She knew that if she told him the full extent of Bob's call he would insist on staying with her. She also knew that if she requested Carlton to contact Auntie Rosie that would set the alarm bells off too. She decided to play down the call.

Carlton turned as he saw Naomi approach. He said, "Everything okay?"

"They found the getaway vehicle used by the mortuary attendant."

"And Darke?"

"No."

"And that's it? You were on the phone that long for that."

"Bob also told me about some stuff that Helen had been working on."

Carlton nodded and looked at his wife. He knew when something wasn't right. He said, "Okay, let's enjoy today, and you can bring me up to speed when we get back to Alan's tonight."

Alan heard the mention of returning to his place and said, "We aren't going back guys."

Naomi and Carlton turned and said, "What?"

"We aren't going back to Dunnellon tonight, we're staying here at Julie and Steve's, and then tomorrow we're going to their condo in St. Augustine."

Naomi said, "But we haven't got our stuff."

"Yes you have," said Debbie, "we put all your gear in your suitcases, then stowed them in the trunk of our car. We wanted it to be a nice surprise for you."

Carlton didn't like surprises, and he especially didn't like anybody interfering with his suitcase and belongings.

Naomi saw the look on Carlton's face and said, "Wow, thanks guys – that was very thoughtful of you… " She cast a warning look at Carlton and said, "…we've never been to St. Augustine before. How long are we staying there?"

"Two nights," said Alan, "tomorrow and Saturday, then we part company on Sunday. You fly back Monday, and we all go back to work."

Naomi looked at Carlton, and then back at Alan. She said, "It sounds perfect, thanks."

Chapter 35

Friday 24th November 2006. St. Augustine, Florida.

It had been a crazy day in St. Augustine. It was Black Friday, the day after Thanksgiving. It was the busiest shopping day in America, and everywhere had been thronging with people. Naomi, Carlton, Julie, Steve, Debbie and Alan, had walked around the historic Castillo de San Marcos, watched the gun-firing ceremony across the Matanzas River, taken the train trolley tour, and had wandered through the delightful streets of America's oldest city. Everywhere abounded with attractions for the ubiquitous tourist, but none of it detracted from the quaintness of the place, it underlined its enduring vibrancy.

As the party walked along the top end of St. George Street, Steve turned to Alan and said, "There it is."

Everybody looked up and saw a signboard advertising, *'The Mill Top Tavern – Food & Spirits – Live Music Daily.'*

"Now let's hope that he's playing today…he usually is."

Naomi sidled up to Alan and said, "What's Steve talking about?"

"Do you recall saying that you'd heard a song named *'The Kennesaw Line'* written by Don Oja-Dunaway?"

Naomi recalled not only the song, but the psychic episode in which she'd heard it. She said, "Yes, I do."

"Well the Mill Top is where Don performs."

"And he's here today?"

"Steve believes so, but we'll soon find out…"

A few minutes later they arrived and Carlton gave Naomi a nudge. He said, "Look at the address…"

Naomi looked to where Carlton was pointing and saw that it was nineteen-and-a-half St. George Street. She looked at Carlton and said "Nineteen-and-a-half?"

Carlton shrugged and said, "Don't ask me!"

The Tavern was a converted, one-hundred-and-thirty year old Mill, complete with a redundant water wheel.

"We need to go upstairs," said Steve.

Seconds later they entered the upstairs bar and found an empty table for six in front of the stage. The singer looked down, saw Steve, nodded, and smiled. It was Don.

Following lunch and drinks Don finished his stint on the stage and joined them at the table. He introduced himself to everybody, but very soon became fascinated by Naomi and the work that she did.

Naomi too was fascinated by him – because she couldn't still figure, why, of all the songs that she could have heard during a psychic episode, it had been one written by him. In the end she came to no conclusion, just a profound feeling that she'd met somebody who might one day make a difference to her life.

One hour later, having enjoyed their meal and Don's unique style of country singing, they headed back to Steve's beachside condo for an hour's rest before heading out for dinner.

Back in Charleston, Helene Gibsonne de Lyon looked about her house. Everything was ready for the visit of the sceptical woman from St Andrew's and her friend. She checked her appearance in the living room mirror, fluffed up her medium-length blonde hair at the sides, and then sat down. As she did so, her bra strap bit into the flesh of her back under her left shoulder. She reached round, slipped her hand underneath it, and felt a sharp edge on a label. She tried to smooth it down, sat back, and felt it chafe again. She let out an exasperated gasp, looked at the clock on the mantelpiece, and went upstairs to change it.

She slipped her voluminous, waist-hugging, white blouse over her head, and then let out another frustrated sigh, because that had messed up her hair again. She threw the blouse on her bed, reached around, undid the strap of her bra, and then threw that on top of the blouse.

At that second, she heard her front door open, and then close.

She frowned, looked at her watch and said, "That you Sam?"

Nothing.

She moved closer to her bedroom door and called out, "Sam – is that you?"

Nothing.

She picked up her blouse, held it in front of her breasts, and walked out onto the landing. She leaned over the handrail and was about to repeat her call when she heard a noise come from her kitchen. Seconds later she heard another noise, and then another. She tried one last call, "Sam?"

Still no reply.

She pulled on her blouse, went to her bedroom, and grabbed hold of the phone. A cacophony of sound erupted from the kitchen. She heard pots and pans falling from their overhead hangers and a host of things bouncing off the tile floor. She ran into her son's bedroom, snatched his signed baseball bat off its place of honour, and then crept down the stairs, ready to dial 911 in an instant.

She approached the kitchen, took a deep breath, and pushed the door open. On her centre console she saw pots and pans scattered everywhere. She said, "What the hell…" and then heard the front door slam. She spun around, saw Sam, and said, "Damn!"

Sam saw the baseball bat and said, "Good Lord honey, what is it?"

Helene said, "Something's happened in my… " She saw Sam's eyes widen and look over her left shoulder.

Before she could respond, she felt one hand clap over her mouth, and another grab hold of her wrist with such force that she dropped the bat. Her right arm was then forced across her stomach in a vice-like grip. She then saw a man stand up from behind her sofa and grab Sam.

"Listen to me bitch," said the man holding Helene, "do as we say, and you live. Don't – and you die. Do you understand?"

Helene nodded.

"Good." The man removed his hand from Helene's mouth and looked at Sam.

Sam said, "Please don't hurt us…"

Helene felt the phone in her left hand. She manipulated it so that she could dial and hovered her finger over the number nine.

"My name is Muz – which one of you bitches is the psychic?"

Helene pressed the number nine. She heard the faint dial tone, but nobody else did.

"We both are," said Sam.

Muz scowled and said, "Which one of you knew my name?"

Helene pressed the number one.

Sam opened her mouth to respond but was cut off.

"I haven't got all fucking day!" said Muz, "Which one of you bitches knew my name?"

"I did," said Helene.

"And I did," said Sam.

Muz frowned, looked at Sam, and said, "*You* – how did you know my name?"

Helene pressed the last number one, made sure that nobody had heard it, and then tried to press the 'send' button. She felt the phone start to slip out of her hand and in an attempt to keep hold, she squeezed, and a flurry of key tones sounded.

Muz said, "What the fuck?" He spun Helene around, saw the phone, and knocked it out of her hand. He then grabbed the front of her blouse and yanked her forwards. It ripped from neckline to waist, exposing bare skin. He looked down, grabbed Helene's neck with his left hand, and pushed his right into the open blouse. "Nice tits sweet cheeks," he said, squeezing her nipple between his forefinger and thumb. "And if you want to keep them, you won't do anything stupid like that again!" He glared into Helene's eyes, and said, *"Got it?"*

Helene couldn't speak because of the hand constricting her airway. She nodded.

Muz pushed Helene back against the wall, swept up the baseball bat, and held it under her chin. He said, "Now – how do you know my fucking name?"

The front doorbell rang.

Muz and Lennie whipped around and looked.

Muz turned back and said, "Are you expecting somebody?"

"Yes," said Helene.

"Well get rid of them."

Helene looked down and said, "Dressed like this?"

Muz looked at Sam and said, "You get rid of them."

Sam knew that their best chance of help lay with their visitors. She said, "I can't."

Muz hissed, *"What?* – What do you mean you can't?"

"I can't."

"Don't play games with me lady – get rid of them!"

"I can't," said Sam, "'cos they'll see from my face that I'm scared. I'll give the game away."

Muz looked at Sam's face and realised that she was telling the truth. She looked terrified and tears were streaming down her face. He said, "Shit!" He looked at Lennie and said, "You get rid of them."

The doorbell rang again, and then they heard the door handle turn.

"Hello," called a voice, "it's only us…"

Muz yanked Helene into the kitchen.

Lennie slammed Sam against the wall of the living room, and put his hand over her mouth.

"Helloo…" said Carole, "…Miz Gibsonne de Lyon?"

Janet and Carole walked into the living room and then shrieked as they saw a man whirl around with a gun aimed at their faces.

"Backs to the wall!" yelled Lennie.

Janet and Carole backed up and stood next to Sam.

Carole let out a cry of fear as she saw Muz appear holding Helene with a torn blouse and her left breast exposed.

Muz pushed Helene towards the other women, and said, "Stand over there and keep quiet."

"What now?" said Lennie.

"I'm thinking."

"What if more people come?"

"Shut up – I'm thinking!"

Helene had a brainwave. She said, "More are coming – including the Sheriff."

Lennie said, "Shit, that's all we need…"

Muz glared at the women and then turned to Lennie. He said, "I'll watch the front while you tie 'em up and get them into the van."

Twenty minutes later, Lennie turned to Muz as they sped away from Helene's house. He said, "So what's on your mind?"

"We're not taking any chances with these bitches; we're going to put them somewhere where they can't escape. Then we're coming back for that fucking Deacon."

Chapter 36

At 12:55am the *SS Georgiana* arrived off Dewees Inlet, and then turned southwest onto a heading of 250 degrees towards the lighthouse on Sullivan's Island.

Being a new moon that night, the sky was as black as the devil's waistcoat, but Captain Davidson, a retired British naval officer, had experience of running the Federal blockades into Charleston, and he knew where he was going. They'd already managed to avoid a patrolling schooner and steamer, but he knew that there would be worse to come.

The *Georgiana* was a brig-rigged, iron hulled, propeller steamer of one-hundred-and-twenty horsepower with a black-painted jib boom and two heavily raked masts. Her iron hull and smoke stack were also painted black whilst on her clipper bow the figurehead of a woman, the poop deck, and the iron rails around it, were all painted white. She was just over two hundred feet in length; weighed five-hundred-and-nineteen tons gross weight, and carried a crew of one-hundred-and-forty men. She was pierced for fourteen guns, but twelve of them, much to the disdain of the crew, were still in the hold. Down below she was carrying rifles; musket balls; two state of the art Whitworth breech loading cannon, four Blakely rifled cannon, medicines, liquor, china, and a host of other valuable, assorted merchandise.

But the most precious part of the cargo, were the boxes of gold.

Captain Davidson looked at the black smoke belching up from the stack, and cursed the cheap bituminous coal that he was burning because he knew that it could give away their position, but due to Confederate cutbacks he'd had to take it instead of the almost smokeless, anthracite that he'd used on previous occasions.

He looked across the bridge deck to his First Lieutenant, a grizzly, tough American named Jim Morrow who'd been with him since leaving Liverpool. He said, "Is the cowl ready, and in place Number One?"

"It is sir."

"And the hatch to number four hold open?"

"Yes sir."

Davidson nodded and said, "Good. – Keep her on this heading. It's eight nautical miles to the lighthouse on Sullivan's Island, and four to the rendezvous, so reduce speed to eight knots, and with luck we'll be there in half an hour."

Morrow nodded and said, "Very good sir."

"And post a lookout on the starboard bow to watch for that signal light."

"Yes sir."

Davidson looked at his pocket watch and then back up to the attentive Morrow. He said, "Now just let's pray that the Good Lord is looking out for us Jim, because if not, it's going to get damned hot around here within the next thirty minutes."

The *Georgiana* steamed down the unmarked Maffitt's Channel at eight knots, half of her capable speed, and kept to her charted course of two nautical miles off Long Island.

Aboard the U.S. Armed Yacht, *America*, a lookout spotted smoke from the *Georgiana's* stack. He yelled, "Vessel on the starboard quarter!"

All eyes turned to where the lookout was indicating.

"Fire as she comes to bear!" shouted the Second Lieutenant.

The gunners ran to their posts, but they were too late. The *Georgiana* steamed by before they were ready, and the only shot fired, missed.

The *America's* Captain watched in disdain. He yelled orders to give chase, and to send up signal flares to alert the rest of the blockading fleet.

Aboard the *Georgiana*, Davidson reached for the electric telegraph and altered it to 'full speed ahead'. The vessel surged forwards. "Mister Morrow," he said, "make adjustments for the increase in speed and watch for that signal."

Morrow, who was standing on the starboard bridge wing, called, "I will sir." He strained his eyes in the dark and then spotted something. He raised his binoculars, said, "Sir, dead ahead!" and passed the binoculars to Davidson.

Davidson looked at where Morrow was indicating and said, "Damn their Yankee hides." He turned to the helmsman. "Turn five degrees to starboard Mister Caines and hold your course."

Alerted by the flares from the *America,* the masthead lookout aboard the flagship of the Union's South Atlantic Blockading Squadron, the *USS Wissahickon*, had seen the approaching blockade-runner. He yelled, "Runner on the starboard quarter!"

The Third Lieutenant called, "Gunners, trail your canon round thirty degrees aft and wait for my signal!"

As the *Georgiana* raced by, the *Wissahickon* opened fire. An eleven-inch shot slammed through her port bulkhead and crashed out of the starboard side in a hail of screaming wood and metal. Everywhere was in uproar, but nobody was killed. Up on deck the hands could hear the gunnery officers aboard the *Wissahickon* giving commands to fire on them.

Davidson felt the massive thud. He snatched the cap off the engine room voice pipe and yelled, "Tie down the steam release valves, and don't let them go 'til I say so!" He rammed the cap back and prayed that the increase in boiler pressure would give them another couple of knots' speed.

Down below, the engineers stared in alarm as the pressure levels climbed and overloaded the boiler.

The *Georgiana* started to gain sea room.

Ahead, the Federal Sloop-of-War, *USS Housatonic* caught sight of the approaching blockade runner. Inch by inch she changed position in an attempt to intercept them, but the *Georgiana* swept past before she could bring herself to bear.

At the harbour entrance, the blockading fleet of monitors, gunboats, and picket boats saw what was happening, and began moving into position to prevent the runner from entering.

Aboard the *Georgiana* a cry went up. "Sir! Light on the starboard beam!"

Everybody turned and looked. A signal lamp flashed two dashes and one dot – Morse code for the letter 'G' – 'G' for *Georgiana.*

And then disaster struck. A lucky shot from the *Wissahickon* slammed into the stern of the *Georgiana* and slewed her violently to starboard.

Davidson yelled into the voice pipe, "All stop and report!"

Several minutes later an engineer raced up the bridge steps.

"How bad is it?" said Davidson.

"We've lost steering sir."

"And the prop?"

"Okay as far as we know."

"Right, get back to your post and wait for my command." Davidson called, "Mister Morrow."

"Yes sir?"

"We've lost steering. Prepare to launch as planned."

"Here sir?"

"No, we've still got the prop and that Yankee appeared to knock us onto the correct heading. We'll steam at full speed ahead and ram her into the shallows."

Morrow said, "But… "

"Please do as I say – and run a white light up the stern jack."

"To signal our surrender?"

"Yes – but post a dozen armed marines under the stern counter."

Morrow frowned and said, "Sir, if you're planning what I think you are I would be very uncomfortable with that, the men aboard those vessels are fellow…"

"Do as I say mister! I won't have those damn Yankees attempting to board my ship without giving them something to think about first."

Morrow drew in a deep breath and then nodded. He conveyed the Captain's orders to a crewman and then watched with intense disapproval as the white light was run up.

Davidson leaned over the bridge wing and yelled, "Deck crew – fit the stack cowling."

Two dozen strong crewmen manhandled a large cowl over the top of the stack and diverted the billowing smoke into hold number four.

A lookout aboard the *Wissahickon* saw the change and called, "Her smoke's stopped sir!"

Lieutenant Commander John L. Davis, commanding the *Wissahickon* nodded and turned to his First Officer. He said, "All right Number One, they must have vented the boilers – order all stop. We don't want to venture too far out of the channel or we could hit the bottom."

"Very good sir."

"And lower the longboats."

"Yes sir."

Twenty minutes later, Davis watched as his men approached the stationary vessel.

Crouching below the stern rails of the *Georgiana,* the dozen armed marines waited.

Morrow watched the approach of the boarding parties and was filled with apprehension. He looked at the resolute face of his Captain and said, "Sir, this isn't right, we're under a white… "

Davidson turned and glared. He said, "Don't you dare question my authority Mister Morrow! This is war goddamn it!"

Morrow bit his lip and looked down. He looked back up and said, "With your permission, sir – I'd like you to note my objection to this course of action."

Davidson said, "Noted," and then turned back to look at the approaching longboats with ice-cold eyes.

The unsuspecting men approached the stern of the *Georgiana* and then looked up in alarm and disbelief when they heard the order, *"Marines – take aim, and fire at will."* Above them rifles appeared over the stern deck rails. In blind panic they started to row back as a shower of cartridge shells whined into them.

Aboard the *Wissahickon*, the Captain was horrified. He said, "My God! – Those treacherous bastards!"

The First Lieutenant said, "Shall we return fire sir?"

"No, we might hit our own men – and unlike those reb curs, we have honour!"

Aboard the *Georgiana*, Davidson yelled for the cowl to be removed, rammed the telegraph handle forwards, and then yelled down the voice pipe, "Flank speed!"

The water below the stern boiled as the prop sprang into action, and the vessel surged ahead.

The watching blockaders were stunned as the *Georgiana* suddenly burst into life and disappeared into the moonless night.

The Officer-of-the-Watch aboard the *Wissahickon* turned to Davis and said, "Your orders sir?"

Davis considered his options and said, "She can't go anywhere, the entrance to the harbour is blocked, and she won't dare turn back this way. And by God, if she does after that act of consummate treachery, we'll show her no mercy!"

Aboard the *Georgiana*, Davidson kept his eyes glued on the blinking light in the distance. He knew that the depth would soon shelve away. He went out onto the bridge wing and yelled, "Marines, standby the charges. Bosun, be ready to launch the boats!"

He went back into the bridge, opened the voice pipe, and yelled, "Engine room – prepare to cut the pipes – and the minute we hit, smash the pumps and douse the fires!"

He went back onto the bridge wing and shouted, "Deck crew, bring those boxes on deck and load them into the pinnaces." He then went back into the bridge and waited.

The impact came with such violence that men and equipment were thrown across the decks. The bow ploughed into the sandy bottom, dug deep, and brought the *Georgiana* from twelve knots, to a dead stop in a matter of seconds.

Above the chaos, the Captain shouted, *"Now! Everybody! Proceed as planned!"*

One hour later, the longboats from the *Wissahickon* approached the stern of the *Georgiana* again. Above they could see smoke and flames burning from several fires, and they weren't sure if it was another trap.

Onshore, the contents of one of the boxes of gold had gone, and so had the majority of the *Georgiana's* crew. Twelve members including the Bosun remained, ready to row two small jolly boats to Venning's Landing across the inland waterway.

Captain Davidson shook the hand of Lieutenant Joliet, and said, "Good luck Lieutenant, we've done our part, now it's up to you."

Joliet said, "Thank you sir, we'll do our best." He saluted, then turned to his Sergeant and said, "Okay Sergeant, carry on."

Sergeant Schmidt saluted back, and then called to his men, "Right lads, let's get these boxes across to the jolly boats – it's still a long way to Charleston, and you know how cranky I get if I miss my breakfast."

Chapter 37

Del Morrison checked around him, slipped into Casey's old shed, and shut the door. He cleared away some sacking, revealed the small refrigerator that Casey had shown him a few weeks' previously, and flopped down onto his old chair.

He'd received an unusual phone message from Janet telling him that she was staying over at Carole's following their Black Friday shopping spree, but he hadn't paid much attention to it. His mind had been on Julie. He'd tried calling her, but he'd drawn no response, and it had frustrated him.

Still feeling aggravated at not being able to take advantage of Janet's absence, he sat back and thought about things. He recalled the conviviality and innocence of those days prior to meeting her, and prior to learning about The Fire of Mars, and out of the blue, he felt an unexpected pang of regret.

He reached down; extracted one of Casey's favourite Bud Light's and snapped it open. "To you buddy," he said as he held the can up and took a drink.

He felt on the edge about so many things.

How he'd got away with the cock-and-bull story that he'd concocted to Janet about finding kids driving the mechanical digger, he still didn't know. He'd no idea why he hadn't heard anything from Muz and Lennie since Casey's death and he presumed that they'd given up on the stone and disappeared. He knew that he'd lied to the police, and that the Sheriff viewed him with a massive amount of suspicion. He knew that the psychic woman had warned Janet about him, and that even Lesley-Ann was suspicious about him. But worst of all, he knew that he was responsible for poor old Casey's death.

He took another drink of beer and considered his position. Could he confess all and get Janet's forgiveness? Should he tell the Farlingtons the true location of The Fire of Mars and then get lauded for that? Could he restore that innocence and get some peace of mind?

The phone in his pocket emitted a tone informing him that he'd received a text. He opened it and saw that it was from Julie. It read, *"Beware! The following contents could cause offence…"*

He frowned and then heard another text arrive. Attached to it he saw a photo of Julie standing outside wearing a cerise, diaphanous blouse, a black miniskirt, black stockings, and black, high-heeled shoes. Her strawberry blonde, hair was blowing off her shoulders in a mild breeze, and she looked amazing. He guessed that Lorraine must have taken the photo, but he didn't see anything offensive about it.

The phone buzzed again. In the next photo, he saw Julie sitting on a wooden stool with her legs apart. Her miniskirt was hitched up, showing her tempting looking mound covered by a near see-through, leopard skin print pair of hipster panties with a black floral waistband and tiny string of faux diamonds hanging down at the front. Her blouse was now open, exposing a deep cleavage that went down to her navel.

He sucked in his breath, expelled it slowly, and put the can of beer down.

The phone buzzed again. With shaky fingers he opened the next photo.

Julie's breasts were now fully exposed and her nipples stood out like two small walnuts. She'd put her fingertips into the waistband of her pants, and was pulling them down.

Del gasped, and said, "Fuck!" He looked through the windows of the shed, saw that nobody was approaching, and then undid the zip of his trousers. He slipped his hand inside his boxers and started stroking his stiffening penis.

The phone buzzed again. He opened it and his mouth fell open.

It was a close-up leading from the top of Julie's black stockings, to her fully exposed vagina. He drooled as he saw the narrow strip of fluffy blonde pubic hair that led to her clitoris, and then at her soft, pink, protruding inner lips which were wide open.

He looked closer and saw from the moist, swollen look of them that she was excited.

The phone buzzed again and a text appeared asking, "Wish you were here babe?"

Del texted back, "Yes – you look so goddamned hot! I want to fuck the life out of you. xxx"

Seconds later he received, "So why don't you get hold of that big hot cock of yours and tell me what it feels like? xx"

His penis was rock hard. He texted, "It wants to be inside you – *right now*..."

He received, "Oh baby – why don't you stroke it and tell me all about it? That's what I'm doing to my pussy right now..."

He grunted with a deep desire and stood up. He looked out of the shed windows, pulled his penis out of his pants, and started to masturbate with his left hand.

With his right, he alternated between photos of Julie with her pants up, and then with them down. As he drew close to ejaculating he put the phone down on Casey's bench, zoomed right in to her vagina, and swapped hands. He felt the usual tightening sensation below his testicles, lifted his head up prior to exploding, and saw Muz staring through the window in front of him.

He was mortified, but couldn't stop from ejaculating. As he stuffed his penis back into his pants he felt sperm spewing everywhere. On his hand, on the zip of his fly – and on the inside of his trousers.

The shed door snatched open; Muz looked down and said, "Jesus H Christ! – What the fuck are you doing?"

Lennie stepped from behind Muz and saw too. He said, "Ooh shit Deacon... busted!"

Del didn't know what to do with embarrassment; he blurted out, "I, I, I was er..."

"Jerking off," said Muz.

"What got you turned on Deacon," said Lennie, "a pumpkin pussy?"

"I – er..."

"I'm not interested," said Muz, "put it away and clean that shit up."

Del saw a roll of paper wipes on Casey's bench and attempted to clean himself up whilst Muz and Lennie watched."

Muz shook his head and said, "I've said this once, and no doubt I'll say it again – you sure aren't like any other Deacon I've met before…"

"And who's the patron saint of jerkers," said Lennie, "Saint Jack-off?"

Del knew that there was nothing that he could say or do to explain his actions. Instead he said, "Okay, okay, so you got me – what are you doing here in broad daylight, and what do you want?"

"What do you mean, what do we want?" said Muz. "You know what we fucking want!"

Del shook his head when he thought about the trench and the conditions inside it. He said, "It's not going to be that easy. The further the workmen have gone down the worse it is. Because we're so close to Church Creek the water table is high and the bottom of the trench is filled with a sticky, gooey mud."

"So why don't we use that digger out there?" said Lennie.

Del closed his eyes and explained what had happened when he'd attempted to use it.

Muz shook his head again and said, "You really are one dumb son-of-a-bitch! Did you think that you could just get into one of those things and drive it?"

Del nodded.

Muz then became suspicious and said, "And what were you doing trying to get that stone alone? Were you trying to double-cross us?"

"No! I saw an opportunity and just took it!"

"And nearly blew it for the rest of us you fucking numb nuts!"

"Okay," said Del, "I realise my mistake now, but my story was believed and we've still got a shot at it."

"And this time Lennie'll drive the digger."

Del said, "He won't be able to because after the last episode, the key's been kept in the parish house overnight."

"In a safe?" said Muz.

"No – on a hook inside the front door, but you can't…" Del saw the look on both faces and didn't finish the sentence.

"When does that thing leave?" said Lennie.

"The contractors were supposed to be leaving today, but they're doing an exhumation on Monday, so they won't be going until at least Tuesday night."

"Right," said Muz, "we'll do it Monday night."

"You can't do it Monday," said Del, "they might not have finished the exhumation by then."

Lennie frowned and said, "Why, how far are they going down?"

"It's not a case of that. It's what they might encounter once they start. Sometimes it can last for days."

"We're doing it Monday night," said Muz, "and you're going to be here."

Del was shocked and then adamant. He said, "No I'm not."

Muz leapt across the shed and grabbed Del by the lapels. He rammed him against the shed wall and said, "Do you love your wife?"

"Course I do – what's that got to do with it?"

"And do you want to see her alive again?"

"Yes."

"Well listen to me shit-for-brains. Me and Lennie have got your wife and her buddy – and those two psychic freaks – locked up somewhere nice and private and unless you do as I say, you ain't never going to see her again."

"What? Where are you keeping them?"

Muz said, "Yeah, like I'm going to tell you…?"

"And what about the others?"

"Never mind about them – they're for me and Lennie to have some fun with."

Del had a dark thought and then said, "All right, I'll do as you say, but how do I know that you'll keep your word after what happened to Casey?"

Muz gripped Del's jacket tighter and nearly lifted him off his feet. He said, "You don't jackass, but I will guarantee that you won't see her again if you don't do as I say."

Del looked deep into the eyes of Muz and then said, "Okay – Monday it is then. And if that stone's there, we'll get it."

Muz stared at Del for a few seconds longer and then backed away. He said, "Good – be here at midnight." He then looked at Lennie and said, "Let's go."

Lennie nodded and the two men disappeared.

Del waited until the two men had gone and then dropped down onto Casey's old chair. He looked at the stains on his trousers and said, "Shit!" He tried to wipe as much off as he could with water and tissues, and as he was doing so, the dark thought passed through his mind again.

He didn't want to see Janet again; he didn't care about her any more. And as for Carole and the two psychics – well...

He saw the Bud light on the bench and took a deep swig. His eyes narrowed as he calculated the odds of trying to engender a situation in which he got his hands on the ruby, got Muz and Lennie to kill their captives, and then tipped off the police causing a fatal shoot-out.

He took another drink and settled down into the chair. "There has to be a way," he said as he looked out of the window deep in thought. "There has to be a way…"

Chapter 38

Helene looked around and tried to assess where they were. She couldn't move freely because duct tape had been bound around her wrists and ankles, and she couldn't speak because another piece had been plastered over her mouth.

The journey from her house had taken no more than three quarters of an hour, and when they'd been blindfolded and manhandled out of the van, she'd picked up the distinctive aroma of trees, flora, and fauna. She'd heard a couple of vehicles passing by at speed and the ground underfoot had been soft on the short approach to the building. They'd had to climb three steps before entering, and once inside the floors had been wooden, uncovered, and hollow sounding. Everywhere smelt musty and damp, and when they'd been locked into their room, they hadn't had to negotiate any steps or stairs.

Before the men had ripped the tape off their eyes, she had known that they were in the back room of a deserted shack, close to a busy main road, and close to Charleston.

The one thing that she needed most was her psychic ability to connect to Sam, but that wasn't going to happen. Sam was too scared to do anything.

She looked at the others.

Carole had had to endure some kind of vile sexual assault, because she'd been taken away during the previous night and returned several hours later with torn clothing and missing underwear. She was battered about the face, and appeared to be in deep trauma.

She caught the eye of Janet and held it for a few seconds.

Janet saw and somehow knew what Helene was thinking. She looked at the dishevelled figure of Carole, and then back at Helene, and then thought about the green bag with white handles.

Before the men had covered their mouths with duct tape, she'd got it across to them that she'd been on her period, and by some miracle, they'd allowed her to keep the bag because it contained her wipes and tampons. They'd removed everything else though, including her mobile phone and wallet.

She saw Helene look at the bag. She looked at it too. It was lying by her side. She looked back at Helene.

Helene raised her eyebrows, nodded, and then shut her eyes tight, indicating that Janet should do the same. She saw Janet looking and trying to comprehend – and then saw her nod, and close her eyes.

It was almost instant, and Janet couldn't believe it. It sounded as though Helene had just said, "The bag! The bag!" She opened her eyes and saw Helene look at the bag. She frowned and looked at the bag, but didn't understand. She looked back at Helene and saw her indicate for her to close her eyes again.

She did, and it happened again. This time she heard "The mirror – in the bag!" She opened her eyes, nodded at Helene, then swivelled round and hooked the bag handles. She put her hands inside, unzipped the small compartment, and felt the tiny, credit card-sized mirror slotted inside. She slipped it out of its holder, extracted it, and by twisting her wrist bindings, began to saw away at the duct tape.

Nothing happened.

She realised that the edge of the mirror was too smooth. She looked up in despair, and saw Helene raise her eyebrows. Without thinking, she shut her eyes and listened. She heard the words, "Break it." She opened her eyes, nodded to Helene and then pressed down on a corner.

With a sharp crack, a shard broke off.

Everybody looked, and then in unison, looked at the door. They sat transfixed but soon realised that the sound had drawn no response.

Janet picked up the shard, and within seconds she'd freed her hands.

This became the most terrifying time of her life. Her heart was beating like crazy. She looked at the door and knew that if she made the faintest sound, she could attract the men. It felt as though a steel band had been placed around her head and tightened.

She saw the look of terrified apprehension on everybody's faces. She freed herself and everybody else, not daring to make a noise, and being ready to react to the slightest sound.

Helene whispered, *"Sam, Carole, the door opens inwards – sit with your backs against it and be ready to push if necessary."*

Sam and Carole did as they were bid.

Helene scanned the room and saw that the door was the only way out. There was a tiny window high up on the back wall, but if they'd been able to reach it, they wouldn't have been able to climb through it. She was just about to give up, when she spotted a dirty mat in the corner of the room. She crept over to it – being careful to stick to the outside edges of the room in case the floorboards creaked – and lifted it up.

Underneath was a piece of cardboard. She lifted that and saw a broken floorboard. She looked through, saw daylight, and realised that it led to the crawlspace under the shack. She grabbed hold of the jagged edge of the board and heaved upwards. The two nails holding it in place started to lift, but she didn't have the strength to break it free it on her own. In despair she turned to the other girls who each had a go, without success.

Helene whispered, *"Look for something to lever it up…"*

A search revealed nothing that would do the trick. Then Janet had a brainwave. Her apparent ability to be able to communicate with Helene had rocked her to the core, but once she'd accepted it, she'd become a convert, and she recalled Helene advising her to buy the green bag because one day it would save lives. At first she'd attributed that to finding the mirror, but the mirror wasn't the bag.

She picked it up and saw that it was a simple bag with no end panels, two stitched-on long handles, and a small interior zipped pocket. She stared at it trying to figure out how it could help, and then the penny dropped.

She snatched up the mirror shard, sliced the stitching down the sides of the bag, and opened it up. She then twisted it, and walked across to the others. "Let's try this," she said, as she looped the bag under the end of the broken floorboard.

Helene and Sam took one side, whilst Janet and Carole took the other.

Helene mouthed, *"One – two – three!"*

They all heaved together, pulling and straining, until the board snapped free with an enormous *crrrack!*

All eyes turned to the door.

Nothing happened.

They realised that they were alone, and then in near frenzy, used the removed floorboard, to lever others up until they opened a hole big enough for them to drop through.

They emerged from under the shack, saw that they were at the rear, and then ran along the path to the road in front.

Janet said, "It's Highway 17!"

Helene leapt out in front of an approaching car and raised her hands.

The car stopped and a young man stepped out. He saw the state of the friends and said, "Are you ladies okay?"

On the opposite side of Highway 17, Muz and Lennie had just finished an alcohol-fuelled lunch, and they were speculating what they would do to their respective women once they got back.

"I'm having that psychic," said Muz, "she looks like she's got a bit of fire in her."

Lennie lifted his head up, burped, and said, "Yeah, and I'm having…"

Muz suddenly hit the brakes and said, *"Shit!"* He realised that he'd made a mistake stopping and then accelerated away.

Lennie looked across the Highway, and saw three police cars and an ambulance, all with flashing lights, outside their shack.

"Holy Christ!" he said, "Isn't that…?" He saw one of the women look across the road and point as they sped off.

"There!" said Helene, "That's the van!"

On the opposite side, a young police officer turned, noted the licence plate number and went back to his vehicle to radio the details in. A few minutes later he rejoined the women and said, "That van was stolen four days ago from outside a diner in Savannah, but we've notified the Highway Patrol and they're looking for it as we speak."

Inside the van, Muz was furious; he'd seen the cop go to his vehicle, and he guessed that it wouldn't be long before every car in Charleston was looking for them.

"Fuck!" he spat out, "How did those bitches get out?"

Lennie shrugged and said, "Beats me…"

Muz turned and walloped Lennie on the arm and said, "Did you ever say my surname in front of those bitches?

"Why?"

"Why do you think meat-head?"

"No – I didn't, but I guess that it didn't make a difference anyhow."

Muz whipped around and said, "How do you figure that?"

"If that blonde one with the nice tits knew your first name was Muz, she more'n likely knew your last name was Appleton."

Muz seethed and said, "We should've finished them all off when we had the chance."

Lennie nodded and said, "Sorry bro – what are we going to do now?"

"Ditch the van, lay low, and see if we can get that ruby on Monday night."

Lennie was shocked. He said, "You still want to go back to the church – even after everything that's happened?"

"What else are we going to do? We've got no money except the few dollars we got from those bitches, we can't use their credit cards now, and we have to get as far away from here as possible."

"And as quick as possible," said Lennie. "We have offed two people don't forget!"

Muz looked at Lennie and said, "It's a good job one of us has brains."

"What do you mean?"

"The cops won't be expecting us to stay here after those women have blabbed, and there's probably dozens of fingerprints all over the shack, so the last thing they'll expect is for us to go back to the church."

"I don't know about that…"

"We're in the shit anyway, so do we go, and end up with nothing, or do we stay, and try to get that stone?"

Lennie said, "I don't know…it doesn't seem…"

"We're going," said Muz, "and that's an end to it. We'll double-bluff the pigs, get that stone, bury the Deacon, and get the fuck out of Charleston."

"Whoa, whoa, wait a minute. What do you mean bury the Deacon? Why?"

"Because I've had it with him; he's brought us nothing but bad luck, and I want his ass good and dead."

Chapter 39

"Thy purpose firm is equal to the deed.
Who does the best his circumstance allows,
Does well, acts nobly; angels could do no more."
Edward Young (1683-1765)

0440 Hours, Saturday 21ˢᵗ March 1863. South Carolina Railroad Depot, Charleston

Ira was frantic with worry. He turned to Adam and said, "This is ridiculous! When you said that you'd come up with a plan I thought that you meant something credible – something that might have a chance of working…"

"Stop worrying; the best plans are often the simplest."

"*Best plans?* Best plans? – This isn't a plan at all, it's a death sentence!"

The friends stopped talking when they heard the approach of marching soldiers. Through the darkness they saw a Confederate Master Sergeant leading five privates.

Ira's desperation soared. "Please stop this now brother – before they get here!"

"For Pete's sake Ira, calm down, I've got everything under control; trust me."

Adam nodded as the detail of men halted in front of him.

Weims snapped to attention, saluted, and said, "Master Sergeant Weims reporting for duty sir."

Adam returned the salute and then said, "A word alone if I might Master Sergeant."

Weims said, "Certainly sir," and followed Adam away from Ira and the detail.

Out of earshot Adam said, "Is everything set up Gil?"

"It is."

"And you know exactly what you have to do?"

"I do."

"Any other problems?"

"No, once I'd informed Harrison in Richmond that I intended posing as an undercover NCO in the detail guarding the gold before it leaves for Wilmington, he gave me carte blanche."

"Good." Adam nodded across to the five soldiers. He said, "What about your men?"

"Not one's a conscript, and once they've got their hands on their share, they'll disappear quicker than goose shit off a shovel."

"And the engine driver has no idea?"

"None."

"What time is he connecting to the coach?"

"0530, and we depart at 0600."

"Fine; now, before we rejoin the men, run the plan past me one last time."

Weims looked at Adam's serious face and said, "After you leave I will return with six more hired soldiers and we'll transfer the 'iron ore' from the car in siding number four to the cart at 1000 hours. If questioned we'll say that it's being taken to Fort Dorchester where it will be met by another detail. We'll then meet Lucius and Jacob at Quarter House Tavern.

Once we arrive at the Prioleau place, Lucius and Jacob will take their shares, the Prioleau's will take theirs, and Bart will take his, Ned's and your shares. Lucius and co. will leave Charleston along the River Road, and Bart will leave via the Fort Dorchester Road, and we will all leave on different days.

My men and I will row the remainder up Church Creek, and then use the church's escape tunnel to get the remaining gold to the vault at St. Andrew's where it will stay."

Adam nodded and said, "Good – now, you do know that you'll get word from Wilmington before the end of today that the gold never arrived, don't you?"

"Yes, I'm expecting that. I'll tell Harrison that I'll leave for Wilmington tomorrow morning to investigate. I'll visit St. Andrew's early in the morning, leave Reverend Drayton his share, and then give the boys their shares. After that I'll go to Wilmington and the guys will disperse and go their own ways. When I return to Charleston I'll collect the remaining gold from St. Andrew's vault and keep it until you return."

Adam was surprised and said, "You told Reverend Drayton?"

"Yes, he's a wily one and that's a fact. We never could have done it without him finding out, and with the war restricting sales from his plantations, I think that he thought his contribution a gift from above."

"I knew that he was a canny guy, but I never would have figured he'd be a willing participant in this venture."

"Trust me brother, John Drayton didn't get his plantations by honesty and prayer alone…"

Adam raised his eyebrows, extracted his pocket watch, and looked at the time." He said, "Right, good luck Gil, let's go."

He walked with Weims back to the detail, and saw the look of despair on Ira's face. He ignored it and said, "Fall in men."

The seven 'soldiers' fell in, two abreast, with Weims at the front.

"Master Sergeant," said Adam, "I have to go to the telegraph office to collect the goods car key, and to send a wire to Wilmington. Do you know where you have to go?"

"Yes sir."

"Good, then – detail – to your posts…quick march!"

Weims led the detail towards siding four. As they approached, a Senior Private snapped to attention.

"Stand easy," said Weims.

"Thank you Master Sergeant," said the Senior Private.

"Anything to report?"

"No Master Sergeant."

"Good, then you are relieved."

The Senior Private said, "Thank you Master Sergeant," turned and then called his men to attention before leading them away.

Weims waited until the retreating detail was out of earshot and then said, "Corporal, post your men around the car, and you come with me."

Ira nodded, and did as he was told. When he turned back to Weims, he saw him standing fifty feet away, and looking at one of the nearby cars.

He walked over to Weims and said, "Have you seen it?"

"Couldn't rightly miss it…"

Ira turned and saw it in siding number six. "Holy Mother," he said, "talk about conspicuous…"

Weims turned and saw the huge red cross painted on the door. He looked at his pocket watch and then back up the track to where the points were. He said, "You re-post the men, I'll throw the switch."

In the telegraph office Adam waited until he'd seen the clerk wire the message that he'd be leaving on time, to his contact in Wilmington. He looked at the clock on the office wall and noted that it was 5:20am.

He thanked the clerk and headed towards siding number four. He got halfway and then heard the approach of a locomotive. He turned, snatched out his pocket watch, and saw that it was 5:25am. He prayed that Weims and Ira had done their part.

The engineer saw Adam and nodded as his huge black loco, coal-tender, and single passenger car, trundled past. He reached the points and heard the familiar clacking sound as the train rumbled over. He leaned out of the cab, saw that he was approaching a goods car, and then applied the brakes. He saw the troops on duty around it, and gathered that he was at the correct one.

The loco backed into the coach and then stopped as soon as the driver felt the familiar lurch.

The coal man stepped down from the cab, walked to the rear, connected the goods car to the passenger car, and then went back to the loco, and climbed aboard.

Adam arrived and saw that the train had connected to the car in siding six. His heart was beating like a hammer.

He walked down the side of the loco and saw the engineer staring at the goods car and scratching the back of his head.

Adam approached and said, "Good morning, is everything in order?"

"Kinda," said the engineer.

"Kinda?" repeated Adam.

"Yessir," said the engineer in his deep southern drawl, "but I must've got my wires crossed however."

"How so?"

"I was led to believe that I'd be connecting to the car in siding number four...and nobody said nothing about it having a red cross painted on it."

Adam was horrified; his simple plan was on the verge of backfiring. He said, "So why did you connect to this one?"

The engineer turned to Adam and said, "The switch was thrown to siding number six, and when I looked I saw the soldiers guarding this car, so I presumed I'd gotten it wrong."

Adam drew in a deep breath and said, "Perhaps you'd better go check with your Depot Manager that we have the right car then."

The engineer frowned and said, "I don't have a mind to do that Captain. He is one tetchy son-of-a-bitch who doesn't like to be disturbed before 7am. If I was to go knocking on his door at this time, he'd have a fit and make my life hell for the next month or more."

Adam nodded and said, "I see." He pondered for a couple of seconds and then said, "Maybe we can resolve this without disturbing the Depot Manager." He called across to Weims and said, "Master Sergeant – here if you please."

"Yes sir."

Adam waited until Weims was close by and then said, "Is this your first post here Master Sergeant?"

"Yes sir."

"I see. And before you arrived, had you been told which siding to go to?"

Weims saw the look of perplexity on Adam's face, and said, "No sir, I was told that I'd see which car was being guarded, and to relieve the detail at 0500 hours."

"And this was the car that was being guarded?"

"Yes sir."

"And did anybody say anything about it being marked with a red cross?"

"Yes sir, when I questioned the Corporal in charge of the previous detail, he said that it had been painted on the car so that the Yankees wouldn't damage it if it came under fire."

Adam was relieved by Weims quick-wittedness. He nodded and said, "Very well Master Sergeant, get your men aboard."

He turned to the engineer and said, "Everything does seem to be in order, but if you'd rather double check…?"

"No sir," said the engineer, "I guess somebody made fresh plans and didn't update the controller – happens all the time…"

"Well if you're sure?"

"Yes sir, if you'd like to climb aboard we'll get underway."

Adam felt his equilibrium settling, and said, "Fine, I'll just have a quick word with my Master Sergeant and then we can go."

The engineer nodded and clambered back up into the cab.

Adam walked across to Weims and saw him salute. He returned it in case anybody was watching, and then said, "Damn, that was too close for comfort."

Weims looked around and said, "Nothing we couldn't handle." He stepped closer and then added, "The key to the padlock is where your brother said it would be."

Adam turned and saw that nobody was watching. He removed the goods car key he'd picked up from the telegraph office and handed it to Weims. He said, "We're trusting you Gil. You're either going to end this day with a lot of good, grateful friends, or you'll be watching your back for the rest of your life…"

"Stop, please," said Weims, "I give you my solemn word that you, your brothers, and your friends can trust me. We all want to be well set up when this war ends, and I certainly don't want to spend the rest of my life looking over my shoulder."

"All right, but it isn't over yet either," said Adam.

"I know." Weims extended his hand and said, "But when it is, we'll all be rich. Trust me."

Adam looked into the eyes of Weims, shook the offered hand, and said, "Okay, be safe, and God go with you."

Ten minutes later, Weims saw the train disappear out of the depot. He looked at his pocket watch and saw that it was exactly 6am. He drew in a deep breath, said, "Right Gilbert – breakfast first, then we got plans of our own to attend to…"

Chapter 40

"Are you Naomi Wilkes?"

Naomi turned around and saw an attractive looking man, whom she guessed would be in his late thirties, standing, looking at her.

"Yes I am," she said.

"My name is Spencer Prioleau; I am a forensic archaeologist from the South Carolina County Coroner's Department, and I have been put in charge of this disinterment."

Naomi shook the offered hand and said, "Hi, it's nice to meet a fellow archaeologist, though my jurisdiction is in the north of England."

"I gather so ma'am; I just needed to ask you a couple of questions before we proceed."

Naomi nodded and said, "Okay, shoot."

"Are you the person who started all of this business off?"

"Yes and no. I took possession of an old, but recently discovered letter dating from the 1820's indicating that a very rare and valuable ruby was buried here, but I would have to say that the person who started it all off was the man who wrote the letter, and first buried it here, Valentine Chance."

Spencer nodded and said, "I see. And what alerted you to this particular spot?"

Naomi turned around and pointed in the direction of the approaching Del Morrison. She said, "Deacon Morrison was told by his groundsman that he had discovered the whereabouts of an unmarked grave, for somebody named 'Matthews P. F.' and this fitted perfectly with a clue that had been left in the letter written by Valentine."

"A clue? This Valentine Chance guy didn't just outright name where he'd buried the stone?"

"No, he stated that he was leaving the clue for his 'wastrel sons' to solve so that they would learn that great riches weren't easily come by, but in case he succeeded his sons, he sent a copy of the clue to his father in England, so that any other family member might find it if they hadn't."

Spencer thought for a second and said, "So the stone may have been removed at any time in the past?"

"No," said Naomi, "it couldn't have been unless it was come upon by chance, because the first part of the clue involved finding a metal shard, that led the way to solving the second part, and my distant cousin Alan..." she pointed to Alan, "...was the one who found that intact."

Spencer raised his eyebrows and said, "A fascinating tale ma'am, and I can see why you are all excited."

"Please call me Naomi – 'ma'am' sounds so formal."

Spencer smiled and said, "Okay Naomi, but if I slip into it every now and then, it's just force of habit." He paused and then said, "Now, if you'll excuse me for a few minutes, I'll just have a quick word with the Deacon."

Naomi looked around at the tranquil scenery of old St Andrew's. It seemed to have a serene quality about it. She breathed in the scented aroma of the local flora and fauna, and wished that Carlton hadn't had to fly back to England.

Her mobile phoned buzzed indicating that she'd received a text.

She retrieved the phone from her bag, half-expecting a text from Carlton, but then opened it and read, "California." She stared at her phone for several seconds expecting it to inform her that only a partial message had been received, but nothing further happened.

She noted that the text had been received from an 'undisclosed sender.'

"Everything okay cuz?"

Naomi looked up and saw Alan approaching. She put the phone back in her bag and said, "Yeah, fine, I think. I just got a weird text..." something clicked in her mind. She snatched the phone out of her bag and looked at the text message again.

Alan saw the look of perplexity on Naomi's face and said, "What's wrong?"

Naomi paused before answering and then said, "Earlier this year, I received three notes each containing just one word. One was 'hive,' the second was '2Delta2,'and the third was 'male.' Now I've just received a text saying 'California.'"

"Hive, 2Delta2, male, and California? Does any of that make sense to you?"

"No – so why would somebody send them to me?"

"Maybe because..." Alan heard Naomi's phone buzz again, and stopped speaking.

Naomi opened up the message and saw that once again, it was sent from an 'undisclosed sender.' She read,

"California.

Why not pay us a visit and let us show you what the Golden State has to offer!

Click here for more details."

She looked up at Alan and said, "False alarm; it was an advert."

Alan smiled and said, "Good, but it doesn't explain those other odd notes."

Everybody turned and looked when Spencer called, *"Okay Jake – let's go!"*

Jake started the engine of the mechanical digger and drove it across to where Spencer was indicating.

Seconds later a police car stopped in the drive and Sheriff Bonnie-Mae Clement stepped out.

Del saw Bonnie-Mae and tried to avoid her by slinking down behind a couple of workmen as they walked across to the site above the burial vault.

Reverend Hughes appeared on the steps of the parish house, and was about to join the others when he saw Bonnie-Mae indicating for him to stay put.

"Is everything okay Sheriff?" he said.

"No Father it is not; I have a veritable cascade of questions to ask, and I have no intention of leaving here without getting them answered."

"Anything I can help with?"

"No Father, but Deacon Morrison needs to do a whole mess of explaining otherwise he'll be joining me down at headquarters for the foreseeable future."

"Oh dear – sounds serious; not anything that will adversely affect the good standing of this church I hope?"

Bonnie-Mae considered her answer and then said, "I hope not Father."

"And have you had the results back about the poor unfortunate found in the burial vault?"

"We have, she was female, obviously, she was between eighteen, and twenty years of age, and the carbon 14 result showed that she had died in the latter part of the nineteenth century, sometime around 1880."

"Goodness gracious," said Marshall, "that's a surprise. I had entertained the idea that she'd been placed in there somewhere around the early 1800's or so. I never would have figured that she'd have been put in there as late as that."

"Me neither, and Heaven only knows what was going on back then, but I guess we'll never find out."

"And were there any clues to who she was?"

"No sir, she was Caucasian, there were no obvious wounds to the skeletal remains, and the only conclusion that we can draw is that for some reason or other, probably related to witchcraft given the inverted cross…"

"Or maybe some kind of race issue?" interrupted Marshall, "If she took up with the wrong man? That kind of thing was very severely dealt with back in the day."

"Could be – crosses were featured when race crimes were committed back then, but it was still an extreme measure to lock her up in there, and let her starve to death."

Marshall shook his head and said, "Good Lord, it doesn't bear thinking about. And what kind of Godless creatures would do that to another living soul?"

"We'll never know Father, we'll never know."

Marshall decided that he needed a distraction. He said, "Shall we join the others? It looks as though the dig is about to start."

Bonnie-Mae nodded and walked to the designated site with Marshall. She saw Del, cast him a scathing look, and watched him wither.

All eyes turned to Spencer as he said, "Okay Jake – take off the first six inches."

Jake dropped the arm of the digger within the top boundary of the delineated ground, and then slowly withdrew it.

Naomi felt a pressure on her left shoulder and heard the moaning start again. Her heart rate increased. It sounded as though whoever was in the ground was aware of the disturbance, and was trying to be heard.

A few minutes later, Spencer stepped down onto the exposed earth and looked around. He knelt down, scraped at a couple of places with his small hand trowel, and then stepped out. He said, "Another six Jake."

Everybody watched in fascination as the digger went deeper down.

By the time that the excavation had descended two feet without result, Del had begun to feel smug. He knew that he'd been successful in luring everybody away from the real grave site and he waited with anticipation for the first exasperated comment.

"Another six!" called Spencer.

Jake lowered the mechanical arm and removed another six inches of soil.

Spencer held up his hand and said, "Okay, hold it!" He hopped down into the hole and looked around. Everything still looked natural. He scrutinised the whole area, picked up one or two stones, and then climbed back out. He looked at Jake and said, "Three inches this time…"

The arm of the mechanical digger lowered, and scraped away another three inches of topsoil.

Once again Spencer stepped down and looked around.

Standing at the edge of the hole, Marshall looked at his watch and noted that it was 10:30am. He had to attend a meeting of the church elders in the parish house at 11am, and he knew that he'd have to fend off more than a few searching questions about the disinterment.

"Nothing," said Spencer, as he climbed out again. He turned to Jake and called, "Another three…"

The mechanical arm lowered again and removed another three inches of soil.

As Spencer walked towards the hole, he heard Marshall say something. He turned to look at him, misjudged his footing, and slipped over the edge. He fell in, landed on his side, and felt something bang into his ribcage.

Once the mayhem had settled and the offers of help had been dismissed, he turned and looked at the spot where he'd fallen. He frowned, retrieved his trowel from his leather pouch, and started to clear away the soil.

Seconds later Naomi said, "What's that?"

Spencer looked up and said, "Not sure ma'am." He continued clearing dirt from around the protruding object until his trowel scraped on something hard. He stopped, and then tapped down with the point of his trowel.

Everybody heard a dull metallic sound.

The smugness evaporated from Del's face, he stepped forwards, and looked down.

Spencer looked up at Naomi and said, "This isn't a coffin ma'am."

Naomi looked at the metal object sticking up from the ground and said, "So what is it?"

Spencer looked at the object and then back at Bonnie-Mae. He said, "Sheriff you need to see this – it looks like some kind of door handle…"

Chapter 41

Bonnie-Mae watched as Spencer cleared away the soil and revealed a metal door.

Peter Purewell, who'd arrived seconds earlier, was the first to make the connection. He walked to one end of the hole and said, "Guys, that's the same as the other one."

Naomi walked around to the metal door on the vault, made a mental note of the details, and then looked at the exposed one. She said, "Peter's right, they're identical."

"So that raises three questions." Bonnie-Mae looked from face-to-face and then continued, "One – what is that door doing there? Two – where did it come from?" And three, why was it put there?"

Naomi walked back to the vault entrance, walked down the steps and looked at the metal door.

Peter followed her and said, "See anything?"

Naomi glanced up and said, "Not offhand..." She inspected the door and doorway looking for any reason why there could have been two doors, but she found none. She went inside and felt a shiver of apprehension. She couldn't help looking behind the door, even though she knew that the remains of the young woman had been taken away.

Although it was gloomy in the vault, there was enough light for her to be able to see. She walked to the side opposite the doorway and inspected the wall for evidence of another portal but saw nothing. She then examined everywhere else with minute detail, but still drew a blank.

By the time that she'd re-emerged, she'd drawn an audience.

Bonnie-Mae was the first to speak. She said, "Did you see anything to explain the other door ma'am?"

Naomi looked up from the base of the steps and said, "Nothing, but maybe we're looking in the wrong place."

Nobody spoke.

Naomi climbed back up the steps as Spencer arrived. She said, "The interior of the vault has been lined with asphalt…"

"That would have been to waterproof it," said Spencer.

"And it would have concealed any signs of disturbance to the inner skin of the vault," said Naomi.

Peter said, "So are you saying that we need to expose the outer skin to see if another door had been there?"

"Correct."

"Interesting as that may be," said Spencer, "the only thing it would reveal, is another entrance, or exit, on the other side."

"No, I disagree," said Peter, "I've studied the construction of a lot of these nineteenth century vaults in numerous locations throughout the States, and I've never seen one with two doors."

Spencer pondered for a few seconds and then said, "Maybe so, but, what would it show us even if we did expose the brickwork and find evidence that a door had at one time been in place? It's not as though we'd have found some mysterious entranceway, leading to a hitherto undiscovered place. We already know what's on the other side – the vault!"

"Depends which way you're looking," said Naomi.

Spencer, Peter, and Bonnie-Mae turned in unison.

"Sorry ma'am," said Bonnie-Mae, "what did you say?"

Naomi looked at the Sheriff and repeated, "It depends which way you're looking."

"What do you mean?" said Peter.

Naomi looked around the curious faces and said, "We're all assuming that the door is leading into the vault. What if it wasn't?"

"Then it'd be leading out, obviously," said Spencer.

"It's not obvious at all," said Naomi, "if it was another entrance or exit, why isn't it still there. And what is the door, assuming of course that it came from this vault and not the other, doing, lying on its side, two-and-a-half feet under the ground, at the head end of this vault?"

Silence.

Naomi looked at the blank faces and said, "Why don't we apply the same principle that we used to discover this door?" She turned and pointed down the steps.

"And what was that?" said Spencer.

"An equilateral triangle," said Naomi.

Spencer frowned.

Peter said, "Naomi figured that the steps down to the vault had to be approximately forty-five degrees in elevation, and used the principle of an equilateral triangle to work out where the top step must have been."

"Ah," said Spencer, "of course, so if your theory is right, we should be able to apply the same principle under the door that we've exposed, and find the entrance or exit steps there?"

"No," said Naomi, "if my theory is wrong, we'll find steps there."

"Wrong?" said Bonnie-Mae, "But you said…"

"Spencer has already gone down two-and-half feet at a distance further away than the top step this side of the vault, and he hasn't exposed anything other than the door."

"Right," said Peter turning to Naomi, "so if steps had been there, we'd have found evidence of them by now?"

"Unless it was destroyed by the placing of the door there," said Naomi.

"Wait, wait," said Bonnie-Mae to Naomi, "let me get this straight. Will you be right about finding steps there, or wrong?"

"If my theory is correct, we won't find any steps there," said Naomi.

"Then what did you mean when you said 'it depends which way you go through the door'? You can only go in or out; there ain't no other way for Pete's sake."

"Yes," said Naomi, "but we're only thinking about the burial vault."

Bonnie-Mae felt her prickliness start to rise. She said, "Because that's what we've been talking about isn't it? What else is there to think about?"

Spencer felt the tension level rise and cut in. He said, "Guys, guys, all of this is beside the point. We're here to see if there's a burial below that door. Whether or not there's another doorway in this burial vault is irrelevant, because its discovery, or not, wouldn't achieve anything anyway."

Naomi looked down at the floor, and then back up. She knew that her response would be contentious. She said, "On the contrary, it may answer everything."

Silence descended.

Naomi saw everybody staring at her with puzzled expressions on their faces. She said, "Look, right now we're not getting anywhere. Let's lift that metal door and see what's underneath it; then we may get our answers."

Spencer looked at his watch and said, "Agreed… "

"No, hold your horses' cowboy," said Bonnie-Mae. She turned to Naomi and said, "What did you mean that it may answer everything?"

Naomi looked at Bonnie-Mae and said, "Okay – we've all been speculating that the door we found could belong to this vault because it matches the one in situ." She pointed to the open door. "And if at sometime in the past it had been installed on the opposite side of the vault, what would have been the purpose? Peter's told you that he made an extensive study of burial vaults and he's never seen one with two doors. So, assuming that the door outside did once belong to this vault, why was it installed?" She paused for a few seconds to let her words sink in. "To me," she continued, "there would have been no point in going to the expense and work of it, if it had just been another ingress or egress point, so it must have been installed for another purpose."

Bonnie-Mae let out an exasperated sigh and said, "But there is no other dad-blamed purpose! You can only come in or go out of the vault!"

"Yes… "

"Then what the hell are we standing here jawing about? Let's get back to work and get this goddamned disinterment over with. I have much better things to do with my time than standing around yacking over inconsequentials!"

Naomi stood her ground; she said, "I agree that you can only go out of, and come in doors, but what you seem to be assuming, is where you go into and out of!"

Bonnie-Mae was nearly beside herself with frustration. She said, "*The freaking vault!* Where the hell else could you go?"

"Now you've arrived at what's on my mind."

Bonnie-Mae said, *"What?"*

"We have been presuming that we can go in and out of the vault through both doors – if indeed there was another door in situ – but there are steps leading down to this door. So far we've seen nothing to indicate steps going down to the other side."

"But…"

"But nothing," pressed on Naomi, "if there *was* a door in place, and there are no steps going down to it, where did it go to?"

A stunned silence fell on the place, until Spencer said, "Wait a minute, are you hinting that a door from the vault could have gone somewhere else?"

"Yes."

Bonnie-Mae was speechless.

"What? To a tunnel or something?" said Spencer.

"Whoa!" said Peter. He turned to Naomi and said, "You've just triggered a memory. A couple of years back I was contacted by an author from your Country who was writing a novel involving St. Andrew's, and he told me that he'd heard rumours of an old Confederate escape tunnel going from here to Church Creek. I told him that I knew nothing about one, but now here you are mooting that one could be here."

Bonnie-Mae looked at Naomi with a new respect and said, "Ma'am, please accept my sincere apologies for my emotional outburst. You have once again impressed me with your cold logic."

Naomi smiled and said, "Thank you."

Spencer said, "Ma'am, you just made this dig one hundred percent more interesting! Anybody care to join me while we go for a look see?"

Everybody followed Spencer back to the site. Upon arrival they saw that Taffy's men had brushed the remaining soil off the door, and that they'd dug a small channel around the outer edges, allowing them access to it.

Spencer hopped down into hole and threaded a length of rope under one side of the door. He climbed out, handed an end each to two guys, and then checked that they were ready.

He looked at Naomi, saw her nod, and then said, "Right – all together. One, two, three – *lift!*"

Chapter 42

Saturday 21ˢᵗ March 1863. Florence, South Carolina.

The train started to slow down as it approached the junction of the South Carolina Rail Road line with the North Eastern Rail Road line at Florence railroad station.

Adam looked across to Weims' four 'volunteer Confederate conscripts' and said, "Are you clear what you have to do?"

"We are," said the self-appointed leader, an abrasive acquaintance of Weims, named Ezra Hicks. "We wait aboard until the loco has taken on fuel and water, and then jump off as the train's pulling out. We then ride to Conway and wait 'til Gil arrives. After that we take our cuts and disperse."

Adam looked at Ira who shook his head and then looked down.

"Your nigger buddy don't look none too sure," said Hicks, "he ain't afraid is he?"

Ira leapt to his feet and said, "Who are you calling a…"

As quick as a flash, Hicks drew his pistol and aimed it at Ira. He said, "Don't you get sassy with me boy, 'cos I'll shoot you dead." Before he could utter another word he felt a sharp pain in the back of his neck. He turned and saw Adam holding a vicious-looking Bowie knife under his chin.

"Drop the gun," said Adam.

Hicks dropped the gun.

"Now," said Adam, "There's two ways we can do this, one where you end up sliced into jerky strips, and the other with a red cheek. Which is it going to be?"

Hicks looked at Adam and said, "What?"

Adam nodded and said, "Right, I choose." In an instant he slapped Hicks across the face with such force that it knocked him off his feet.

Hicks's three associates reached for their guns but stopped when they saw Ira pointing a sawn-off shotgun at them.

Hicks looked up from the carriage floor, saw Ira training a gun on his companions, and saw that Adam was now aiming his Colt 45 at him. He said, "Okay, okay, let's not be too hasty here boys. We're all on the same side, right?"

Adam looked down and said, "Do you punks know how easy it would be for me and Ira to shoot you all and then blame you for the gold not being on board?"

Hicks looked at Adam's face and then at Ira's – he saw Ira nod. He said, "Like I said, let's not be too hasty..." he turned to Ira and said, "...I apologise if I caused offence with my nigger remark, I..."

"You've just got a big flapping mouth which you don't seem able to control," said Adam. He looked at Ira and said, "In fact we could be doing these three boys a big favour if we silenced it altogether; leastways then, they might have a chance of escaping with their share, without no big mouth giving the game away."

"And they'd have his share too," added Ira.

Hicks gulped when he saw the look of anticipation appear on the face of his three associates.

"Boys, boys," he said, "please, we're in this together – please..."

Adam looked at Ira and said, "What do you think?"

"Shoot him, he's a liability."

Adam pulled back the hammer on his pistol and raised it.

Hicks covered his face and pleaded, "Please, no..."

Adam held the gun in place for a few seconds and then lowered the hammer back onto the percussion plate. He said, "Get up."

Hicks got up.

Adam kicked the dropped pistol to one side and said, "Can we all trust you?"

"Yessir, Yessir, you can..."

Adam turned to everybody else and said, "It's up to you boys."

Nobody spoke.

"Seems like nobody's willing to take your side big mouth..." Adam pulled back the hammer again.

Hicks dropped to his knees and said, *"Please, I beg you, I'm sorry for my remark, I won't go letting anybody down…"*

Adam lowered the hammer again and said, "Right get up." As Hicks stood up he grabbed the front of his tunic and nearly lifted him to his toes. He leaned right into his face and said, "One slip, one tiny remark, and I'll let it be known that you were the one responsible for the loss of the gold, and you'll have every lawman and reb soldier from here to Tennessee on your tail. Do you understand?"

Hicks nodded.

Adam held his steely gaze for a few seconds longer and then let go.

Ira looked at the nervous faces of Hicks's companions and said, "The same goes for you boys. Do you understand too?"

The three young men all nodded.

The air crackled with tension for a few seconds, and then Adam looked out of the window and saw that they were about to arrive at Florence railroad station. He turned back to Hicks and said, "Do we have an understanding?"

"We do," said Hicks.

Adam hesitated, and then said, "Okay, you know what you have to do. Let's get about it."

The train ground to a halt.

Hicks picked up his gun and went with his three associates to their guard positions around the rear coach.

Adam and Ira stepped out of the carriage and saw the engineer walking towards them.

"You boys take your job seriously," said the engineer, nodding to the four soldiers on duty.

"We sure do," said Adam. "How long before we're on the move again?"

The engineer said, "As soon as we fill the tender and take on water we'll be off; should be no more than half an hour or so."

Adam turned to Ira and said, "Right Corporal, I'm off to the telegraph office to inform Wilmington that we've arrived safely at Florence. You stay here with the detail."

Ira saluted and said, "Very good sir."

Adam nodded and walked towards the telegraph office. His heart was beating ten-to-the-dozen and he wasn't sure if it was nervousness or the thrill of excitement.

He'd felt the same on each occasion he'd been faced with danger – even when he was a boy – and though the sensation usually carried a dire warning with it, he was still elevated by it.

Thirty minutes later, the train lurched forwards. Hicks and his three associates stood by to leap off as it cleared the confines of Florence railroad station.

They watched as the train gathered speed until one of Hicks' men said, "Damn it Ezra, we're gonna break something if it goes any faster."

No sooner had the man spoken when everybody heard a loud bang. They rushed to the carriage windows and looked out. Dead ahead was a left-hand curve, concealed by a large storage shed.

"What was it?" said Ira.

"No idea," said Adam.

Seconds later they heard another bang.

"That was from the line," said one of the men.

"Is somebody trying to blow us up?" said Hicks.

"Bang!"

They looked again.

Ira said, "That was on the line too."

Seconds later, they felt the train slow down. It turned the bend, cleared the storage shed, and then they saw a troop of Confederate soldiers signalling for the engineer to stop.

"Holy Mother!" said Hicks, "what's this?"

Adam said, "Remain calm. When the train stops, take up your positions around the carriage and wait for my orders."

The train stopped. Hicks and his men jumped out and took up their guard positions. Adam and Ira waited by the carriage.

A Confederate Colonel rode up and dismounted.

Adam saluted and said, "Is there a problem sir?"

The Colonel returned the salute and said, "I am Lieutenant Colonel Ambrosio José Gonzales, and I am here to relieve you of this duty."

Adam said, "It is an honour to meet you sir, your exploits for the Confederacy are legendary, but I must insist on seeing some documentation to back up your order."

Gonzales turned, snapped his fingers, and a young Lieutenant rushed forwards.

"Get my bag," he said.

The Lieutenant got the bag and handed it over.

Gonzales extracted an official looking document, and Adam recognised the Presidential Seal in the top right-hand corner.

"These have been signed by President Davis, instructing me to relieve you of this duty, outside of Florence railroad depot."

Adam looked at the paperwork, verified Gonzales's claim and noted that the date of the orders was the same as the date of his Presidential Orders. He handed them back and said, "I don't understand sir, why wasn't I instructed to hand over this command in my orders, and why the deception?"

"Nobody is questioning your loyalty Capitan Holdsworth; this is just a small part of a much bigger plan, and even I do not know all of it."

Adam nodded and said, "I understand. So what are my orders now sir?"

"You and your men are to return to your individual units."

Adam raised his eyebrows and said, "Very well, thank you sir."

Gonzales said, "So now, the only thing left to do is to verify your cargo. Do you have the key to the carriage?"

Adam's heart rate went through the roof. He put his hand in his pocket, retrieved the key, and handed it over.

Ira looked at the number of Confederate soldiers and realised that they would not survive any kind of confrontation. He prayed that Adam would pull them through it – as usual.

"Come with me Capitan," said Gonzales.

Adam didn't know what to think. He wondered if Weims had double-crossed them, or if anybody else had been onto them. He considered the possibility that Gonzales might be playing out a part in order to trap him. The escape options shot through his mind like quicksilver, and he too concluded that even with Ira and Hicks's men, they would not survive an armed confrontation with the Colonel's troops.

Gonzales walked to the carriage, didn't say anything about the huge red cross, and took hold of the padlock. He lifted it up, and was about to insert the key, when he stopped and looked closer.

Adam's heart was beating so quickly that he thought he'd pass out.

"Oh… " said Gonzales, "…I see that you have not broken the security seal."

Adam was confused; he hadn't looked at the padlock and he didn't know what Gonzales was talking about. He said, "Sir?"

"The Confederate security seal on the padlock Capitan – I see that you haven't broken it."

Adam said, "No sir, I saw no need."

"So you weren't curious about the contents of the carriage?"

Adam stepped closer and said, "I am aware of the contents Colonel, but this carriage has been guarded by hand-picked men since it arrived in Charleston. I saw no need."

Gonzales said, "Hmm, admirable sentiments Capitan." He looked deep into Adam's eyes and then looked at the padlock again. He hung onto it for a few seconds and then let it go.

"Very well Capitan Holdsworth," he said, "you are relieved of this duty. You may return to your unit."

If Adam could have got hold of Ned right then, he'd have kissed him. He didn't know how his brother had managed to put a Confederate seal on the padlock, but he had.

He snapped to attention, saluted, and said, "Thank you sir, and good luck with the rest of the trip."

"Thank you, but luck plays no part in this endeavour. It is all about planning."

Ira looked sideways and could have choked.

Adam turned to Ira, said, "All right Corporal, recall your men, they are relieved."

Gonzales said, "My Lieutenant will provide you with horses for your individual journeys Capitan." He bowed his head and added, "Vaya con Dios."

"Adam said, "Thank you sir," saluted once again, and walked away with his heart still hammering in his mouth.

Chapter 43

The metal door was raised until it was vertical, Taffy steadied it, and everybody else looked down. Nothing was there except natural soil.

The two men lifted the door out of the hole and laid it down nearby.

Spencer inspected the exposed surface and then stepped down onto it. He looked around, picked up one or two stones, and then said, "Nothing." He looked up at Jake and said, "Okay, another six inches."

Jake manoeuvred the digger and then removed six inches of soil.

Spencer stepped down again, found nothing, and asked Jake to remove another three inches.

The process was repeated, and once again Spencer called up to Jake, "Okay, another three… "

"Stop!"

Everybody turned and looked at Naomi.

"Do you mind if I make a suggestion?"

Spencer said, "No, be my guest."

Naomi stepped closer to the hole and said, "Using my logic about the steps on the other side, we can see that if they'd been here, we would have seen evidence of them here by now – but we haven't. So if we're considering the possibility of an escape tunnel, wouldn't it have descended at roughly the same thirty to forty degree angle?"

Spencer turned and looked at the northeastern side of the burial vault and said, "But we aren't excavating a tunnel or the vault, we're looking for a burial."

Naomi said, "In my humble opinion, the door changes everything."

Spencer saw that the edge of the dig was no further than six feet from the burial vault and said, "I see, so if that door led to steps down, and they descended at forty-five degrees, then the roof of the tunnel would have to be at least another four feet down from here?" He pointed to the southwestern end of the hole.

Naomi said, "Yes; and if we are right, it's unlikely that there will be a burial where we are looking."

"Because the tunnel would have gone straight through it," said Peter.

"Yes, and our nineteenth century ancestors fervently believed in the sanctity of the grave."

Del, who was watching the proceedings with growing concern, said, "I wouldn't put money on an escape tunnel being there."

Everybody turned and looked.

"Why?" said Spencer.

"Because of the water table; if the top of the tunnel is six feet down, then the bottom of it is at least another five feet down. That would make the whole thing well below it, and it would have flooded in a very short time."

"Unless it was sealed with asphalt the same as the vault," said Peter.

"Or maybe, if there is a tunnel there – that could have been why it was sealed up?" said Spencer.

Del didn't know what to say. He shrugged and said, "Maybe…"

"The point is," said Bonnie-Mae, "if our English friend is correct, we're digging in the wrong place." She turned and looked at Naomi and said, "Isn't that right ma'am?"

Naomi said, "Yes it is, and my name is Naomi, Sheriff."

Bonnie-Mae nodded and said, "Thank you ma'am." She turned to Spencer and said, "We should be digging up against the northeastern side of the vault."

Spencer looked up at Marshall and said, "That would be up to Reverend Hughes."

Marshall looked at his watch and saw that it was 10:50am; he knew that the meeting with the churchwardens started at 11am, and he didn't like being pressured into making spur-of-the-moment decisions, but he knew that the meeting could take over an hour. He looked from face-to-face, saw the looks of anticipation, and said, "I can't see what harm it would do under the circumstances."

"Excellent," said Spencer.

Half an hour later, Taffy had marked out a three-foot wide strip running the full width of the burial vault, in red marker dye, and everybody waited with baited breath.

Spencer surveyed the area and then called, "Okay Jake, three inches."

Jake manoeuvred the digger to the edge of the plot and pushed the lever controlling the mechanical arm. It snaked out, reached the far end, and descended. He drove it three inches into the soil, and then retracted it.

Everybody watched as the topsoil curled into the bucket.

Spencer examined the exposed surface, stepped down, and pressed the point of his trowel into the soil near the vault. He looked at Jake and said, "Okay, another three inches."

Jake pushed the lever forwards once again, and the mechanical arm snaked out. He drove it another three inches into the ground, and then pulled the lever backwards.

As the bucket approached the vault, everybody heard a crunching sound.

Jake stopped the movement, lifted it, and swung it out of the way.

Spencer stepped into the hole, knelt down near the vault, and started to clear soil with his small hand trowel. Seconds later, he looked up and said, "We got something…"

Del was horrified; his plan was going wrong – again. He closed his eyes and cursed his run of bad luck. He had hoped that by the end of the day, nothing would have been found and that anything to do with the vault would have been put well and truly to bed, but like everything else, since he'd decided to steal the ruby, it had gone to hell in the proverbial handcart.

He'd received a call from Muz warning him to be at the church at midnight or he'd face the consequences, and the only comfort he had was that Janet had gone to stay with her sister after being released from the hospital following her ordeal.

He looked across at the tunnel site, shook his head, and wondered how many more things could go wrong.

Naomi opened her mouth to say something, but then felt an intense pain on her left shoulder. She gathered that it was something to do with the new excavation, but it wasn't accompanied by any sound.

She reached up to her shoulder and began to rub it.

"Looks sore honey."

Naomi turned and saw Jackie, the warden, standing behind her. She said, "It is."

"Then why don't you let me fix one of my momma's herbal remedies for you? I have all the ingredients in the parish house and it won't take but half an hour to fix."

Naomi smiled and said, "That's very kind of you, but I wouldn't want to put you to any trouble."

"It's no trouble at all. We all used to swear by momma's remedies, and before she passed into the Lord's hands, all the neighbours and kinsfolk used to come to her with their ailments."

Naomi frowned and said, "Aren't you supposed to be in the meeting with Father Marshall and the other churchwardens?"

"Not on this occasion." Jackie looked around and then leaned closer. She said, "I suspect that I am one of the subjects of the meeting."

Naomi raised her eyebrows and said, "Good I hope?"

Jackie smiled and said, "I hope so. It's my birthday next week, and I think that they're planning some sort of soirée for me, because it's also my fifteenth year at St. Andrew's too."

"Oh, congratulations on both counts."

"Thank you dear – now you wait here and I'll be back in two shakes of a lamb's tail."

Naomi watched as Jackie headed towards the parish house; something had triggered in her brain and she wondered if she was right.

Jackie stepped into the parish house, and straight away the moaning started.

Naomi frowned, walked across to the excavation site, and tried to home in on the exact place from where the sounds were coming.

Spencer saw her looking and said, "I think that you were right, this looks like something substantial." He nodded to the side of the vault.

Naomi smiled, and continued to sweep her gaze from side-to-side, hoping to intensify or decrease the sound as she looked. But despite her best effort, she couldn't identify one particular place from another.

Taffy noticed Naomi rubbing her shoulder, and said, "You okay English?"

Naomi looked up and said, "Yes, I think so, I get plagued by shoulder twinges every now and then, but today seems to be worse than most."

"Can I get you an aspirin or something?"

"No thanks, Jackie's gone to the parish house to get me one of her mother's herbal remedies."

"Not anything you could get off a shelf at Boots then," said Taffy with a smile on his face.

"No, I guess not!"

"Taffy – can you fetch me a shovel please?"

Taffy turned when he heard Spencer. He called, "Sure, two seconds…" he turned back to Naomi and said, "Are you sure that I can't get you anything?"

"Yes, I am fine thanks – you go."

Taffy smiled and headed for the works van.

Naomi looked as she heard Bonnie-Mae ask Spencer, "Any of it making sense?" but before she heard him reply, her phone buzzed again.

She took it out of her bag and saw that she'd received a text. She opened it up and saw the single word, 'Tyson' sent from an undisclosed sender. Her heart rate increased and the already painful pressure on her shoulder intensified.

She walked away from the dig, perched down on a nearby seat, and took out her notebook. She wrote down, 'California' and 'Tyson' and placed three large question marks behind them.

She knew that something was wrong, and then, in her head, she heard a desperate female voice say, *"The mound! The mound! – Get out quick…"* She wheeled around and looked at the dig. The moaning stopped. She jumped to her feet, ran back to the site, and looked at everything as though her life depended upon it. She was staring with such intensity that she didn't hear anybody approach, and then a voice said, "Here you are my dear, try this."

She whipped around and saw Jackie standing with a glass in her hand. She didn't know which way to look, at Jackie or the dig.

She ignored Jackie and stared at the ground, but that was it – it was the ground. It wasn't a mound, it was flat...

"Honey?" said Jackie.

Naomi turned around and looked at Jackie in such a way that she saw the look of concern appear on her face.

"Whatever is bothering you so?" said Jackie.

Naomi didn't know what to say; she turned and looked at the dig and realised that whatever she'd experienced had passed, and that it wasn't anything to do with the present excavation.

She turned back to Jackie and said, "I'm sorry, I didn't mean to be rude but I was trying to figure something out."

Jackie smiled and said, "It's fine – now why don't you drink this and see if it helps?"

Naomi thanked her, took a sip, and said, "Mmm, it tastes like honey with something in it."

"Honey is the main ingredient, but it's the other things that should help you."

Naomi took another sip and said, "Can I ask you a personal question?"

"Sure, I have nothing to hide."

"Are you from Charleston?"

"No, I came here fifteen years ago after the last of my family passed away, and now the folk of St. Andrew's are my family."

Naomi smiled and said, "That's nice."

"Yes," said Jackie, "I couldn't have been made more welcome. It felt like I fitted in right away; and because I have lots of free time, I'm happy to get involved with the events and socials we put on here. And I do believe I've become a permanent fixture in that kitchen!"

Naomi smiled and sipped more of the herbal drink. She said, "This is really good..." she paused and then said, "did you come here because of the climate?"

Jackie smiled and said, "If I'd have wanted nice weather, I'd have gone to Florida! No, I came to Charleston because way back in history my family originated from here, so when I had the choice, I thought that it would be good to come back to my roots."

Something clicked in Naomi's mind; a wild idea that she wouldn't share with anybody else. She said, "So, do you know of any remaining family connections with Charleston?"

"Just the one," said Jackie. "Off King Street, between Price's Alley and Ladson Street, there's a small street supposedly named after my great great great grandfather, who settled here after the Civil War."

"Oh wow," said Naomi, "I'll have to look out for it before I leave. What's the name of it?"

"It's…"

"Naomi!"

Naomi turned and saw Spencer indicating for her to join him. She turned to Jackie and handed the empty glass back. She said, "Sorry Jackie, I have to go, can I get back to you later on?"

Jackie smiled and nodded towards the parish house. She said, "Sure – you'll know where to find me."

"Of course, in the kitchen – and thanks for the drink, it was very nice."

"It was my pleasure," said Jackie.

Chapter 44

Naomi walked across to the dig site and saw the look of excitement on Spencer's face. She looked into the hole and saw that he'd exposed what appeared to be roof support timbers.

"Man, if this isn't some sort of tunnel I'll eat my hat," said Spencer. "I haven't ever come across anything like it before, and it's ticking all of my happy boxes!"

"I can see that from your face," said Naomi. She turned to Peter and said, "And you had no idea that this was here?"

"None – and we've done extensive stabilising work here. As I told you before, we completely dismissed the idea when the English author guy put it to us, because of the water table."

Naomi looked at the exposed timbers; they were approximately six inches wide, by four-and-a-half feet long. Spencer had exposed eight of them, but he hadn't attempted to see how thick they were. She guessed that at least six inches on each end would have been used to secure them, making the tunnel – if there was one – three-feet-six-inches wide at best. Being mildly claustrophobic, she shivered at the thought of having to traverse somewhere that narrow underground.

"Here we go," said Spencer, "it's descending."

Naomi looked and saw that he'd cleaned the earth off the ninth timber, and that it wasn't flat like the others, but canted down.

Spencer cleared the soil from the tenth and saw that it canted down at the same angle. He looked up and said, "Taffy, can you go to the van and fetch the crowbar and large trowel?"

Taffy nodded and walked across to the van.

Naomi edged closer, looked at the angle of the timbers and said, "Thirty degrees…"

"My guess too," said Taffy, "which would mean that it will have to keep going down at this angle for another twelve feet, to get six feet of earth above it?"

"Correct, and even at that depth it could have been prone to collapse."

Spencer looked up and added, "Not if they timber-lined it properly."

"In which case the tunnel's got to be flooded," said Naomi.

Spencer frowned and said, "If the roof timbers go down another six feet, and the tunnel itself is five or six feet high, it must have been some operation – so maybe not."

Naomi said, "You can't line timber planks with asphalt."

Spencer considered his answer and said, "Hmm, I don't know. Our ancestors were an ingenious lot, I'll bet they would have given it a good go." He looked at Naomi and said, "Let's expose a few more timbers and then we'll lift a couple to see what's underneath." He turned towards the van and shouted, *"Taff! Can you bring the flashlight too?"*

The word "flashlight" had everybody crowding around the dig site – all of the SCDHEC workmen, Bonnie-Mae, Del, Jackie, Alan, and Debbie.

Bonnie-Mae said, "I have my camera in the patrol car, do you want it?"

"No thank you Sheriff, if I need it, I have one in my car." Spencer looked at everybody once Taffy had handed over the lamp and tools, and said, "Right, let's see what's here."

Using the trowel, he scraped the earth from between the sixth and seventh timber until he was satisfied that he'd reached the right depth. He then reached for a crowbar with a ninety-degree bend at one end. With the straight end he prised the timbers apart, and then lowered the angled end between them. He twisted it so that it hooked below the timber, and then exerted an upwards pressure. The plank began to lift. He stopped, slid the crowbar along another foot, and repeated the procedure. The plank lifted some more. He then extracted the crowbar, and scraped the earth away from the opposite side. He inserted the angled end of the crowbar halfway along, exerted the upwards pressure, and the whole timber lifted out of its one-hundred-and-forty-three-year-old resting place.

At a nod from Spencer, Taffy took the timber and laid it down to one side.

"Can you see anything?" said an eager Alan.

Spencer looked up and said, "We'll remove three, and then have a good look."

One-by-one the timbers were lifted, and even before the last one was up, Spencer and Taffy were getting excited.

Spencer couldn't help himself; he turned and beamed at Naomi. He said, "It's a tunnel okay! And I don't know what it's like at the bottom of the steps, but it's bone-dry here!"

The pressure on Naomi's shoulder was intense. Jackie's herbal remedy hadn't helped, but she knew that it wouldn't. No moaning ensued from the dig, and she turned to see if Jackie was still there.

She was.

With a big grin on his face, Spencer switched on the flashlight and checked to see that it was working okay. He then laid flat on his stomach and aimed the light into the tunnel.

A few seconds ensued, and then those closest to Spencer heard him make an odd sound. He appeared to slither forwards a few inches as though he wanted to get a better view; he made another grunting sound, and then slithered forwards some more. Then without warning, his body shot forwards, and disappeared over the edge. Everybody heard him fall with a thud and make a gasping sound.

Taffy shrieked, "Jesus Christ... " He looked up at one of the workmen and said, "Quick Mal, get the other flashlight!" He then looked into the hole and yelled, *"Spencer! Spencer, are you okay?"*

No response.

"Spencer – Spencer – can you hear me?"

Mal ran back and handed the flashlight over.

Taffy looked into the hole and said, "I can see him." He looked back at Mal and said, "Get the ladders." He then wrenched three more roof support timbers away and threw them to one side.

Mal lowered the ladders into the hole, and watched as Taffy descended.

Bonnie-Mae had retrieved her flashlight from the patrol car, and joined Mal as Taffy descended. She called, "Be careful down there, and watch where you're putting your feet."

Taffy reached the bottom which was six feet down, and noted that the tunnel was about four feet wide. He switched on the flashlight, looked down, and saw Spencer at the bottom of a flight of steps. "Spencer," he said, "Spencer, are you okay?" He saw Spencer stir, and walked down until he reached the penultimate step. He stopped dead as he saw the skeletal remains of a human hand.

Spencer came to, opened his eyes, and rubbed the back of his neck.

Taffy said, "Are you okay?"

Spencer looked up and said, "I think so…"

"What happened – one minute you were looking in the hole, the next you were gone!"

Spencer said, "It was weird. I started looking around, and then it felt as though something grabbed my throat and started to choke me. I wriggled a bit thinking that I'd trapped my shirt or something, but the more I moved the tighter it got, suddenly the pressure increased, and over I went." He rubbed the back of his head and said, "I must have hit my head 'cos I don't remember the rest."

"Are you guys okay?"

Taffy looked up and saw Bonnie-Mae looking in.

"I heard you talking and figured that you didn't need the paramedics – is that right?"

"It is Sheriff," said Taffy, "Spencer's a bit knocked about, but he's okay." He looked at Spencer and said, "You are okay aren't you?"

Spencer grimaced, altered his position, and said, "A few bruises maybe, but yeah, I'm okay."

Taffy said, "Look at this." He aimed the torchlight at the skeletal remains of the hand.

Spencer leaned around and said, "That's what I'd seen when I looked in, only it was a whole skeleton…" He looked behind him, retrieved his flashlight, and tried switching it on – nothing happened. He said, "This lamp's had it, hand me yours." He swivelled it behind him and saw a jumbled mass of bones, and fragments of badly decayed clothing.

"Shit," he said, "I've made a mess of this haven't I?"

Taffy said, "Looks like it." He looked around and said, "I'm amazed how dry it is down here, can you see anything further down?"

Spencer lifted the torch up and shone it down the tunnel. He said, "Holy Mother of God! What the hell's happened here?"

Taffy was shocked too, he said, "Stone me, I wasn't expecting that…"

Strewn out, as far as the limited light from the lamp extended, the two colleagues saw the skeletal remains of another three people lying on the floor, draped in fragments of clothing.

Taffy said, "Shall we take a closer look?"

"No, I've screwed up enough forensic evidence by falling on this character; let's not screw up any more. We'll open up more of the roof timbers and do it by the book."

Taffy watched the arc of light dancing at the end of its range as Spencer talked, and then he saw something. He said, "Hang on – pass me the flashlight." He took the lamp and aimed it down the tunnel. Something glinted in the gloom. He said, "There – did you see that?"

"Yes I did."

Taffy held the lamp steady and said, "Can you make out what it is?"

Spencer said, "Try adjusting the focus."

Taffy gripped the torch lens and swivelled it around.

The arc of light narrowed.

"Right, try again."

Taffy held the flashlight up and saw further down the tunnel. Without thinking he said, "Fuck… "

"Is that another body?"

"It is."

"Can you see what was glinting?"

Taffy lowered the narrow arc of light and swept it from left to right as he retracted the beam along the tunnel floor. Something flashed, and he held the lamp steady. He turned to Spencer and said, "Good grief, is that what I think it is?"

Chapter 45

At 10am seven 'Confederate soldiers' arrived at the depot.

Weims, resplendent in his Captain's uniform marched into the depot manager's office and presented his orders. He also held his breath.

The clerk read the orders, said, "Siding Six," and handed them back without looking up.

Weims couldn't believe his luck; he walked out with his instructions and couldn't credit that nobody had noticed that the goods coach from siding number six had gone, whilst the coach in number four was still there.

He climbed aboard the wagon and signalled for the men to proceed. He knew that apart from his wagon driver, a long-time associate named Able Vanhoose, an irascible Dutchman, that the five other 'conscripts' had been hired for this purpose alone, and couldn't even question about being taken to siding number four.

He patted the left-hand pocket of his tunic for the umpteenth time to make sure that the key was still there.

They arrived at the siding, and noticed that nobody else was around.

Weims hopped down from the wagon, and walked across to the goods coach, inserted the key in the padlock, and opened it. He cast the chain to one side, and then opened the sliding door. Thirteen boxes sat in the middle of the coach floor, two-abreast, two-deep, with one on top.

Weims was shocked into temporary immobility. Adam had informed him that there would be seven boxes, each containing two, twenty-five pound bars of gold. Now here he was, staring at thirteen boxes. He didn't know what to say, and he didn't know what to do. His mind went into overdrive.

'Had he gone to the right siding?' – But he knew that he had. He stepped back and looked around, just the same. 'Had he got the right coach?' – The key had fitted the padlock. 'Was there double the amount of gold now? Was it even gold still in the boxes?'

He knew that he hadn't the time to start breaking boxes open and looking. He turned to Vanhoose and said, "Okay Able, get the boxes onto the wagon, and make sure they're covered with the tarpaulin."

"Right – *sir*," said Vanhoose with a grin on his face.

When they'd finished loading the wagon, Weims checked that he was happy with the tarpaulin, and then as an afterthought, closed the goods coach door, re-threaded the chain through the handles, and padlocked it.

Five minutes later they departed the depot.

By 2pm, everything had gone like clockwork. Weims had met Lucius and Jacob at the Quarter House Tavern. They'd ridden to the Prioleau Estate and the boat had been waiting for them, thanks to Jim.

Following a quick check, he'd established that one box held two gold bars and that the others contained gold coins. He'd also worked out by weight, that each of the boxes of coins contained ten thousand dollars.

Prior to crossing the Ashley River, and in line with Adam's instructions, he'd overseen the distribution. He'd given Jim a box and a box each to Lucius and Jacob for their families. He'd given Bart, who'd been staying at the Prioleau place, a box for himself, one for Ned, one for Adam, and one for Ira. He'd then set aside one box to be shared by Vanhoose and his 'conscripted' men, and one for him. That left the three boxes of coins and two gold bars that had to be transported up the escape tunnel to St. Andrew's and given to Reverend Drayton to put into the vault. .

Following a late lunch at the Prioleau estate they parted company. Lucius and Jacob crossed Bees Ferry and headed back to pick up granny and the rest of the workers from the Prevost Plantation and Bart took a small wagon that Jim had given to him and headed off along the Fort Dorchester Road with his boxes to meet Adam, Ned, and Ira.

Weims finally shook hands with Jim Prioleau and said, "Thanks partner, I hope that you survive the conflict."

Jim smiled and said, "I'll try." He then said, "Are you sure where you're going?"

"Yes, I checked it out last Monday with Reverend Drayton."

"Excellent, then good luck, and watch out for the current, it can run fast on the ebb tide."

Weims said goodbye and walked down to the boat. It was bigger than he thought.

Vanhoose, and the five 'soldiers' held an oar each and their share of the gold was stacked with the remaining boxes in the bottom of the boat.

Weims climbed aboard, and was then rowed to their destination at the top of Church Creek.

"Right," he said, pointing to a spot on the ground, "I'm going to light the lamps along the tunnel, while you guys unload the boat. Take the boxes to that spot over there, and don't enter the tunnel until I get back, got it?"

The men nodded and set about their tasks.

Weims walked across to the concealed trapdoor, cleared away some foliage, and opened it. He then parted a thicket and retrieved a thick branch around which he'd wrapped some oily rags. He lit it, cast a last glance around, and then went down the steps into the tunnel.

As he lit the oil lamps along the tunnel wall he marvelled at its construction. It was rock-solid, bone dry, and a real testament to somebody's mining and construction skills.

One-by-one the lamps illuminated the way until he felt the ground start to rise, he then stopped, and didn't light any more. He didn't want anything shedding light on his, and Vanhoose's handiwork of the previous week.

Holding the torch in front of him, he reached the steps at the far end of the tunnel, walked up, and saw the solid wall of timbers dead ahead. He couldn't begin to comprehend how the men would feel once they realised that they were trapped in, with no way out, and he quickly put it out of his mind.

He retraced his steps, and before stepping out into daylight, made sure that the fuse lines that he and Vanhoose had installed were out of sight.

He emerged into the South Carolina sunshine and drew in a deep breath. The tunnel was four feet wide and five-feet-six-inches high, but it still felt too claustrophobic.

He saw the men waiting for instructions and said, "Right, give me one of the bars out of that box. That'll be for Reverend Drayton tomorrow morning."

"Yeah, very Reverend," said one of the men, "I expect he'll be besides us when we get to Heaven won't he boys?"

The men laughed.

Weims could see that they were beginning to enjoy the thought of getting their hands on their shares.

"All right," he said once he'd been handed the bar, "there's three boxes and one bar to go up the tunnel to the church. In case we get any snoopers, I'll guard the boat and Vanhoose can guard our shares, you five guys take the rest up the tunnel."

The men nodded and set about picking up the gold.

Weims watched until they were about to depart and then said, "Guys – wait." He saw that one man was carrying the bar, and that the other four were holding the three boxes between them. He said, "I've just had a thought, leave one of those boxes here, and one of you go ahead with the torch in case any of the lamps has gone out. It can get mighty dark and spooky in there."

The smallest guy, a scrawny nineteen-year-old said, "I'll take the torch!"

"And whoever volunteers to do the return trip with the last box gets free drinks all night tonight, right boys?"

A cheer went up and nods of agreement were passed around.

The torch bearer lit his torch, and one-by-one they disappeared into the tunnel.

Weims snatched his pocket watch out, looked at Vanhoose, and said, "Two minutes."

Vanhoose ran across to a thicket, retrieved a second, smaller torch, and lit it. He stared at Weims waiting for the signal.

Weims watched the second-hand reach twelve and then said, "Go!"

Vanhoose went to the tunnel, took two steps down, and faltered. He thought about the five guys and what would happen to them. He looked down the steps and then back at Weims.

"Go on!" said Weims.

Vanhoose looked down the steps once more and said, "I can't, it isn't…" He stopped speaking when he saw that he was looking down the barrel of a handgun. He looked back at Weims and said, "What are you doing?"

"Go and light the fuses!"

"I can't – we can't do that to the men, they have as much right to a share as we do…"

Weims's face contorted into a snarl. He said, "This is your last chance Vanhoose. Light the fuses."

"I can't…"

Underground, the sound of the shot echoed along the passage. The two men at the back stopped and turned. One said, "What was that?"

The other said, "It sounded like a shot."

A shout went up from the man carrying the torch. He said, "Where's the door?"

"What?" said the second in-line, "What are you talking about?"

"The door," said the scrawny nineteen-year-old, "where is it?"

The second man put down his box, walked up the steps to the torch bearer, and peered over his shoulder

The torch bearer turned and said, "Look." He held the torch in front of him. He waived it about from side-to-side and said, "Where is it? Vanhoose said that the door to the church was here."

"The second man looked at the wall of solid timbers and then the penny dropped. He yelled, "No! It looks like we've been had boys! Quick, get back to the other end!"

The confused men dropped their loads, and began to run back.

At the other end, Weims pulled Vanhoose's body down the steps, and uncovered the fuse lines. He heard footsteps and shouts as the men ran back towards him. He snatched the last fuse line out of its hiding place and jammed the torch under it. Within seconds it spluttered into life. He ran back towards the exit and lit the other three on the way. He then ran up the steps, threw the torch to the ground, and slammed the trapdoor shut.

In the tunnel the first man felt the ground start to incline and then saw something glowing in the distance. He stopped dead and the others almost piled into his back.

"What's that?" said one of the men.

The first man turned, opened his mouth to speak, and was then blown off his feet by the force of the first explosion.

Three more explosions followed in quick succession and a huge pall of dust engulfed the doomed men as they lay on the tunnel floor with screaming ears.

One-by-one they opened their eyes and saw nothing but stark and terrifying blackness. The blast had expelled every lamp in the tunnel.

Above ground, Weims let the rumbling subside and then waited in silence until he was sure that nobody was coming to investigate. He then covered the trapdoor with foliage, and secreted the gold bar and two boxes of coins in nearby bushes.

He smiled to himself. He had more than enough for the present, and he knew where to go if he needed more.

Everything had gone perfectly.

Chapter 46

00:30am Tuesday 28th November 2006. Sheriff Bonnie-Mae Clement's Apartment

Bonnie-Mae lay wide awake in bed.

Work permitting, she tried to be in bed before midnight, and within seconds she would be asleep. But something was playing on her mind.

Two weeks' earlier, on the 14th November, the psychic, Helene Gibsonne de Lyon had informed her that her gold cross, the one that had belonged to her mother, was in the filter of her sister Darlene's swimming pool. She hadn't known how to react, and she hadn't said anything in return, but she'd visited Darlene, and had been given the cross. She'd been told that it had been found in the filter of the swimming pool, which may not have been such a wild stretch, except that she hadn't been in the pool before she'd lost it.

Nobody had been able to explain how it had got there. Darlene's two children had been questioned by their parents and they'd denied ever knowing about the cross let alone taking it and dropping it in the pool. The only conclusion that she'd been able to draw was that the chain must have come undone, because it wasn't broken, and had somehow become entangled or stuck to somebody's footwear and been launched or dropped into the pool.

Regardless of the plethora of how's, why's, and wherefores, one simple question remained. How on earth did Helene Gibsonne de Lyon know where it was?

She laid there with the cross between her forefinger and thumb and couldn't come up with a single rational explanation.

She glanced up at the face of her digital clock and saw that it was 12:38am. She let go of the cross, shut her eyes, and turned over onto her right side.

The phone rang.

She cursed, switched on her light, picked up the phone and said, "Clement."

"Bonnie-Mae, it's Beau, I'm sorry to disturb you but we just had an unusual phone call from that psychic."

Bonnie-Mae sat up, unable to believe that she'd spent the last half hour or more thinking about her. She said, "The de Lyon woman?"

"Yes ma'am."

"At this time in the morning? – What kind of unusual call?"

"She wants you to go to St. Andrew's now."

"What? Now? What kind of stupid request is that?"

"She didn't stop to explain," said Beau.

"What do you mean?"

"She put the phone down."

Bonnie-Mae drew in a deep breath and tried to calm herself. She said, "Okay, start from the beginning and tell me everything that she said."

"The phone rang in the office less than five minutes ago. I answered and Helene Gibsonne de Lyon told me who she was. She said she had an urgent message for you. I asked if it could do in the morning, as you were probably asleep. She said, no, it was urgent. She said if you argued with me, I was to say to you, 'You got the cross back okay – now go to St. Andrew's.'

Does that make any sense to you?"

A shiver ran down Bonnie-Mae's spine because she'd just picked up the cross that afternoon. She said, "Have you sent anybody to the church?"

"No ma'am, I rang you first."

Bonnie-Mae looked at the clock; it was 12:47am. She said, "All right, I'll go. Who's on patrol?"

"Wayne Parker."

"Okay, tell him to meet me at Church Creek Mall and tell him not to pass the church on the way there. I'll see him in fifteen."

"Okay, thank you Sheriff – sorry to disturb you."

At 1:05am Bonnie-Mae pulled alongside Parker's patrol car in Church Creek Mall's car park.

Parker got out, leaned down to Bonnie-Mae's window, and said, "Here we are again, in the middle of the night, and heading back to St. Andrew's."

Bonnie-Mae raised her eyebrows and said, "What can I say?"

"You can tell me why you're here instead of your bed."

"It's complicated and I'll explain later. Right now we need to get to the church – we've had a tip-off."

Parker climbed in the passenger seat and said, "I sure hope it ain't like that night last May…"

Bonnie-Mae put the car into 'drive' and cruised as quietly as the engine would allow on the approach to the church, but before they'd got within one hundred yards of the drive, they could hear the distinctive sound of the mechanical digger's engine. She looked at Parker and said, "Send for back-up."

She let the car creep along the road with the lights off until it was blocking the drive from the church. She looked down it and could see three men. One was driving the digger, and two were standing nearby watching. They appeared to be excavating the trench that the SCDHEC men had sunk.

She looked at Parker and said, "Tell back-up to approach quietly, with their lights off, and to stay at least a hundred yards from the church drive. I want to see what these jokers are up to."

Down at the church, Del and Muz watched as Lennie scooped successive bucketful's of gooey sludge from the trench in the car park. They weren't being careful about where it was being dumped, and everywhere was a mess.

Del looked at the plumes of black smoke emitting from the exhaust of the digger and heard how noisy it sounded in the still night air. He shook his head and said, "This is crazy, it's suicidal, we shouldn't…"

Muz turned and grabbed Del by the lapels. He yanked him closer and said, "I've just about had it with you! From the day that we ran into you…"

"Yeah – literally," said Del.

"Shut the fuck up!" Muz glared into Del's eyes and then said, "I said – from the day that we ran into you you've been nothing but trouble! We've gone on wild goose chases, we've kidnapped people, and we've even killed two goddamned people since meeting you, and all because of you and that fucking ruby. So if

you think that we're leaving here tonight without it, you've got another think coming!"

Del opened his mouth to say something, but before he could speak, Muz slapped him across the face.

"Don't even speak to me asshole!" said Muz, "We're staying until we get that ruby, and that's it." He stared at Del for a few seconds and then pushed him away. "Now pick up one of those spades and start sifting through that shit in case the box has rotted and all that's left is the ruby."

"It's not necessary."

"What? What do you mean?"

"If the ruby's there, it'll still be in the box."

"What are you talking about – how do you know that?" said Muz.

"Because of the high water table. Wood can't rot in airless mud." He paused and then added, "It's made up of cellulose, hemicellulose, and lignin, and if the organisms that break it down can't get air, they can't do it. It's simple biology."

"And what if Lennie busted the box with the digger smart ass?"

"Then…" Del caught sight of something over Muz's left shoulder. He'd stared up the drive of St. Andrew's in all lights, day and night, and he knew every inch of it. Now it looked different; his alarm bells switched on.

"Then what?" said Muz.

Del looked back at Muz and his mind was so ablaze, he forgot what he was talking about. He said, "What?"

Muz said, "Wake up shit-for-brains! I said 'what if Lennie busts the box with the digger?'"

"Then we'd see busted fragments of it lying in the mud – and so far all we've seen is mud."

Muz looked at the mud splattered everywhere and said, "Well keep your fucking eyes peeled, and watch out for intruders?"

Del nodded and waited until Muz had turned away. He moved into a different position and looked up the drive from behind a tree. His heart nearly stopped – he saw the Sheriff's car blocking the entrance.

He looked back at Muz, watched him walk to the edge of the trench, and then look down into it with his torch. An idea started to form. He looked at Lennie and saw that he was engrossed in what he was doing.

He waited until Lennie was bringing the bucket down, and then without hesitation, ran across to Muz and slammed into his back.

Lennie couldn't believe his eyes. He saw Muz lurch forwards, hit the side of the descending bucket, and then fall underneath it. Man and bucket dropped into the trench and out of sight. As quick as a flash, he yanked at the lever to lift the bucket, but in panic, pulled at the wrong one, and withdrew it.

At the top of the drive Bonnie-Mae and Parker saw the sudden action. They leapt out of their car and started to run down the drive whilst unholstering their sidearms.

Lennie was panic-stricken. He looked down at the bucket and saw it drawing towards him in the trench. His mind went blank. He stared at the controls and saw his hands still in place, and then as if stung, he yelped and let go. He looked out of the cab window and saw the Deacon staring in the trench with his hands up to his mouth.

He leapt out and said, "What the fuck did you do that for?"

Bonnie-Mae and Parker raced around the bend and shouted, *"Police! Get down on the ground."*

Lennie spun around, saw two officers, and knew that the game was up. He turned to Del and said, "You treacherous bastard – you're going to pay for this…" He reached into his jacket for his handgun. He heard Bonnie-Mae yell, *"Raise your hands in the air now, or I'll fire!"*

Lennie ignored the call.

"Sir – this is your last warning. Get your hands in the air or I'll fire!"

Lennie grabbed the gun, and pulled it out of his pocket in blind hatred.

Bonnie-Mae fired and saw Lennie drop like a stone. She remained stock still for a couple of seconds and then approached the body whilst being covered by Parker. She kicked the dropped handgun to one side, knelt down next to Lennie, and saw that his eyes were half-open. She holstered her weapon, felt for a pulse, and then turned to Parker. She said, "He's dead."

Chapter 47

Naomi approached the drive in her hire car and saw police tape stretched across the entrance. She drove to the edge of the tape and saw a police officer from the Sheriff's department approach. She got out of her vehicle, and said, "My name's Naomi Wilkes, and I'm here with the team carrying out the excavation on the tunnel."

"Sorry ma'am, but not today. This is a crime scene and I'm not allowed to let anybody through until forensics have finished."

"A crime scene? What's happened?"

"I'm sorry, I'm not at liberty to discuss what's gone on here, but if you are part of the excavation team, I guess that you'll find out soon enough."

"Can you at least say what kind of crime was committed here?"

"Sorry ma'am."

"I only ask because I'm concerned that something may have been removed from the dig."

The police officer turned around when Naomi looked at the tunnel excavation site. He looked back at Naomi, leaned closer, and said, "If it's any comfort ma'am, none of this investigation concerns that dig over there."

Naomi frowned and said, "Oh – at least that's something then." She looked behind the police officer and felt a pressure exert itself on her left shoulder. At first she thought that her attention would be drawn to the tunnel area, but it wasn't, it was to the trench. She looked at the police officer, raised her eyebrows, and said, "One more question – please?"

The police officer hesitated and then said, "Ma'am?"

"Is this new investigation concerning the trench in the car park?"

The police officer's demeanour changed. He said, "Is there something that you're not telling me Ms Wilkes?"

"So it is?"

"I repeat – is there something that you're not telling me Ms Wilkes – something that we should be aware of?"

Naomi didn't know how to answer; she didn't want to say anything about her psychic feelings because she knew how much that offended religious folk. She said, "I am a professional archaeologist and if I can lend anything to the proceedings, I'd be glad to."

The police officer stared at Naomi for a second or two and then said, "Please wait here."

Naomi saw him walk away a few paces and speak to somebody on his personal radio.

A few seconds' later he returned and said, "The Sheriff says to let you through."

Naomi smiled, got back into her car, and drove under the tape as the police officer held it up. She saw the Sheriff waiting for her further up the drive.

Bonnie-Mae hadn't slept since arriving in the early hours, and was beginning to feel the effects. She watched as Naomi drove up, and stepped out of her car. She walked up to her and extended her hand. She said, "Ma-am – Naomi isn't it?"

"It is, please call me that."

Bonnie-Mae nodded and said, "Thank you for your offer of help."

"What's happened here?"

"We've had a double killing."

"My God…" Naomi saw the look of disapproval on Bonnie-Mae's face and said, "…sorry Sheriff." She then said, "Is it anybody we know?"

"Not you, but we do. The deceased were known criminals who were wanted for questioning over a series of crimes. Robbery, extortion, kidnapping, assault, aggravated sexual assault, and possibly murder. The list was extensive."

"Good grief! So what were they doing here, and how did they end up being killed?"

"One died when he was pushed under the bucket of the mechanical digger as it was being lowered into the pit, and I shot the other when he attempted to use his firearm."

Naomi looked across at the trench. The mechanical digger was stationary at one end with the arm raised, and mud was splattered everywhere. She looked at Bonnie-Mae and said, "What were they doing?"

"Now we get to the interesting bit. According to Deacon Morrison, they were looking for that ruby. El Fuego de Marte I recall."

"How does Deacon Morrison figure in all of this?"

"That's the second big question – and one that I intend to get to the bottom of."

Naomi frowned and said, "He wasn't here too was he?"

Bonnie-Mae looked at Naomi and said, "I see that I have kick-started that inquisitive mind of yours." She paused and then said, "But in answer to your question, yes, he was here. He was the person that could have been shot, if I hadn't acted as I did."

"But why were they digging here if the Deacon believed the old Matthews' grave to be over there?" Naomi glanced in the direction of the tunnel.

"According to Deacon Morrison, he went out of his home late last night to put out some garbage, and was grabbed by the two deceased who brought him here. They told him that they'd heard rumours of a rare and valuable ruby being buried here, and they forced him at gunpoint to tell them where. He said, that in order to preserve the integrity of the proper dig site, he told them that the Matthews' grave was below the trench."

"And they believed him? Two dangerous men drag an innocent church Deacon to a graveyard in the middle of the night – they presumably saw all of the paraphernalia around the proper dig site, yet the Deacon manages to convince them that the grave is situated below an excavated stormwater drain?"

"According to him – yes."

Naomi was aware of the pressure on her shoulder and the almost magnetic pull towards the trench. She looked at Bonnie-Mae and said, "In that case, he was either a very convincing liar, or he knows more than he is letting on."

"And I will be exploring that assertion to its fullest extent in the coming days." Bonnie-Mae looked at Naomi with slits of eyes and added, "But if you don't mind me saying ma'am, Naomi – I get the distinct feeling that you may know more than you are letting on too."

Naomi was impressed. She looked at the Sheriff and said, "Okay, you aren't going to like this, but I am psychic."

Bonnie-Mae's mouth fell open, and she looked straight down at the floor. She then turned around and started to walk away.

Naomi was shocked. She thought that she'd upset or offended the Sheriff. She watched, as Bonnie-Mae seemed to be wrestling with herself. She heard her say, "Hot damn!" and then saw her turn and walk back.

"All right," said Bonnie-Mae, "what have you got to say?"

Naomi hesitated and said, "Does this bother you Sheriff?"

"Everything about it bothers me ma'am, but I got to tell you – right now I don't know what to think about you guys and it's driving me plumb crazy."

"It's not something that I could easily accept," said Naomi, "and having the gift, if you can call it that, draws more scepticism and derision than thanks."

Bonnie-Mae looked down and then back up. She said, "Okay, let's have it."

"Would you mind if I walked over to the trench?"

Bonnie-Mae turned and looked. She saw the forensics team packing up, and she knew that both bodies had been removed. She said, "If you have a queasy stomach don't look in the trench, there's still, er – evidence in there."

Naomi nodded and said, "Okay." She walked towards the trench and almost at once, the odd feeling of being ushered overtook her. She stopped and said, "I can feel it now."

Bonnie-Mae stopped and said, "What?"

"A feeling as though I'm being pushed towards the trench."

"And have you ever had a feeling like it before?"

"Only here; everywhere else I hear voices, or see things. At this trench it feels as though I'm being guided somewhere."

"All right – why don't you just go with it and see where it takes us?"

Naomi nodded and let the feeling guide her. She walked across to the trench, then turned left and started to walk away from the church. The feeling pushed against her. She stopped, turned one-hundred-and-eighty degrees, and walked again. The feeling was behind her. She continued until she felt the pressure push against her from the front once more. She did another one-eighty, and walked until the pressure on her front started again. She then stopped, turned around, took two paces forwards and looked into the trench. She wished that she hadn't.

The base and sides of the trench did contain evidence of the previous night's crime scene…graphic evidence.

One of the forensics team saw Naomi blanch. He said, "Would you like me to cover it over ma'am?"

Naomi turned and said, "No, thank you." She looked at Bonnie-Mae and said, "Whatever's drawing me is right here." She pointed down.

They both looked into the trench. First from one side, and then from the other, but saw nothing.

Bonnie-Mae said, "I may not be a forensic archaeologist, but I can't see anything other than mud and dirt."

Naomi cast a glance at the traces of evidence from the night before and said, "Apart from the obvious unnatural material in here, neither can I."

Bonnie-Mae ignored the 'unnatural material' comment and said, "Do you think that we should open up a wider section?"

Naomi shrugged and said, "I don't know, I'm drawn to this spot, but it isn't an exact science. Maybe instead of wider, we should be going deeper."

Bonnie-Mae looked into the trench and said, "Surely the folks from the eighteen hundreds would have experienced the same problem with the water table wouldn't they?"

"You'd think so."

"So if we're having difficulty going any deeper, they would have too."

Naomi looked into the trench again and saw how viscous the mud was. She said, "Yes, I suppose they would."

"So there must have been an optimum level at which those folks could have buried a body round here?"

"True…"

"And anything below that would have been like trying to teaspoon water from one side of a boat to another?"

"Yes."

"Then if your instincts are right, and my logic is right, maybe what's drawing you here is the last resting place of your relative, and not anything physical?"

Naomi recalled that most of her psychic episodes were to do with the intangible. She looked at Bonnie-Mae and said, "That's a good point Sheriff, and difficult to dispute."

Bonnie-Mae nodded and walked all around the trench looking at every angle until she arrived back at Naomi's side. She said, "I'm blowed if I can see anything other than mud, so why don't we dismiss this side of the yard and get back to work on the tunnel?"

Naomi looked into the trench once more and then said, "Okay – when can we resume work on it?"

"Forensics have just about finished now. I'll let the DHEC guys get on with their work here this afternoon, and you can resume on the tunnel tomorrow morning."

Naomi thanked the Sheriff and promised to return at 8am next day. She started to walk back to her car, and felt the pressure exert itself on her left shoulder. She turned to look at the tunnel, but realised that she was looking at the wrong thing. She turned to face the trench once more and the pressure intensified.

Bonnie-Mae looked up the drive and saw Naomi staring towards the trench. She looked down and said, "Hot damn," once again…

Chapter 48

At 3:30pm Naomi sat at a table in the dining hall of the parish house with Reverend Hughes, Sheriff Clement, Peter Purewell, Spencer Prioleau, and Taffy Brewer. Jackie had provided everybody with coffee and homemade cookies, and had disappeared back into the kitchen.

"This," said Marshall, "has been one of the most extraordinary periods in my life. When I first got to hear about the Matthews' grave I didn't give it much thought. In my wildest dreams I never would have believed that as a result of it, we would discover the remains of a Confederate escape tunnel, five bodies, and all that gold!" He turned to Spencer and said, "Do we have an estimation of its value yet?"

"At the start of business in New York today, the price was six-hundred-and-forty-six dollars per ounce. We found one gold bar weighing twenty-five pounds and two boxes of gold coins each weighing twenty-five pounds. That in weight alone, amounts to seven-hundred-and-seventy-five thousand, two-hundred dollars, but the numismatic value of the coins may be much higher."

"Numismatic value?" said Marshall, "what is that?"

Spencer turned to Marshall and said, "In the simplest terms, it is the collector's value. It often exceeds the value of the gold itself because people want it, and with those coins and bar being linked to the Civil War its value could be up to five times more."

"And it doesn't get more convincing than being found with five dead rebel soldiers," added Taffy.

"And have you come up with an explanation of why they were trapped down there?" said Marshall.

"We've examined the full length of the tunnel now, and it appears to have been the result of an extensive collapse at the Church Creek end."

"So why wasn't the tunnel flooded if the proofing was compromised?" said Peter.

Spencer said, "That's one of the mysteries right now, and we don't have an answer for it."

"And what do you think that they were doing with the gold?" said Taffy.

"My guess," said Spencer, "is that they were hiding it."

"In the tunnel?"

"It appears so; we know that the vault end had been sealed for whatever reason, so maybe they thought that it would be a good place to conceal something like that."

"And then it collapsed whilst they were in there?" Peter recalled how claustrophobic it had been in the tunnel and blanched at the thought of being trapped in. He said, "Poor devils… "

Naomi thought about the words 'through here' that had been scratched into the north-eastern wall of the burial vault. She wondered whether the unfortunate woman who'd been sealed in had experienced the same moans she had, and that perhaps she'd been deemed a witch who'd been able to communicate with the dead. She shuddered at the thought that had she been living in those times, she too may have suffered the same fate.

She looked around the table and decided against saying anything.

"And as exciting as all of this is," said Spencer, "it does get better."

All heads turned in his direction.

"One hour ago, I received a telephone call from a colleague of mine in the Federal Reserve Office who confirmed that the coins and gold bar were part of the missing bullion from a vessel named the *SS Georgiana* that sank off our present day Isle of Palms in 1863."

A gasp of dismay came from the assemblage.

"*Part* of the missing bullion?" said Peter, "How much was supposed to be there?"

"When it left England bound for Charleston, it was carrying three-hundred-and-fifty pounds of gold, with a present day value of just over three-and-a-half million."

"Wow," said Naomi, "so most of it is still unaccounted for?"

"Correct, the vessel was discovered by marine archaeologist E Lee Spence in 1965, and numerous items have been recovered from her, but the gold has never been found."

"Except for our bit," said Peter.

"And have we established who it belongs to?" said Marshall.

"We believe so Father," said Bonnie-Mae. "It was gold destined for the Confederacy from England, so it belongs to the government."

"Even though there is no Confederacy any more?"

Bonnie-Mae smiled and said, "No – after the war it became a part of the Union, and all that belonged to the CSA, went to them."

Marshall said, "So we find three-quarters of a million dollars' worth of gold and we get nothing?"

"It's the way that the system works Father. Where it's acknowledged that the original owners of treasure trove can't be located, often because they're long dead, the find is deemed in some States to belong to the finder. In other States, to try to prohibit unlawful trespass in search of treasure, the find is deemed to belong to the person on whose land it's found. But in this case, we know who the owner of the gold is – it's the government."

"Perhaps we should have taken a leaf out of old Reverend Drayton's book, Marshall," said Peter, "he was known to have been a bit economical with the truth when it suited him."

Marshall glanced at Peter and then at Bonnie-Mae. He said, "Maybe..."

"Surely all isn't lost though is it?" said Naomi. "In the UK the government always claims right over treasure trove, but in most cases they give a percentage to the finder and the landowner."

"Naomi's right," said Spencer, "and most of the American States base their treasure trove laws on British statute." He paused, looked around the group, and then said, "And for your info I have requested that a percentage be given to the church in my submission report."

"How much?" said Peter.

"Twenty percent."

"Good Grief," said Marshall, "that's er..."

"Just over one-hundred-and-fifty thousand dollars," said Naomi.

A stunned silence fell on the room until Marshall said, "One-hundred-and-fifty thousand? My, my, my – that would stand this church's finances in very good stead."

Spencer smiled and said, "I believe too that we could be in with a very good chance of getting it because the Mayor of Charleston, who is up for re-election very soon, has seen this project as one of his re-election platforms." He saw the looks of excitement on everybody's face and then added, "But please don't bank on that amount, and don't make any plans for it until we get a confirmation that it will be awarded."

"No, of course not," said Marshall, "but if you'll forgive a moment of weakness, I do think that this calls for coffee and cookies right now!" He looked around, leaned forwards, and said, "And if I'd been old Reverend Drayton, I might have been tempted to get a few beers from our much missed Casey's beer stash!"

Everybody smiled and commented, but not Naomi. Something about 'Casey's stash' caused the thumb to press on her shoulder. She said, "Who's Casey?"

Everybody fell silent until Marshall said, "He was our ground-keeper."

"*Was* your ground-keeper? Doesn't he work here any longer?"

"No ma'am, Naomi... " Bonnie-Mae was trying to get it right. "...he was murdered two weeks ago."

The pressure increased on Naomi's shoulder. She said, "Why?"

Bonnie-Mae looked around the room and said, "Under normal circumstances I wouldn't be allowed to discuss any part of an ongoing investigation, but because I believe that Casey's death is linked to the unusual occurrences that have been taking place at this church, I will tell you that we are linking his death to the two men whose bodies were removed from here last Tuesday."

Naomi tried to rationalise the feeling that she'd experienced at the mention of the ground-keeper's name, but nothing clicked.

"And old Casey had a secret stash?" said Peter.

"Marshall turned and said, "Yes, in his shed – he thought that it was his secret, but most of the church officials knew about it."

Peter shook his head and smiled.

"It was fine," said Marshall, "and he never overdid it."

Naomi felt the pressure increase at the mention of the shed. She said, "And did he keep anything else secret in there?"

"No," said Marshall, "only his beer."

Bonnie-Mae looked at Naomi with a frown on her face. She'd had several tastes of Naomi's mental acuity and wondered where she was going. She saw Naomi nod, look down, and then reach up to her left shoulder and rub it. She said, "Are you having a moment of er..." she looked at the faces around the table and changed tack. She said, "What's on your mind ma'am?"

Naomi looked at Bonnie-Mae and said, "I don't know..." She fell silent for a few seconds and then said, "Didn't I hear mention that it was Mr. Peters who told Deacon Morrison where the Matthews grave was?"

"You did."

"So, how did *he* know?"

Silence descended upon the group, and they looked at one-another with frowns upon their faces.

"And how long had he worked here?" said Naomi.

Peter said, "The best part of twenty years."

Naomi looked down again and mulled things over for a few seconds. There was something about the trench and the unusual feelings that she'd experienced when she was near it. She looked up at Taffy and said, "Did Mr. Peters tell you where to sink the stormwater trench?"

"No, Deacon Morrison did."

Bonnie-Mae's alarm bells went off full tilt. She said, *"Deacon Morrison?"*

"Yes Sheriff."

Bonnie-Mae turned to Marshall and said, "And Father, did you tell Deacon Morrison where to sink the trench?"

"No I did not. He told me that Mr. Brewer had informed him where it should go."

Taffy raised his eyebrows and said, "Hey, wait up a minute – I didn't inform anybody about anything. I received orders from my office to report to Deacon Morrison and he told me that due to unmarked burials being in situ beneath the present day car park, he would instruct me where it was safe to sink the trench."

The mention of the unmarked burials triggered something in Naomi's brain. She said, "How many burials are there below the car park?"

Marshall said, "Just one or two and they were very early interments. We tried to contact the deceased family members, but none could be located so we deconsecrated the ground, and the car park extension went ahead."

The pressure on Naomi's shoulder went haywire. For the first time since setting foot on American soil, she heard a male voice utter, "Ahh… " The sound was so real that she spun around and looked behind her.

The action wasn't lost on Bonnie-Mae.

Naomi turned to Marshall and said, "Do you have a record of who was buried there?"

Marshall sat back with an awful dawning of realisation. He looked at the inquisitive faces, and then said, "The records are kept in the storeroom."

"And...?"

Marshall anticipated Naomi's question and said, "Casey was in charge of that too."

Bonnie-Mae leapt in. She said, "Wait right there. Let me get this straight Father – did you instruct Deacon Morrison to have the storm drain sunk while you were on vacation?"

"No, I did not. In fact I was annoyed that he'd gone ahead without getting my permission."

Behind the door to the dining hall, Del stood with a horrified look upon his face. He'd walked in in time to hear most of the conversation and he knew that the game was up. He looked at his watch and figured that he had an hour at best. He exited the parish house and almost ran back to his car. He had to get to Julie, and get out of Charleston.

"So," said Bonnie-Mae, unaware of Del's rapid departure, "you went on vacation and Deacon Morrison got in touch with DHEC. He asked for a stormwater drain to be sunk in the car park, but then designated the exact area, because of historic burials. He then informs us, that Casey has informed him, that the Matthews' grave is adjacent to the old burial vault. Is that right?"

Everybody nodded.

Bonnie-Mae looked at Naomi and said, "Ma'am, Naomi, when you first arrived, did you believe that the Matthews' grave would be found where Deacon Morrison said it was?"

"I thought it unlikely."

"Why?"

"Because the Matthews' grave dated from the 1820s and all of the others nearby dated from the 1700s." Naomi reached into her briefcase and extracted a copy of the church's visitor information sheet. She threw it on the table and said, "If the diagram on the leaflet is accurate, look at the symmetry of the historical plots. How could a grave situated between plots six and seven have gone unrecorded, if it was put there at least one hundred years later than the others?"

Silence descended on the room.

Bonnie-Mae was fascinated to see if Naomi had arrived at the same conclusion that she had. She turned to her and said, "So, in your opinion, given all the latest revelations, where would you think that the Matthew's grave is sited?"

"I don't think that there can be any doubt about it," said Naomi. "It's below the trench in the car park."

"Yes ma'am!" said Bonnie-Mae. She turned and looked at the shocked faces around the table. "And that," she said, "is why those two perpetrators and Deacon Del Morrison, were digging there last Monday night."

"What?" said Marshall aghast, "Are you implying that my Deacon has been complicit in deceiving us all, and that he was aware of the real whereabouts of the Matthews' grave?" He paused and then added, "And that he was trying to get hold of the Fire of Mars for himself?"

"I am," said Bonnie-Mae.

"And that he was in cahoots with those two thugs who kidnapped and assaulted his wife?"

"And killed Casey Peters? – Yes sir I am. And when I get a hold of his sorry ass, he's going to wish that he'd never heard of that goddamned ruby, you just mark my words..."

Chapter 49

Del checked to see that Janet's car had gone, and then pulled up into the drive. Before getting out of his vehicle he dialled Julie's mobile number. He waited for a few seconds and then heard a tone indicating that the number was out of service. He frowned, dialled again, and got the same tone. He thought for a couple of seconds and guessed that she'd either changed her phone, or set up a new number.

He exited the car, ran into the house and threw all of the clothes that he wanted into a large suitcase. He manhandled it down to the car and heaved it into the trunk. He then ran back inside, tapped in the numbers to their fireproof, under-floor safe, and removed the ten thousand dollars that he and Janet kept in there in the event of emergencies. Next he ran into his study and removed all of his personal documents, driving licence, insurance certificates, bonds, social security forms, and everything else that he could think of.

When he'd finished, he looked around and figured that if he had missed anything, he could replace it once he'd started his new life with Julie. He looked around one last time, then picked up his briefcase and headed for the front door. He opened it, and saw Janet pull into the drive behind his car and stop.

He dropped the briefcase out of sight and tried to think of any excuse to leave, but his mind went blank. He heard the engine stop, saw Janet open her door and put one foot outside, and then he heard her cell phone ring.

Janet answered and said, "Hello, Janet Morrison."

"Janet, this is Bonnie-Mae, where are you?"

"At home, in my car, in my drive."

"Is Del with you?"

"No, he's standing in the doorway looking at me right now."

Bonnie-Mae considered her options. She wanted to say 'act naturally and delay him until we get there' but she didn't know whether Janet would be able to remain calm and dispassionate if she heard that Del was wanted for questioning. She also wasn't sure how he'd react if he found out that the police were on their way to arrest him.

She opted to play it safe. She said, "I need you to trust me on this – don't question what I'm about to say, and don't give anything away in your reactions. Do you understand?"

"I do."

"Good – tell Del that Carole's been involved in an accident and that you have to go to accident and emergency right away. Then you are to drive to my office. Is that clear?"

"Yes, it is."

"Good – then do it now."

Janet said, "Okay, bye." She got out of her car, said, "Carole's been involved in an accident, I've got to go to A and E right now."

Del couldn't believe his luck. He said, "Is she okay?"

"I'm not sure right now, but I have to go..."

"Okay – I'll see you when you get back. Give her my love, and I hope that it isn't too serious."

"Will do, bye honey."

Janet got into her car, backed out of the drive, and drove away.

Del snatched up his briefcase, slammed the front door shut, and then sped off to Julie's trailer in Walden Street.

At St. Andrew's church, Naomi watched as Sheriff Clement sped off with the blue and red lights flashing atop her vehicle. She turned to face Taffy and Spencer and said, "Are you sure about this?"

Spencer looked at Marshall and said, "It's okay with me as long as Father Marshall is happy."

Marshall said, "Jackie told me that you have to leave first thing tomorrow, is that correct?"

"Yes, I'm driving to St. Augustine, meeting my cousin Alan and his wife, and we're spending the night with their friends Julie and Steve at their condo by the beach."

"It sounds delightful," said Marshall, "but if this is your last day in Charleston, the least we can do is to see if that ruby is where you say it is."

Naomi smiled and said, "And I'm very grateful to you. It would have driven me crazy to think that I was so close, but never got the chance to look."

"Well let's get to it," said Spencer. He nodded to Taffy, waited until he'd positioned the mechanical digger, and then turned to Naomi. He said, "Right – give us your best guess."

Naomi approached the trench, and felt the familiar ushering feeling. She manoeuvred until she believed herself to be in the right place, and then pointed down. She said "Here."

Taffy lowered the digger arm into the trench, scraped away a bucketful of pluff mud, and deposited it onto a large plastic sheet that had been laid out in the car park.

Naomi and Spencer looked into the trench and saw the hole almost immediately fill up with more gooey sludge. They then looked at the mud on the sheet and saw nothing there either.

Spencer signalled to Taffy to repeat the process.

In North Charleston, Del turned into Walden Street, and drove down to Julie's plot. He got out of his car, walked to the door, and then saw a huge man appear from behind the trailer. He stopped dead as he saw the man ignore him, and start banging on the trailer door.

"Julie, Lorraine! – It's me – open up!"

Del walked up to the man and said, "Can I help you?"

"If you're a cop," said the man.

"A cop? No I'm not – why do you need a cop?"

The man turned and said, "To help me find my partner and sister."

Del was stunned; he said, "Partner and sister? What are...?"

The man said, "Buddy, I don't know who you are, but my name's Dave Nicholls. Julie's my partner, and Lorraine's my sister. So who are you, and what do you want?"

Del stared at Nicholls in shock. He said, "I'm, I'm – my name is, Del. Del Worthington – I'm the maintenance man for the park."

"And what do you want?"

"I er, want to know where they are. I did some work for them and they haven't paid me."

"Well, you'll be lucky to get it bud, 'cos this isn't the first time that these two screwballs have taken off without paying their bills."

Del couldn't believe his ears. He said, "They've done it before?"

"In Baltimore, Lancaster, DC, Vegas...you want more?"

"They just take off? Why?"

"Unpaid rent, debts, jealous lovers...you name it."

"Jealous lovers? I thought you were..."

"And you were right, I am Julie's partner. We got two grown-up boys together, but when she met my psycho sister, she went off the rails. Drink, drugs, men, women – now she's one screwed-up, sick puppy..."

Del was mortified. He said, "And you've no idea where they've gone?"

"Do you think that I'd be knocking on this trailer door if I knew smart ass?"

"No, I guess not; I just wondered..."

"Forget it bro. I hope that they didn't owe you too much, 'cos you sure as hell ain't going to see 'em again. They could be in the freakin' Bahamas by now."

Del stared at Nicholls in disbelief, then nodded, and turned away. He walked back to his car and climbed in. He stared out of the windscreen for a few seconds, and then realised that he had to get the hell home before Janet returned.

He started the engine, rammed the gear into drive, and screeched away.

Back at St. Andrews, Naomi and Spencer looked into the empty trench for the umpteenth time and saw nothing.

Naomi glanced at the huge pile of gooey mud that was oozing towards the edges of the plastic sheeting and knew that they were on a loser. She looked at Taffy and Spencer and knew that they were indulging her.

She said, "We're wasting our time aren't we?"

Spencer pursed his lips and then said, "We'll try two more, and if we still get nothing, I guess we should call it a day."

Naomi nodded and said, "Okay." She wandered to the left of her position beside the trench and felt the pressure push against her. She turned and walked in the opposite direction and once again, felt the pressure usher her back to the self-same spot.

"You'd better step back," said Spencer.

Naomi nodded and stepped back.

Taffy dropped the arm of the digger into the pluff mud and scooped up another bucketful. Nothing was in it. He lowered the bucket for the last time, dug it in deep, and withdrew it.

They watched as it lifted out of the trench, spewing and spilling grey goo.

Taffy deposited it on the pile.

There was nothing in it.

Naomi looked in the trench, and saw nothing but the smelly, goo re-levelling itself. She turned to Spencer and said, "Well, that's that then. Thanks for trying."

"I'm sorry; I know how much this meant to you."

Naomi nodded, and saw Taffy approach.

"Sorry English, it may not look it because of the mud re-levelling itself, but we've gone down much further than the average burial depth here. If anything had been in there we'd have found it by now."

Naomi smiled and said, "I know – thanks for trying though."

"Come on," said Spencer, "let's get a coffee in the parish house and tell Marshall that we're through."

As Naomi walked away from the trench she felt the pressure on her body, but she didn't feel anything on her left shoulder, and she didn't hear any voices. She drew in a deep breath and presumed that she'd been experiencing some kind of echo from the past; the memory of a place that had been touched by a distant ancestor.

She looked over to the tunnel dig site, and realised that since it had been exposed she hadn't heard moaning from there either. That seemed self-evident.

Then something clicked. She'd never resolved why the moaning had ceased whenever Jackie had appeared. She recalled her saying that she'd had a distant forefather who'd settled in Charleston after the Civil War, and she'd mentioned a small street being named after him, but she hadn't established which it was.

She followed Spencer and Taffy into the dining hall and sat down.

Taffy went for the coffees, and Spencer went for Marshall.

Within the hour, it was time for Naomi to leave. Everything that needed to be said had been said, she'd thanked everybody for their kindness and for being so accommodating, and she'd promised to keep in touch.

Marshall said, "I'm sorry that you didn't get what you came for, but I've got to say, if it hadn't been for you and your family, we might not have been about to get our hands on some much needed funds for the parish."

Naomi smiled, and said, "It was my pleasure, and for the record, I love it here, and I love Charleston. In fact, I intend getting up early tomorrow morning and having a last drive around the city before I leave." She looked to one side, saw Jackie, and said, "And I want to see the street that your ancestor owned."

"It's not a proper street," said Jackie, "more of a large yard than anything else."

"And what was its name?"

"Weims Court, named after my old forefather Gilbert I'm told. Apparently he ran a detective agency down there that survived until the late 1940's."

The thumb pressed down on Naomi's shoulder and she thought that Jackie had said something relevant, but when she couldn't make any links she said, "Well, I'll be sure to take a photo of it for my album before I go."

She thanked everybody once again, gave them all a hug, and left St. Andrew's for the last time.

Chapter 50

Naomi sat enjoying one of her last all-American breakfasts, and recalled how much Carlton enjoyed the pancakes and maple syrup. She'd been missing him like crazy, and though she'd known that the last week in the USA had been more about business than a vacation, she couldn't wait to see him again.

She smiled as she cut into the warm pancake, and was about to put it into her mouth when she heard her phone buzz. She extracted it from her handbag and saw that it was from Carlton, telling her that he loved her and was looking forward to her return.

Before she closed the text section down, she noticed the '*Tyson*' message and realised that she hadn't given any further thought to it. She put the phone down beside her breakfast plate. She recalled all of the other single word messages that she'd received. They were Brahma, hive, 2delta2, male, California, and Tyson. She was about to write them down on a spare serviette, and then she hesitated. She looked in her pocket book and noted that of the six words received; only Brahma, California, and Tyson had capital letters. She wrote down BCT, and then h2m. She then wrote Bh2, the first letters and number received, and wondered if that was the start of a Bournemouth, England, postcode – but the mCT didn't match that.

Bh2mCT – it didn't make sense. She stared at it all through her breakfast, and then texted everything to Helen Milner, her co-researcher, in England. She looked at her watch, saw that it was 9:30am and knew that it would be 2:30pm in the UK. A minute or so later, her phone buzzed again. It was from Helen. It read:

Fascinating – I'm on it. Looking forward to your return. H.

The phoned buzzed again; it was a text from Sheriff Clement.

Sorry I didn't get the chance to say goodbye.

Deacon Morrison was arrested at his house last night and is in custody awaiting trial. Thank you for your invaluable assistance at St. Andrew's church, and I'm sorry that you didn't find The Fire of Mars.

I wish you a safe journey home and hope that you like what I sent you.

It's been an honour ma'am. (Sorry – Naomi!)

Best wishes,

Bonnie-Mae Clement.

She smiled, and put the phone down. It had been a ride, and she'd enjoyed every minute of it, but she couldn't imagine what the Sheriff of Charleston could have sent her.

At 8pm that night she sat in one of the lively restaurants in St. Augustine with Alan, Debbie, Julie, Steve, and Don from The Mill Top Tavern. The conversation was lively and animated, the ambience of the crowded room couldn't have been better, and the presence of Don made up in part, for the missing Carlton.

Everybody had finished their meals and they were waiting for their hot drinks when Naomi felt the need to spend a penny. She excused herself and went to the ladies room. Minutes later, whilst checking her appearance in the mirror, she realised that she needed to re-apply her lipstick. She looked in her small handbag, rummaged around and couldn't get to it without removing some items. She took out her mobile phone, and saw that somehow it had switched off. She switched it on, and then set about re-applying the lipstick.

She heard the phone's start-up tone, and then in quick succession, she heard it indicate that she'd received three texts. She put her lipstick back in her bag and read the first text from Helen.

I think that I've got that one-word message conundrum but it doesn't make sense. If I'm right, you'll get one more word and I'd put money on it being 'Centauri.'

Keep in touch

H

The second was from Carlton.

Hi gorgeous, my life is too empty without you in it. I'm taking Monday off to meet you at Gatwick. Please pick up at least 3 large Hershey bars and a litre of vodka from duty free, and if you want to, because you've really missed me, you could get me a nice prezzie too! (A soft leather wallet maybe...!)

Undying love babe,

C. xxxxx

She smiled and recalled Carlton's instant liking for Hershey's chocolate. She made a mental note to pick some up. She opened up the third text; it was from an undisclosed sender. It read, *"Centauri."*

She was stunned; that was the word that Helen had predicted.

She walked back into the restaurant and saw that the waitress was delivering their drinks. She sat down, waited until everybody had theirs, and then she told them about the series of one-word messages. She wrote them down as she'd received them, and pushed them into the middle of the table.

The words were passed around in silence, but Julie and Steve started to speak at the same time.

Steve said, "You go first..."

Julie smiled, turned the list to face Naomi, and said, "It's not that hard to figure out. Some of the words are easier than others, but for me the give-away was 'Tyson.'"

Steve looked at Naomi and said, "Me too."

"It had to be preceded by Mike," said Julie, "then Centauri had to be preceded by Alpha. If you then realise that all of the words have to be preceded or followed by another, and at least two of them are from the phonetic alphabet, it isn't hard to figure the rest." She retrieved the list, took out her pen, and wrote a word in front of each of the others with the single exception of the word Brahma. She then turned the list around and pushed it to Naomi. It read:

Brahma

Bee – hive

R – 2delta2 or 2D2 (R2D2!)

Alpha – male

Hotel – California

Mike – Tyson

Alpha – Centauri.

Julie said, "It's Brahma, twice. The first word is Brahma, and the one-word clues spell out Brahma." She looked at Steve and said, "Do you agree?"

Steve nodded and said, "I doubt that it could be anything else."

Naomi frowned and said, "Brahma, Brahma? How does that make any sense? My colleague and I looked up Brahma on the internet and saw that he was one of the Indian Trimurti, or Trimurati."

"That's interesting," said Steve, "I can't say that I'm familiar with it."

"It's a concept in Hinduism in which the cosmic functions of creation, maintenance, and destruction are personified by the forms of Brahma the creator, Vishnu the maintainer or preserver, and Shiva the destroyer or transformer."

Steve nodded and then frowned. He said, "And if that's so, somebody sending you the name of an Indian God, twice, doesn't make sense to me either." He turned to Julie and said, "Honey?"

Julie shook her head and said, "Me neither."

"What about Emerson?" said Don.

All heads turned in his direction.

Don said, "Ralph Waldo Emerson – he was one of my favourite nineteenth century American poets. One of his most enigmatic pieces was named 'Brahma.'"

"Do you know it off by heart?" said Naomi.

"I know bits of it, but it would spoil the piece by quoting bits. You need to read it all."

Alan said, "Wait a mo, I can get it on my cell from Wikipedia." He connected to the internet, opened up Wikipedia, and typed in *'Brahma (poem)'*. He waited for a few seconds and then said, "Okay, here we go..." He remained silent as he read the words.

Naomi felt a pressure start on her left shoulder. She watched as Alan's look of interest turned to something altogether more serious.

Alan finished reading, looked at Naomi with a look of deep concern on his face, and said, "If this is what somebody meant you to receive, it's worrying. I'd be watching over my shoulder if it had been sent to me." He handed the phone to Naomi.

Naomi read out loud:

"RALPH WALDO EMERSON
November 1857

Brahma

If the red slayer think he slays,
Or if the slain think he is slain,
They know not well the subtle ways
I keep, and pass, and turn again.

Far or forgot to me is near,
Shadow and sunlight are the same,
The vanished gods to me appear,
And one to me are shame and fame.

They reckon ill who leave me out;
When me they fly, I am the wings;
I am the doubter and the doubt,
And I the hymn the Brahmin sings.

The strong gods pine for my abode,
And pine in vain the sacred Seven;
But thou, meek lover of the good!
Find me, and turn thy back on Heaven."

A shiver ran down Naomi's spine. She knew who had sent the conundrums.

Don said, "Are you okay Naomi? You look as though you've seen a ghost."

Naomi looked at the concerned faces around the table and said, "I've not seen a ghost, I've received messages from one."

Debbie recoiled and looked at Alan. She said, "Alan, you know how I..."

Alan glared at Debbie and said, "Not here!"

"What do you mean?" said Steve to Naomi.

Naomi said, "I believe that these messages have come from, or at least via, a man who we believed to be dead up until a week or so ago. But his body disappeared from the morgue."

"Good grief," said Steve, "who was he, and how could he be sending you the texts?"

"Not 'was' – it's 'is'. I'm convinced that he's alive. He's a man that I've crossed swords with on a couple of occasions, but the last time he held me responsible for exposing his underground drug making facility in the north of England."

"Goldarn it Naomi," said Don, "you did that?!"

"Yes, and he's tried to have me killed on at least two, maybe three occasions that I know of."

Steve and Don's mouths fell open.

Don said, "I can't believe it! Why didn't the police arrest him?"

"They did; then one day he was found dead in his cell. His body was taken to a mortuary pending a post mortem, but two days' later it had gone."

Steve said, "How?"

"No idea, but the driver who transported his body from the cell to the morgue was found at the bottom of a reservoir strapped into the front seat of his car."

"Good Heavens..." said Don. He looked at Naomi's troubled face and said, "You don't think that he's here in the US do you honey? 'Cos if he is..."

"No, I don't believe so," said Naomi, "I think that he's waiting for me in the UK." She hesitated, looked around the table, and said, "I'm sorry guys; I have to send a text."

She saw the nods of approval and then removed her phone from her bag. She wrote:

Hi Guys,

I'm now convinced that Adrian Darke is alive. I'm sure that he's the one who's been sending me the weird texts.

I arrive back Monday morning and I'll contact you as soon as I can.

Best,

Naomi

She addressed the text to Bob Crowthorne and Helen Milner, pressed 'send' and put the phone back in her bag.

She looked around the table and saw that all the joviality had gone. She said, "Come on guys, this is my last night here and I'm not going to let that idiot spoil it. I've sorted him out before, and when I get back to England I'll sort him out again."

Don grinned, lifted up his glass, and said, "And damn it if I don't believe you too lady – Way to go Naomi!"

Chapter 51

Sunday 3rd December 2006. Orlando International Airport,
Florida

Naomi sat in the main departure lounge close to the shops and restaurants. She had an hour to wait until she was called to her boarding gate, and having had a snack and coffee, she decided to wander around the duty free outlet to buy Carlton's Hershey bars and vodka, and maybe even a suitable wallet if she saw one.

Within forty minutes she'd made her choices, and was pleased that she'd found a wallet that Carlton would like. She walked across to the check-out and placed her items on the counter.

"Afternoon ma'am," said the girl by the till, "may I have your boarding card please?"

Naomi smiled and said, "Okay." She reached into her handbag, took out a leaflet, and handed it over.

The girl frowned and said, "Sorry ma'am, this isn't your boarding card."

Naomi looked and saw that she'd handed over the small visitor leaflet from St. Andrew's. She apologised, took it back, and handed over her boarding pass.

Back in the concourse she plonked herself into a seat and attempted to stuff the boarding pass, receipts, and St. Andrew's information sheet back into her already overfull handbag. She placed the boarding pass in a front pocket in an upright position for easy access and stuffed the receipts into her jeans' pocket. She then recalled that she had more information leaflets from the church in her suitcase, and decided to leave that one on the seat next to her, so that somebody else could read it while they waited.

Before putting it down, she looked at it one more time. It was a simple piece of A4 paper that had been folded into three. The front cover contained an old print of the church, and times of worship on it. Overleaf was a plan of the church showing a walking tour of the oldest burial plots around the perimeter.

She smiled when she saw plot seven, the burial holding vault. It looked so simple and uncomplicated on paper.

She was about to fold it up and put it down when something caught her eye. It was an arrow at the top right-hand side of the plan indicating true north. Then she saw that plots three and four to the left of the arrow were aligned unlike the rest.

She felt a sudden tightening around the temples. She stared at the page for a few seconds longer and saw that it wasn't plots three and four that were misaligned, it was the whole church.

All Christian churches were supposed to be aligned east/west, but St. Andrew's wasn't – it was aligned southeast/northwest. That meant that whoever had buried their loved ones in plots three and four had known about it, and had addressed the situation at the time of burial.

A pressure began to manifest itself on her left shoulder. She looked at the written details of plot three and saw that it belonged to one Elizabeth Nairn whose husband had died in 1715. That indicated that as early as the mid-seventeen hundreds, folk had been aware of the church's misalignment.

She snatched a pen out of her handbag and as accurately as she could, drew in the trench that Taffy had sunk. She clapped a hand up to her mouth and said, "Oh my God..."

She could see the mistake.

When Casey had informed Del where the Matthews P. F. grave had been located, he'd ordered a trench to be sunk on the same alignment as the church, but by the time that the grave had been dug, everybody would have known that that alignment was incorrect.

As the pressure increased on her shoulder she recalled how she'd been ushered to one spot beside the trench – and that had been her biggest blunder. She couldn't believe how stupid she'd been.

She snatched her mobile phone out of her bag and dialled Taffy's number. She heard him answer and said, "Taffy, it's Naomi, we've made a huge mistake."

"What do you mean a huge mistake?"

"We dug for the ruby in the wrong place."

"But you told us where to dig," said Taffy.

"And I got it wrong. Deacon Morrison had asked you to align the trench with the church, so that he could be sure to cover the full length of the old grave."

"And..." said Taffy.

"But the church's alignment is wrong – it's southeast/northwest, not east/west. By the eighteen-hundreds, the gravediggers had been well aware of the misalignment and had compensated for it."

Taffy said, "Bloody hell English, that means..."

"...that we should have been digging below where I was standing, not in the trench next to it!"

"Because the grave was offset...?"

"Exactly!"

"Whoa, whoa, that puts the cat back amongst the pigeons..."

The airport's public address system cut across their conversation, announcing that the passengers on Naomi's flight should proceed to a boarding gate.

Naomi said, "I've got to go Taffy, they've just called my flight."

"Okay, the heavy plant's still at the church; we'll ask Marshall's permission to dig tomorrow and see if anything's there."

"All right, but please let me know if you find anything. You've got my number."

"Course I will – now safe journey and I'm sorry."

"Sorry? What are you sorry about?"

"That you've got to go back to England and not Wales."

Naomi laughed and said, "Yeah right! Keep in touch – bye." She put her mobile phone in her pocket, picked up her bag, and headed for the boarding gate.

And every step of the way she kicked herself for being so stupid.

Chapter 52

Tuesday 5th December 2006. The Historic Research Department, Walmsfield Borough Council Offices, England

At 2:30pm Naomi looked across to Helen and said, "I'm really looking forward to Christmas this year."

Helen looked up and said, "You've only just got back and you're looking forward to Christmas?"

"Yes, I loved it in the States, and I loved the hot weather in Florida, but nowhere feels as good as home at Christmas."

Helen leaned back in her chair and said, "Go on then, we've got all the unimportant stuff like your family history out of the way, what were the clothes shops like?"

Naomi smiled and said, "Excellent, there was this one shop in Charleston..."

Her laptop indicated that she'd received an email.

Helen said, "Ignore that, it'll be about work."

Naomi cast a sideways glance at her monitor and was surprised to see that the email was from Stephen Page, the man with whom she'd become professionally involved in the Malaterre case. She said, "It's from Steve Page..."

"Stephen," corrected Helen, "he hates being called Steve."

"And with your shaky history together, you should know."

Helen looked down and said, "As a matter of fact, I was going to tell you something about him today."

Naomi looked at Helen and said, "Sounds interesting."

"We, Stephen and I, have started seeing each other again."

Naomi couldn't believe her ears. She said, "I thought that you'd given up on him."

"I had; kind of. Then he sent me this beautiful bunch of flowers and a card inviting me to dinner at a function he had to attend in York. And we...we...went..."

"You went?"

"Yes, we went. – Together..."

Naomi raised her eyebrows and said, "Together, together?"

"Yes."

"No! You're not saying *together, together,* are you?"

"Yes."

Naomi let out a shriek and said, "And...?"

"And it was kind of wonderful."

Naomi clapped her hands up to her mouth.

"And we've been seeing each other ever since."

"And he feels the same?"

"He says so."

Naomi said, "OMG!" and then looked at the email subject box. It said 'Personal.' She said, "So what does he want with me?"

She went to open it and then saw two more arrive in her inbox. One was from Taffy Brewer in America.

She opened it up and read it.

Hi English,

Hope you arrived home safely yesterday.

We've found it...

Naomi leapt to her feet as though she'd been stung. She said, "No! *No!*"

Helen looked and said, "What? What did he say?"

Naomi didn't answer; she dropped back into her chair and continued reading.

...it was exactly where you said it would be.

It was in an old wooden sea chest with a flat lid, in incredible condition, and it had carvings on the lid. In the centre was a cow's head with horns that had been cut short, and either side of it were the initials 'V' and 'C' if any of that makes sense to you.

We would have been in touch yesterday, but because of the mud in the mechanism, it took a good locksmith until this morning to get it open. Anyway, that's all dross.

The Fire of Mars, or 'El Fuego de Marte,' according to Father Marshall, was in there, and in layman's terms, it's a bloody whopper!

We had a specialist jeweller down here, (whose eyes nearly popped out of his head when he saw it), and he reckons that it's somewhere between eighteen and twenty carats in size – making it the largest ruby ever found!

Check out the attached photo.

Naomi looked up and saw that a jpeg file had been attached.

Helen said, "*N* – what did Stephen say?"

"It's not from Stephen – not this post anyway, this is from Charleston – they've found the ruby."

Helen was astonished. She said, "El Fuego de Marte?"

"Yes, look." Naomi clicked on the jpeg file and watched as it opened.

The uncut ruby filled the screen. It was oblong in shape, and from the outermost edges to the very heart of the stone, it was the deepest red that they had ever seen.

"Wow," said Helen, "that looks magnificent, and what an appropriate name!"

"And damned near priceless I'd say," added Naomi. She clicked back onto the text and continued reading.

"Here in Charleston we're still reeling at its sheer size and magnificence, but Bonnie-Mae has taken it for the present."

Helen said, "Oh – who's Bonnie-Mae?"

"She's the Sheriff of Charleston."

"Only I forgot to give you something."

"Let's finish this, and then you can show me."

They both continued reading.

"She's told us that according to State law, because we know who owns the ruby, it'll be given to your cousin from Florida, when he gets here.

Needless to say, he was mega- excited, but I guess that you've heard from him by now too."

Naomi looked at her inbox and saw that the other email was from Alan. She continued reading.

"Anyway, I thought that you should know about it ASAP because if it hadn't been for your insight we may never have found it. So well done you!

And right now, I'm forced to admit – much against my will – that every now and then some good things do come out of England. (But not often...if ever...).

Best wishes from us all and have a great Christmas.

Taffy xxx

PS – Deacon Morrison was charged with numerous crimes yesterday, including being an accessory to Casey's murder. He's being held in the State Penitentiary until his hearing in February."

Helen looked at Naomi and saw the look of emotion on her face. She said, "And well done from me babe. You did it; you finally brought the Whitewall saga to an end."

Naomi looked at Helen and said, "My grandfather Frank was told by his old Aunt Charlotte, that one day, Maria's Papers might make him rich, or his children, or his children's children, and though it isn't how she expected, she had been right.

Because of those papers, and everything else that we've revealed, Alan and his side of the Chance family will now own the largest and most valuable ruby ever found."

Helen said, "And that deserves two teas and two Mars Bars – on me."

Naomi smiled, and then remembered something. She said, "Before you go, you said that you'd forgotten to give me something?"

"Oh yes, it arrived Monday." Helen walked over to her desk, removed a bulky envelope from her drawer, and handed it over.

Naomi looked at the back and saw that it had been sent by Bonnie-Mae from the Sheriff's Department of Charleston. She opened it up and found a 'With compliments' slip, a Certificate, and a small leather wallet.

"What is it?" said Helen.

Naomi read the certificate and then opened the wallet. Inside was a badge. She looked up and said, "In recognition of my services to St. Andrew's church and the Sheriff's Department of the City of Charleston, I've been made an Honorary Deputy Sheriff!"

Epilogue

*February 2007. The abandoned St. Mary Cross Animal Research
Unit, Skelmersdale, Lancashire*

"My God," exclaimed Naomi. She heard the woman behind her
say, "You need to be quick now Superintendent; alarms may have
gone off inside there."

Crowthorne turned to Leo and said, "You wait here with the
ladies," he turned to his men and said, "...okay in you go." He
grabbed the handle, yanked the door open and stepped aside,
expecting to see his men rush in. Instead, they stopped dead.

"What the hell...?" said the first policeman.

Crowthorne turned, looked through the door, and saw that it
was jet black inside. He frowned, pushed past the first man, and
walked into the doorway. He looked in all directions, but the only
thing that he could see, was that he appeared to be standing on the
top landing of a metal fire escape. He stepped forwards one pace,
and listened. For several seconds he strained his ears in the dark,
but heard nothing. He turned to the woman behind Naomi and
said, "Was it like this when you came here?"

"No it wasn't, it was well lit."

Crowthorne looked down into the stygian darkness and said,
"How far does this go down?"

"About thirty feet."

"Thirty feet?" repeated Crowthorne.

"Yes, and it leads directly into the central lab," The woman
frowned and said; "can't you hear anything?"

Crowthorne turned and stepped back onto the landing. He
indicated for everybody to stand still and keep quiet. For several
seconds he listened, but heard nothing. He stepped back out of the
metal door, looked at Naomi, and said, "Your ears are younger
than mine, see if you can hear anything."

Naomi nodded, stepped onto the landing, and in that instant, the door slammed shut behind her.

In the loading bay, Crowthorne jumped back in alarm and said, "What the hell?" He turned to one of his officers and said, "Quick, open the door again!"

The young PC yanked at the handle, but nothing happened.

"Shit," said Crowthorne, "Shit!"

On the other side of the door Naomi was petrified. She grabbed her torch out of her pocket, and switched it on. She shone it down and said, "Hello?" but received no reply. She then said, "I don't mean you any harm, but you have to cooperate with me." She heard nothing. She waited for a few seconds longer and then attempted to look around.

It was weird – the light from the beam didn't reflect off anything. It was as though she had gone to her back door on a moonless night, and shone the light into space. She stayed rooted to the spot, aiming the beam left, then right, and then up. It was the same. She saw nothing. She then aimed the light down and attempted to see how far the steps went down, but then she became more puzzled when she couldn't see.

A pressure started on her left shoulder and she knew that something wasn't right. Her breathing became more rapid and she began to be gripped by a sudden desire not be there.

She said, "Stop it, get a hold!" and then shone the torch straight up to see if she could see any part of a ceiling - but nothing was there. She frowned and wondered if she was looking into space, and then switched the torch off to see if she could see any stars. It was pure jet black.

And then she heard it; breathing - below her. Every hair on her body stood on end and her eyes widened in fear. She heard the soft pad of something step onto the metal staircase below.

She panicked and tried to switch on her torch, but in doing so, dropped it. She tried to catch it, but instead, sent it flying into space. In the breathless, petrified silence that followed, she expected to hear it hit something below, but no sound came at all.

And then she heard whatever it was, breathe again, and start climbing up the steps...

If you enjoyed this novel, look out for the next;

'The Hallenbeck Echo'

Other novels by Stephen F Clegg;

'Maria's Papers'

'The Matthew Chance Legacy'

The Emergence of Malaterre'

<u>**www.stephenfclegg.com**</u>